THIEF OF LOVE

By

Gerry Cramer

Thief of Love

This book is a work of non-fiction. Some names of characters are a product of the author's imagination for their privacy and safety. Resemblance to actual events, business establishments or locations is coincidental in entirety.

Thief of Love Copyright 2005
All rights reserved.
Printed in the United States of America

No part of this book may be used or reproduced in any manner. For information write to:

M. B. Rodeo Publishing House
117 East Miami Trail
Bay View, OH 44870

Library of Congress Control Number: 2005905900
ISBN: 0-615-12908-0

Printed in the United States by Morris Publishing
3212 East Highway 30
Kearney, NE 68847
1-800-650-7888

Thief of Love

To the Memory of --

Robert Johnson (Bobby) who entered into my life for a season. I treasure his memory and the time we spent together, but the moment is gone.

He was a fearless, spirited man who energized people around him by his presence.

Why did I write this book?

The purpose is a Memorial to Robert (Bobby) Johnson.

Thief of Love

Acknowledgements

Many of the individuals I want to acknowledge are people I have grown to know very well. Others among those I wish to acknowledge have been in my life for years and I continue to value their friendship, while some others have gone on to be with our Lord.

First, I want to extend my heartfelt appreciation to my critique partner, Karen Plunkett-Powell. With her contributions my book is more interesting. Karen was a caring, kind and gracious person. I thank God for that kind of caring. Karen passed away two and a half years before this book went to press and I miss her very much.

For editing assistance, deep appreciation to Victor West, my talented editor who gave me much needed support and encouragement. Pacific Literary Services--thanks a bunch. You knew what I needed the most.

To Barbara Allen, My Personal Secretary, whose work is incredible, who always managed to finish in a timely fashion and made the road to finishing this book possible.

And especially to Mary Norris, a champion artist who drew the cover illustration by my design. Her talent and contribution is very much appreciated.

A hug of course to all those who make my life meaningful: Stella, Cristy, Nancy, Fred Jr., Angie, Ashley, Robert, Josh and Billy Angelo (Lewie), Jim and Ellie, Roy, Brandy, Jennifer, Christy and Tommy.

Mother and Dad, you're not here with us but not forgotten.

Thief of Love

Chapter One

Sara Bringard walked into the factory's no-smoking break room and slid heavily into one of the six booths. The drone of the air conditioner and loud volume of the CNN News Channel made her head ache; an overwhelming assault on her already taxed senses. Sara had spent most of the hours of her shift taking stock of her future; she knew she had to make changes in her life, but was unsure about what. . . or how.

She'd been at Advance Motors Global work force as a bearing maker for twenty-five of her forty-four years. In their recent state-of-the-business meeting, management had announced that the plant would soon be up for sale and the market was shifting to favor cash-generating, value-oriented suppliers. Consequently, the generation-three bearing business was too competitive for the AM manufacturers; and the bearing business, once AM's shining star, was destined for the sales block.

Distracted by the loud volume on the TV, Sara rose to turn down the sound, then went to the vending machine for coffee.

Sara was still recovering from the painful breakup of a ten-year relationship that had left her celibate for the past year. Her former fiancé, Matt Wilson, had accepted a sixty-thousand-dollar buy out and invested his money in a t-shirt and souvenir shop in Aruba. He'd left Ohio and Sara to pursue his dreams, and now Sara felt a deep loneliness, yet she still wasn't ready to start a new romance.

Sara checked the time on the wall clock, thinking that her friend, Shea Robbinett, would be there any minute. Sara had promised Shea she'd meet her for coffee, but dreaded the conversation that would no doubt follow. In spite of Sara's irritation, every time she and Shea talked, the topic turned to romance. Shea just couldn't accept that Sara was happy with her Christian, single lifestyle.

Sara's born-again experience and her church were filling the void. For now, her primary goal was to grow in God's word. But Shea didn't see things Sara's way.

After twenty years at the AM plant in Bristol, Connecticut, and corporate down-sizing, Shea had transferred her quality-control position to the Ohio operations. Sara and Shea had 'clicked' instantly. Sara found that Shea was so interesting to talk to that Sara found herself depending on her for good company. Shea was a big-city girl, not the church-going type; she led what Sara considered a promiscuous lifestyle, and, while Shea had been kind to her, Sara was starting to feel stifled by Shea's constant pressure to find Sara another man.

There were footsteps in the corridor, and Sara was just turning to look toward the door when Shea dashed into the break room, saying, "Sara, you must listen to me this time. Christy called me. She's recently placed a voice message on the Romance Connection -- a nine-hundred-number hotline ad and voice-message system." Shea was buzzing with excitement as she had blurted out the words with a soft urgency.

"Shea -- " Sara tried to interrupt her as Shea slid into the booth across from where she sat, but Shea was unstoppable.

"I'll give you the phone number. Just put in a short message on the voice mail and the charge will be on your next phone bill. Christie says the response is great and the men are hunks."

Sara sighed and ran her fingers through her hair, rolling her eyes as she said, "I've told you before, Sara, I don't wan romance. I'm not interested; nor am I looking for anyone right now. My life has been full of bad choices with far-reaching consequences."

Shea smiled. "Honey, life can be better with the right person in it. Let's face it, two are better than one." She winked naughtily as she said the last.

Sara sighed again and shrugged, making it clear she wasn't interested in being set up, or discussing it further. She turned conversation to the topic of the impending sale of the AM plant, and, all too soon, their break time together was over.

As much as Sara hated to admit it, Shea's enthusiasm had in fact rubbed off on her. Sara thought about it all night and soon realized that she was in need of companionship. The next morning, she followed Shea's advice and registered her message and phone in the Romance Connection system.

Over the next few days Sara received a handful of calls. Among the callers was a certain Bryan, who told Sara he lived in Denver, and that he worked full time as a chef in a popular restaurant, and part time as a ski instructor. They talked for a half hour, but Sara didn't feel a connection. After some further conversation, she was honest and told him, "No, thanks."

Another call came from the Motor City -- Detroit. A man who identified himself as 'Bill' said he was a car salesman. He didn't seem to have much on the ball, with an easily detected drinking problem, especially clear since he called when the bars closed -- after midnight and in the very early morning hours. <u>So much for candidates number one and two</u>, Sara thought.

Sara let the ad run another week, disappointed to realize that the next wave was after just one thing. The pattern of the sexist calls was basically the same. The first began by describing in graphic detail how he wanted to be turned on. "Come on, baby, I want you to. . . " he said in a cold, dead tone, breathing rapidly into the phone.

At first, Sara was so shocked she said nothing, the silence weighing heavily on her mind and spirits. Then, unable to hold back any longer, her voice hardly quivering -- more from her anger than fear, she said in a steady voice, "Quit calling, pervert. There's a state hospital holding cell for sexual deviates like you!" She clutched the phone firmly, and waited. He stopped talking; his rapid panting continuing on the line. Her patience exhausted, Sara continued, "This isn't a phone sex internet line. Yours isn't the first sick call I've received, so the police are monitoring and recording my calls!" The line clicked and went dead, but, before he hung up, Sara had the satisfaction of hearing his heavy and rapid breathing interrupted by a gasp of fear and surprise.

Sara hung up the phone and lay back, huddled tensely in her bed, moving her head restlessly on the pillow. She was feeling dirty from the demeaning telephone calls. She waited tensely, for the most frightening threatening calls always came late at night.

The phone rang again. Sara thought about ignoring it, then decided to answer one last call before shutting it off for the night. She reached for it, hesitated, then, her hand trembling, lifted the receiver and slowly brought it to her ear.

"Hello, Sara." The voice was unfamiliar; the call sounded like it came from a long distance. "Did I get you up from bed?" His tone was almost apologetic, and sounding relaxed yet sincere.

Sara fought to keep her voice steady as she asked, "Who is this? It's very late to be calling."

"I'm sorry to interrupt your sleep, but I needed to know what you were doing tonight," his tone was still soft, almost caring, but with an edge she now detected that had a slight but cold firmness. "This is your Louisiana lover," he said, adding, "I'll see you Saturday night."

"You'll what?" Sara asked, her voice no longer steady as a sudden, icy fear gripped her heart. She swallowed, gathered her strength and fought back. "Where are you calling from -- the Eastern time zone, or the moon?"

He reacted with a low laughter that had no warmth in it. "Do not despair. I'll soon be there. I'm near you, but I must say goodbye for now, darling." Then, the line clicked and went dead.

Sara sighed, hung up the phone, and hugged her pillow, puzzled and frightened by the strange call. She regretted getting involved in Shea's and Christy's romance hotline idea and decided to cancel the service the next day.

Suddenly, it was morning; Sara had fallen asleep and there had been no more calls that night, so she had slept through. In the light of day, and without any further annoyances the night before, she decided to give the Romance Connection another chance.

For the next few nights the phone didn't ring, then, the mysterious caller was on the line again. "Hi, Sara," he said, then asked, "How are you, my sweetheart? Did I wake you again?" This time, his laughter was derisive and cruel.

Sara felt a shiver go up her spine, causing her whole body to quiver. She tried to steady her voice before she answered, "Yes, you woke me up, damn it! Do you think you're scoring points or are you just trying to frighten me?"

His voice suddenly changed, and he spoke into the phone in a very rapid and breathless tone. "Don't hang up on your Louisiana lover! Have you ever been raped?" His breath came in short, shallow gasps. "I'm going to. . . " Unable to control her anger and suddenly overwhelmed by fear, Sara hung up. The phone again stayed silent for several nights. Then, three nights later, it rang.

At first, Sara vowed to not answer the call, but it kept ringing. Finally, she set her jaw, squared her shoulders, picked up the receiver and held it to her ear.

His tone was now firm, direct, as if assuming control, "Is that how you like it, Sara -- in the ass?"

She wanted to scream obscenities at him, to shout at him that he was just crazy, but held herself back.

His soft chuckling was colder than ever as he said, "Get me off, you . . ."

Unable to contain herself any longer, Sara drew in a deep breath and used what had worked so well before. "You're not the first slimey creep to try to terrorize me like this. The police are taping your calls and have traced your number, so -- "

Again, she had the satisfaction of hearing her tormentor gasp in fear as the line suddenly went dead.

Her hand shook as she replaced the phone on its cradle. It took almost a half hour for the effects of her panic -- the shaking hands, the quivering in her stomach, the shuddering throughout her whole body -- to wear off. But the revulsion did not wear off. Still feeling dirty, Sara took a long, hot shower, lathering her whole body and even washing her hair as she tried 10to make herself feel clean again. Still feeling soiled, she dried off and lay on her bed, still a bit shaky as a consoling thought came to her: She was probably rid of the disgusting little worm who called himself a man; but he was stuck with himself, that night and for the rest of his life.

As Sara lay on her bed she recalled that through her reading she had learned that many of the most grisly crimes committed by serial rapists and murderers came from an explosion of anger in the type of men who resented and hated women and who often resorted to calling and terrorizing women they thought of as being vulnerable; not usually the kind of woman who would strike back, as she had done by turning their obscene calls against them.

The next day, in the break room, Sara was so depressed she felt she had to confide in Shea. "I cringe when my phone rings. I hardly answer it anymore."

Sara very surprised at Shea's reaction. " Well," Shea said, "they probably expect you'll be home at that time." Not only did Shea not seem shocked, in fact, her mood was casual -- nonchalant. "You don't arrive home from work until midnight. What do you expect?" Shea stooped to adding her own insult to Sara's already injured spirit by boasting, "Your calls aren't like mine. Mine start around 5 p.m."

Shea paused, letting the bite of her words sink into Sara before asking, "So, what was the message you posted?"

Sara stifled a hot retort, counted to three, smiled and said, "It goes kind of like this: Attractive redhead, mid forties, a very sensitive and gentle person who, in a relationship with the right person, would be extremely affectionate. Seeks companionship with a good-looking man with honorable intentions." Sara stopped, sighed, swallowed, went on. "I want to find someone who knows how to have fun in life. I'm an automotive worker on a factory floor. Mid-sixties income. Divorced. . . " She let her words drift away, looking to Shea, who was now studying her nails.

Sara suddenly grew pensive, staring into her half-full cup of chamomile tea as she told Shea, "Now I realize how naive I was with the Romance Connection. My posted message will be out of the system as soon as they update the Romance Hotline. I don't need to meet anyone this way. It seems dangerous."

"Dangerous?" Shea laughed. "Well, I met several good-looking, high-moral, decent, well-groomed males," she said, then paused for effect, adding, "Not one pervert. I can't believe what you're saying is true. They're all gentlemen, comfortably well off, seemed stable in every way, paying my flights to New York and Dallas. Do you think I'd go that far to meet a pervert?"

Sara sneered, her voice so tight she could barely get out the words as she said, "My telephone number will be changed midweek. Shea, I wish you well; but a situation like this can be dangerous yet instructive at the same time. I'm determined to make more sensible choices in relationships from now on, and in how I meet people."

That night, Sara received her first call from a man named Bobby Johnson, who said he was in Monterey, California. Although he seemed to be a nice guy, Sara was unsure from her past experiences, but tried to keep her composure to avoid being rude to him.

"All I want is to be happy, to find a nice lady and make her happy too," Bobby said in a soft tone, adding, "I'm a definite hand-holder and hugger." He seemed gracious and kind, and didn't sound like he was manipulating her. She enjoyed his portrayal of himself as a cowboy. "I ride and rope. I've been taught the workings of a ranch from the ground up. I work a long hard day at the ranch," he said. "I like to go out, but also need someone who'd be happy at home just getting junk food and watching videos; and -- as happy as I am roughing it when I'm a competitor in rodeos -- camping out."

Over the next few days, Bobby would phone her at different times, telling her he was calling her from the ranch and updating her about his job and riding in the rodeos.

Thief of Love

Relying on her intuition, Sara listened closely and didn't pick up on any violent attitudes, although Bobby did seem high-spirited. She soon regarded him as a special friend, and looked forward to his calls. When he described himself and his lifestyle, as he told it, it all seemed so different from hers -- working all night, riding, roping cattle, and sleeping during the day at the bunkhouse. Her past dread of the phone ringing was replaced by the fear that it wouldn't. His words were reassuring, giving her hope for the future.

"What I want to find is a partner," Bobby told her. "I don't want to compete with a woman, but I want to share with and enjoy life with her. I hope we can find things we both like to do together, but I have no problem with her having interests she doesn't have to include me in. I just want for us to be happy."

Suddenly, Sara was plunged into uncertainty and despair when Bobby didn't call for three days. Then, on the fourth evening, the phone rang. Sara tried to let it ring -- to not let him think she was as anxious to talk to him as she really felt, but, by the third ring, she grabbed the phone, her breathless "Hello?" a little too loud and urgent, she realized as soon as she had said it. "Hello, Sara," he said.

"Where have you been, Bobby?" she asked, silently kicking herself for sounding so desperate. She paused, cleared her throat. "I miss talking to you when you don't call. You're very unpredictable." Her tone was now slightly less tense.

"We have to try to not let the day-to-day stuff get to us," he said. "We have to keep the big picture -- our whole lives together -- in sight.

"I like to ride my horse into the mountains; it clears my mind. I stay out there until I unwind. If I don't call you, don't be concerned. I'm fine. Don't worry; be happy, baby," he said in a matter-of-fact, upbeat tone.

He sounded so sincere Sara couldn't resist taking what he said as the truth. "Don't you have a woman, Bobby?" she asked.

"Not for a year or so," he said, adding, "I did live with my ex-girlfriend for a couple of years. But we're not together anymore. So, I'm unattached ever since."

He hesitated, as if waiting for Sara to say something, but she didn't know what to say, so he continued. "I met my last girlfriend while visiting my daughter, Dawnette. I was driving semi, passing through Salt Lake City, Utah."

"You have a daughter in Salt Lake City, Bobby?" she asked.

"Oh yeaaah; she's a doll baby -- twenty-one years old and a ski instructor," Bobby said, pride in is voice.

"Do you ever see Dawnette, Bobby?" Sara asked.

"I call her and she sent me a Father's Day card last year," Bobby replied.

Sara unexpectedly popped the next question, to see what he'd say when she caught him off guard. "Are you calling any other ladies on the Romance Connection?"

"I did call a couple," he said, then asked, "Why?"

"I just need to know if you have someone else." She wanted to be honest with him.

"No, baby. The others didn't work out; there's no one but you now," he said, sounding sincere.

Sara continued her interrogation. "Have you ever been arrested for committing a crime?"

The line was silent for a moment. "I'm not a righteous man, but I've never been in the joint," he said finally.

Knowing that his reference to jail as "the joint" meant that he probably had in fact done some time behind bars, Sara

Thief of Love

asked, "What did you do?"

He kept his voice low, trying to keep her calm, Sara realized. "I was charged with a misdemeanor -- assault upon the police. There were two of them beating me with billy clubs, and I fought back; you know, like Rodney King. I was also charged with resisting arrest and disorderly conduct. Since then, I stay out of L.A.," he said, adding, "I was born there; but I don't get homesick. My ex-wife and two sons are there too. My mother and father are dead and buried nearby. I've been up here in Monterey for a time with David, my brother. He lives in Seaside, and works in Salinas, for California Armor Company, welding and building government armed cars."

When she didn't respond, Bobby continued, "David is <u>tops</u> -- dynamite! He's an intelligent, sensitive man with high moral standards -- law-biding citizen at that."

Sara decided to put her suspicions aside, accepting his seeming honesty as a good sign, for now, and asked, "Where is Seaside?"

"Within low miles of Monterey," Bobby replied at once, obvious relief in his voice over the fact that she had given him a chance to continue. "You can see the ocean from David's house. When I'm not at the ranch working, I spend time with David, fishing out on Fisherman's Wharf. I love the sound of the ocean at night. When the fog is in, I can hear the fog horn as it moos against the chilly, peaceful night air."

"Chilly, in Monterey, California?" Sara asked.

"The temperature stays the same in Monterey year round--about seventy degrees in the day; but it cools down in the evening. It's so beautiful out here," he told her. "What do you say, honey, in the next few weeks if I fly you out here? We can sit outside and watch the whales and dolphins together by the ocean. This can be the beginning of a beautiful relationship. Think about it. For the next few weeks, I won't call you because I'll be out riding cattle -- hustling herds to ranches in Texas to make money for you, honey. If I buy you a plane ticket, will you accept my offer? Can you come out? I want to be face to face with you and hold you in my arms," he said, his voice as casual and relaxed as if he'd just asked her the time of day.

Sara was so surprised she was taken off guard; it was almost as if he had delivered a surprise punch line to a joke. She had to keep herself from laughing as she replied, "Bobby, let's take it slow and careful, okay? I don't even know what you look like. I want to find someone who needs me, gains pleasure from me and appreciates my support. I want to get to know him."

Bobby said, "I have dark hair and steel-blue eyes, with a tanned complexion. I'm a cross between Charles Bronson and Clint Eastwood -- macho."

"Oh, so you look like a movie star?" Sara asked, chuckling, then said, "I bet you have a lot of girlfriends."

"Some girls like me, some don't," Bobby said. "What does my lady look like?" he asked.

"I'm tall -- about five foot, eight inches, with reddish brown hair."

"A long-legged woman?" Bobby asked.

"Well, I guess you could say that," Sara said.

"I love it," he said, sounding enthusiastic.

Generally, over time, as each began to know how to deal with the other, their interactions improved. But, Sara noticed, as the calls keep coming in, he seemed to be deliberately delaying her visit. But, she accepted that, presuming he might be busy with work, as she was; besides, she thought, she hadn't planned on going to California till he brought up the idea, and she also thought it might be better to try to get to know him even better over the phone before their first face-to-face meeting. On the other side of it, she felt a deepening loneliness as each passing day reminded her that time would wait for no one.

"What do you think about us getting together soon?" he finally asked. "If two people want, of course, they owe it to themselves to be together." He paused a moment while his words weighed on Sara's sense of isolation and longing, then said in an almost grand tone, as if making an announcement, "I'm coming to Ohio, baby!" She didn't know what to say, and flustered into the phone as she said, "I -- well, that is. . . I, uh --"

He cut off her stumbling words with a plea. "Give me a chance to make you happy. It's up to you. Your tomorrow can be anything you want it to be; a time filled with happiness; a vibrant togetherness. Just believe in me, baby. You won't be sorry."

The coaxing allure of his low, crooning voice coupled with Sara's own self-doubts and absence of a companion proved stronger than her power of resistance. She knew that he knew she was vulnerable to his persuasive conversation because she found herself going in the direction Bobby wanted to take her. Despite her wanting to take it slowly, he convinced her that his visit to her would be a good next step.

En route to Ohio by Greyhound Bus, Bobby called her from San Francisco. Sara still wasn't sure if he was coming or not; he could have been calling from anywhere; he could even still be in Monterey. Her heart tightened at her confusion. She wondered how she could get involved in a relationship with someone she'd never even met before, and had doubts about where it would take her.

In his next calls Bobby said he was in Cheyenne, then

Thief of Love

Omaha; she no longer doubted he was coming now; with each of his updates he sounded more excited, and she was infected by his mood, feeling herself becoming excited as well, despite her misgivings. During the call from Omaha he said, "When I transfer in Chicago, I'll be delayed six hours, but I'll be -- for damn sure -- ready to get off this bus loaded with skinheads!"

He still sounded excited, but on edge now too. "They're getting to me -- messing with my beaver hat. I hope I don't have to teach them some manners," he added.

His last words made her concerned; but, she felt, it was too late to call off their meeting.

"I'll arrive in Sandusky tomorrow at ten thirty. Try and get down to the bus station. Wait inside and surprise me. When I get off the bus I'll find you."

Sara experienced a momentary chill; a feeling of foreboding; of post-excitement depression setting in. Her sense of discomfort about their meeting kept her awake most of the night as her mixed emotions assailed her from every side. <u>I need to have a clear mind</u>, she thought. In the morning she mediated her conflicting feelings. It had been a long and sleepless night; but now she knew she was prepared for the start of a strong relationship, if that was what fate, and God, had ordained for her.

Thief of Love

Chapter Two

It was ten forty Tuesday morning when the Greyhound bus with "Cleveland" on its destination board pulled up in front of the Sandusky bus depot.

Inside, Sara sat upright with anxious anticipation on a long bench in the curbside waiting room. Looking out the big plate glass windows with curious eagerness, she saw the passengers filing toward the front door of the bus as it slowed to a stop directly in front of where she sat.

The bus door opened with a whoosh of compressed air, and the tired travelers began stepping outside and going to the rear to claim their baggage.

Bobby had said to stay inside, so Sara remained seated and turned her head toward the assembled passengers near the baggage compartment, noticing a man, his face weathered like a Cordovan, wearing a Levi jacket with a black Western hat pulled down low over his brow. He carried a dark duffel bag strapped over his shoulder, turned away from the baggage claim area and entered the station, pausing just inside the door, appearing to feel a bit awkward.

Sara knew it had to be Bobby. His eyes held a kind expression. He cast a sidelong glance toward Sara, and she could feel his eyes penetrating her. He had recognized her just as she had him.

Sara stood, standing tall in her black coat and faded jeans, with trendy store logos on her sweatshirt and black blazer.

He winked.

"Hi, Red," he said, his voice booming, adding for all to hear, "I like what I see." His face broke into an infectious smile, which she returned.

Thief of Love

"How did you recognize me without a picture?" she asked.

"My sites were set on you, baby, before I left my seat," he said, his enthusiasm making his words a confident boast.

His confidence melted her reserve. "That's all right," she said, seeing his obvious eagerness. Even though he might have been forward, he did seem independent, and Sara was happy about that.

Knowing that first impressions are limited, she still didn't expect to see him in such a condition. However, on a Greyhound bus for three days, without shaving consistently, it would be difficult to look spruced up. His hands were shaking, and she knew it wasn't from nerves. He looked like he might have a drinking problem, but no one is exactly as they first appear she thought. Perhaps he had lost his direction in life after his divorce, she reasoned. He didn't exactly fit the Clint Eastwood/Charles Bronson image he projected on the phone, but his weather-beaten skin, tanned by the sun, made him look very rugged -- if he wasn't an authentic cowboy, then she never saw one.

Her intuition wasn't always correct, Sara knew, but she saw beyond his shortcomings. Though she was expecting something else, she saw that he had a lot of heart, and his eyes looked kind as he smiled in a good-natured way.

He surveyed the room. "Where's the nearest phone?" he asked. "I need to call the ranch."

Sara pointed, "All the way to the rear of the building, near the restrooms."

Bobby turned and quickly went toward the phone banks, taking long and quick strides. He stepped into a booth next to the mens restroom and closed the door.

Sara waited a few moments, and Bobby reappeared, stepping out of the phone booth and returning to the waiting room. He gave Sara a quick nod, sighing deeply as if relieved at making his phone connection. "All right," he said. "I'm finished. Let's get out of here."

He led the way out of the bus station. Sara zipped up her jacket against the cold as she and Bobby returned to the baggage pickup area, the earlier crowd of passengers now mostly dispersed to their destinations.

The Greyhound's diesel engine threw strong, pungent fumes into the brisk Ohio winter air as Bobby gave his claim ticket to the baggage attendant. "Run this number," Bobby said.

The attendant sorted through the three remaining items of luggage, then shrugged, handed back the ticket and said, "Sorry, not here."

Bobby frowned, shook his head. "This is unreal," he said as he turned, marching back inside confidently, gazing steadily ahead.

Sara followed as Bobby entered the office, almost shouting as soon as he stepped inside, "Where in the hell did you people put my luggage?" All conversation in the room stopped as voices dropped and there was an awkward silence.

Bobby crossed his arms over his chest and adopted a defiant pose in the center of the room.

A tall man wearing a gray suit and blue necktie rose from his desk at the rear of the office and hurried to Bobby's side. "May I help you, sir?" he asked.

Bobby glared at the man, then fairly spit out his words as he said, "Where the hell's the manager?"

"I'm the manager," the man said, lowering his voice in an effort to encourage Bobby to do the same, but the tactic didn't work as Bobby's stare grew in intensity and hostility, his face reddening.

"This is bullshit!" Bobby shouted, adding, "Trace down my luggage, man!"

The manager held up his hands in supplication as he said, "Hold on! Hold on!" He held out one hand, and Bobby just stared at it. "I'll need your claim check," the manager said.

Bobby harrumphed, handed the manager the ticket and resumed his insolent stance.

The manager's smile was gracious as he took the claim check to the nearest console and scanned the computer for a moment, then returned to Bobby, speaking softly again as he said, "I'm sorry, sir. I know you're concerned, but don't worry, Mister Johnson; your luggage was taken off in Chicago by mistake. Please, just leave your phone number and I'll get back with you as soon as I know when the baggage will arrive here."

Bobby continued to scowl as he accepted the pen and pad of paper the manager retrieved from the counter and offered him, scribbling Sara's phone number in an impatient manner.

The manager took the pad, put on the most optimistic face he could muster and turned away.

"Well, get on it; and I don't mean tomorrow," Bobby said, his voice now calmer but still with a hard edge, his irritation obvious as he stormed out, leaving Sara to follow him once more.

His long legs made one stride for every two of Sara's, so she had to hurry to catch up. When she was still several feet behind him, he turned around and asked, "Where are you parked at?"

She pointed to the north side of the bus depot as they went -- Bobby taking long strides, Sara half running to keep up with him -- around the semicircle of brick-paved sidewalk. His boots thumped solidly on the brickwork as he strolled boldly between the rows of parked cars, on the opposite side of the pavement ahead of her.

Sara went to her 1998 Buick Park Avenue and said, "Right here. The passenger side is open."

Bobby stopped, turned, looked over the hood and smiled. "Hey, hon," he said, "I need to ask a favor." Without waiting for an answer, he continued. "Can I please borrow money off of you to buy a pint?" His tone made it sound more like an order than a request. "I have a check coming from the ranch for my share of hauling a herd of horses to various western ranches. I'll call when we get to your house, and they'll forward my check."

Sara stiffened, struggling to shake off fierce feelings of futility she said in a quiet, steady voice. "I guess so."

They got into the car, pulling the doors shut against the cold. She put the key into the ignition while Bobby turned on the radio and scanned the stations. As she drove out of the parking lot, he found a station playing the Kentucky Head Hunters. He turned the volume up high, blasting loud music into her ears. The sound made her suddenly aware of the tension headache that had been bothering her all morning.

"Bobby," she said, "Please turn that down."

He scowled, turning the music down a little -- just barely.

"It's still too loud," she said as she turned onto the main road toward her house.

His frown deepened as he turned the volume down just a little more.

With an exasperated sigh, Sara reached over and turned the knob till the music was at a comfortable level.

"Can't hardly hear it now," he said in a sulking tone, like

a five-year-old.

With Bobby's obvious resentment of authority, even in its mildest form, Sara immediately realized it was questionable if she could tolerate a long-term relationship with him.

He started drumming his fingers heavily on the dash and singing along with music -- also too loud -- until the song finished.

"This is beyond belief," she said. "What absolute arrogance."

Bobby's sudden laughter erupted. He sounded genuinely amused; clearly enjoying her discomfort. Her low tolerance for his arrogance seemed to lift his spirits. He suddenly reached over and touched her hand, saying, "I'm sorry, Red; I'm just a little too tired. It was a long trip, and those skinheads that got on the bus in Denver kept razzin' me about being a cowboy till I thought I'd explode." He held her hand to his lips and kissed it. "Your hand's soft, but cold," he said, continuing to hold her hand in front of his lips, blowing warming air onto her chilled fingers.

The warmth spread from her fingers to melt her cold, hard mood. "You're a mystery man, Bobby. You know, you make me edgy," she admitted without thinking.

He looked serious, then his face broke into the slightest smile. "Hell, I'm no mystery man," he said. Studying her. Then, his tight little smirk relaxed, and he broke into a grin, as if waiting for her to join him.

Sara shook her head, then had to cover her mouth as she stifled a laugh.

"Hi, baby," he said, his tone pleasant. "Glad to meet you."

She nodded. "Okay; we'll start over. "Glad you're here, Bobby."

Thief of Love

Without warning, he slid across the seat, putting his arm around her shoulder. "Give me a kiss," he said, gripping her jaw and turning her lips toward his, planting a quick kiss on them.

Sara raised her chin, lifting her jaw out of his grasp, turning her head so she could see out the windshield. "Bobby, I can't see the road if you turn my face to the side."

He laughed and gripped her shoulder tight. "We've got to get closer tonight," he said, his tone soft, almost romantic.

In spite of her better judgment, the sense of mystery and excitement about him kindled her interest.

Bobby looked away, surveying the street. With his free hand he reached into his pocket for a cigarette, then said in husky and eager voice, "How close are we to a carry out? I'll buy my bottle there."

"A few miles on up the road, we'll run into a drive-through, but you can't buy high-powered alcohol there."

At his look of confusion, she explained. "Here in Ohio, we have state liquor stores where you can buy bottles of liquor, and get carry-outs of beer and wine in grocery stores."

He shook his head, smiled and said, "Let's get moving to the state store then."

They settled into silence as she drove along the state highway. The car began to get chilly inside, so Bobby pushed the temperature control level all the way over into the heat zone, then resumed looking out at the countryside. He blinked as if to relieve some eyestrain, then glanced over at her. "The farmland stretches for miles," he said. "The country is so flat and dull -- it looks the same, with no hills or mountains all the way to the horizon."

"No, Bobby, not all of Ohio is flat," Sara said as she shook her head, keeping her eyes on the road. "We're close to

Thief of Love

the lake frontage. Ohio Amish country is rolling hills; about a one-hour-twenty-minute drive south from here; Holmes, Tuscarawas, and Wayne counties; the heart of the Amish farms. Buggies roll along the narrow, hilly roads; and farmers, children and their horses roam the rolling countryside. The foothills of the Appalachian Mountains begin about there." Sara nodded ahead and to the right. "You'll see farms about ten miles south of the Lake Erie shoreline. Ohio scenery is different from out West in many ways, but beautiful. About a quarter of a mile out of town, on State Route 4, you'll start to see farms and barns. Farming and agriculture are big in Ohio."

Opening his window, Bobby gazed up at the noonday sun shining through the clouds. "I'll land a part-time job exercising horses and shoveling out stalls in my spare time. We'll get a newspaper and I'll check the classified section," he said in a motivated tone. His flashing blue eyes suddenly seemed shadowed with a quick change of thought. "The wind is strong out there. Whipping up something from the northeast?"

"Typical February and March weather -- strong winds in Ohio," Sara said with a nod. "You may have to hold your hat on out there, Bobby."

He looked glum. "I wonder if I made a mistake coming to this gawd almighty forsaken country," he said in an almost whining tone. "March wind, rednecks, and redheads."

Sara thought he was kidding, but a sidelong glance revealed he was still frowning.

"And a Republican state," he added, his frown turning into a crooked smirk.

<u>How obnoxious -- he needs an attitude adjustment for sure</u>, Sara thought.

It was a few minutes before noon when they arrived at the

state liquor store. She turned right into the public parking lot across the street, just beneath the fifteen-minute parking sign.

"Let's go," Bobby said, his mood improved now that the liquor store was just across the street.

He climbed out, and, again, Sara followed a step behind.

Sara started to cross the street, jaywalking. But Bobby continued on the sidewalk, going toward the traffic light a half block away. Sara cut across the street and watched as Bobby stayed on the other side, stopping at the red light.

When the light changed, he crossed, accosting her as he came closer, "What's with you people in Ohio anyway? It's against the law in California to jaywalk."

Sara's mood was of calm exultation as she said, "Jaywalking is illegal in Ohio too; but the police are busy with more important matters, I guess. Maybe that's why you have so many drive-by shootings out in California -- more than we do here, even in Cleveland."

Her satisfaction increased as he fumed quietly and stalked past, ignoring her as he opened the liquor store door, letting it close in her face as he went inside.

Sara waited there outside the door, holding her purse. She watched as he stood just inside the door, scanning the fully stocked shelves.

A man carrying a brown paper bag stepped away from the cashier's counter, approaching the door. Sara stood aside, and the man opened the door and went out, holding the door open for her. "Why, thank you," she said, adding, "Such a gentleman."

Sara stepped inside, casting sidelong glance at Bobby, her good feelings growing as she saw that he had seen the man's polite gesture, and heard her reply, although he pretended that he hadn't.

Thief of Love

    He snatched up a bottle with an impatient gesture. "Just get me a liter of Black Velvet," he said, his words bitten off. "A liter will last me till I get my check from the ranch."

    She was stunned by his ill-mannered demand that she buy him the liquor.

    Bobby reached out his hand, clutching hers. "Let's pay for this." He arched his eyebrows.

    She turned away.

    He stepped around her and studied her face from the side. She knew he could see in her eyes that she felt disappointment and sadness; that she feared it had been a mistake allowing him to visit her.

    "Look, baby, I'm sorry. It's been a long trip, with skinheads bugging me to boot; I'm just too tired, remember?"

    She nodded, sighed, turned to look directly at him but didn't know what to say.

    "I'll feel a lot better when I get to work and have some money rolling in," he said, trying his best to prompt her into a better mood.

    But all Sara could feel was dread. Feeling helpless, all she could do was look at him.

    "Aw, come on, baby; give us a kiss," he said, reaching for her.

    Sara thought of the men who were too aggressive, pushing women to give them what they wanted, no matter how the women felt. She turned away, saying, "Bobby, please, not in front of people inside the store." First his rudeness, then his insensitivity and invasion of her privacy all left her hurt and confused -- cold loneliness mixed with hot anger. She suddenly blushed, embarrassed to be seen in public in such a state, studying him intently for a second.

Thief of Love

Bobby looked around as if in search of something or someone to help him out of his situation, then sighed and said, "I'm sorry if I sounded disrespectful. I regret it if I did, but you should observe traffic lights. You're my friend and I'm worried about you." He put his arm around her shoulders again, pulling her a little closer.

She felt a momentary chill, then, reluctantly, almost as if struggling with herself, she leaned into him.

"Goodness, you are going to have to lighten up. Okay, foxy lady?" He took his arm from around her shoulders, stepped behind her, reached up and massaged her shoulders.

The tension that had kept her from relaxing all morning began to lessen. Sara believed he wanted to make her happy. She nodded, breaking into a slight smile. She turned toward him, staring at him for a few seconds. His expression on his face was a mixture of earnestness and amusement at the same time. Her smile widened, she nodded, opened her purse, stepped up to the cashier's station and put twenty dollars on the counter.

Bobby set the liter of Black Velvet down and waited for the clerk to ring up the sale and bag their purchase.

They started toward the door. Outside, a cluster of traffic went by. Among the cars, a passing police cruiser slowed down, the officers inside scanning the interior of the liquor store.

Sara noticed Bobby was now moving slowly and carefully. He didn't step outside, instead he stopped just inside the door and stood, watching. He felt in his pocket for a cigarette, fingered it, then took a moment to light up. "What do you think they're looking for?" he asked at the police car pulled out of sight.

She shrugged. "I don't know, Bobby, but it's not <u>me</u>!"

Bobby nodded absently. "I know that; you're too

honest."

She stood there, waiting for him to open the door. "They probably just take a look inside liquor stores to see if everything's okay, instead of hunting for jay walkers."

He didn't laugh or even grin at her attempted humor, instead saying, "I don't like cops."

She nodded. "They like to give out parking and speeding tickets. I have two on record."

"See what I mean? He scowled, taking another drag on his cigarette. "I can smell cops. L.A. cops patrol the street with battering rams. They come unannounced to your house in the middle of the night while you're asleep, and just knock the door down."

"Ye Gods," Sara said. "Battering rams?"

Bobby nodded. "All you see is hundreds of poked holes and big gashes in the wall. Your house looks like a demolition derby when they get through." Bobby's eyebrows lifted and he sighed.

Sara's eyes opened wide. "Can they do that?"

"They plant so much evidence, you don't stand a chance when they're out to get you." He cast an unreadable look at her.

Sara was feeling suspicious of him again.

Bobby stared at her in silence for a long moment. "Smile," he said, prompting her. "Don't worry, baby." He reached over and patted her shoulder. "What do you say we head to your house and have a drink?"

They settled back in her car. Bobby took the liter of Black Velvet from the bag and poured a drink between his eager lips. Sara started the engine and up the car into gear, then headed away from downtown, toward her house on Taylor Street.

Bobby settled into an easy comfort after a few more sips

from the bottle before she parked in front of her home. He looked up and seemed to study her pale gray, two-story Cape Cod with a glassed-in front porch and black shutters. With a brief glance toward her he said, "Let's get a move on," his tone impatient.

Sara ignored his lack of good manners, got out of the car and, closing the door behind her, started around as Bobby hopped out, retrieved his duffel bag and slammed the passenger-side door shut.

They headed toward the porch. "Give me the door key," Bobby said; it was an order, not a request.

She handed him the key. He reached for the partly opened storm door, shaking his head in disgust as he asked, "Don't you people know how to shut a door around here?"

Sara wondered why he was so bothered just because the storm door wasn't shut tight as he gripped the knob of the heavy oak front door, inserted the key in the deadbolt lock, and opened it, handing the key back to her.

Without observing the proper etiquette or protocol, he marched inside, with Sara right behind.

Bobby frowned at the exposed ceiling beams in the foyer, then advanced into the living room as if he, not Sara, owned the place. She tried to view the room through his eyes: the wallpaper was in soft hues of blue, green and purple. Natural earth tones dominated the furnishings. An Amish horse bridal mirror was straight ahead. The decor was Southwestern and Pennsylvania Dutch, with handcrafted Amish furniture. A couch, loveseat, two big chairs, coffee table and end tables in Amish Oak completed the scene. Sara was proud of her home; but Bobby didn't seem impressed.

"Where's the kitchen at?" Bobby suddenly asked.

Thief of Love

She led him into the kitchen.

He paced around, went to a kitchen cabinet, opened it, pulled out a glass and poured himself two fingers of Black Velvet, neglecting to offer her any.

"Do you have Seven Up?" he asked, his tone polite, in contrast to his actions.

Sara went to the pantry, retrieved a twenty-ounce bottle and handed it to him.

Bobby mixed the Seven Up with one half whiskey in the glass, pulled a chair out from the kitchen table and sat down.

Sara noticed that his hands were shaking as he downed over half his drink in one gulp. Sara sat opposite him as he finished his drink and lit a cigarette. "Guess I'm gonna like here in Ohio for a while," he said as he mixed himself another drink, his hands steadier now.

Sara eyed him closely. His 'for a while' remark made her think he wasn't sure if he'd stay long. She thought that when his check from the ranch came in he'd move on. <u>Maybe he doesn't really like what he sees</u>, she thought, feeling a twinge of disappointment, while realizing that might be for the best.

Bobby ground out his cigarette in the glass ashtray she kept in the center of the table -- for guests because she didn't smoke herself. He downed the last of the whiskey in the glass and stood up, saying, "Excuse me," as he moved his chair back from the table. "I'd like to shower and shave."

Sara stood and led him into the living room. "I'll show you upstairs, Bobby." He followed her up the stairway with his duffel bag. She guided him to the bedroom where he emptied his personal belongings from the duffel bag onto the bed: a plastic bag of soiled underclothes, a toothbrush and toothpaste, shaving cream and a razor, cigarettes, an address book and clean underclothes. There was also a red cap with black print in small letters across the top that said, 'Paso Robles, CA.'

Sara showed Bobby to the bathroom, giving him a clean bath towel and washcloth. He placed them on the back of the toilet and looked into the mirror above the vanity, then took off his shirt and stared at his reflection, wearing jeans and, above his narrow hips, a belt with a large silver buckle. "I've only gone since yesterday without shaving."

"Your beard grows back quickly then, doesn't it? She asked as she stepped back into the hallway, still facing him, adding, "I'll get out of your way, Bobby -- so you can clean up."

Looking in the mirror at her, he smiled. "You remember what a smile is, don't you?" he said, coaxing instead of trying to intimidate her, adding, "Smile." "You know -- the corners of your mouth turn up like this." He demonstrated by pushing the corners of his mouth up with his fingers.

His antics made her smile. It wasn't a broad but genuine.

He nodded. "It's what people do when they're happy."

Her smile faded a little as she wondered if she really was happy.

"Be happy; don't worry," he said.

His prompting made her smile widen again as she turned away and went down the stairs, thinking how funny he could be, and how he had swept her off her feet immediately on the phone, but also that he was very unpredictable.

Sara relaxed on the sofa, and, moments later, she could hear the sound of the shower water and, within another minute, Bobby's version of the Randy Travis hit "Forever and Ever." Her thoughts about him sent her heart racing, even as she was wondering what would happen next -- whether he would enjoy nightlife, or like a quiet night at home, cuddling up next to her, just watching TV.

Chapter Three

About four thirty, the phone rang and Sara answered it.

The caller began with the introduction, "My name it Ted Mitchell. I'm a scriptwriter for the Clay Bennett Show -- a nationally syndicated T.V. talk show. One of our future segments will be devoted exclusively to a story about the Romance Connection."

"Well, I don't think I'd really enjoy any publicity about myself, with or without the Romance Connection," Sara said.

"May I speak to Bobby Johnson?" he asked.

Sara felt momentary confusion, followed by irritation. "How did you know Bobby Johnson would be here?"

"He told me," Mitchell said.

"When did he do that?" Sara asked.

"Before he left Monterey," Mitchell replied.

She couldn't keep the irritation out of her voice as she told him, "Bobby is taking a shower," and asked, "Is there a message?"

"Yes. Please tell him that Ted Mitchell called."

"What do you know about Bobby?" Sara asked.

"Oh, a little bit, actually. Good old Bobby's name keeps coming up on the Romance Connection. He's a charmer with the ladies. He's done nothing wrong, even though women are sending him money cross-country and throughout the southwest to come and see them. He's clever and prolific."

Sara couldn't keep the alarm from her voice as she asked, "What else should I know about him, Mister Mitchell?"

He laughed. "We've kept in touch with Bobby about various aspects of his personal life from the time we focused on the Romance Connection. He's quite a talker, and knows what he wants."

Sara thought for a moment. This Mister Mitchell seemed to know a lot about Bobby. She found herself wondering if this was the routine way talk shows worked. They seemed to be investing an awful lot of time and money for just one interview. She heard Bobby turn off the shower, and quickly asked Mister Mitchell, "What exactly is it you want with Bobby?"

"We're in the preliminaries -- very early development stages -- of producing a story about the Romance Connection. I'm writing the script. It would probably be a good idea for you and Bobby to keep your schedule flexible for a last-minute interview. You may find something coming your way that will occupy you and be profitable at that. We're in hot pursuit to include Bobby in the script."

"Would you please call back tomorrow?" Sara asked.

"Okay," Ted said, asking, "What time would be good to catch him?"

"Probably about dinnertime," Sara said.

As Sara and Mister Mitchell exchanged good-byes, she could hear Bobby open the door to the bathroom, and, a moment later, the bedroom door closing. She felt good about her decision to question Mister Mitchell for information about Bobby while he was in the shower, not wanting to linger on the phone to wrestle with what she was sure would be Bobby's annoying questions about the conversation. She wanted to consider her thoughts and be in touch with her feelings in private.

Sara felt a terrific disappointment. What had Bobby done? she worried. She knew he hadn't been completely honest with her, which was never a good sign. A series of possibilities troubled her mind. <u>Could it be possible I may get burned real bad?</u> she wondered. Then she thought maybe she was being too suspicious. Maybe what Shea had seemed to be suggesting was right -- maybe Sara was bringing some of the bad luck on herself with her own negative attitudes and paranoia. She decided to dismiss her worries for now, and to give Bobby a chance to prove himself, not wanting to condemn him merely because of a strange call from someone she didn't even know.

But, still, Bobby's not being forthright with her made Sara decide to call and consult with Shea.

"Well, what did you think at your first face-to-face meeting with him?" Shea asked.

"My first, almost irresistible impulse was to send him back to California," Sara said, her voice firm.

"Right then?"

"Yes. He might have good looks and sex appeal, but he's tough-talking -- not street talk, but very blunt; and at times he's uncomfortable to be around because he's self-centered and overly confident. That's his biggest problem."

"Well," Shea said with a sigh, "give it time; don't be too hasty, honey."

"I do know one thing for certain, Shea. If he is going to hang out with me, he's going to have an attitude adjustment. Can you come over? You can see for yourself."

"It won't be for a couple of hours. I have an appointment with my hair dresser," Shea said.

"I hope it doesn't take too long; try to get a move on it. I need to talk to you. A man called from the Clay Bennett T.V. cable talk show, a scriptwriter. I couldn't believe what he told me; he's in hot pursuit of Bobby about including him in a story devoted exclusively to the Romance Connection."

"Oh boy," Shea said, adding without hesitation, "I'll be there. I want to hear about this."

They exchanged good-byes and Sara hung up.

"Who was that on the phone?" Bobby called down the stairs.

"Just my friend, Shea. She's coming over in a couple of hours to meet you."

Without any modesty, Bobby trotted down the stairs wearing only a bath towel wrapped around his waist, his hair still wet, but combed. Sara's eyes zeroed in on his athletic body. His shoulders, chest muscles and arms were tattooed.

As he headed for the kitchen, she noticed a large forest scene across his back, shoulder to shoulder. The ink wasn't in bright colors but subdued tones. Then her attention was drawn to the way he moved -- with the grace of a man accustomed to taking charge, and without a trace of self-consciousness.

Sara was baffled. Bobby acted as if he owned the place. She watched through the open kitchen door as he opened a cabinet, and retrieved the bottle of Black Velvet. Without asking her permission, or even looking in her direction, he poured himself a glass of whiskey and Seven Up. Then, in a leisurely manner he sat in a kitchen chair just as the phone rang.

Sara answered it.

"Who's calling?" Bobby shouted from the kitchen.

"I don't know yet," Sara called back to him, then said into the phone, "Yes?"

"Ted Mitchell here. Is Bobby Johnson in?"

"Oh, hi, Ted. This is Sara," she said, then asked, "How are you?" She thought she'd make a point of showing Mister Mitchell that he'd forgotten proper telephone etiquette.

Ted stuttered and stumbled. "Oh, uh, s-sorry. I-I'm fine. And you?"

Without responding to Ted, Sara held out the receiver

Thief of Love

toward the kitchen, shouting, "Bobby, it's for you."

He growled as he stood slowly and adopted a relaxed pace as he went to the kitchen doorway, saying, "Isn't there a phone in the kitchen?" He paused, then added, "This is a personal call, you know."

Sara didn't try to keep the sarcasm out of her voice as she said, "Well, excuuuse me; the phone's beside the refrigerator."

Without thanking her or any extending any other courtesy, he turned abruptly, stalked to the kitchen phone and picked it up, saying, "Bobby Johnson here." He paused a moment, then said, "Man, what is with you? What do you want? What kind of story are you writing?"

There was another pause, then Bobby said, "Sounds tough."

Sara stood with hands on her hips and stared at Bobby, then wandered back and forth across the living room, listening and watching his face as he said, "Yeah, yeah, man. I'll go with it!" Then, he glanced at Sara, turned away from her and lowered his voice, but she could still hear him as he said into the phone, "Call back in a couple of hours. Okay, man?"

With that he hung up the phone, returned to the kitchen table, finished his drink then headed into the hallway and called to her, "I'm going to call the bus station about my clothes."

Sara shrugged as he returned to the phone and dialed the number. She heard his low conversation, but paid no attention to what he was saying and, after a moment, he hung up again, returned to the hallway and said, "Come on; let's go get my clothes."

<u>Just like that</u>, she thought, <u>with no asking, even a warning; with the expectation to get going, right now.</u>

Sara sighed, put on her parka and her gloves, then had to

wait while Bobby went upstairs, put on his clothes and came back down.

They went out to the car and she started the drive to get his clothes. After they had gone about two blocks, Bobby leaned over to check the speedometer and gas gauge. Sara was driving at the thirty-five-mile-per-hour city speed limit; the gas gauge was at one quarter.

"Stop and get gassed up," he said. "Then I'll drive." It wasn't a suggestion, just a matter-of-fact order.

His manner of trying to take over irritated her, so she turned it back on him. "Do you have a driver's license, Bobby?" she asked.

"Yeah, but I'll need to send for it," he said, adding, "I lost my wallet."

She shook her head. "You can't drive my car without a license, or proof of being licensed in California. My insurance won't cover you if we have an accident."

"<u>Son of a bitch</u>," he said, slipping into a brooding, childish mood.

Sara continued on at the speed limit. After a moment, he looked over at her and said, "So, you want to drive -- <u>drive</u> already!" He looked out the window and added, "What are you waiting for, Christmas?"

Sara tried to relax as she sped up slightly.

He lit a cigarette, puffing hard, inhaling deeply.

The trip continued in silence until they arrived at the bus depot. When Sara parked, Bobby hopped out of the car, walking jauntily down the parking lot without waiting for her. She got out of the car and was only halfway down the parking lot when he entered the office. As Sara entered the depot, Bobby was receiving his baggage -- a green army bag about five feet long

Thief of Love

and three smaller bags; two looked light, the other heavy.

"Help me carry these bags," he said, not asking, without even a `please.'

She picked up the two smaller, lighter-looking bags, pushing through the door herself, not holding it open for him or waiting. She could hear him grumbling behind her all the way to the car as he struggled with the two heaviest bags. Sara popped open the trunk, tossed the two bags inside, went around and resumed her place in the driver's seat while Bobby tossed the heavier small bag into the trunk, closed it and loaded the large bag into the backseat. He climbed into the passenger side and remained sullen, probably still from the disappointment of not being able to drive her car.

Sara started the engine and drove toward home as Bobby lit up a Camel, switched on the radio and scanned the stations.

"I'm not a smoker," she said.

He ignored her.

She decided to try kindness instead of confrontation. "Are you hungry, Bobby? We can stop at McDonald's and get a sandwich and fries."

He shrugged, then said, "No, let's stop at a bar. I'll have a couple of drinks, and we can shoot some pool."

Sara thought that might be better than sitting around her house getting on each other's nerves. "Okay," she said. "I'll take you to Eve's Korner; it's near the house. They have food service and a jukebox -- the music sound system is stereo; and they have a pool table. You'll like it there."

He nodded. "Okay, but don't take to me where your boyfriends go."

"I don't have any boyfriends," Sara said, then sucked in a deep breath and puffed it out as she added, "Not anymore."

Thief of Love

She parked in front of Eve's; they could hear the loud Country Western music as they got out of the car and went inside.

Bobby didn't hesitate once he got inside the room, heading straight for the bar.

Sara followed and called after him, "Don't sit at the bar, Bobby. I'd rather sit at the tables. Bars are for the men, okay?" He turned toward her, gave a one-shouldered shrug and even smiled as he said, "Be my guest then. Okay, sit at a table. Give me a few bucks and I'll get us a couple of drinks."

Sara handed him ten dollars.

"What are you drinking?" he asked.

"I'll take a Bud," Sara said.

Bobby went to the bar, bought their drinks and returned to the table. He set his seven and seven down, popped the top of her Bud and poured it into a glass for her. He slapped the change -- a five dollar bill and several quarters -- onto the tabletop, pulled his chair out and sat down next to her, then dragged her chair closer to his, reaching his arm around her neck and suddenly kissing her.

While Sara was still stunned from his seemingly impulsive yet casual advance to the kissing stage, he pulled four quarters from the pile and pointed with his jaw toward the jukebox.

She sipped her Bud; he took a gulp from his; they rose. She stayed by his side as he led her to the jukebox, inserted the quarters and pressed the selections for Garth Brooks, Billy Ray Sirus and Travis Tritt.

The jukebox immediately started playing Garth Brooks' latest as Bobby put his arm around her, singing in rhythm and swaying with the music.

Thief of Love

Sara could tell he was a hard-playing cowboy, and caught him checking out the bar filled with women, who had all dressed to be alluring, did their best to be seductive, and thought themselves to be irresistible.

Bobby looked the pool table. "I'll shoot you a game of pool, Red," he said with a grin.

She felt a sudden apprehension. "My name is not 'Red'; it's Sara," she told him in a firm tone.

"Okay, Sara," he said as he nodded, reached for two pool sticks and offered her one.

"I don't play well, but I'll try." she said.

"Go for it," he called out with a gusto Sara was sure was meant to impress the other ladies.

They played two games; she could see her lack of experience and skill made the game a lot less than thrilling for him, so, when a handsome young man of about twenty-five picked up a pool stick Sara returned to her seat and took a sip of beer.

She watched Bobby and the young man have fun playing pool and throwing it back and forth, then thought to check her watch. It was seven thirty. Her eyes darted about the room, never still, always watching some of the other women who were watching Bobby.

She thought about Shea coming over as Bobby returned to the table for the five dollars change he had brought back from the bar, but said nothing. He took enough quarters to keep playing pool, ignoring her completely.

A colleague from the plant, Calvin Patrick, wearing his United Autor Workers solidarity jacket with a Fedron Chassis A.M. emblem on it, came into Eve's and went over to play the jukebox. He saw Sara sitting alone and nodded. She nodded in return and, after Calvin made his selections and bought a Miller Lite at the bar, he joined her at the table.

"What's doin'?" Sara asked.

"Just on a thirty-minute break from work for dinner," he said, asking, "How come you're not working tonight?"

Just then, Bobby Johnson appeared at the table, standing with his hands in his pockets, glaring at them. Sara saw the suspicious condemnation in his eyes.

"We've got a problem here," Bobby said, his voice an angry growl.

Calvin looked up in surprise and set down his beer.

"She's with me," Bobby said, fire in his tone. He put his foot on an empty chair and kicked it aside. Sara's anger flared like a sudden storm. She jumped up and stepped between them.

"That's enough, Bobby!" she said through clenched teeth.

Bobby leaned aside to continue glaring at Calvin, who stared right back, remaining cool as he picked up his Lite and took a sip.

Sara stepped between them again, blocking their view of each other. "Cool it right now, Bobby Johnson. Take it easy. Cal and I are co-workers -- friends for many years. Lighten up!"

Bobby scowled as he half shouted, "We're out of here. Get your purse; let's go." He turned and started for the door, then stopped and glared back, silently prodding her to follow.

Sara shook her head in disbelief as she started across the room toward Bobby.

Bobby grunted at her and said, "Come on; I told you about your boyfriends. Get moving, now!" He marched ahead of her to the door.

Sara longed to apologize to Calvin Patrick for the rudeness, but she didn't want to give Bobby any excuse to continue or escalate the confrontation. <u>What a turkey</u>, Sara thought as she followed him out the door.

On the way out, Bobby turned the `open' sign around so it read `closed' as he pushed the door open. He didn't look back to see her turn the sign back around as she trailed behind.

The air felt cold and thin; Sara shivered with a sudden chill. Her mood plummeted into misery as she followed Bobby to the car, thinking: <u>He's an alcoholic -- without question. He's trouble.</u>

Bobby remained silent as they got into the car. She started the engine and drove once more for home. Just as she pulled out of the parking lot he jerked his head back and said, "It's the end for you for sure. I'm leaving in the morning."

She shot a quick glance toward him, and looked away. This time Bobby was motionless -- no cigarettes, no music, no conversation. He just stared ahead like he was in deep thought, fury and disgust in his eyes.

They pulled up in front of the house. Bobby got out of the car quick as lightning. She was surprised but a bit flattered -- and surprised that she was flattered -- by his jealousy. He opened the rear door and pulled out the large bag. She popped the trunk and he removed the heaviest of the three bags there. She got out, retrieved the two lighter bags, closed the trunk and followed him up the steps, where he stood sullenly outside the locked door.

She set down the two lighter bags, unlocked the door, and, without waiting, stepped in ahead of him, dropping the bags in the foyer and going into the kitchen to get herself a drink of water.

She heard him drag the bags inside, close the door, and carry all the luggage upstairs. As she listened, she heard him seized by a fit of deep, gagging, choking, coughs -- lasting nearly

Thief of Love

a minute -- but she resisted the temptation to rush up to see what was wrong. As long as she could hear him, she knew, he was still breathing.

Within a few minutes, Bobby came downstairs, having changed into black jeans and a red tee shirt with 'Paso Robles County Fair' on the front -- matching the cap he had worn earlier. He marched into the kitchen with his jaunty walk, retrieved a glass, the Black Velvet and Seven-up and made himself a drink. Although still silent, Sara could see that his mood was more relaxed.

She just stood by the sink, wondering what she would say to him when the doorbell rang. Sara went into the living room, looked out and saw Shea's Coupe DeVille. She opened the door and Shea stepped inside just as Bobby was coming into the living room. Shea looked at Sara, then Bobby and back to Sara again, searching their eyes intently.

"Bobby, I'd like you to meet Shea -- who's a very good friend of mine," Sara said, adding, "Shea's the one who prompted me into posting a message on the Romance Connection."

He said nothing so Sara continued with a smile. "Shea became a close friend after we met when her plant closed in Bristol, Connecticut -- a sister A.M. operation -- and she transferred here. Our anniversary of employment dates are close: mine is October 28, 1968; hers is November 28, 1968."

Shea went to the sofa and slid onto it with the grace of a goddess, motioning Bobby to sit in a nearby wingback chair. Sara noticed that Shea carried a designer handbag with a long leather strap, which she set on the end table. Sara thought Shea's classic features would get anyone's attention, even without the careful application of makeup.

"I'm so pleased to meet you, Bobby," Shea said, putting her freshly manicured, dainty fingers into his hand.

He shook her hand and held it till she slowly eased it away. "It's good to meet you, Shea," he said.

Sara surveyed Shea's long, curly blonde hair, which made her look even more gorgeous and feminine, and saw that Bobby was eyeing Shea curiously. But Sara wasn't jealous of her; she knew she could always hold her own with men.

"So," Shea said, "tell me about yourself."

Bobby shrugged. "Not much to tell."

"Well," Shea continued, "what do you do for a living?"

"Ranch hand, mostly," Bobby said in an offhand way.

"My, that's exciting," Shea said, adding, "and I'll bet the money's good too?"

Bobby fell silent for a few moments as if adrift in another thought world, oblivious to her question.

Shea shrugged and got up. "I'd like to take your picture with Sara," she said, seeming to want to impress Bobby, and Sara, with her personal importance. Shea walked across the room, dropping her hips with every step, confident his eyes were following her strut. She turned to catch him looking and, dangerously close to the immodest, shook her head, laughing and wrinkling her nose.

"No pictures," Bobby said, quickly on guard. "We're not here to pick assignments for show and tell." Bobby obviously felt uncomfortable. He cleared his throat deeply, choking for a moment again, then crossed his arms over his chest as if to demonstrate his determination.

Shea remained cool and self-contained, almost emotionless. "You're calling the shots, Bobby," she replied. Bobby smirked. Shea continued. "Well, this is pretty impressive -- you coming all this way from the Pacific coast, and being pursued and sought after by a national cable T.V. talk show. What's involved there, anyway?" Shea had suddenly turned to ask Sara, catching her completely off guard as she struggled for an answer.

"Uh, you'll have to ask Bobby about that. Why don't you while I go upstairs and straighten things up a bit?" she finally said, excusing herself with what she was sure was a sick look on her face.

Sara left them standing in the living room as she proceeded upstairs, where she quickly sneaked into the bedroom. Inside, she made a brief survey of Bobby's personal belongings. She carefully and quietly opened the large duffel bag, hoping it would give her some clues about Bobby -- the real Bobby, not the one he pretended to be. Inside, she found a book titled, "What Women Want; What They Don't Want." Underneath the book, behind a manila envelope with a sheaf of what appeared to be legal papers, some photographs included a picture of a beautiful young lady in her twenties wearing a ski suit, standing atop a snow-covered mountain on a perfectly clear day, the blazing blue of the sky contrasting with the pure white of the snow and her tanned, almost peaches-and-cream complexion. Alongside her were two children, also dressed for skiing -- a boy about six and a girl around seven. Sara turned the picture over. 'Dawnette' was printed across the back. She had a medium build and long blonde hair, and Bobby's steel blue eyes, leaving not a doubt in Sara's mind that she was his daughter.

"What are you doing up there," Bobby yelled from downstairs.

"Just straightening up," Sara called back, hastening to close his bag, go the dresser and start moving her bric-a-brac --

Thief of Love

perfume bottles, compacts, tissue box, hairbrush and other cosmetic items -- into one corner.

"Stay out of my room," he shouted.

Your room? Sara thought with bitterness. I let him use my room and now he thinks it's his.

"Get down the steps," he yelled again, his tone now more of a growl.

Sara came down to find Shea on the phone. Speaking in a strong, firm voice and clicking her nails on the table Shea said into it, "I'm Bobby Johnson's manager -- Shea Robinette from Bristol, Connecticut. I reside presently in Sandusky, Ohio."

Sara threw a contemptuous glance in Shea's direction, frowning in disgust.

Shea glanced at Sara, disregarded her discomfort and continued talking into the phone. "My understanding from Bobby is that you'd like to invite him on the Clay Bennett show; is that correct?"

Before Ted could answer, Shea turned on the speaker phone.

"That's correct. There's no need to be formal though." Ted's tone was relaxed and his words clear. "We've considered a story idea about the Romance Connection, with some of the main focus on Mister Johnson."

"How so," Shea asked.

"We'd like to include Bobby and a couple of the ladies he met through the nine hundred number phone hot line. He has quite a gift with the ladies, I've learned." Ted chuckled into the receiver. "We've been in hot pursuit to keep up with Bobby's latest location. We tracked him down before he left Monterey, California. Women just seem to gravitate to him."

Shea was taking notes on a pad as she said, "He is quite

Thief of Love

impressive." She crossed her legs, knowing it would inch her silk skirt up her thighs, and that Bobby would look.

Sara threw her another contemptuous glance, which Shea also ignored.

Bobby calmly regarded Shea's exposed flesh while Ted rambled on. "I understand Bobby is powerful in many ways, due to his rough-and-tumble background."

Shea spoke clearly, emphasizing her words. "A short while ago, I spoke with Bobby and he's agreed to be flown to New York to appear on your program."

"Sounds good," Ted replied. "The show will be videotaped in two weeks. Bobby will be flown to and from New York, and will have a complimentary room in one of the city's better hotels."

Shea looked to Bobby, who shrugged and turned away. "And what else?" Shea asked.

"Oh," Ted continued, "Joyce, from El Paso; Texas, and Lori, from Monterey, California; have been invited too."

"Let's talk more about what Bobby wants," Shea said, her voice rising. "We're talking business here -- you and me; okay?" Shea continued, her words coming faster as she spoke. "Bobby will require a package of one thousand dollars cash, and a new pair of Justine or Durango leather Western boots, plus, he'll need to eat while he's in New York and I'm sure your program can arrange for Bobby to have his meals taken care of, and not in any of the second class places either."

"I don't know about all this," Sara interrupted, eyes wide, asking, "Why are you pushing this and egging it all on? I just met Bobby. You're going to kill the romance before it goes into motion. You're interfering with my peace of mind, happiness, hope for the future."

Thief of Love

Shea cradled the phone, covering the mouthpiece with her other hand till Sara stopped speaking, then held the phone to her ear and continued, ignoring Sara's words. "Ted, are you still there?"

Bobby's body language signaled defiance as he studied Shea's face, giving her no look of support in his facial expression either.

He looked to Sara and said, "So, you're worried about my affairs. I can't believe it."

Shea and Bobby watched her as Sara said, "Well, are you tempted? Keep this in mind, Bobby Johnson; I want you to think about it." She spoke in a commanding tone. "If you're going to be with me and stay in my house, you will not go on cable T.V. with other women whom you've slept with. Joyce and Lori are probably lowlifes and sleazy. You'll probably be in bed with them before you come back," she added in stifled exasperation, tears clouding her eyes.

"That sounds like a threat," Bobby said, his expression hard and his eyes cold.

He snatched the phone from Shea's grasp. Shea looked up at him, shock running through her.

Bobby spoke into the phone in a firm tone. "Hey, man," he said, his gaze on Sara's face. "Let me talk this over with my lady tonight. I'll call you tomorrow."

Sara walked past him and back into the kitchen.

"It's your call, Bobby," Ted said, a chuckle in his voice. "Go on, call me back at a good time. I'll look forward to hearing from you."

Bobby handed Shea the phone, and she hung up, but kept writing in her notepad. She looked at him, raised one eyebrow, flicked her hand and said, "You'll have a good future if you can do what I tell you. If you don't go on the show with Lori and Joyce, the deal's over before it starts." She spoke with more determination as she continued, "I'll included Sara in the package. She'll also get a paid trip. Sara, don't sabotage this." She slammed the notepad down with the last words.

Bobby shook his head in disbelief. "Seems like you have it all planned out your way! What I need is a rousing roll in the hay with two obliging tramps and a pair of eager parted thighs. Get real." He paced the room with his jaunty gait.

Sara slammed back, her adrenaline flowing. "I don't give a damn what you like." She nodded at Shea. "The two of you will make great partners -- Romance Connection Soaps. You should go on T.V. and take on the world and everyone in it on your own terms and on your own turf! You characters are a show of its own!"

"That's a laugh," Bobby said, then muttered under his breath in a sarcastic tone.

Shea looked toward Sara, her words coming through clenched teeth as she said, "I think you owe him this one." She leaned back in the chair and smiled at Bobby mischievously. "Look at your boots. Couldn't you use a new pair?"

Bobby looked at her with an aloof, cold expression.

Shea's chin snapped up, her words coming sharp as she said, "Anyone can be bought, if the price is right." She shifted in her chair, removing her suit jacket. She shifted again, thrusting her chest forward, showing off her breasts.

Sara wondered if Bobby would be swayed by Shea's flirtations. Her nerves were raw from the silent, charged tension that had come between them.

Bobby stared steadily at Shea then said, "No one's going to buy me, Shea. Sara and I are in this together." He began

Thief of Love

pacing again.

Shea reached into her leather handbag to retrieve a tube of lipstick and hand mirror. She pretended to look into the mirror, but instead scanned the room, watching Bobby. As he turned in her direction, she batted her long eyelashes flirtatiously.

Bobby met her eyes, but made no response.

Shea's smile was seductive.

Sara coughed as Shea's antics became too embarrassing. "I think she kind of likes you, cowboy."

Bobby looked at Sara in surprise -- as if he didn't think she would have understood the interaction between him and Shea.

"Well, are you tempted?" Sara said, and waited, looking from face to face.

"Fer God's sake," Bobby said, looking at Shea and shaking his head. Then, in a more serious tone, he turned toward Sara and said, "Thanks partner." He nodded toward Shea. "She's easy on the eyes and has a smooth personality. Right now though, I think I'll hang tight with my foxy redhead." He put his arm around Sara and looked into her eyes. "I'm a talkative guy but not stupid. There'd be no reason in the world for anyone else." He leaned toward Sara, kissing her and putting everything he had into it.

Shea sighed, stood, pulled her jacket and purse from the sofa and said, "Oh, people, it's getting late. This has been a unique evening, for sure." Her tone was sociable and gracious.

Sara stepped out of Bobby's embrace and escorted Shea to the door.

Shea turned back, looking at Bobby. "Good nigh-yight, Bobby," she called, singing out to him.

"See ya'," he said, his tone abrupt.

Thief of Love

Sara knew the danger from Shea had been averted only by Bobby being alert enough to duck and dodge her beckoning, from first meeting to final call.

As Shea went out the door, Bobby asked, "Like to rent a movie tonight?"

Sara shrugged. "It's been a long day. I have cable; maybe we can find something to watch and order a pizza."

Bobby smiled. "Sounds good to me."

After the pizza was gone and as the movie ended, Sara found that, somehow, they had gotten very cozy together. A kiss led to another, then a couple, and then a lot more. She knew she shouldn't let herself be so weak, but it had been too long since Matt left.

Bobby looked into her eyes and said, "I'm tired. Come on along to bed."

Sara hesitated, sitting still on the sofa, her whole body stiffening.

After another passionate kiss, Bobby said, "I get scared when I sleep alone; come on along."

She relaxed a little, but remained unmoving next to him.

"You know how I feel about you, girl," he said, adding, "It's one o'clock in the morning already." He stroked her neck and kissed her ear, whispering, "Come on."

Bobby's attentions suddenly brought Sara to a blazing readiness. She allowed him to pull her from the sofa and lead her up the stairway. They stopped at the top of the staircase, directly opposite the master bedroom door.

Sara started to pull away, stepping toward the guest room at the end of the hallway.

He held onto her wrist. "Where are you sleeping?" he asked.

Thief of Love

"I was going to sleep at the end of the hallway. I planned for you to sleep in the master bedroom," Sara replied.

He leaned down and kissed her. The sensation of scratching stubble from his mustache, the feel of his lips, teeth and tongue on hers brought moans from both of them.

His hands were soft, moving slowly over Sara's neck and shoulders, enticing her. She leaned to thrust her breasts against him and she held him tight, kissing his lips until he became hard. She ground into him, her thighs gripping his loins. His breath was heavy, his hand with a firm grasp on one of her breasts. Sara had no doubt of his lovemaking skills as he led her into the bedroom, guiding her to the bed.

Overcome with sudden passion, she pulled back the covers as his jeans dropped to the floor. Within seconds he had helped her out of her clothes, and she allowed him to take her. Tonight, she would have to be content with what lovemaking would allow, and she knew finding out would take them closer to the brink of heaven or hell -- whatever tomorrow would bring.

Thief of Love

Chapter Four

Over the next few days, Bobby's inclusion in her life set Sara out of her normal routine. The first day they sorted out his clothes; everything was musty and smelled of cigarette smoke, as though they hadn't been washed for awhile, just quickly packed. As they stood before her washing machine he said, "Here's a rolled up, damp tee shirt; put it in the first batch."

She nodded. "Okay, Bobby; but let's not mix whites with colors -- we don't want to bleach out the colors when we get the stains out of the whites."

He mumbled and grumbled to himself as he rummaged through the clothes, picking out the dark colors and sorting the whites.

Sara noticed he had several designer shirts, in bright colors that threw off a lot of energy. She thought that his taste in casual as opposed to work clothes was good. She liked the sporty casual style of his jeans and a few pair of dress pants, as well as his heavy-lined coat and high-top boots.

After he sorted a pile of dark clothes, shirts and pants, Sara set them in a wash basket before she put them in the laundry chute. She noticed two long-sleeved navy blue uniform shirts and pants to match. The appearance of the work clothes set off a strange agitation within her, and she felt compelled to ask, "Bobby where did you work to wear these uniforms?"

He lifted his head with a slow reluctance, staring at the clothes. After a long pause, he said, "I worked for Brewer and Banner -- an upscale amusement company in California. They travel a three-state circuit to places in California, Nevada and Utah."

Sara noticed that the name label across the front shirt

pocket wasn't 'Bobby Johnson,' but 'Bob Haynes.' "Why is this?" she asked.

He stared at the name, but didn't reply.

"Who's Bob Haynes?" she asked.

He shrugged. "Oh, Bob Haynes was my celly's name. He died while he was at a California men's colony. We were together for several years," he added, his face sad, his tone subdued.

His response didn't allay her suspicion. "Why do you have his clothes?" She knew from his reactions that something was wrong.

Bobby flashed a quick grin, restrained it and said, "I'll be doggoned. They're not his shirts; they're mine. I used his name in order to keep a low profile in California."

"Why did you think you needed to do that? Sara asked.

He shrugged. "The newspaper ran a few articles about me." He fell silent, not elaborating.

"Are you a fugitive?" Sara asked suddenly, dropping his shirt into the washing machine.

Bobby's eyes flared and glittered with anger. "No! Hell no!" he said, half shouting. "I'm not on the run. You can even ask my sister, Megan; my Aunt Betty; or my brother David. I'm not a runner, I face my problems." His tone was insistent, sincere.

Sara wasn't satisfied, but decided not to press him any more at the moment, making a mental note to file the subject for a later discussion.

Over the next few days Bobby spent a lot of time in 'his' bedroom, keeping the door shut and only permitting Sara in to clean when he said it was okay. She wanted to get in there to check it out and sort through the papers in the manila folder, but felt it was too risky. If he caught her, it would make her attempts to investigate more difficult, so she decided wait for the right time.

Already, Bobby was taking possession of the house. Sara was forced to listen to his morning grumbling until he got some alcohol. Ever since the morning after, she regretted spending that first night with him, and now refused to sleep with him, using the excuse: "I can't sleep with you because you snore. It keeps me awake most of the night." She talked to him less and less, holding back her feelings.

"I didn't come this far to be treated like this," he said, his friendly demeanor fading fast. "I want to work this out with you."

Sara slept in the back bedroom. Late at night, she heard him talking on the phone. There was an extension on the night stand next to her bed, and, feeling very tempted, she reached for the it, trying to avoid making any noise that would signal him that she was eavesdropping.

As soon as Sara held the receiver to her ear, the sound of a woman's voice suddenly alerted her. Her feelings of resentment overcame her caution, and she couldn't remain silent. She shouted into the phone. "Who are you talking to?"

"Look, bitch, get off the phone or I'll come back there and rip it from the wall," he said, his voice trembling with anger, adding, "And get your ass up here, right now."

Sara was overwhelmed by her anger as she shouted back at him, "Screw you, Bobby! Don't you think you're running over me, especially in my own house." She slammed down the phone, hopped out of bed, threw on a robe and hurried down the hallway, her mind in turmoil. She burst into 'his' room, shouting, "Get the hell out of my house!"

Thief of Love

"You don't really want me to, and I will not!" Bobby shouted back at her as he hung up the phone. He jumped up, stalked around the room and then stepped in front of her.

Sara glared at him, her expression hard and cold.

He sighed, lowered his voice and said, "Look, don't love me so much that I feel smothered. The truth is you're jealous."

"What an inflated ego you have." She shot the words at him.

He backed off, looking regretful. "I'm over two thousand miles from my home; just stay out of my private calls to my sister and my cousin from Virginia. It's possible we'll be able to stand each other until my check comes from the ranch. Then I'm outta here."

Sara doubted his story about his sister and `cousin' was truthful.

* * *

After the first of the month, phone bill arrived in the mail. Sara wasn't surprised but disappointed and upset at the large number of his calls apparently made to other women. He had even called the number of the Romance Connection. Recently, however, he had made a point of extending little kindnesses to her, which made her wonder if the calls had been farewells and a cancellation of his Romance Connection membership. She tried to put aside her unpleasant pangs of jealousy. The very thought of him being able to attract romance with sensitive women over the phone made her feel ill.

When Sara asked him to pay for his calls, he said, "As soon as my check's here from the ranch."

"You've been talking about that check for weeks," Sara said.

"I don't know what's taking so long; I'll call about it,"

Thief of Love

Bobby said, starting toward the phone on the kitchen wall.

"Give me a direct answer," she said, asking, "Who, exactly, was that woman I heard you talking to on the phone."

He frowned and said, "That's my cousin, Ellen, in Virginia." Then he scowled and added, "No more questions, okay? I don't want to hear any more suspicious probing or remarks." He stared at her, his eyes cold.

She stared back.

"Wait. I know where to get some money." He went into the living room. Sara followed.

Bobby picked up the phone, dialed a number, hit the speakerphone button.

Sara listened to the ringing on the line, then heard, "Ted Mitchell here."

"Hey, Ted, it's Bobby Johnson," Bobby called out toward the phone speaker.

Without hesitation, Ted said, "The deal's off, Bobby."

Bobby looked surprised. "Off? Why?" His voice was weak and quivering.

"We have to make hard choices all the time," Ted said, adding, "Our research people investigated and report that you did lengthy prison time in the seventies for assaulting members of the L.A.P.D. Is that true, Bobby?"

In the following brief silence, Sara stood and watched Bobby through a haze of anger. Bobby was deceptively quick, confident and decisive. He raised his palms to her, as if to demonstrate he was unarmed.

"Hey, no harm! I'm a hard battler -- none better when trouble comes down, but I wasn't in any crime scene or violence directed against the L.A. Police. I'd been running wilder than a jack rabbit in southern California," he said. "But, I want to settle down with someone to love. Just for the record: I'm not those women's fantasy outlaw either."

The line went dead as Ted hung up.

Bobby picked up the phone and kept trying to get through to calling Chicago, but didn't get past an answering machine, and the receptionist at the network just sent his call through to the answering machine again. He even tried to call Ted's house, but another answering machine picked up the call there too.

Sara guessed that no matter what Bobby's record had been, Ted had probably changed his mind because she wouldn't go along with the script they were writing about Bobby's life with women he met on the Romance Connection hot Line. Even with Bobby denying his criminal involvement, the L.A.P.D. angle would have made a hotter story for the Calvin Bennett Show. She decided she had done enough damage by not cooperating with the T.V. show idea and left him alone about his prison time, for now.

Sara had to get to work on second shift, so, without saying good bye, she left. During the shift, she found it hard to keep her mind on her work as her thoughts strayed to Bobby. He was a chore to live with at times; just after switching to second shift she had come home at eleven forty to find him looking through her mail. He handed her most of the envelopes, then threw down a piece of junk mail from a televangelist, contempt on his face as he said, "These guys are no good; they're just taking advantage of your good heart."

She appreciated his loyalty, and believed he wasn't at all the dangerous man she had first imagined. Sometimes, he would do his best to please her, but the relationship unfolding between her and Bobby was still very tenuous. He had shared a few confidences, and she had refrained from prying into his private life.

Then things reverted. Sara returned home from afternoon shift; it was eleven forty-five p.m. She found Bobby slumped in an easy chair, clicking his way through the television channels.

She could tell he was in a frenzy and something was bothering him, so she asked, "Bobby, what's wrong?"

He forced himself to look into her eyes, then said, "Shea is a back-stabbing friend."

Sara sat on the sofa and asked, "What did she do to make you so upset?"

Bobby turned off the T.V. and put the remote on the table. "Shea called, wanting me to go out with her to the comedy club tonight," he said in a low tone.

Sara frowned. "What did you tell her, Bobby?"

Bobby's expression suddenly became troubled. His voice dropped to a nervous whisper. "She told me if it were you and you had the opportunity, you wouldn't consider her feelings."

Sara sighed in exasperation. "Shea loves to play people against each other. She's done it all her life. I'm used to it, but I'm offended." Sara's voice quivered with anger and the sobs she held inside. "She's not pulling this off; I'm calling her for a woman-to-woman talk."

Sara picked up the phone and pushed the speed dial button.

Shea answered on the second ring.

Sara held one hand over the mouth piece as she said, "Bobby, listen," and switched the speaker phone connection on.

"Shea, this is Sara, Sara said, then asked, "What's the deal?" Her tone was insistent, demanding.

Thief of Love

"What are you talking about," Shea asked, innocence in her voice.

"Why did you call my home, for my boyfriend, while I was working, trying to take him out behind my back?"

"What?" Shea sounded surprised. "Is that what he told you?"

Sara was breathing fast, and her words came out in puffs of anger. "He said you're a back-stabbing friend; that you went out of your way to show the other side of your nature."

Shea kept up her defense. "Sara, I'm appalled that you'd think I would have asked him that. What I did do was call for him to give you a message; and he asked me to come pick him up." Her tone had been indignant, but now dropped to a friendly respect. "Now, are you going to let yourself be deceived and distracted? Think about it. I didn't do it."

Deeply hurt and not convinced by Shea's story, Sara swallowed hard. "I still want to know, Shea -- if you can't be my friend all the time, why this? Your focus is more on what you want. It appears the friendship we have is divided whenever there's a man on the scene."

Shea resumed her indignant tone. "I don't want to talk to Bobby, so tell him for me: I wouldn't waste my time on a charlatan."

Bobby could hear every word Shea said and started to say something into the speaker, but she had already hung up.

"Whenever there's a call, I'm checking the caller I.D. first. If it's from Shea Robinette, I won't pick it up. The answering machine can record the message," he said to Sara.

"Right now, I feel the same way myself," Sara said.

Thief of Love

Chapter Five

Over the next few weeks, Bobby changed his tack, going out of his way to become almost gracious. He would tell neighbors with the utmost sincerity that they were engaged to be married as soon as he gained steady employment. "After we have a beautiful church wedding, all I want is to cherish Sara for the rest of my life," he told them.

His charm and warmth had their effect on her, and she agreed to rejoin him in the master bedroom. A natural chemistry seemed to take hold between Sara and Bobby. She saw that he had a lot of good thoughts about things, and she drew them out of him. He shared with her his hope of someday operating the largest cattle ranch in the state of Ohio. Sharing his hopes and dreams, and having steady companionship in her life again -- along with her keeping house, fixing meals and showing hospitality -- brought Sara a real sense of joy and fulfillment.

But it was still far from perfect. Sara spent the better part of most mornings listening to Bobby complain. He got up early and was jittery in the morning, but would be bored and listless by noon.

"When you have steady work you'll feel better," Sara told him one morning, then watched as -- restless, irritable and discontented -- he picked through the want ads. He found fault with many of the offerings before even calling them, but went out on an occasional interview. However, she soon realized he either sabotaged any job interview he was lucky enough to get by claiming he couldn't do the work, or found a reason not to go after he was hired, such as, "I don't feel well today," or, "It's too far away," or, "I got no car." He even used these excuses for refusing jobs that she thought would be perfect for him.

Thief of Love

    Worse, Bobby began calling California almost every day, bemoaning his situation to his friends and family. He even blamed the weather for his problems with remarks such as, "The weather in Ohio sucks. There are clouds and it's overcast all the time -- no sunshine."

    Sara tried to help him in every way she could. She studied the classified ads, provided leads, and helped him prepare a resume. She gave him rides to interviews or money for taxis if she had to work when he had an appointment.

    Finally, one day at breakfast, exasperated, Sara told him in a firm tone, "Stop your whining and do something about your life. You can't glory in the sunshine during the winter in Ohio. We live close to Lake Erie where we have seasonal overcast and clouds during the winter and early spring."

    He remained sullen, staring into his coffee cup.

    Sara started to clear the dishes away. "Bobby, everything big begins with something small. You can't start out with the biggest cattle ranch in Ohio; start with what you have. Look at a beginning point as an opportunity," she said. "What I want in a partner isn't difficult. Remember what you said to me on the phone from Monterey? I want the same thing: I don't want to compete with my partner in life; but I do want to share with him and enjoy life with him and, if he needs my support, I'll be there."

    He got up from the table, went to the kitchen drawers, dug out a paper, pencil and ruler, returned to the table and began drawing.

    Sara started washing dishes. "What are you drawing?" she asked.

    Still working intently, he said, "The layout for the biggest cattle ranch in Ohio. It's a champion plan. Like you said, I'm at the starting point of my biggest dream and goal. It will emerge," he assured her, as if shaken out of his doldrums.

Seeing that he was still lost in his fantasy, Sara rolled her eyes and shook her head as she turned her attention to the dishes, saying, "Welcome to the real world, Bobby. It won't fall into your lap, and will definitely not be easy."

He threw the pencil and ruler down on table, leapt up and headed toward the back porch, assurance still in his voice as he called back, "It won't be today or tomorrow, but it's going to be a kick."

Sara decided not to press Bobby for promises. She was after deeds, not words. She did realize he was still setting himself up for failure by setting unrealistic goals, and felt somewhat sorry for him, recognizing that he obviously had very little money and no chance of getting that cattle ranch if he wouldn't work toward his goal.

Their unfolding relationship was still very tenuous, and often almost completely broke down. His drinking soon assumed more serious proportions, beginning many afternoons and continuing almost every night. He had shared a few confidences with her, and she tried to refrain from invading his privacy. It soon became apparent, however, that Bobby had health problems. He complained about pain in his stomach, and she noticed that he sometimes carried a styrofoam cup, occasionally spitting phlegm into it. He told her, "The pain is kicking me in the ass; if I don't have a drink of whiskey, I'll suffer.

"I think it would be better if you have a medical checkup, and maybe get some medication -- not alcohol -- to relieve the pain; in fact, the alcohol could be the problem."

"What's that supposed to mean?" he asked, his words a challenge.

Thief of Love

"Like maybe ulcers," she said.

He laughed. "I'll have to just call you Mary Poppins, my nurse; okay, hon?"

"Okay; and your nurse says you're going to apply for medical attention through the Veterans Administration Service," she said.

His smile turned to a frown. "Yeah, well, I tried that before, but I lost my social security card, and they won't give me a new one without my birth certificate, which is at my sister's place."

Sara sighed in exasperation. "All right; just call your sister and have her send it to you."

Sara's exasperation grew because Bobby's sister, Megan, who lived in Tucson, required about ten calls from Bobby before she finally forwarded his birth certificate.

When Bobby's birth certificate at long last arrived, Sara drove him to the social security office. She felt lighter, more hopeful than she had in a long time as it seemed he did in fact have a sister out west. She thought that possibly, someday, her life, and his, just might return to normal.

Bobby's often gregarious personality and affinity for children enabled him to make friends with most of the kids in the neighborhood. He listened to them and made everything they said seem important on a personal level. At first Sara was resentful, wanting Bobby to herself, but after she thought about how alone he was -- -away from friends and family in California, and especially while she was working -- she realized he needed to be with people.

Through the neighborhood kids Bobby met Sandy and Rob, the parents of fifteen year old John and seventeen year old Jerry -- a young man ready to join the Army after he graduated from high school. The boys drew energy from Bobby's motivation. Sara thought it was too bad he couldn't motivate himself as well.

At first it didn't seem that Bobby was interested in seeking other women. Somehow, he made Sara believe she was his and he was hers wholeheartedly. But inconsistencies began to appear.

Thief of Love

Chapter Six

One Friday, Bobby said, "These days, I miss going out to the cowboy joints. If you're going to master the two-step you can't work seven days a week." He paused, then asked, "Did you ever dance with a cowboy?"

Sara frowned at his comments and question, then said, "I'll be missing a lot of extra overtime money if I don't work tomorrow."

"Come on, be a good sport," Bobby said.

"Oh, I am a good sport; but, since I'm the only one earning the money to support two people, well I'm sure you can understand."

"Of course I can," he said, adding, "It'll be something to remember -- your first cowboy dance."

Sara thought of Matt Wilson, her ex-boyfriend, who only took her out dancing three or four times in all their time together. She did miss going out to dance, and thought it would be fun. Matt was a rocker; he could sure shake it up when he danced. Unfortunately, it seemed all he had wanted was to work and make money. Now, Sara realized, she was doing the same thing -- working every day. But Matt had faded into the past -- she now recognized that truth, after meeting Bobby. Bobby was a motivator, and he kept everything going in a social setting, which made him a lot of fun to be with. He was blessed with a gregarious and exciting personality, which drew people to him. 'Oh, well. . . " she finally said, wilting with embarrassment; once she set her mind on anything she hated giving up on it.

Bobby smiled. "Great. Let's go tonight."

Sara nodded. "Okay. Give me time to get ready."

They went to Eve's Korner, and, to Sara's chagrin, she

Thief of Love

discovered Bobby had already met a Country and Western group --- 'Southern Comfort' -- who played there Wednesday evenings, during pool league. She silently fumed as she realized he had been going there Wednesday evenings while she was at work on second shift. Soon, with the band playing and Bobby and everyone around him having a good time, Bobby's charisma made him almost impossible to ignore and she found herself drawn into the atmosphere. When he asked her to dance Sara accepted and suddenly realized that she had been having a good time for over an hour.

Jake Lewis, the band's drummer, joined them at a table, along with Jake's daughter, Tammy, and her boyfriend, Russ. Sara was pleased that Bobby had made some friends in Ohio; and his former sullenness had disappeared.

"You know how I get along with youngsters, Sara," Bobby said. "Russ is twenty-one and Tammy is eighteen. Russ owns and operates a motorcycle repair shop."

Russ nodded and said, "I'm going to give Bobby a job."

"Oh, really; doing what?" Sara asked.

Russ glanced at Bobby and said, "Aw, he can hang out and answer the phone. I'll teach him the trade."

"He's going to pay me decent wage," Bobby said, excitement in his voice.

"You bet," Russ said with a nod as he took a drink from the nearly empty beer glass in front of him.

Sara saw Bobby watching Tammy, with more than just a casual, friendly interest she thought. She looked toward Tammy and saw that she was fluttering her big brown eyes and flashing a toothy white smile in Bobby's direction.

Thief of Love

Bobby saw Sara catching their mutual admiration and began looking around the room as he said, "Anybody like a drink?"

Everybody at the table gave Bobby an order, and, with the one hundred dollars in his pocket Sara had given him as they left home, he stepped to the bar, then returned with a glasses of beer and set them all around.

Tammy looked at the beer bottle in front of her, then up at Bobby, her gaze telling anyone who saw her that she had an intense interest in this handsome cowboy man. "Thank you," she said.

Bobby sat back in his chair, pulling Sara closer to make more room for Russ, who was a big but agile man.

Sara sipped her beer as she listened to the idle chit-chat at the table and surveyed Russ's fiancée. Tammy was young and sexy, but with an air of self-confidence beyond her years. Sara could see that despite her aura of innocence, Tammy could easily present a problem, being underneath a wily seductress who could put almost any guy under a spell.

Tammy looked at Bobby, and all eyes shifted to him as she said, "You're a hot number when it comes to dancing. Come on, Bobby, let's see the Western stuff you're made of -- let's dance."

Tammy's golden hair waved rebelliously and her voice was low and alluring; but it didn't need to be because Bobby nodded and said, "You can bet your sweet life it's a dance," as he fairly leapt to his feet, almost brushing Sara aside when he rose and stood waiting for Tammy to join him.

Russ seemed unconcerned and merely continued an involved discussion with Jake about whether playing drums or riding a motorcycle would make you go deaf sooner.

Thief of Love

Sara watched Bobby and Tammy attentively as they stepped across the floor. Sara thought, <u>Tammy is sexy and alluring, and she certainly knows how to use it; and Bobby is a cold-hearted asshole.</u>

For the rest of the night, Tammy asked Bobby to dance every dance -- slow or fast.

Sara didn't like this from the start, and, after a few dances, neither did Russ. Finally she could take it no more and said, "I believe someone has stolen my partner," when they returned to their drinks between dances.

Bobby's eyes widened. "Now, now, no need for this," he said, his voice taking on an indifferent tone.

"Why don't you quit then?" Sara asked.

Tammy pushed at her freshly curled hair and studied her well-manicured nails. "I wasn't looking for trouble -- just wanted a dance," she said.

"<u>A</u> dance, as in every dance all night? Look somewhere else," Sara said, her voice quivering in anger.

Russ fixed Tammy with a steady gaze. Bobby looked away form them, in Sara's direction.

"Speak up! I expect you to cut in," he said, drawling in his cool, slow way.

Sara slammed her hand on the table. "It doesn't make any difference how many good and bad sides you have. When we're together, we're supposed to be together. I'm not supposed to have to deal with you dancing with another man's partner."

Bobby just smiled at Sara as if nothing had happened, saying, "Baby, don't worry. From now on, I'll just give you the sign to cut in, and go on ahead."

Sara shook her head. "It isn't my fault her boyfriend can't dance, and that you dance with a flirty girl like Tammy, so she can put her arms around you; play up to you in front of me -- someone she's never met."

"That's enough," Bobby said, his tone hot, making it a command.

"Yeah, and enough of that, too," Russ said, taking Tammy by the hand and leading her onto the dance floor.

Sara surveyed Russ as he and Tammy joined a line dance: With his curly blond hair, he cut a handsome figure in a tight muscle shirt, despite the fact that his love handles made it bow slightly at the waist. His jeans were low slung, showing just the heels of his cowboy boots. Bobby was in much better physical shape despite the fact he was twice Russ's age.

Bobby was clapping his hands loudly and with enthusiasm as he shouted, "Yeah! Yeah! Come on, get down!"

Applause from other tables and the bar immediately broke out. "Right on," Bobby was shouting. He jumped to his feet, held up his arms and wiggled his hips like he thought he was something hot.

When the music ended, he noticed Sara as she drew sharply erect, astonished by his little act after what she had just told him. She sent him an accusing smile.

Bobby looked at her for a minute, suddenly subdued as he once more sat with his date.

"I 'spect you oughta be moseyin'," Sara said in a cowboy drawl.

"Aw, Sara," Bobby said, his tone almost whining, "We were just funning. Tammy is the doggonest pretty youngster I ever seen."

"Love isn't love without trust," she said.

His chin dropped, making a small circle as he said, "Baby, you don't understand. Bobby Johnson loves you, but he's

Thief of Love

a wild and fun-loving man."

She studied him as he started tapping in time with the music on the table with a beer bottle when the band played a new tune. Searching him with tears welling up, she struggled to keep them from spilling out as she wondered what his sudden use of the distant third person meant. Was he being sincere or removing himself from the equation by referring to himself as if it were someone else? The tension and conflict grew within her as she fought with herself over becoming tangled in another lost love affair or remaining alone.

Sara started thinking out loud, telling him, "I'm a stand-by-your-man kind of woman, not a standing woman waiting passively while other women make passes at my man."

Now subdued, his reply sounded lame as, his arrogance gone, Bobby seemed sincere when he said, "I know I'll have to change the whole way I am. Give it a little more time and I'll be different; I promise. Someday you'll have my whole heart and soul. You'll never know how much I really care about you. For now, I can't help being me. I'm the way God put me together. My spirit cries 'No!' but my flesh is awful weak."

Sara felt that her unpremeditated, caring overture had been rebuffed. "You're not a born again Christian, Bobby. It will never work for us," she said, staring at him as if he were dreaming. "My desire is to have a Christian man; and so far it seems I haven't made contact with you on this. Now, I think it's time for us to go home," she said as she rose and walked out the door, forcing him to scramble to keep up with her.

Outside, Sara deliberately and steadily went to her car, started the engine and put it in gear, not waiting or caring if Bobby went home with her or not.

Thief of Love

Bobby barely had time to open the passenger side door and hop in before the car started to move. They remained silent all the way home. Sara slept in the guest bedroom that night.

Thief of Love

Chapter Seven

The next days were an emotional and physical whirlwind. Sara asked Calvin to let her know if he saw Bobby in Eve's Korner while she was at work, so she knew Bobby was secretly stepping out, which, whether he went home with another woman or not, she considered to be cheating.

Sara struggled to come to terms with the mess she'd gotten herself into; the inconsistencies in bobby's personal life. Sara realized clearly now that for him the newness of their relationship had worn off. Bobby now preferred leaving Sara at home and partying with Russ. Her sole consolation was that Tammy wasn't invited along with them either.

At first he just arrived home late, then it turned into arriving home at dawn or even morning. Anxious and worried, Sara would call the motorcycle shop, but the phone there was hardly answered, or when Bobby did answer he had a ready excuse.

"I'll be late coming home; I'm working my butt off," he would tell her.

Sara was learning the hard way that Bobby was not a man to be led around by a woman. Certainly any woman who fell in love with him would be in for a ride as rough as going bareback on a wild and free-ranging mustang horse.

Despite her private vows to herself to remain aloof and go it alone, Sara tired of being left out and challenged him, "Bobby, I have to know: Is there another woman?"

"No!" Bobby said, half shouting, as he began to rail at her, "You're just jealous, and a bitch. No wonder men turn homosexual -- dealing with super bitches like you." He sounded furious as he heaped his scorn upon her.

Thief of Love

    Arching an eyebrow, Sara wondered if this was Bobby's way of throwing her off or confusing her so she couldn't think straight. Either way, she felt it wasn't fair. "I won't let you get by with this, Bobby. Something is up. You're nothing but a drunken womanizer," she yelled at him as he slammed the door.

    Sara watched from the window as Bobby stomped down the porch steps, his boots echoing on the stairs. She stepped out into the fading sunset, watching him wave his Western hat as if he were departing on horseback. She was suddenly overcome with rage herself as she yelled, "Don't come back, you son-of-a-bitch! You're out of here!"

    Bobby turned. "I read your letters. You're sending money to those hustling preachers," he yelled while he was fading into the distance as he went down the street.

    Sara's eyes were stinging from the cold wind, but that wasn't what brought tears to her eyes. She swallowed her anger and felt her stomach lurch from the effort. Feeling a sense of closure, as if fate had somehow taken it's course, she thought, <u>I'll send offerings to ministries if I want to.</u>

    Disgusted and tormented, Sara returned to her bed -- her own bed, in her own bedroom now that she had told him he was out of there. She lay in the dark, wondering and confused. Minutes became hours and still she couldn't sleep. Bobby was later than his usual overdue time to return home, although she had no idea why she should care.

    Then, just as Sara decided he would not be returning, she heard a vehicle nearing her house. She rose from the bed and parted the drapes. Looking out from the upstairs bedroom window, she could see Russ's truck, and heard an exchange of a few words as the truck door slammed shut. Russ drove off, and Bobby's boots thudding up the steps onto the front porch seemed

Thief of Love

to echo in the late-night stillness.

Bobby's knocking on the front door was sharp and insistent.

With her muscles tensing, Sara started down the steps into the foyer. The light was off downstairs, but the glow from upstairs made light on the stairway. Sara saw on the grandfather clock in the hall what it was three a.m.

He knocked again, louder.

Sara opened the tiny safety-security portal in the front door and looked out.

"Sara! Open the door!" he shouted into her face.

Shocked, she said nothing and made no move to let him in.

He glared at her and continued shouting. "I'll kick it down. Do you hear me? If it's hell-raising you want, you've got it. It won't embarrass me when your neighbors hear me kick your door in."

After an instant of uncertain delay, Sara unlocked the door.

Without hesitation, Bobby pushed open the door and lunged for Sara, grabbing her shoulder with his rough-knuckled hand. He charged inside and, gripping her shoulder, pushed her head back up against the wall. Expecting a fist in her face, Sara trembled in fear. At the same time, she felt a surge of anger that he could treat her that way.

His expression turned cold. "I told you I'd never hit a woman. Chill." It was an order, not a suggestion. His voice became a snakelike hiss. "Don't you <u>ever</u> lock me out again, understand?"

Her rage grew at being mistreated so in her own house and, unable to restrain herself, Sara fought back. "You're more of a creep than I imagined."

Bobby expression went from cold to hot again as he shouted in Sara's face. "I don't mean to rock your world, Poppins, but I have told you before: I can be your best friend or your worst enemy!"

Sara didn't know how to respond, so resumed her silence.

"Sara, will you marry me?" Bobby asked suddenly.

"Marry you?" She could only repeat the words, incredulous, staring at him as if she were dreaming, but thinking he must be insane. The hurt and anger within her grew until, disregarding the possible harm he could do to her, Sara answered with a definite, "No, I don't want to marry you!" Tears of anger and self-pity began welling out of her eyes.

He leaned closer to her, studying her face intently.

Sara's expression hardened, and her eyes were alight and burning with vengeance. She pushed him away so suddenly she almost lost her balance.

Bobby stumbled back, saying, "You never cease to amaze me. Get upstairs in bed." He pointed up the stairs.

She nodded. "I'm going to bed, Bobby, but alone," she said, her voice hard and cold.

Sara stormed up the steps and went into her room, but neglected to lock the door as she threw herself onto the bed and pulled the covers over her.

She could hear Bobby moving with awkward slowness up the steps; then, suddenly, he pushed the bedroom door open, holding onto the frame to keep his balance. He took two steps and collapsed on her bed, sobbing and reaching for her, so bold, so sure of himself.

"No!" she shouted at him. "Get your hands off me!"

Bobby backed off as her words and gaze lashed him with

Thief of Love

cold fury. Then he jerked his head up, the sudden realization of her rejection like a blow to his face. He muttered a curse under his breath and rolled over on his side. Instantly, his cursing fell silent as he passed out.

* * *

Early the next morning, Sara crept out of bed, moving slowly toward his pants, which now lay on the floor next to the bed. She glanced in his direction, but he was still asleep, snoring loudly. Reaching into his back jeans pocket, she found his address book and snatched it out quickly. She couldn't resist opening it and flipping through the pages: name after name, phone number after phone number, address after address, woman after woman. Then Bobby woke up abruptly leaped out of bed.

"You're busted, tramp!" he yelled in her ear as he snatched the book away. "Stay out of my business!" His voice was cold and unforgiving. "It's all private, personal, and confidential," he said in a deep, dramatic tone.

Sara remained slightly rigid in shock and fear. She now appreciated just how devious Bobby could be. She had thought he had carelessly cast his pants on the floor and was fast asleep; but he was setting her up all along.

"That's it. I mean it; get out of my house!" Sara shouted at him.

Bobby sat back on the bed, narrowing his eyes at her, his hands clasped and pressed against his chin. There was no movement whatsoever on his now expressionless face.

Sara shouted at him again. "You have to leave! I can't deal with you anymore."

He finally moved, taking his hands away from his face, as his expression now relaxed. His voice was low and steady as he said, "Thanks a lot. If not for bad luck, I'd have no luck at all.

Thief of Love

All I did was play pinball last night with Russ."

She stared at him in disbelief. "Since you met Russ, you run all over town day and night. You're seldom with me. You may as well move in with him!"

He smiled and shrugged. "So I'll cut Russ loose. Besides, I can't hang out with him anymore because he's on pills and cocaine, and he smokes pot. I just can't be around drugs!"

"Is it the drugs? Is that what this is all about?" Sara asked.

Bobby shook his head. "No," he said, sounding exasperated. "I can't be around drug users."

Sara thought about how alcohol made Bobby lazy. She wasn't sure if he was doing drugs, especially considering the way he abused alcohol.

His eyes searched hers for a long, silent moment. He swallowed dryly, without his usual first Black Velvet for the day to make it easier. As he seemed to realize she was refusing to humiliate herself by letting tears fall, he looked amazed.

They stood in utter silence for a moment. Sara leaned against the door. Seconds passed. Bobby's expression softened further. He sighed and said in a more relaxed but serious tone, "I won't step out of this house without you. I'll stay in here while you're working and not go anywhere. Please, let's make this work."

Sara's anger began to subside.

Bobby reached for her hands; she didn't resist as he held them. "You're as pretty as a wild rose, and compassionate. I'm beginning to know and understand you. You're a beautiful person, and I can't lose you. I'm a strong man, and I won't let this go easily. I'll do my best to make you happy."

Sara felt her resolve weakening as he wooed her with his

Thief of Love

sweet words.

He held her hands more tightly and looked deep into her eyes as he said, "Please don't make me go back to California. I really like it here."

Sara felt a sudden resurgence of doubt, anger and distance from him. She found it hard to believe this man who was now showing her such tenderness in his eyes. She remembered the uncaring, arrogant, demanding person she had first met. She didn't take her hands away but said in a firm, resolute tone, "I won't deny that I feel something for you, Bobby; but I realize nothing can come of this."

He looked puzzled as, disappointment in her voice, she said, "You seem to talk so straight to me, but fabricate lies that sound so reasonable that I always believe you. You're seldom really drunk, but never totally sober either."

Bobby's expression, eyes and tone became desperate as he said, "I'll go through rehab for you, if that's what it takes to keep you. You'll never know how much I care."

Sara shook her head and showed a sad smile as she said, "You're a double-minded man, Bobby. You have no commitment to the heart. Your first love is your alcohol. I'm number two. You'll always be committed to your alcohol -- your first love."

Thief of Love

Chapter Eight

For the next seven days, Bobby did his best to behave himself. He rose early every morning, as though he had some purpose to his life. Then he hovered near the phone in case someone called too early and disturbed Sara's sleep. After all, she was the one in the household who worked on the factory floor until almost midnight.

On Tuesday morning Sara was awakened by the sound of someone coming up the stairway. The thick carpet on the steps didn't keep her from hearing the footfalls.

There was a soft tapping on the door.

"Yes?" Sara asked.

Speaking in a low tone, Bobby said, "Sorry to wake you, honey. Can I ask you a favor?"

"What is it, Bobby?" Sara called, adding, "You can come into my room."

She sat up in the bed, switched on the light and repositioned the covers around her waist.

Bobby came in slowly, holding a cup of steaming coffee in a foam cup, saying, "Coffee's ready."

"Thank you," she said, reaching for the cup.

Bobby handed her the coffee, stood erect, shifted on his feet, his hand rubbing the top of his head as he said, "Workpower Temp Agency called a few minutes ago. They offered me a job opportunity with a Jeep plant in Toledo. They set up an interview for late morning. The only drawback is the weather is hellacious."

Sara threw the covers aside, turned in the bed and put her feet to the floor, rose and opened the Venetian blinds. Outside, the sky couldn't be seen for heavy snow clouds.

Thief of Love

Bobby stood behind her, blinking and trying to adjust to the sudden brightness of the cloudy yet day-lit skies.

"It will be a pleasure to take you," Sara said, her tone cheery as her mood. She headed for the shower, dropping her nightclothes into the laundry chute on the way and drawing a warm flannel shirt and jeans from the closet as she passed.

Bobby sat on her bed to wait as she stepped into the bathroom shower.

In a few minutes Sara was showered, dressed and leading Bobby to her car, asking him, "Where to?"

"Downtown, on Jackson and Water Street. I was told to stop by Workpower for a work slip with directions," he said as she started the car.

"I believe I know where you're going," Sara said, nodding happily as she pulled away from the curb.

As they drove toward the Workpower office, Sara looked over at Bobby; he seemed happier than she'd ever seen him.

He smiled at her. "I feel so connected to find someone who's this patient and understanding. That's what I love about you."

Embarrassed, she kept her eyes on the road ahead as he continued. "You listen to what I'm feeling. You know, if everything works out in this job, I'll do my loving duty. I'll buy you anything you want, need and desire. If it takes me getting out of bed at three in the morning to buy you a nut ice cream sundae, so be it. I'll do whatever it takes to make you satisfied. Whatever it takes, you got it, baby!"

Overcome by his words, in near euphoria she said, "Gee, Bobby, you don't really have to do anything -- with your flamboyant persona and silver tongue. You'll have your own money. Just love me tonight." As she said the last, she almost bit off the words, but, too late, her true feelings had betrayed her and gotten out.

Bobby's smile widened, suddenly, he leaned over and kissed her.

"Bobby, I can't see," she said, pulling her lips away and looking past his head through the windshield.

"The best is yet to come," he said, hugging her.

Sara covered his hand with one of hers and told him, "I haven't been shown this much caring for a long time."

She nodded ahead, through the windshield, where snowflakes were beginning to flutter toward the pavement. "You're aware Toledo is sixty miles from here?" she asked.

He nodded. "That's the drawback," he said, adding, "Ohio weather."

As soon as he said the words, snow began to blow across the road like bleached white sheets.

As they approached the city center, heavy duty snow removal trucks appeared, plowing their long blades through the streets, pushing the heavy snow aside. Following behind them were trucks spreading rock salt on the on the pavement to keep it clear, at least for a while.

By the time they drove through town, heading north on Columbus Avenue, the snowfall was so thick Sara could barely read addresses on the buildings. As they headed to the bay front, she turned left onto Shoreline Drive, then pulled into the parking lot at the Jackson Street Pier and left the engine idling.

The Snow squalls became more intense, leaving visibility at almost zero. Sara couldn't even see across Sandusky Bay to the Lake Erie Islands. The farthest she could see was Cedar Point Boat dock.

Thief of Love

Sara pointed through the windshield. "Jackson Street is that way. "I'm not familiar with Workpower Temp Agency; and I can't see out there now, Bobby. Watch for lights on the first floor of buildings and, when you see some, walk in and ask for directions."

As he got out of the car, a blast of cold air and swirling snow invaded the dry and warm interior.

"What power in nature. Ohio weather is awesome," Bobby said, closing the door and walking toward Jackson Street.

Sara turned the radio on, scanning for a weather report. The local news station was announcing a list of school, business and government office closings. Unfortunately, Fedron Chassis wasn't on the list. However, roads were closing on rural routes; and a semi had jackknifed on the Ohio Turnpike between Sandusky and Toledo, further blocking traffic.

Sara kept her pessimism in check and tried to meditate for a minute. She ran the automatic window down to view the desolate street. A gray Chevrolet passed, leaving fresh sets of tire tracks in the rapidly deepening snow. She could see Bobby coming across from the corner. The snow and wind were picking up, forcing him to look down. When he opened the door, another gust of cold air surged inside the car. He stomped his feet and climbed in, slumping, then leaned forward and rubbed his hands in the flow of hot air from the heater.

"This is impossible," Bobby said, his voice tense. "There's no way in hell we could even attempt this one." He shook his head. "I wanted this job, big time." His face stiffened as he put his arms around her, and they held on tightly to each other.

"Go ahead and let's get out of here," he said. "There's no sense sitting here worrying about the Jeep plant. I was told at

Thief of Love

Workpower that the weather advisory made an announcement to stay off all roads if possible."

As she started the car, Sara had the sudden eerie feeling he would drown his sorrow when he got to the house.

During the trip home, Sara had to use all her driving skills, bred in so many Midwestern snowstorms, to keep the car on the pavement and moving steadily ahead without slipping or sliding off the road or into a sideways spin.

The was already tension in the air by the time they entered the house, and, as she suspected, Bobby's first acts were to rush into the kitchen, drink a glass of Black Velvet, and call his aunt in California.

While Bobby had been quiet and subdued till he made the call, he suddenly became talkative once his aunt was on the phone. "Shock does funny things to you," he told her. "I've been in shock since I've been in Ohio. I lost my job because of this God-forsaken Northwest Ohio weather. Drop some wisdom on me, Aunt Betty; help me understand. I need some Southern California wisdom."

Sara moved closer to Bobby but he backed away as if wanting her out of the conversation entirely. He continued talking long distance for about ten more minutes. When he hung up, he didn't give Sara his attention; instead calling his. She listened to his one-way conversation as he left a message:

"Hey, David, what's up? It's Bobby. It's eleven thirty. What are you doing? Ah, man, I'm just going to check in with you. I just lost a good job. Um. . . I. . . I - I need to talk to you. My fingers are crossed, so I'll get another one soon. Can you call me? I'm thinking about calling the ranch. Hope everything is okay and going well. Just give me a call when you get a chance. Later, man. Bobby."

Thief of Love

    Sara was sympathetic but more than a little miffed herself. There were two Bobby's -- the one who was controlled by alcohol, arrogant and cocky; the other one caring, loving, and wanting to plant some roots and settle down. All he seemed to feel he needed was a kick from alcohol and a job to take care of his security for himself and his lady.

Chapter Nine

Much of that afternoon was squandered in bickering. She knew what the problem was. She could feel the changes that she had undergone with Bobby's alcohol consumption. In the midst of the chaos, he ran out of booze, and had been dry for about an hour.

Sitting in the living room, she was on the couch and he sat in an easy chair as the argument about going to get him more Black Velvet intensified.

"Come on, let's hit it," he half shouted, half snarled at her.

"Damn you," she said, her tone firm, adding the challenge, "Do you have any collateral?"

"You'll learn about collateral once I send to L.A. for the Diablos to come shoot up your house. Hey, Bitch, can you handle when the Diablos come torching your house to the ground? So, come on, let's hit it." It was obvious he could barely contain himself. His hand windmilled the air as he yelled at her through clenched teeth.

Incensed at the threat, Sara flared in anger. "I want you out of here -- out of my house, and out of my life!" she shouted.

Bobby's face clouded with anger. He leapt up from the chair, pounding his fist on the end table.

"Get out," Sara said, adding, "or I'm calling the police."

He scowled at her, shouting, "You ain't nothing but a factory-working bitch. You ain't shit, bitch!" He fled from the room, charging up the stairway, stepping with the assurance of a man who had seen violence in many forms. He stopped and stood for a moment at the top of the curving stairway, then turned and went into the master bedroom.

Thief of Love

    The tense silence that followed made the hair on Sara's arm stand on end. She felt disgusted and was tired of arguing with such an unreasonable man. She pondered what she should do next when she heard a loud thump coming from the bedroom. Even as she jumped from the chair and ran up the stairs, Sara knew something was wrong.

Thief of Love

Chapter Ten

"Bobby!" Sara shouted as she reached the top landing. Pushing open the bedroom door, she saw Bobby's still form lying on the floor, blood on the carpet around his head. More than half hysterical, she dashed to the phone and punched 9-1-1 on the keypad. The dispatcher answered on the second ring; Sara was nearly breathless as she said, "I have an emergency at five fourteen Taylor Street. My boyfriend is lying on the floor with blood oozing from the back of his head."

"Is he breathing?" the dispatcher asked.

Sara broke into a sob as she answered, "Yes."

Bobby started moaning and mumbling incoherently, ". . . it's the calf ropin', not the steer rassling." The words weren't clear, but he spoke with bravado and gusto, his voice reverberating through the room.

"Is that him talking?" the dispatcher asked.

"That's him; he's a rodeo cowboy," Sara said, breathless as she began to hyperventilate.

"Exactly what happened?" he asked.

"I don't know. I was downstairs when I heard a loud thud on the ceiling in the room above where I was sitting. I hurried to his bedroom and found him on the floor."

"Just stay beside him, but don't move his head, neck or back. Help is coming. I'm sending a fire rescue squad to five fourteen Taylor Street. Do I have the address correct?"

"Yes, you're correct," she replied.

"I have to answer other calls now," the dispatcher told her.

"All right," Sara said and he hung up.

Within what must have been a few minutes but seemed

like hours, she could hear a siren whooping and wailing in the distance.

"I'll be right back," she called to the semi-conscious and still mumbling Bobby as she hurried out of the room, raced downstairs and hustled out into the cold to meet the rescue squad.

As the ambulance rounded the curve from Ohio Boulevard, Sara flagged it down.

The two emergency medical technicians -- one male and one female -- hopped out of the rescue van and rushed to the rear, opening the large doors and removing a stretcher with collapsible, wheeled legs and a medical satchel from inside.

"Where is he?" the male, an overweight, blond and blue-eyed man wearing eyeglasses asked.

"Follow me," Sara said, holding open the front door as the E.M.T.s pushed and carried the gurney and satchel inside and into the foyer, then she squeezed past them and raced up the stairs.

At the bedroom door, Sara gesture and stood aside as the emergency medical techs rushed inside.

The female, also slightly overweight, a black woman of about thirty, who wore her hair short -- very short, almost a crew-cut -- crouched and leaned over Bobby.

Sara stepped into the room and stood just inside the door as the woman looked up at her, asking, "What's his name?"

"Bobby," Sara said.

The woman nodded and turned toward Bobby again, gently lifting open his eyelids one at a time and shining a tiny, handheld flashlight into each as she asked him, "Bobby, can you hear me?"

Bobby just moaned, whether in reply to the question or response to his pain Sara couldn't tell.

Thief of Love

The female attendant looked up to Sara again, wide-eyed as she asked, "How did this happen?"

Sara sighed and shrugged. "I'm not sure. He'd been drinking Black Velvet part of the afternoon. We were arguing about a job. He ran out of booze, and started demanding for me to take him to the state liquor store. I refused to take him and told him to get out. He staggered up the steps. I heard a loud thud on the floor above the living room. I rushed upstairs and found him like this."

Expressionless, both medics looked into her eyes, then to each other.

The male crouched and nodded as he examined the wound, then looked at the bedside furnishings. "It looks like he hit his head on the corner of the night stand." He pointed. "The blood splashed against the wall and ran down the side of the night stand."

The female attendant loosely placed some gauze pads over the bloody wound while Sara struggled to keep from crying out as she reached for the tissue box on the dresser. She wiped her eyes, smearing her mascara, then halted, not sure of her thoughts as the E.M.T.s collapsed the gurney's legs, laying it flat on the floor beside Bobby.

"Mild to severe concussion," the female medic reported to her partner as he removed a backboard from underneath the stretcher's thin mattress, laying it on the floor along Bobby's other side.

One medical tech crouched in either side, they gently and carefully rolled Bobby partly onto his right side as the female slid the backboard under him; then they both eased him onto the board, amid his groans of pain and delirium.

Sara watched in open-mouthed fascination as the two

rescuers continued their perfect teamwork when they lifted Bobby on the backboard and onto the stretcher. After a few seconds, with the male going to the end closest Bobby's head and the female standing near his feet, they lifted the gurney and locked its legs into the upright position.

Sara stepped aside as they rolled Bobby into the hall and eased him down the stairs.

Sara followed. Not wanting to interfere but unable to stifle her anxiety, she asked as they reached the foyer, "How bad is it?"

"The wound is wide and deep," the female attendant answered as they lifted the gurney over the doorsill and wheeled it across the porch. "He has a mild to severe concussion, and needs immediate attention at the emergency room," she said in conclusion as they carried Bobby down the stairs, rolled the gurney to the back of the ambulance and lifted it inside.

"You coming with?" the male attendant called out as they folded the gurney down and locked it into place.

"Yes," Sara said, pulling her keys from her pocket, closing and locking the door and rushing to the back of the ambulance, hopping inside just as the female attendant also climbed in and closed the doors, and the male got into the driver's seat and started the engine.

They started on their way, and the swaying of the ambulance around corners and down the streets, along with the wailing of the siren, made Sara feel dizzy and disoriented.

She watched as the female medic bent over Bobby, raised his eyelids and again shone the beam of a small flashlight into his eyes. His eyelids fluttered and his eyes rolled.

"Bobby, can you hear me?" the attendant asked again, then placed a headset on and punched a number into a keyboard and said into the hands-free microphone, "Subject male, forty-five years old, left occipital head trauma -- wide and deep; mild to severe concussion."

The paramedic covered the mouthpiece and called to the driver, "E.T.A.?"

"Eight minutes," he replied.

Sara only half heard as the female continued her report to the emergency room staff, "E.T.A. eight minutes, pulse. . . "

Ten minutes later, the emergency room waiting area floor felt hard and cold under Sara's feet as she paced like a caged tiger. She expected to just collapse at any moment as fear and confusion ran through her. It seemed that Bobby's troubles were her fault; that she should have persevered to get him to the new job; that she could have taken him to the liquor store; that she shouldn't have been so hard on him -- telling him to get out in the aftermath of an Ohio snowstorm; that she should have done something about the end table that may have cost his life.

A petite nurse of about forty who looked to be Hispanic and with an appearance Sara could only think of as 'cute' flashed a warm smile as she approached. "Ms. Bringard? Mister Johnson is being treated by Doctor Lee; he's a very good doctor, and the patient is in excellent hands."

"Thank you," Sara said, a little relieved but still very anxious.

"I'll tell you more about Mister Johnson's condition as soon as I know anything. In the meantime, an admissions clerk needs to talk to you. Will you step this way, please?"

The nurse led Sara to a half-partitioned cubicle and introduced her to a young white man of about twenty-five who wore his dark blond hair in Jamaican-style corn-rolls.

The clerk was sitting behind a tiny desk and cheerfully

asked Sara to take a seat.

Sara complied as he leaned forward in his chair and said, "Good evening. I need to ask you a few questions about Robert Johnson, please."

Sara nodded. "Okay," she said.

"What is your relationship to Robert?"

"I'm his fiancée."

"Please spell Robert's last name."

"J-o-h-n-s-o-n."

"His age please?"

"Forty-three."

"In case of emergency, whom should we contact, and at what phone number?"

Sara paused, unsure exactly how to respond, then said, "He lives with me, at five fourteen Taylor Street." She lowered her head and leaned forward. "You can contact me, Sara Bringard, at my home. The number is five-five-five, eight-seven-three-five."

"Does he have an insurance carrier for medical benefits?"

"No," Sara said. "He asked for a medical card at Human Services about a month ago, but hasn't received a final approval. But he is a veteran though. Doesn't that qualify him for veteran's medical benefits?"

The clerk leaned back and shrugged. "That's not for us to decide, although Robert can apply for assistance through the Veteran's Administration Services, on Columbus Ave."

Sara knew the location. It was a huge hospital wing where several thousand disabled veterans were in-patients, taken care of by state and federal workers.

The petite Hispanic nurse approached again.

The admissions clerk looked up at her.

Thief of Love

The nurse smiled at Sara and said, "The emergency room doctor has admitted Robert. He'll be placed in a semi-private room after he comes back from x-ray."

The admissions clerk nodded and said to Sara, "You may go back to the emergency waiting room. If I need you for any future information, I'll send for you, or call you later."

Sara sat in the waiting room for over an hour before she spotted the emergency room doctor -- a slight Asian man with a pencil-thin moustache -- standing near an elevator, holding a clipboard and writing.

She approached him unnoticed. "Excuse me. I hate to interrupt your work, but I need to know Robert Johnson's medical condition," she said with more assertiveness than she felt. She crossed her arms across her chest as the doctor looked at her.

He seemed irritated as he stopped writing, sighed and said, "I'm waiting for radiology. He's just out of x-ray; when I get their report I'll make my prognosis." The doctor pursed his lips, regarding Sara from beneath lowered eyes as he rubbed the back of his neck. She suddenly noticed how tired he looked as he continued, "The back and left side of his head revealed multiple linear abrasions with severe contusions." His tone changed and became softer. "I coaxed him to consciousness after I stitched up the wound. I've ordered complete bed rest in a ward for a couple of days. He'll go there from x-ray." Having done his duty by informing her of the facts, he picked up his pen to continue his written report.

"Thank you," Sara said as she moved back toward the waiting area. As she passed the enclosure where the rescue squad had brought Bobby Sara could see vinyl pads and gloves scattered on the table next to the E.K.G. machine. In the doctor's station she could hear a nurse's voice. She stepped into the cubicle and tucked back the curtain. Bobby was lying on his left side on a hospital bed, facing the wall. Sara went across the aisle to where Bobby lay. He appeared to be awake and alert, and tried to smile.

She smiled back at him, noticing his cloudy eyes as she whispered, "Everything is going to be all right."

He looked confused as he held out his hand. She held it in hers and squeezed it.

"If you need to talk, I'm here for you," she said.

"Hi, baby," he mumbled.

"How are you feeling?" she asked.

"Like I've been on a trip to hell," he said, slurring his words.

"I need to ask you an important question. Are you eligible for Veteran's Benefits? The hospital admitting clerk asked me to find out if you had medical benefits."

His eyes darted across the room in nervous uncertainty.

"I've misplaced my DD-214 discharge papers from the army. I'll call my sister, Megan. She'll send me what I need." He said it as if he believed Megan would to this for him; Sara had an unexplained doubt about it though.

Sara nodded. "I told the clerk that you applied a month ago at Human Services for a medical card but that you hadn't received final approval yet."

His expression was childlike as he stared in confusion. "I'll just check out of here," he said, adding, "I can't pay the bill."

Sara shook her head. "No, don't do it, Bobby. That would be foolish. Medicaid can back-date ninety days once you're approved. You need a good checkup and bed rest."

He nodded, sighed and whispered, "Thank you for caring. I love you, baby." He looked up at her, then turned down his eyes.

Sara looked out into the corridor and saw the nurse exchange papers with the emergency room doctor. She crossed the hallway and stepped into the room, smiling at Sara as she said, "Hello. Robert is ready to go to his room now." She went to Bobby's bed, unlocked the wheels and started to push it out of the emergency room cubicle and into the corridor. Sara followed as the nurse rolled Bobby through the winding hallways and to another set of elevators, where several other people were waiting to step aboard.

After a very few seconds, the elevator door opened. People quickly stepped out and those waiting outside filed in and crushed together to make room for her, the nurse and Bobby's gurney.

When they got off on the third floor, the nurse dropped off a sheet of paper as they passed the nurse's station and continued on, wheeling Bobby into room three eleven.

After Bobby was settled in, Sara dropped into a black leather chair beside his bed. He reached out his hand for hers and gripped it tightly, like a frightened child. Sara tried to console him by caressing his hand.

His face paled, then slowly reddened to a flush. "You're my Sara Poppins," he said, adding, "Bobby wouldn't know what to do without her." She didn't know if his referring to her has 'Sara Poppins' instead of 'Mary Poppins,' and to himself in the third person was the result of his injury or just fatigue.

They sat in silence for what seemed like a long time, till a young, perky nurse of average height who looked like Filipina entered the room with an energetic pace. "Good evening," she said in an upbeat tone. Then she quickly went to Bobby's side and took his pulse. He lay still, looking up at her, studying her while she placed a blood pressure cup around his arm, pumped it up and let it deflate. He rubbed his free palm against his eyes and breathed out, wheezing heavily. She finished her tasks, wrote the results in a handheld clipboard, smiled at them and stepped out.

Bobby suddenly seemed wide awake and fidgety, looking around the room then peering at the doorway. Sara could see suspicion in his eyes as he glanced toward her. "Get me a Camel, please. I need a smoke." It was a demand, not a request.

Sara shook her head. "You know there's no smoking in a hospital, don't you?"

He nodded, his expression glum.

She saw the disappointment and bitterness in his eyes, then relented, saying, "You'll have to go in the bathroom and shut the door." Sara glanced toward the door guiltily, opened her purse and removed a pack of his cigarettes, which she often carried for him, tapped the pack on her wrist, pulled one out and handed it to him, along with a book of matches.

Bobby sat quickly, then swayed, still woozy.

"Are you sure you want to do this?" Sara asked.

A determined look appeared on his face. Sara sighed, rose, took his hand and helped him as he stumbled and hesitated across the room toward the tiny bathroom.

After enough time to smoke about half a cigarette, Sara heard the toilet flush, and Bobby emerged, seeming even more unsteady as she helped him back into bed.

"I feel light-headed," he said as he lay down.

Sara chided herself mentally. What if he had fallen in the bathroom and hit his head again -- would he have died? She pursed her lips, then shook her head in disgust at their little conspiracy. "That was some chance we took," she said, biting the words off.

Bobby just smiled and flipped one thumb up, "We did it, didn't we baby," he said.

Sara's anxiety melted away. She tried to suppress a grin as she said, "I must confess, you dazzle me."

The Filipina nurse suddenly re-entered, stood just inside the door and scanned the room. There was a coldness in her eyes she looked from Sara to Bobby and back again.

Sara couldn't hold her gaze and looked to Bobby.

Bobby grinned at the nurse and asked in a self-assured tone, "Hey, hon, can you please assist me with a remote for my T.V.? I can't miss watching tonight; my cousin comes on at eleven thirty."

The nurse seemed startled by his request, saying nothing for a moment that stretched into another as she held his gaze before she finally asked, "Who's your cousin, and what program is it?"

"Don Johnson, Miami Vice," he said, his reply automatic and without hesitation.

The nurse laughed, in spite of herself it seemed to Sara, proving that she wasn't the only one susceptible to his humoring charm. The nurse nodded and said, "All, right" as she turned to leave, stopping at the doorway to fix first Bobby then Sara with a firm look as she added, "You know, there's a no-smoking policy in this hospital." She left without waiting for either of them to reply.

Moments later, a candy striper who appeared to be all of seventeen years old, with honey-gold hair, cyan-blue eyes, a toothy grin and even freckles -- the epitome of the Midwestern

Thief of Love

farm girl, bounded enthusiastically into the room, cheerily saying, "Hello. I heard you'd like T.V. service."

"Yes, we do," Bobby said, trying to keep his tone casual and his expression matter of fact, even though, as Sara could plainly see, he was drawn to the girl's attractiveness.

The candy striper beamed as she told him, "The daily cost will be two dollars, seventy-five cents."

"That's absurd," Bobby said, his tone not hostile but bemused, adding, "So you people Ohio hospital management won't serve your patients with complimentary T.V.?"

The girl just kept smiling at him and shrugged.

Bobby shook his head and exclaimed, "Ha!" adding, "You know what? Your hospitals in Ohio are cheap!"

The girl's smile didn't fade even a little as she said, "Sir, the cost of service will be two dollars, seventy-five cents each day.

It was Bobby's turn to shrug. "Okay, whatever; get a move on," he said.

The girl turned and stepped through the door, calling back over her shoulder, "I'll be by with a remote.

Evening was approaching. Sara rose from the chair, yawning and stretching as she checked her watch.

Bobby looked at her with a sharp, suspicious expression in his eyes. "What's up, Poppins?"

Sara went to the mirror, checked her makeup and said over her shoulder, "It's late; I'm heading home."

His tone was cold as he said, "Have it your way. Don't bother yourself any further. Just don't worry over me. If I die, bring a few flowers to my grave once in a while, if you think of me."

Knowing the thought of her leaving touched something

deep within him made Sara feel a twinge of pity. She turned toward him, seeing his face pale, but contained as his features set in a scowl. "Look at the bright side, Bobby: You're not a man doomed to die just yet. The hard time for now is over. When you regain your strength, you won't be so pessimistic. How can I help encourage your healing when already you see yourself dead inside?"

Sara could see that her well-intentioned words of comfort did nothing for Bobby's mood as she reached for her navy wool coat on the back of the leather chair. She put it on, removed her gloves from a pocket, picked up her purse and handed him ten dollars. "Here," she said, "You might want a candy bar or a newspaper, and to pay for your cable T.V."

Bobby's expression didn't soften as he said, "Fine. Just lay it on the desk."

Sara kissed his cheek without saying another word, then turned and left the room without hesitation. When she arrived outside Sara stood for a moment taking in the beauty of an Ohio winter evening. The streetlights had come on, casting a fuzzy amber glow in the falling snow, which carpeted the streets with a layer of sparkling white diamonds.

There were four taxis at the nearby cab stand. Sara hailed the first and he pulled up in front of the hospital main entrance. Within minutes she was safe and warm in her own cozy but empty house.

Right away, Sara noticed the message light flashing on her answering machine. She pushed the `play' button and heard Bobby's voice saying just two words in a whisper, "Call me."

The second caller hung up, but the third call was from Sara's mother. Her voice sounded high-strung and tense. "Sara, your neighbors, the Wallaces, called me and said there was an emergency at your house -- that your cowboy friend was taken to the hospital. I've never known anyone who trusted people so much. You know very little about this man you moved into your home. Sara, mark my words, one day you're going to come home from work and find everything you own taken or, worse yet, you'll get your throat slit. Ditch him at the hospital while you still have the chance."

Sara shook her head. In her telephone conversations with her mother she had told her a little too much about their relationship. Now her mother had no respect for Bobby, and certainly no sense of compassion. Of course, she knew her daughter was a fighter when she believed in something; that she'd stick to a fight till it's right. She knew that somehow it's always easier to tell the next person how to swim when you're not in the water yourself.

Sara didn't return her mother's call. Instead, she undressed and put on her nightgown. Suddenly, she felt an overwhelming sense of not just loneliness but of being alone, in an empty house; a house that had not been empty -- that had known companionship -- for an appreciable time. Bobby's presence seemed all around her, accenting his absence. She wandered through the master bedroom, feeling like an intruder in her own house as she surveyed his clothes, his Western boots and his beaver cowboy hat in the foyer. The house felt so cold and empty without him.

She went to the dresser and opened one of the drawers that Bobby used. Inside, underwear was scattered about in disarray, pairs of socks were balled together, a shaving kit and a manicure set rested upon a bed of haphazardly folded and stacked t-shirts. Protruding slightly from the pile of t-shirts was the corner of an envelope. Sara hesitated for a moment, then

Thief of Love

grasped the envelope with her thumb and forefinger and, moving reluctantly and ever-so-gingerly, her hand trembling, she drew it out and held it up. The envelope was blank, but she could feel some paper inside. Dreading what she might find, Sara opened the envelope and retrieved the folded sheet of paper from within. Casting her hesitancy aside, Sara quickly unfolded the paper and read:

    Honey, hope we can meet soon, if it's meant to be.

A photo fell out and onto the dresser top. Sara picked it up and stared at it. It was a snapshot of a woman of about thirty-five, with dark blond hair and chestnut brown eyes. She turned the picture over. Written on the back was the dedication:

    To Bobby, the face behind the voice.
    I love you, Ellen from Virginia.

Sara tossed the note and photo down and rummaged through the drawer, looking for she knew not what, at once not accepting but forced to accept what she had found. Now she remembered how she felt the first day she and Bobby met, and the phone calls from the scriptwriter leading her to the discovery -- Bobby's false sense of intimacy he had portrayed to other women. He had called Sara on his ex-fiancée's telephone in Monterey. Had he continued on Sara's phone likewise? Just who was this Ellen from Virginia? Surely it wasn't one of his cousins, as he had told her. The images that ran through her mind were more than she could bear.

    Suddenly overwhelmed with the stress of the day, Sara collapsed onto the bed, cried and drifted to sleep, her spirit and mind plunged into despair.

Thief of Love

Chapter Eleven

Sunlight shone through the curtains as Sara was awakened by the trilling of the phone. Still groggy, she just lay on the bed and stared at it. After the phone rang at least ten times, and continued to ring, she rose and checked the caller I.D., which displayed the hospital number. She began considering ways to punish Bobby. She remembered her mother's words of warning recorded on the answering machine: `Get him out of your life while you still can to survive this.' Sara decided to not answer his call.

The phone rang almost incessantly for the next hour. Sara checked the clock; it was half past seven. The phone rang again, and Sara glanced at the caller I.D.; this time it was her mother. She picked it up, saying, "Hello, Mother."

"Why haven't you called me back? I've been at my wits end, girl. You don't know anything about this Bobby Johnson."

"Mother, you know Bobby is in the hospital. He hit his head on the night stand and was rushed there by the rescue squad. I was with him until late last night."

"Your father and I don't want you mewing over that man. Even the smoothest con man needs a willing mark. Don't sit and let things build up into something worse happening,' she said, anxiety in her voice.

Sara sighed in exasperation. "Mother, I don't need your pep talk. I'm not complacent." As she spoke, her voice cracked. She felt more guilt-ridden over the conversation than heartbroken over Bobby as she continued, "It goes without saying, Mother -- you're not the least bit concerned how Bobby's recovering. He could be in a life-threatening crisis for all you care. In truth, I'm trying to deal with this catastrophe myself. I don't need to talk

Thief of Love

with you about any of this right now. Later, Mother." She hung up, frustrated by her mother's comments and attitude.

Sara turned on the T.V. The update of weather conditions reported all roads cleared and open. When Sara heard this, she slipped on her robe and house slippers, went downstairs to the foyer and looked out the door. The morning looked crisp and clear. She went out onto the front porch. The sunlight had been deceptive; it was very cold. Still, she stood on the porch taking in the clear, cold day till her teeth began to chatter, and the phone started ringing again. Without stopping to think, Sara hurried inside, picking up the receiver.

"God, I miss you, baby," were Bobby's first words. "Where have you been?" he asked.

"Yeah, right, Bobby, sure you do!" she said, adding, "Do you recall a conversation when you told me that Ellen was your cousin from Virginia? It was hard to believe you had a penniless, favorite cousin on the East Coast when you came all the way from the West Coast."

"What are you reading my mail for?" he asked. "I don't read your mail when it comes in from Irving, Texas; from your T.V. hustling preacher man. Are you holding something back? I don't know what's going on with you while you're constantly getting mail from him."

She said nothing to his tirade.

"Can you hear me?" he asked.

She remained unresponsive.

"Can you hear me?" he asked again, then went on. "Now wasn't that a stupid question? If she'd answer, I'd at least know I haven't lost my hearing. She always holds center stage, you know that for sure, Bobby!"

Those words pushed every emotional button Sara had.

Thief of Love

She screamed into the phone, "When you get out of the hospital, you're out of here! I'm tired of your bogus tales."

"You know we love each other," he said, his voice softening. "Can't you see your loss of trust has provoked all this? Get over here to the hospital and pick me up. If you don't come in thirty minutes, I'm discharging myself."

Sara took a deep breath before responding. "There are no words to describe strongly enough how I feel right now. You've lied so many times to me that my trust has crumbled. Up until this day, I could only speculate as to who Ellen was. There's nothing left to wonder about. The evidence is in her note and picture she sent you."

He snorted and chuckled. "Pure nonsense."

Again, Sara held her silence, and Bobby continued, talking fast. "Could it be that there's more than meets the eye with your T.V. evangelist? It comes with the territory -- T.V. evangelists are hustlers; quit sending them money."

"They are absolutely not hustlers," Sara said. "They're on T.V. to give hope and build a climate to grow faith. You're worried about my money. You try to manipulate my mind, Bobby. You say it's always my fault, never yours!" She slammed the receiver into its cradle.

For the next twenty minutes, Sara paced around the house dry-eyed, adrenaline rushing through her. She knew that when she sent money to support Christian T.V., it was for a good cause, not for drawing a preacher man to herself. Then, in spite of her inner turmoil, by her own choice, she dressed and headed for the hospital.

Upon arrival in Bobby's room, Sara stepped inside quickly and with eagerness, sitting in the leather chair next to him so she could watch his expression.

Thief of Love

"I thought you'd never get here," he said, placing his hand on her shoulder, giving it a nudge. "I just want to tell you something before it's too late."

She waited in silence for him to continue.

"Sara, if something happens to me, I want you to have everything I own; everything I own down to the smallest picture, and my trust fund in California, go to you, okay? I'm contacting my attorney," he said.

Lifting an eyebrow, Sara shrugged and said, "If you like. But I didn't come back to see what I can get out of you; I came back to see you. By the way, how are you?" she asked.

He looked away, forcing her to lean to the side to see his expression. "Like I've been punched, kicked and shot," he said, lowering the volume on the T.V., but not bothering to turn it off.

He struggled out of bed, looking into the mirror above the small sink. As Bobby surveyed himself, he combed his unkempt, black hair. He looked at Sara through his reflection in the mirror and said, "Bring me a drink; I need to relax."

Sara was so stunned she could only sputter, "W-w-w-hat? Did I hear you clearly?" she asked, feeling her blood grow hot.

Bobby just flashed a casual smile and said, "I think you heard me clearly, Poppins." He walked on unsteady legs to the window, pulled the curtain aside and stared down at the parking lot, calling to her over his shoulder, "Reach me my clothes! I'm outta here."

Sara sat in stunned silence before saying, "Wait just a minute. You have a contusion. You're not supposed to even be out of bed. You mustn't leave the hospital."

He just looked out the window, smiling at the sunny day outside.

"Please?" Sara asked, her voice low with the soft plea.

Thief of Love

Just then, a gray-haired nurse who had a no-nonsense face and a wiry body stalked into the room, sized-up the tense situation and demanded of Bobby, "What are you doing out of your bed, Robert?"

Unexpectedly for Sara, Bobby looked embarrassed while he studied the nurse for a moment as he formulated a strategy for dealing with her before saying, "Send a maintenance man over here. How about you taking care of either fixing the heating system or moving me out of this room?"

The nurse fixed him with a firm gaze as she said in a steady tone, "Follow hospital rules and doctor's orders, Robert. I'll take care of reporting to maintenance."

Sara's mind was racing. She thought Bobby must have a mental problem. First he had the audacity to ask her to bring him whiskey in a hospital, then he wanted to just walk out of there, and he told the nurse how to do her job. She realized the booze, and lack of it while in the hospital, had pushed him over the edge.

Bobby slowly stepped back to his bed, as if trying to show the nurse some respect; trying to put on his best front, but a tear rolled down his cheek, revealing some unknown mental or physical pain. He lay down again, picked up the remote and began scanning channels on the T.V.

Without further comment, the nurse made an abrupt about face and marched out of the room, still in charge, so it seemed.

Sara remained in the leather chair while Bobby idly clicked through the T.V. channels.

As the time dragged by, Sara's spirits fell again as she watched Bobby slump into his own bout of depression. They sat, each their combined and separate misery.

But, outside the room, the daily routine continued; the

gray-haired nurse returned, carrying a covered tray -- Bobby's lunch. "Would you like some too?" she asked Sara.

"No, thank you," Sara said, for some unexplainable reason feeling embarrassed.

"How about some coffee then?' the nurse asked.

Sara nodded, and, within a few minutes the nurse returned with a small tray containing a cup, packets of cream and sugar, and a four-cup pot of coffee. Sara thanked her and joined Bobby as he idly watched an old Clint Eastwood shoot-'em-up on T.V.

During that time, a housekeeper and janitor each came to the room, performing their assigned straightening, linen-replacement, litter removal and sanitizing chores.

In mid-afternoon Sara looked up to notice a man standing motionless in the doorway, saying nothing, his gaze seeming focused far away; the bright afternoon light cast deep shadows across his face.

Bobby looked up at him and asked, "Are you lost?"

The man nodded absently, then took a step into the room, saying, "Yes -- I mean no. That is, my father was given this room number," he explained, his eyes scanning the room, adding, "He just came from radiation therapy." He paused and licked his lips.

"Name's Bobby Johnson," Bobby said, then nodded toward Sara, "This here's my fiancée, Sara Bringard."

The man made a polite nod toward Sara, who nodded back, stunned into silence by Bobby's announcement that they were now betrothed.

"I haven't seen him yet," Bobby added.

"Hi there, Bobby." The man said, then nodded toward Sara, saying, "Pleased to meet you, Sara." He looked back to

Thief of Love

Bobby. "My father's name is Everet Siebert. My name is Marcus."

"Howdy, Marcus," Bobby said, his tone more cheerful than it had been all day.

Sara noticed Marcus was a good-looking man, but a tough one to read -- the kind of person who plays his cards close to his vest. She found herself suddenly fascinated by him. He had broad shoulders and stood close to six feet tall. His hair was dark and wavy. She surveyed his clothes: wrangler jeans, a tasteful plaid shirt, Western boots.

He caught her sizing him up and cocked an eyebrow, glancing at her ringless hand.

She flushed and looked away, a small light of desire turning on in her soul.

The Clint Eastwood `Spaghetti Western' had just ended, so Bobby began to scan the channels again, apparently not noticing the exchange of unspoken communication between Sara and Marcus.

At that moment, two nurses whom Sara hadn't seen before entered, pushing the elder Mister Siebert on a gurney. Within moments they had helped him into his hospital bed and left.

Everet seemed only vaguely aware of his surroundings; he just lay on his bed, staring absently at the rapidly changing scenes on the T.V. screen. Sara observed his fair to dark complexion. She guessed he looked to be about sixty to sixty-five. His hair was wavy, with a peppering of gray.

Bobby looked over at him and said, "Hi there, Bud. Looks like I've got good company in this spiffy clean room." Bobby leaned over, his thick-fingered hand extended toward Everet.

Thief of Love

    Everet reacted for the first time, reaching toward Bobby's hand and giving what looked like a weak but good-natured handshake. Marcus took a seat near his father's bed and everyone in the room remained silent as dinnertime came and went, with Bobby the only one eating.
    Throughout the evening, a stream of nurses were in and out, checking Everet's and Bobby's temperature, pulse, blood pressure and respiratory rate.
    The senior nurse -- a tall woman with a pleasant smile -- arrived to administer their pain medications. Bobby took his pills without complaint, but Marcus looked troubled.
    "Are you giving my father generic painkillers? he asked, adding, "He's suffering a great deal of unnecessary pain. Why aren't you giving him Hydromorphone?"
    "We try to keep cancer patients comfortable," the senior nurse said, lifting her composed face and looking him directly in the eyes.
    Marcus looked away and started clenching and unclenching a fist while one foot began tapping nervously on the linoleum floor as he said, "My father needs his Dilaudid increased from one to four milligrams -- and not generic; and I want him to have the same as he was taking at home, Hydromorphone."
    The nurse pursed her lips, expelled a breath through her nostrils, then said, "Sometimes terminal patients are given a shot, if the pill doesn't work and they're in extreme pain; but the shot is to be used only if the medication isn't working and then only every three hours -- no more often than that."
    Marcus looked up at her; she met his gaze; he made no response; she continued. "We sometimes also give a combination of Thorizine and Dilaudid, intravenously injecting

both medications by I.V. I'll talk with his doctor about changing his prescription."

Marcus shook his head vigorously. "Don't set it up. No I.V. push. I want him spared all that."

Bobby looked to Sara and whispered toward her, "A man under pressure."

Sara nodded. "Yes -- a great deal." She turned toward Marcus, saying, "Today, with all the medical science and studies on diseases and cancer, people have a good chance of overcoming these illnesses." Her tone was full of hope, to give Everet a climate to build faith on. Everet smiled and tucked his thumbs into the sheet, pulling it up to his chest.

Bobby nodded. "He deserves that," he said. "Everet seems like a good man."

Everet became more alert, nodded and looked toward Bobby, saying, "Life's precious. That it's also too short weighs on my mind."

"You've got that right," Bobby said, asking, "Where's the cancer at?"

Everet stared past Bobby, through the window at the cloudy nighttime Ohio skies. "I have a metastasized bone." He looked down at the sheet. "The doctors haven't given me much hope or encouragement." A tear gushed out of his right eye and slipped down his cheek. He brushed it away without a hint of embarrassment at having to shed it in front of others.

Sara rose, walked to Everet's bedside and stood by him, putting her arm around his shoulders as she said, "Bobby and I want you to know that we're praying for your healing. Just put yourself into the hands of the Lord."

Everet's face spread into one of the most beautiful smiles Sara had ever seen.

Thief of Love

Bobby nodded. "Pray for him." He broke into a smile. "But don't send any more money for those T.V. Preachers to pray along too."

Sara shot a sharp glance at Bobby, as, frowning, she said, "Why would you want to say something like that?"

Bobby gave an off-hand, one-shouldered shrug. "A lot of reasons -- none we have to talk about now. Forget it, okay?"

Sara silently glared at him.

Bobby looked away and began to play with the control switch of his bed, slowly raising and lowering the head then the foot, and bending it in the middle, first up then down.

Sara turned her attention to Everet as she said, "I'm a born again Christian, and I'll pray for your strength and healing."

Everet gripped her hand, pulling it closer to his face. She could feel his hot breath on the back of her hand as he looked into her eyes.

Sara bowed her head; Everet did the same, and closed his eyes. She held his hand a little tighter as she said, "Dear Father in heaven. In the name of Jesus, coming together in agreement, we ask you for your strength, your Holy Spirit to be with Everet. Please, Heavenly Father, heal his body. We know, Heavenly Father, there is nothing too big that you cannot do. So please give him a miracle healing. Amen."

Everet nodded to himself, and a sob escaped him as he said, "Oh God, please heal my bone cancer." He opened his eyes and looked to Sara; she raised her head and returned his gaze as he said, "I'm so thankful God brought us together." He reached both arms around her shoulders and hugged her with more need than strength, like a man clinging to a life raft in the middle of the ocean.

During Sara's and Everet's interaction, Marcus remained

tight-lipped, with a strained expression on his face, as if the encounter had tried his patience. He rose suddenly and started toward the door.

"See, ya', Marcus," Bobby called after him.

Speaking over his shoulder, Marcus said, "Yeah, later, man." But he had not a word of farewell for either his father or Sara.

Stunned at Marcus' turnaround of mood, Sara shook her head in wonder and shrugged, saying to both Everet and Bobby. "Well, I guess I'd better be going too."

After exchanging courteous goodbye's with Bobby and Everet, Sara returned home for a well-appreciated rest. Unlike the night before, and despite the tension and devastation she had felt all through that night and day -- or perhaps because of the way it had interfered with her sleep for the past forty-eight hours -- Sara fell into a deep, dreamless sleep.

The next morning, Sara arrived at the hospital room just after breakfast.

Bobby looked up in surprise as she entered. "What has you here so bright and early? It was half a day trying to get you here yesterday." He closed his eyes as if to give her a brush off.

She could feel her pulse quicken in a brief flash of anger. Sara looked over to Everet. He was groggy and stared vacantly at the T.V.

The door swung open. Marcus and another man -- short, pale, sleazy looking, with a too-large moustache for his small face and very short hair -- dashed into the room. Sara noticed Marcus carrying a small paper bag. He stepped quickly and eagerly over to Bobby, handing him the bag.

Bobby opened it and peeked inside, briefly studying its contents, then nodded. "Thanks, man," he said, as if they had established a good rapport during her absence.

"May I ask what's in the bag?" Sara asked, her tone soft and innocent.

Bobby brushed her question off with a two-finger salute.

Sara stifled her anger and looked toward Everet, trying to put her thoughts back on him while Marcus and the other man stood looming over him.

The mustached man's face went harder as he made eye contact with her. "My name is Skip." His tone was not cordial but hard and cold. "And I'm going to have to ask you to leave," he added, arching one eyebrow as his thin lips stretched into a sardonic grin.

Sara stood her ground, not moving and meeting Skip's hard stare with her own.

Skip's smile vanished as he continued. "Marcus needs his privacy with his father. Bobby spoke with me earlier. He doesn't want you here while he's recovering from his injury. You put too much stress and anxiety on him."

The man's arrogance and rudeness stiffened Sara's resolve. "Do me a favor," Sara said, "don't talk to me. I don't like where you're coming from and for you to say that I put stress on him!" She stepped closer to Everet.

Skip held his hand up, warning her away from Everet.

Sara stopped, startled by the unexpected confrontation, wondering why all except Everet wanted her out of the room. Bobby remained passive, seeming to ignore the encounter and apparently tuned in to what was going on.

Marcus sat in the leather chair and crossed his legs, looking up at Sara as if just waiting for her to leave.

Bobby finally looked over at her. "Go to work," he said.

Sara sighed, shook her head in disgust, turned on her heel

and deliberately stepped out of the room, wondering what it all meant. On her way out, she heard Skip saying, "Some bitch." The remark cracked in her mind like fireworks, and bit like a bee sting.

As Sara was about to enter the elevator she realized that, amid all of the turmoil, she had forgotten her purse. She made an abrupt about-face and headed back to Bobby's and Everet's room. Her hands were sweating and her legs were shaking as she approached the door. She hesitated outside for a moment, gazing warily inside. Marcus and Skip were nowhere to be seen. She could hear the sound of the bathroom door closing and water being run in the sink. Their voices were muffled, inaudible.

She looked straight ahead, risking only the briefest of glances toward Bobby. He was pouring from the paper bag what looked like Black Velvet into a plastic cup. He looked up and his eyes zoomed in on her, hot as spotlights.

"I just came back for my purse," she said, her voice tight as she moved with deliberate steps toward nightstand where she'd left her handbag. She felt as if she couldn't get out of there fast enough, spinning on one heel and marching with a brisk pace out the door, resolving to herself that as soon as Bobby was discharged, she was sending him back to California.

Sara was tired to the point of a meltdown after returning home. She punched the power button on the stereo and the play button on her cassette deck. The air was instantly filled with the mellow tones of Travis Tritt singing "A Country Club." Feeling drawn by the energy of the music, Sara pulled on her sweats, went to the living room, set four logs into the fireplace and lit the kindling already piled underneath. Within moments, the warm yellow flames radiated their heat into the room. She fairly collapsed into her recliner and tilted it back, facing the sparking firewood.

As Travis Tritt moved on to the melody of "Anymore," Sara meditated on the words, her mood spiraling downward into a case of the blues.

Thief of Love

Chapter Twelve

A late morning phone call set the idea of Bobby's leaving into motion. Sara was just about to put her foot in the shower when her phone rang. Bare feet twitching beneath her, she quickly stepped across the carpet. She checked the caller ID and, even though she didn't immediately recognize the number, removed the phone receiver from the cradle and answered, "Yes?"

"This is Doctor Green's office. He asked me to call Sara Bringard, about Robert Johnson's discharge."

"This is Sara."

"Please hold one moment for the doctor."

Sara toweled dry while during the wait, which was too short as she was more than half wet when she heard the doctor saying, "Hello, Sara. I have some concerns about Robert's discharge. He had a pretty hard blow to his head. His condition is relatively stable; however, I'm not releasing him for a couple more days. He's raised some concerns with me. He complains of pains in his stomach and I'm running tests tomorrow. When he does return home he'll need some counseling for alcohol abuse. The main problem is that he's overly stressed from the drinking."

Sara's thoughts floated back to her job. "I work for Advance Motors Corporation. Our plant has downsized, and we're working three shifts, short-handed. Management has let us know that the company won't honor any personal leaves of absence. Perhaps I can get in touch with his sister out West, or possibly another relative. I haven't spoken with Bobby since yesterday, but I'll call him and speak with him about it and see what his input is. Thank you, doctor," she said and broke the connection.

    With so much bad news coming all at the same time, Sara felt miserable as she finished drying and dressing herself, and called Bobby. As she expected, he was firm in his attitude about leaving, so she put off any further discussion till her next visit the next morning.

    As Sara approached his hospital room, a feeling of dread crept into her. Everything was quiet -- too quiet. She took a deep breath and eased open the door, looking about. She spotted Bobby's empty bed and her eyes darted to Marcus sitting in the chair asleep. Her eyes focused upon Everet. He, too, was sleeping. With a careful tread she crept into the room, past Marcus, inching herself bravely toward the bathroom. She paused, then slowly opened the bathroom door. Her nostrils filled with the smell of soap and disinfectant. She switched on the light.

    The restroom was small, but immaculate and well kept, with its original tile still gleaming white. There was a toilet, a small sink, and a mirrored wall. Sara spotted a single burned match lay on the edge of the sink. Under the sink was a tiny trash can. Inside, she caught sight of a shiny object. She dug into the trash between tissue paper, pushed it aside and saw a blackened teaspoon at the bottom.

    The phone rang several times before Marcus picked it up. "Nothing happening, bro, call later, he said."

    Sara stepped out of the bathroom and studied Marcus. He was in a stupor, nodding forward in his chair, lost in a world of opiate dreams.

    Sara suddenly remembered that Bobby was scheduled for x-rays and wondered how he was doing. On her way out, she was less quiet but neither Marcus nor Everet stirred.

Thief of Love

At the nurses station the staff was engrossed in working on paperwork and charts. Unaware of Sara standing there, Doctor Green entered the cubicle with his usual speed, wiry and intense.

"Excuse me, I need some information," Sara said. Then, in a lowered voice, she asked, "Where's Robert Johnson, from room three eleven?"

Doctor Green looked up and stepped over to Sara. "Robert was scheduled for x-rays at nine o'clock. You can go down to radiology, on the first floor. There's a waiting room nearby. The doctor studied Robert's folder, adding, "Robert has complained several times to the nurses that he has stomach pain, so I've requested an upper GI and stomach testing."

"I know he has stomach pain," Sara said. "He tells me all the time it hurts. I'll just wait in his room until he's finished. Bobby will tell me the test results when he comes back."

"Certainly," the doctor said with an absent-minded nod as he turned back to his paperwork.

When Sara returned to Robert's room, Marcus stirred in his seat, then roused, reaching for Everet's ice water pitcher and pouring himself a glass. Within five minutes, Marcus was again pouring himself a glass of water. After a time, he became more aware of what was going on around him. He started rubbing his nose every few seconds, and suddenly became aware that Sara was in the room. With a sudden burst of energy he began talking.

"Hi, sugar," he said, then asked, "Are you from California too?"

Sara shook her head. "No, I'm from Ohio."

"Bobby told me he adores you, sugar; but obviously he's not a man to be led around by a woman."

Sara nodded. "I know he's taking a day at a time, but takes a nosedive back for another drink, then gets the shakes if he can't get any more alcohol."

"He's his own person for sure," Marcus said.

Sara allowed herself a slight smile. "A very difficult man. Our relationship has been very complicated."

Marcus took another drink of ice water. His eyes closing briefly, he pulled a handkerchief from his pocket, wiping a sudden wave of perspiration from his face.

"Are you coming down with the flu?" Sara asked. "You're sweating, and your nose is red."

"I'll make it," Marcus said with a laugh.

Sara frowned. "You don't want your father to get sick with the flu, do you?"

Just as Marcus started to reply, the door burst open and a nurse wheeled Bobby into the room. His first words were not to Sara but to Marcus.

"Has she been talking about me?" Bobby asked, his tone demanding. "I saw you talking," he said. "I read lips. My parents were both deaf mutes so I picked it up."

Bobby looked to Sara and said, "I have a zest for life you envy; that's why you'll always be my lady. You draw energy from me. I keep you full of life. Right, Poppins?"

As the nurse helped Bobby into his bed, she looked at Sara in amusement. "Is he full of bull?" she asked.

Sara turned her head away and bit her lip to keep from laughing, then looked back at the nurse. "I may have botched romance before, but this one was a fiasco from the start."

The nurse chuckled as she pushed the wheelchair out of the room.

"Have your wounds healed from yesterday's chaos?"

Thief of Love

Bobby asked, his tone lighthearted but also betraying some concern.

Sara thought for a moment, then sighed and said, "No, I haven't. That is, I know how to step back for a while and sort things out rather than dissect the past." She paused, then looked him in the eye. "Bobby, why did you let that throwback hippie talk to me like that? I was shaken. I didn't know what to do. I thought for sure that Skip would be around again today." Her words were in an icy monotone. He's psycho, she thought.

He met her gaze for a brief moment, then looked away. "I wasn't really tuned in to your whole conversation. Then when I felt stronger and started to focus, I felt better about everything, thinking, 'he's a fighter and you're headstrong.' I didn't set out to offend you."

Sara shook her head. "It went deeper than that, Bobby. Everything you said and did was to get me out of this room. What do you mean I'm a headstrong person? He looks like one of those people who breaks a bottle and goes at it like a street brawler."

Bobby shrugged. "Borderline personality. It's a psychiatric term I learned in the joint. He has more than the usual array of skills -- " He stopped in mid-sentence.

"Oh, excuse me," Sara said, rolling her eyes. She pushed herself out of the chair and put on her parka and glasses.

The phone rang.

Sara turned away and didn't even try to listen as Bobby spoke softly into the phone for a moment, until Marcus interrupted, "Give it to me, Bobby." Bobby shrugged and handed him the phone.

Sara turned toward Bobby again, ignoring Marcus as she said, "Your doctor called me."

"What did he want?" Bobby asked.

"If I'd be able to be your caretaker, since he's going to release you in a day or so. He told me he doesn't want you left alone and wants to keep you monitored. I told him I work full time on the factory floor, which makes it impossible. He also recommended that I try and call your sister Megan and I said I thought she'd be great support."

Bobby immediately became animated. "Have you talked to her?" His voice was loud, his tone defensive.

Sara shook her head.

He hoisted himself up on one elbow and started shaking. "Oh no! No! No! You won't call any of my family."

Sara grimaced. "You're getting crazy; that attitude isn't helping."

"My attitude? Who's got the attitude? Don't you understand? I don't want to worry them with any of this. Let's just keep my health and medical problems private, okay? My aunt is too up there in age to put worry on her. She won't take this well and won't rest easy with it."

Sara paced to the window and stared down at the parking lot. "Who's going to take care of you then?" she asked.

"We'll talk about it when I come home. Until then, don't bring me any more ripples. It stresses me out." He picked up a newspaper from the nightstand and began to leaf through it, ignoring her.

Her mood darkening further, Sara looked over at Marcus, who was staring with full attention at a movie on the TV.

Forgetting that he was supposed to be ignoring her, Bobby motioned Sara to approach his bedside.

"Lighten up. Come over here a little closer," he said. "Relax. Look, I don't want to go back to California. I like it here with you. I want to take care of you. You were all alone and lonely until I came into your life."

Sara shook her head. "I think it's not in the best interest for both of us."

"I don't think so," he said in a quick reply, then paused for a moment. "I shared myself with you more than I have with any other person. If I went back to California, it would shake me to the depth of my soul. You know I love you." He put his hand on hers and lowered his voice. "I think I'm going to marry you very soon. We know each other inside and out, and I want to always be with you, share my life with you and love you forever."

"Oh no," Sara replied, becoming tearful.

"You better wake up and smell the coffee," he said. "Most of all, you'll not be able to share my success when I open the ranch." He looked at her intently, with affection -- whether genuine or not -- in his voice. "I know I'd give my life for you. In a sense, I already have. I don't go to bars anymore. I cut myself off from my friends for you."

Sara stood silent.

He looked into her eyes and said, "You're going to miss me when I'm gone."

"I've got to hit the time clock," Sara said. "I'm going to work now."

When she left, Sara found herself smiling as she glanced toward Marcus, who was busy on the phone again.

As she crossed the parking lot, Sara walked with her head down, but when she got into her car she sat inside for a moment before starting it. <u>It's not going to be easy to make him leave</u>, she thought, <u>but I'm sending him back</u>. With renewed determination Sara started the car, turning her attention to driving as she headed toward the plant.

From the hospital, Sara would have a ten-minute drive to work. She glanced at the clock radio in the dash, noting that she could still swing by MacDonald's and make it to work on time. At the golden arches Sara ordered fries and a Big Mac to go. By the time she was done with her fast-food break, she'd arrived at the plant's parking lot. She hopped out and strode through the security gate two minutes before her shift was to begin.

Inside, at the northwest corner of the plant, Sara stepped over to the time clock and swiped her timecard through the overtime equalization options. She punched in, calling for four hours overtime for early Saturday or Sunday, and checked to be sure her options showed up successfully processed. Then she followed her co-workers and headed for her work area in the southwest corner of the building.

That night Sara did a lot of thinking and made plans to send Bobby back to California. When her lunch break came at six thirty, she called him. The phone rang several times before he answered.

Speaking in a firm tone, she told him, "Listen, Bobby. I have something important to say. I don't see any reason for us to continue this relationship."

Bobby started speaking almost before Sara had finished. "Look, it's been beautiful, but I didn't give much of myself. I didn't go out of my way. It's all about money with you. If I had a job and a thick wallet, then I could stay. Couldn't I? I can't keep going on like this either. You're a roller coaster ride for me with your mood swings. I never know from day to day where I'm going to sleep next. If it weren't for Everet, I'd check out of this room. But Everet needs me to keep an eye on him."

Sara couldn't believe how he had twisted everything

around into its opposite. She stared at the phone for a moment, then asked, "How's that?"

"I'm now forced to tell you," he said, then paused, the silence broken by his puffing breath -- probably sneaking another drag on a cigarette, Sara thought. "His daughter keeps coming in here, snatching up her father's morphine pills," he finally said.

"How can that happen with her while Marcus sits there most of the day?" Sara asked, adding, "Is she crazy?"

"He's not here at night," Bobby said in an uneasy tone. "I caught her sneaking in here at two a.m. yesterday morning. She has no values. The pills have made her a thief -- no mercy -- no sensibilities.

"How evil," Sara said in a solemn tone. "When he goes home, he may not even be aware of what was happening."

"I know. . . I know," Bobby said, sounding mournful, "They're vultures. Marcus should probably tell the doctor and consider the possibility of a nursing home."

"I'm worried about him," Sara said. "Oh no, Everet would never go for that. Marcus couldn't do that."

Bobby said, "Goes to show. . . " He stopped there.

"Everet's near death; unable to defend himself," Sara said. "The situation's crazy."

Glancing up at the clock Sara saw that they had been talking longer than she had planned; her lunch break was almost over. They said their goodbyes and she told him she'd be by the next day.

As the night passed, Sara found it difficult to keep her attention on the details of her job, so she asked her supervisor for a pass to leave.

When she settled at home, Sara forced herself to wonder what it would be like to have Bobby gone. As she sat thinking,

Thief of Love

Sara finally realized that in a few days, Bobby would be gone. I don't need anyone, she thought. It's so hard to be alone, but I can't cry in front of him, no matter how much my eyes burn. Any sign of weakness and he'll move in on my vulnerability. Having steeled her determination, Sara didn't hesitate to call Bobby, despite the late hour.

"I'll call the airline and prepay for your flight tonight to Arizona or California, wherever you want to go," she said.

There was a long silence at the other end of the line. No doubt, Sara thought, Bobby's devising a way to get out of this.

"The problem is, I don't have any money, Sara. I need two hundred cash to hold me over until I can get over to the ranch."

"Okay," she said without hesitation, adding, "You got it."

The next day, when Sara picked Bobby up, she couldn't shake an ominous feeling as Bobby hugged Everet goodbye. Her concern about Everet's safety and health grew as they drove away; but she had to turn to more important business. "I can't pay for your flight yet because you haven't told me where you're going."

"You know what?" Bobby said. "All I've seen since I've been here is overcast, gray sky and snow clouds. You all's weather is for the Eskimos and buckeyes. Buy me a westbound ticket for Monterey. I want to see a Monterey sunset tonight. I also need a fifth to lift my spirits."

Deciding to keep him pacified, Sara stopped at the state liquor store, where Bobby stepped out, stood straight, and balled his fists at his sides but stood without yelling, going crazy, or blowing up with the turmoil of emotions he obviously held inside.

Sara handed him ten dollars and he went in to make his

purchase before they continued toward her home on Taylor Street.

Sara left Bobby in the living room while she went into the bedroom for a few minutes of privacy.

Within a few moments, Bobby came storming in.

"Get me the hell out of Ohio quick as possible," he demanded as he strode into the room, standing over her where she sat on her bed. "I'm going to see the sun shine again."

He suddenly dropped to one knee beside the bed.

She watched his eyes and face as the fierce expressions in both softened, and he looked at her with what she couldn't help hoping was renewed affection.

"All I want is one goodbye kiss from you," he said as he brought his lips against hers.

Sara found herself unable to resist, and she threw her arms around him, feeling the pressure of his lips rippling through her. She wanted to hold that kiss forever, knowing the energy she drew from it would stop too soon, and it did.

"This is difficult for me," he said. "I love you, but I'm leaving. Isn't there any lady anywhere who can understand a man's feelings?"

Their mutual weakness had passed. He rose to his feet.

She knew he saw how that kiss, and his words, had hurt her when he said, "Smile, Red. I'd do anything you wanted me to just to see you smile."

Sadness wrapped around her as Sara picked herself up from the bed and began to pull his clothing from the drawers and closets.

Her gloom was overcome by surprise as he suddenly pushed her aside, his tone dripping bitterness as he said, "Don't worry about the way I pack. Let me be alone. All you're worried

Thief of Love

about is getting me out. Call the travel agency. Put your time and energy into that. I'll pack. It doesn't matter in the least to you what or who I am. I'm honest with you. I love you.

"I need a one-way ticket to Monterey, California as soon as possible, leaving out of Cleveland, early afternoon."

Sara wasted not another moment as she went to the phone, dialed the airline and waited for a response, wondering why it took so long. Finally, a reservationist came on the line and Sara asked for the trip Bobby had said he wanted. She was told a flight was leaving Cleveland at four fifteen p.m., connecting at Dallas/Fort Worth at seven forty p.m., and arriving in San Francisco at nine thirty p.m. A commuter plane would then take Bobby on to Monterrey, arriving at ten forty p.m. Sara paid by her credit card without commenting on the charge, which was substantial. Last-minute travel arrangements are always so expensive, she thought.

Bobby packed all of his possessions, came downstairs, and, of course, fixed a mixed drink.

Sara sat on the living room couch and watched as the sunlight glistened off the snow-covered rooftops outside.

After getting a buzz on, Bobby shouted from the kitchen, "Hey, Red, if it was up to me, I'd make my life with you."

He strode through the living room and stepped onto the front porch, leaving the door wide open. He stood outside in the cold for several minutes, breathing heavily before going back inside and upstairs to get his luggage.

After a moment he yelled out as he came down the stairs, "You're a wild and wayward lady. It'll be too late when I get back tonight to see a Monterey sunset. It's the power of the red hair. You got the power, Red. Let's hit it."

He carried his luggage out the still open door, went to the

car and flung it inside in a gesture of contempt. "It's the day of surprises, Bobby," he mused to himself, his tone bitter.

Sara gathered her keys, closed up the house and went to the car, started it and began taking Bobby on his way.

He looked straight ahead out the windshield and, without asking, lit a cigarette, his bloodshot eyes soon squinting against the cloud of drifting smoke. A patch of bright sky appeared, then it clouded up again. He leaned farther toward the window and began to sulk. Within a few moments, Bobby removed the bottle of whiskey from his duffel bag, poured some into a plastic cup and gulped it down.

When they finally reached Cleveland via the Ohio Turnpike, Sara turned onto the Grafton Road exit, pulled into the Park N Fly shuttle pick-up area and stopped.

Bobby slowly began to remove his luggage from the back seat as a shuttle bus appeared.

"Shuttle's coming," Sara said, and, so he wouldn't be too late, she hopped out and helped, carrying one of the bags to the passenger loading zone as the bus stopped.

The driver stepped out, grabbed up Bobby's bags and set them in a luggage rack at the rear of the bus.

"Where to?" he asked.

"American Airlines," Bobby said as he and Sara stepped aboard and took a seat at the back of the bus.

At the terminal, Bobby checked in and they went to the departure gate with only a few minutes to spare.

Bobby turned toward her. "It's difficult to believe nearly two months have passed since I arrived here," he said, his voice soft. He reached up and touched her face. "I'll miss you. I'm going to board the plane real soon; either get it on with me now and we will talk this through or let's just call it quits." The

Thief of Love

undertones in his voice were more like pleading than demanding.

Sara felt dizzy and blown apart, knowing she'd now have to face her loneliness or, scarier yet, might change her mind.

"No, I won't stay," he said, sadness in his voice. "I love you. I want to make you happy. I'll go. It makes no sense to try to explain myself. It makes no sense to me; but I must confess one thing to you: Poppins, I struggle to understand all of this myself too."

The loudspeaker came to life with the words: "Those departing for San Francisco may board the plane."

Bobby extended his arm around Sara's waist as she walked with him to the door.

"Now you promise me something." Bobby's voice was softer, his tone that of resignation. "You promise me I can come see you again," he said as he was about to step out of sight. "One smile, Red."

She nodded, tearful as he walked down the glass-partitioned passageway toward the plane. She held her hand to the window and as Bobby passed he lifted his hand up to hers. Her pain and feelings of isolation intensified to be so close and yet feel glass between them.

"Bye, baby," he called out through the glass, tears in his eyes.

She waved, forcing a smile though expecting to collapse right there; but she knew she had to snap out of it. Tears of anguish weren't going to get done what had to be done.

Thief of Love

Chapter Thirteen

For the next few weeks, Sara worked a lot of overtime to try and fill the void that now made her feel empty and unfulfilled. Only at night, in the privacy of her bedroom, when no one was watching or listening, did she allow herself to cry. Her heart would skip a beat as she meditated on how her meeting with Bobby had set their love relationship in motion. Her mind kept replaying old memories.

<u>If I would have given him more time,</u> she thought, with tears flowing down her face, <u>he could have possibly come through in a positive change and I wouldn't have had to overcome this loneliness</u>. She now felt that all along during her romance with Bobby that a love relationship is more valuable than gold and worth nurturing and tending to with care.

Next, Sara made a decision to try to win old friends back and reconnect to the energy she could draw from them; then she took a step of action. On her personal time at the plant, she took a walk to the northwest corner of the building, looking up and down the grinding lines for Shea Robinette. The oil mist in the air was heavy, so she reached for a terrycloth towelette from the supervisor's desk and wiped the greasy film from her safety glasses, then proceeded with slow and careful steps across the oil-slicked floor of the grinding line.

Sara approached a machine operator standing next to his finish-grinding machine. With his overalls, hat, ear protectors and safety glasses, she couldn't recognize him. He was holding a grinding stone and was just about to change the worn stone on the machine when he saw her coming and nodded.

"Have you seen Shea Robinette?" she asked.

He nodded again. "The parts are running soft in the steel.

Thief of Love

She was by with her audit cart a few minutes ago when an area manager sent her down to check the line. She'll be back shortly."

Sara watched a general service attendant walk his floor scrubber down the aisle. The brushes on his scrubber were down and spinning around, dropping soap on the floor, but the squeegee across the back wasn't picking up the water thoroughly, leaving some in puddles on the concrete floor, although most of the oil has been removed all down the length of the line.

Sara moved out of the attendant's way and sat at the table nearby. Next, the attendant parked his scrubber, took his mop cart from the labor crib and finished the grinding lines with a hand mop, wiping up the puddles. By the time he finished, Shea came down the line, pushing her cart. Walking along with her was a foreman and a quality-control supervisor in white shirt and tie asking her questions. Shea saw Sara but continued to talk with the machine operator, foreman and supervisor. She walked from machine to machine, picking up a few spindle bearings and checking for cracks, then went to the magna-flux booth.

When Shea finished, she walked over to Sara and flashed a broad smile. "I heard Bobby left you; but I'm not surprised. It sure is easy getting hurt these days, isn't it Sara?"

Sara gave an indifferent shrug while Shea kept talking. "I felt offended that you would put our friendship on hold for that womanizer." Shea's voice was getting louder as she spoke.

"Shea, please calm down," Sara said.

"I'm your rock," Shea said. "Wake up and see the light, Sara. He knows which woman needs to hear what. Your social scene suddenly changed after you met that cheap hustler, Bobby Johnson. He's not even a high-class fraud," she said, in rapid fire. "I hoped you'd find a man, but not that kind of man. I know you had to go through whatever you went through with him. You kept your distance from me and other people who love you and care what happens to you and those who seemed to be a part of your life."

Sara couldn't bring herself to tell Shea she missed Bobby. To do that was to acknowledge that he was still in her heart. Shea wouldn't miss that.

"The information given all by itself from the scriptwriter should have been enough. Shouldn't it have been, Sara?"

"I know, Shea. I hurt you. Please forgive me, but I had to disconnect from you and some other people, that's true. I had little control over the situation to avoid raising anxiety between us. I withdrew. I realized once again this was all that was left at the time."

Sara suddenly had an overwhelming feeling remorse. She rested her hand in her shop coat pocket, and drifted into a dreamlike state as she pictured Bobby as she had last seen him, with his hand held toward hers on the window and her own hand pressing back against the pane of glass at Cleveland Hopkins Airport.

Shea stepped along, pushed her audit cart next to the janitor's labor crib, checked her paperwork of the rejected materials from the soft steel of the grinder, and then laid her clipboard on the cart.

"Come on, let's take a thirty-minute break," she said.

"Where to?" Sara asked.

"There could be a few empty seats in the non-smoking break room. We'll go there."

On their way, Shea stopped at the vending machines.

"I'm buying. What would you like, Sara?"

"I'll take a coffee with cream, no sugar," Sara said and pushed the appropriate button. Shea pushed the button for a diet coke with extra ice on the pop machine. They took their drinks into the break room and sat at a table with a wall phone beside it.

"Excuse me, Sara, for a sec," Shea said as she removed an AT&T card from her purse, and an address book. "I'm scheduling an eventful weekend with a high-ranking military officer I met at DJ's Club in Port Clinton last night. He's stationed at Camp Perry."

Sara watched a sitcom rerun on TV while Shea talked absentmindedly into the phone, toying with one of her earrings.

Sara was about to doze off when she suddenly checked her watch, but said nothing.

Shea saw Sara's restlessness and with her hand covering the receiver asked, "How would you like to join Rich, Stephen and me for cocktails after work tonight?"

Sara shrugged. "I don't know about that."

"What's wrong with being wined and dined and wooed?" Shea asked.

"I'll take my time and wait for a good Christian man," Sara said, "and life will be abundant and won't pass me by."

"If you wait for a Christian, you'll be waiting for years and your life will be passing you by," Shea said. "I've included you tonight on my date with Rich. He has a friend, Stephen, who is also a military man. He asked to meet you. I understand he's a hunk.

"I know you feel everything is gone and you have no future, Sara. Let go of all that negativity about yourself. I'm not offering you sympathy; I'm offering support. Stephen is your type. We'll have a blast."

Sara felt embarrassed but kept her composure.

Shea frowned at Sara's continued silence, quickly said a good-bye to Rich and hung up the phone, then asked? "What's

Thief of Love

wrong with meeting Stephen or anyone else, Sara? It's not easy to wait for someone to give you what you desperately long for. I won't say you'll fit real well with everyone and all types of people like I do, but you can hold your own."

"It's easy for you to say that, Shea," Sara said with a noticeable uncertainty in her voice. "You're pretty and radiate a genuine warmth. You make an easy connection with everyone you meet."

Shea clicked her nails on the table, placed her hand on her chin to prop it up, and fixed her gaze firmly on Sara.

"You've never been intimidated by my good looks before. Think about it -- if you don't feel good about yourself, then no one else will. You've got to walk with confidence to make people look at you with confidence. Life's all about changes, Sara. I would suggest, first of all, you should change your blush and lipstick to a brighter color to bring out the highlights in your red hair. Add some eyeliner foundation. You have glittering eyes with a sweet smile and, with your beautiful red hair, after you've freshly teased it, you'll look adorable. Another mistake you make: You should change your clothing to a style with a more alluring look. You want to capture a man's attention. Certainly you don't dabble in modeling or wear high fashion like I do, but you can look as well." Shea put her hand on Sara's shoulder and continued, "You can do it; be strong. He's your type. You'll have a good flow. Go for it."

Sara squared her shoulders and her response held more confidence as she said, "Okay." I'll take an early shower in the women's locker room about ten thirty. Can you wait for me there, Shea?"

"You bet. I can hardly wait till quitting time. When we walk through the gate, it's 'party time'," Shea said, tapping out a tempo with her fingers. "If I'm not in the locker room, I'll be down on the floor. Page me if I'm not. Okay?"

Next Shea opened a large envelope and removed an ad from the Globe Magazine, Sheila Wood `Make a Friend Club' section. With her fingernail, she skimmed through the names of males and used a yellow marker to highlight a couple of good ads she liked.

Sara watched and said. "I thought you had something going with Rich."

Shea's eyes went wide. "I don't enjoy waiting a long time in line at a fast food place where the smell of hamburgers only makes me hungrier. The same with men, because, honey, when I want something, I want it quick. I don't mean anything cheap because I don't date cheap men. If they can't afford me, I don't go. Richard is from another state. When he's gone from here -- out of sight, out of mind -- and that's the way I like it with dating gentlemen from out of town. I'm not involved heavily or seeing them frequently. I'm not fond of dating local men. Just a good time is where it's at."

Sara checked her watch. "It's nearly five ten," she said. My relief will be frantic with me when I get back. The assembly line will be running at high volume, with A.B.S. parts."

Shea nodded as she continued checking out the male correspondence in depth as Sara rose to leave.

"I'll see you at eleven," Sara called back as she hurried out of the break room.

Returning to her work area, Sara offered brief apologies for running late; but the woman working her relief moved on down the line, without giving Sara the courtesy of a reply.

Sara returned to her seat on the assembly line and resumed inspecting the spindle bearing hubs, but her mind wasn't on her job. Instead, she thought she was supposed to share some happier moments and the enjoyment of a friend with some companions, but her heart went back on Bobby. She knew she couldn't keep going on and living in between torments, but would have to do something if he didn't contact her soon -- that she'd be calling someone to find out how and where he was.

By evening, Sara took a paid lunch for working during her personal time, left thirty minutes early and headed for the ladies locker room.

When she got to the locker room, Shea was already showered and dressed in a two-piece black pants suit with a leopard- spotted collar and wearing two-inch heels. Shea nodded at Sara but remained sitting in silence at a table and concentrated on replacing a fake fingernail.

Sara took the duffel bag from her locker and removed a change of clothes. She laid out her bath towel, washrag, toothbrush, toothpaste and deodorant on the bench next to the shower stall.

Shea stepped out of the locker room into the hallway after she received a call on her beeper, then, after a moment, came back in and finished her nail.

"I'm going down," Shea said. "I received a call to report to the north wall maintenance to Ken Stuckey's office for overtime. I'll wait for you there."

Sara took her shower, dressed, put on her makeup, and was finished in twenty minutes. She packed up all her belongings and headed toward the stairwell, stopping along the way, to look out a window, and gaze at the twilight. People were leaving the plant and getting into their cars while others were punching in at the security gate for the night shift.

Shea looked up and saw Sara, and motioned her to the

Thief of Love

northeast door as she too walked to the security gate.

Sara hurried outside, trying to catch up with Shea's long strides. Aa Sara approached, Shea slid on her heels, throwing herself off balance, but she didn't fall, grabbing Sara's shoulder instead. "Oops," she said, hiking up the winding pavement to the security gate while holding onto Sara to keep from falling.

They both punched out and headed toward the parking lot through the many cars. An interior light flashed on in a Jeep Cherokee. There were two men inside. One got out from the passenger side while the other stayed in the driver's seat. He flashed his headlights and, as they walked closer, Shea grinned and waved.

"Hi, guy," she called out.

Shea's date stood out very clearly to Sara. He had a handsome, confident face, with a military bearing -- square-shouldered and broad-chested.

As Shea introduced them, Stephen pushed his forehead with a thoughtful gesture. Sara could see right away that Stephen was a carefree man who quickly made friends wherever he went and with whomever he made contact.

"Hi, Sara," Stephen said, putting his arm around her. Sara tensed, feeling this was forward of him, but didn't say so or move away.

"Hi," she said, her voice soft and subdued.

"Is that all you're going to say?" he asked, his smile as well as his question asking for some conversation as the women climbed into the SUV.

"Hi, I'm Richard," Stephen's companion said as he started the engine.

"I have no idea what interests military men besides wars. I have no real feeling about world travel or anything connected with a service man," Sara said, trying to be completely honest.

"Well, I do," Shea said. "Call your commander-in-chief and tell him Shea Robinette's giving him a direct order to stress the message to Saddam Hussein in Baghdad that I put out a hit out on him, and I want him blown out into the ozone layer." As she said it, she smirked and rolled her eyes, a picture of frustration, with her hands waving up in the air.

Sara slunk down in her seat as if she were outdone again.

Richard threw back his head and laughed with a suffocating arrogance that permeated the interior of the truck.

It was a half-hour drive to their designated nightspot. Already, Sara knew it was going to be wrenching experience.

At about eleven thirty they arrived at DJ's Club. Inside, the hostess took them to a table near the dance floor and almost immediately a waitress appeared to take their order.

"Ladies first," Richard said, looking to Shea.

"I'll have a White Russian," she said.

"I'll have a frozen Margarita," Sara said, adding, "with lime."

Both men ordered seven and sevens on the rocks.

Within a few moments, the waitress returned carrying a tray with their drinks. All four engaged in small talk while the first round of drinks was consumed, and the men ordered another.

It didn't take long for the alcohol to affect the men in ways Sara didn't appreciate, but Shea didn't seem to notice as she twisted around in her seat, posing to show off her seductive top while Sara sat like a statue.

When Sara could take it no more, she excused herself to use the restroom, catching Shea's eyes and motioning with her chin for her to follow.

Thief of Love

Shea caught the signal and accompanied her.

As soon as they were inside the ladies room doorway, Sara came face to face with Shea, immediately coming down on her.

"Some date, Shea. This date of your friend's has hands like an octopus. I feel trapped and harassed."

"Oh, Sara," Shea said, shaking her head. "Different people express themselves in different ways."

"Well, he better start expressing himself in a hands-off way or I'm out of here," Sara said.

"Okay, Sara. I'll try to relay him the message; but, for now, let's just have a good time. Okay?"

Sara nodded but frowned as they returned to their table while the band played a medley of light rock music.

During their short conversation upon returning Shea somehow got Sara's message across by the time Richard swept Shea into his arms and they walked to the dance floor.

Sara looked toward Stephen.

He gave her a let's-get-it-over-with look.

Sara's heart skidded downhill, trying to make the best out of a bad night. A slow dance song was now playing as she and Stephen took to the floor and slow danced; then, fired by a sudden, rash impulse, he bent his face very near hers. He held her close, so close that she could feel his breath in her ear. When she didn't respond, he wrapped one arm around her midriff, pulling her top a bit lower as he ogled the newly exposed flesh of her upper bust-line.

Sara pulled back and forced herself to meet his eyes, saying, "Next time you get fresh, pick some girl your own class and size, you asshole. You are simply horrid. Hands off. No physical, sexual contact is allowed. I'm not like the rest of them."

Sara could see his eyes fill with a look of aggressive authority, and knew he was used to instilling fear in others; but she just confronted his gaze, then broke away and with measured steps returned to the table and sat down.

Stephen followed, avoiding eye contact with her as his face flushed with suppressed rage.

Richard and Shea, oblivious of the strained atmosphere between Stephen and Sara, came off the dance floor just as the waitress stopped by their table.

Richard ordered another round of drinks.

Soon Shea saw that all was not well with the other half of their party, and tried to take the lead in the conversation. She knew all the right things to say, but the icy cold undercurrent of the tension between Stephen and Sara soon drove Shea and Richard out onto the dance floor again.

Sara's mood darkened further when Stephen suddenly said, "If it's money you want, I'll pay your price."

Sara drew sharply erect, astonished. She couldn't speak, only shake her head.

Apparently unaware or uncaring of her discomfort, he continued talking. "We have two adjoining rooms with a swinging door and four beds at our hotel."

Stunned, Sara could only ask, "Why would you want four beds?"

"I may want to move around," he replied, his tone cool and casual.

Still shocked, Sara could only ask, "What did you say? What's with you?" she demanded, her temper rising.

Stephen reached into his pocket, fumbled around, and then threw a picture on the table, saying, "I entertained the

Thief of Love

fantasy that this is a prelude."

Sara's stared at the pornographic photo of a `foursome' in disbelief. "No wonder you're so touchy-freely." Her voice quavered as she continued, "Take me to the car, right now."

Suddenly, Shea was standing over them. "No more of your tantrums, Sara. You're causing a scene."

Stung that Shea would defend this strange and depraved character, instead of taking the side of her supposed friend, Sara said, "Not in my wildest imagination did I consider I would have to go through such an experience, Shea. I can't believe the way you tried to set me up for a swingers' night, and in the sleazy way you did it, too." She winced. "The thought of what you had planned, just like the people in that picture. You were in the plot with them, weren't you?"

Shea looked around at the nearby tables, where people were staring at them, and said in a terse voice. "Oh quiet down, Sara; we'll take you home if you're not up for a good time. "

As they all left and went toward the Cherokee, Shea shook her head and said, "It's too crazy with you. We're getting you back as quickly as possible."

There was venom in her voice, but Sara didn't care.

While they got into the Jeep, Sara said, "Don't worry, Shea, I forgive you, and feel sorry for you."

With that, Shea exploded into a rage. "I don't need your forgiveness. It's my right to do my thing,' Shea said as she sat grinning and tapping her nails on the armrest in a rapid tempo.

"You're not tricking me, Shea, and masquerading me as a slut to get involved with two perverts in a foursome like I saw in that picture. I had the eerie feeling when we were driving over here that you had something else in mind than a nice, normal night out."

Thief of Love

Shea countered by saying, "You know there's nothing wrong with having a good time. I believe that. No one's twisting your arm, you're of the age to loosen up a little."

Sara shook her head. "Our tastes differ. I just don't happen to go for your type of entertainment. You know I just want to have a good time, with no intention being used this way to lure this type of men. You continue to be selfish, as well as controlling people and having no regard for others; and the disrespect and pain you cause me. I feel violated." Close to tears, Sara added as she choked back a sob, "My feelings are hurt really bad."

Richard took a deep breath and glanced in the rearview mirror as they turned into the parking lot.

"My car is over there," Sara said, pointing the way across the parking lot while they drove through the darkness looking for her car.

Richard pulled near her car and stopped the Cherokee, shifting the gearshift into park.

Sara opened the door and stormed out, marched breathlessly back to her car.

Stephen called after her, "You're not still angry at me, are you, gorgeous?" His voice loud and clear, but sharp as he shouted, "I liked what I saw."

"You're history," Sara shouted over her shoulder as she kept walking.

"Let up, you doll," he shouted even louder.

As Sara reached her car and unlocked the door, she could hear Shea saying to Richard, "Honey, let's not let her blow our evening. I'll call Pat. She'll be flattered to be with Stephen. I still want to spend the night with you, honey."

Thief of Love

Chapter Fourteen

Light snow was falling by the time Sara returned home. When she was finally in bed, she tried to get some rest but was unable to relax enough to go to sleep from the deep humiliation. It suddenly seemed necessary and important to call Lori, to be sure everything was okay with Bobby.

Since there were no Monterey, California calls on the monthly statement of her phone bill, Sara called Monterey information and got phone number of a Lori Clark.

She checked her anniversary clock that she had been given at the plant for twenty-five years of service. It was nearly two a.m. but she new that California time would be eleven p.m. so she decided to call.

With each unanswered ring, Sara's anxiety increased. On the fourth ring, the call was answered and a sleepy woman's voice asked, "Hello?"

"My name is Sara Bringard. Is this Lori Clark?"

"I'm Lori Clark."

A sudden nervousness made Sara begin to stammer. "I-I'm Bobby J-Johnson's f-friend from Ohio -- I mean I'm calling for Lori Clark, Bobby Johnson's sister." The words simply would not come out right. "I mean, I-I'm not sure if you're Bobby Johnson's sister or his old girlfriend.

There was a long pause.

"Did you hear me?" Sara asked, adding, "I just need to know."

Finally, Lori said, "I don't know how to deal with people calling for Bobby anymore. I'm Bobby Johnson's ex-fiancée; and I haven't heard from him in three months."

"You're his ex-fiancée?"

Thief of Love

"Yes."

"You haven't seen or heard from him?" Sara asked. "No cards or letters to say `I miss you, Lori?'"

"No cards -- nothing. Like I said, I haven't seen or heard from him in three of months," Lori said with a sigh.

Sara was skeptical of Lori at first, but, as they continued to talk, and although they hadn't spoken before, they fell into a heart-to-heart conversation. Soon, Sara couldn't believe how nice Lori seemed to be, but so very weak, too.

"I've been on a suicide watch since he left me three months ago. What should have been red flags going up to warn me about him -- I seemed to play the warnings down," Lori said.

It was then for the first time that Sara began to see the seriousness of the situation.

"Lori, he knew enough and was practiced enough to fake his way into glittery worlds for his own means of station," Sara said. "That's how he's gone through life."

Lori broke into tears and sobbed. "I would reach out for him in a love-drugged sleep and he wouldn't be there. I endured several nights and days of private torment before the breakdown. When I almost lost my sanity, my doctor prescribed special drugs. I hoped to smooth out the raw edges of memories with a background check -- too late, of course."

Sara said, "I had to distance myself from him, too. He spins fantasies with his tall tales; but I had to bring myself back to reality. I know now that he's just a down-on-his-luck drifter. I just sent him back to California and was curious as to his whereabouts since he was ill when I made him leave.

"He told me he was born in L.A., but didn't go there because of some trouble with the law. He'd say he was calling his aunt and sister, but kept the calls private. He'd give me the

Thief of Love

phone to talk with them for a short conversation, but I could never ask much; he listened the whole time. So, I know very little about him or his past; I only know he told me -- that he was hurt by the rejection of his Jewish family, who disowned him; and that he suffered from his two sons not coming to see him; and was just devastated when his wife divorced him while he was in prison. He confirmed that his ex-wife had custody of the children and he had full visitation rights but he seldom utilized those rights or paid child support.

"I asked him why he didn't visit his boys and he made excuses. He showed me a picture of his daughter, Dawnette. She was a doll and looked just like him, but she was from another time. As a youth, while he took family vacations with his parents in Utah, he met Dawnette's mother.

"A strange thing happened though, Lori, when I took him to apply for social security and veteran's benefits. He was asked about his marital status and wouldn't acknowledge he was ever married or put his children on as beneficiaries.

"He's a complicated person in many respects, but he can be there for others. He proved that to me when he was in the hospital with a man who was terminally ill with cancer. Bobby was there for him.

"I miss being with him, Lori, and he's in my heart and thoughts every day. I pray God will watch over him. I'm more worried than angry that Bobby doesn't call me. I was concerned that something might have happened to him. I just couldn't deal with his drinking and un-productivity, but he had such energy and zest. In a lot of ways, he was good company.

"How did you meet him, Lori?"

"At a carnival," she said. "Here in Monterey, California. He was traveling a three-state circuit, setting up rides and riding

Thief of Love

in rodeos and calf roping. He left the carnival to settle down with me. We were together for five wonderful months, but the magic of the romance was broken when I overheard conversations he would have with other women on my phone. Then, when the phone bill went way up, with calls to and from a nine-hundred number, I reported the calls to the phone company. They checked it out and I was told the calls were made to the Romance Connection, dialed directly from my home. I asked Bobby; he denied everything. He said I didn't know what I was talking about. After that, I called a phone fraud specialist. He gave me the phone number of the Romance Connection, and I reported the calls to them. After that, Ted Mitchell, a scriptwriter for a cable TV talk show, called me and I got bits and pieces of gossip from him about Bobby and his activities."

"I know, Lori. That same man called me the day Bobby arrived at my house, wanting to talk with Bobby to ask him to be the focus of a show they were writing about the Romance Hot Line."

"Through the grapevine, I was told later by Ted Mitchell, after Bobby left, that he was a felon and had spent time in a maximum security prison in California for violent crimes," Lori told her. "Things changed without warning. Bobby asked to borrow my car, he said to check out a job hauling livestock to ranches in the Southwest. I found out later he didn't even go to that ranch. A call came from El Paso, Texas from a Joyce checking to see if he made it back to Monterey. Her main concern for calling was to warn Bobby about a personal check she had written him for expenses so he could return to Monterey. She wasn't sure if the check would clear because there could have been a computer error on her bank statement. I told her I was Bobby's fiancée, Lori, and she was really upset and shaken, and apologized to me. She told me she had met him on the phone. He answered a voice message response system on the Romance Connection that she had registered there. She said he called her for a while and then asked if he could come see her."

Sara couldn't help interjecting, "I know; I had no control over the situation, and I was just tired of worrying about him."

The images running through Sara's mind suddenly hit home, and she had no doubt that if she had become involved in a serious relationship with Bobby he would have taken advantage of her to the max.

"Was he working on a ranch, Lori?" Sara asked.

"He told me often he was going to the ranch, but I wasn't sure where the ranch was," Lori said.

"When he started calling me, here in Sandusky, Ohio, he said he was calling from a ranch," Sara said.

"Sandusky, Ohio!" Lori exclaimed, adding, "I had several hundred dollars worth of calls to Sandusky, Ohio."

"I'm sorry. They must've been to my number, Lori."

"When I talked with Ted Mitchell, he told met that Bobby was talking with several other women on the Romance Hot Line. Some even sent him round-trip plane tickets. He would go see them, spend time with them, and leave. Ted said that Bobby had done nothing wrong; there was just no compatibility with any of them. Bobby has a gift for dealing with women; but Ted believed Bobby was yearning for some one woman to be with."

"What did you do when you found out about Joyce?" Sara asked.

"When Bobby returned with my car, I told him Joyce called and I knew where he had been. He withdrew from sleeping with me and didn't seem to miss me. I asked him where he was, and he said he'd been at the ranch. He said Joyce was a tramp, and told me not to answer the phone anymore."

"What did you do when the phone rang?"

"It mostly went unanswered."

Sara knew everything Bobby had done to Lori had caused her to have erratic behavior, and to become highly medicated. Sara's rage was coupled with disgust at the way he was also looking for easy money.

"Lori, you can still control the outcome if you can just keep your nerves in check. Use your first-rate mind and you can get out of this mess forever. Bobby is a skillful fraud. With him, you'll live in a wondrous kingdom of make-believe. He must have used the money Joyce gave him to come to my home in Ohio. He traveled by Greyhound Bus, giving me the impression he had just quit a job at a ranch and had money coming. No money ever came to my house."

They talked a little while longer, and, after hanging up the phone, Sara found that the images running through her mind were more than she could bear. She had no doubt that if their romantic relationship had continued, Bobby would have taken full advantage of Lori. As she began to understood Lori's state of mind, Sara let the idea go of calling her back.

Thief of Love

Chapter Fifteen

The next day, Bobby called. Sara's heart seemed to jump when she heard his voice.

"Hi, baby, it's Bobby. Can you talk to me please?"

Sara sighed, then said, "Yes, Bobby. I'll talk with you. I just want to know if you're okay. I've been worried about you."

"Baby, I miss you," he said. "Someday, we'll hug and kiss again. Sara, I want to thank you for being my rock and my anchor when I came bringing you troubled waters. I love you for that. You didn't cast me out. Please don't think I'm too hasty in calling, but I can't shake this heavy burden of worry for Everet," he said.

"Where are you calling from, Bobby?" she asked.

"I'm at my buddy Everet's house. He needs me. No matter what, I'm his protector, his support. We have a close bond we share," he said.

"Where's his family, Bobby?"

"The same old, same old with them. I'm keeping check on all of it. He asked me to come back to Ohio. I'm going to spend his last days with him. His bones are giving him problems. He can't be moved around in the bed without them breaking, and returned today from the hospital with pins in his arm from a couple of weeks ago. He walked around like a zombie, bumping into furniture in a catatonic state. He was being left alone, and shouldn't be walking or left alone anymore. I have things to take care of in Ohio; doctor appointments to keep. I'm staying. I'll call you again. Good night."

Waves of dizziness assaulted Sara. She clutched desperately to the headboard of her bed as waves of despair overcame her after hearing of Everet's condition. But most astonishing of all was that soon Bobby would be back.

Sara collapsed back against her pillow, wondering what she was going to do next.

Chapter 16

The next day, Bobby called again. "Listen, baby. I know we're just two broken people who want to put back together our love relationship. But I'm torn between two people who are in need to have someone to pour love into them every day.

"Everet is cancer-stricken, needing compassion and support and home health care. You are the love of my life, who also desires my companionship. Yes, my vision of your love is strong, though to be needed by Everet surpasses you in me. I know you'll never forget it but I've decided to put our relationship on hold and move in with Everet for the next few months."

Confusion, anxiety and stress were made easier for Sara when she realized that, although Bobby had returned to Ohio, he had given her a lot more time to sort out her thoughts, feelings and desires.

In June, the situation reached another turning point -- Everet's health suddenly declined. As his cancer advanced, he fell into a deep coma, then soon died.

Everet's U.S. Government Housing and Urban Development rental voucher expired at his death, leaving Bobby homeless.

At Everet's funeral, Sara stood close to Bobby till the services were over and the mourners had mostly gone their separate ways.

"What are you going to do now, Bobby?"

"I don't know, baby. I won't even have a place to stay as of the end of this month."

"What about going back to California?" Sara asked.

"Right now, till I get my last check from the ranch, I can't even afford to take a bus back home."

"Maybe I could help out," Sara said.

Bobby shook his head. "I can't even go till after my next checkup with the doctors here, in the middle of July."

"Well, I guess you could stay at the house till then," Sara said.

"I don't know if I could do that; you might think I was trying to take advantage of you."

"I can see now, after the way you took care of Everet, that there's a caring, helping side of you."

For the next three weeks, Bobby was all hearts and flowers -- even bringing Sara hand-picked roses and candy.

Then, one day after shift, Sara arrived home to find a police cruiser parked in front.

Thinking the police were in the area to talk something over with one of the neighbors, Sara was shocked to see a police officer coming out her front door, stepping across the porch and down the steps.

Overcome by a wave of panic and fear, Sara hopped out of the driver's seat, slammed the car door and hurried up the walk toward the police officer.

"What's wrong?" she asked.

Instead of answering, the police officer asked, "Do you live here?"

"Yes."

"What's your name?"

"Sara Bringard; this is my home."

"Are you just now returning from work?"

"Yes. Now, what's this all about?"

The police officer's expression and tone of voice remained noncommittal as he asked, "Do you know a Robert

Thief of Love

Johnson?"

"Yes. He's staying with me."

"Well, you had better straighten him out."

"About what?"

"We received a complaint from a concerned neighbor. Take heed that Mister Johnson was accused of consuming alcohol with a male minor on your property while you were at work."

Sara felt as if she were being crushed by an enormous weight as she sighed, fairly wilting as the police officer continued, "If you allow the drinking with underage persons to continue, substantial charges, including felony abuse of a minor, will be filed against Mister Johnson, and you too."

Still stunned, Sara nodded absently, then told the police officer, "I'm sorry. I'll certainly see that this never happens again, even if I have to call you or other officers to remove Mister Johnson from this house."

For the first time, the police officer smiled, reached into a pocket and retrieved a small white business card.

"Don't hesitate to call me. It would please me to personally remove Mister Johnson from the neighborhood."

Sara nodded, took the card and said, "Thank you."

The police officer saluted her with a wave and headed for his patrol car as she climbed the steps with a weary tread and went into the living room, closing the door behind her as she saw Bobby sitting on the couch, watching an old sitcom on TV as if nothing had happened.

"I know you get bored, Bobby, while I am at work. I know you have no one here to talk with, but drinking with kids is off limits on my property. Don't you have any common sense? You're opening the door to serious criminal charges with the state, county and city law enforcement agencies, against both of us."

"Whatever," he said, half muttering the word as he continued to stare at the television screen with an absent, cold look in his eyes.

His unconcerned attitude brought her suppressed anger to the surface. "How the hell do I know what you're doing while I'm at work?"

When he ignored her, Sara made a decision based on another major dilemma she had faced for the past few days and hours. A gloomy labor dispute between General Motors and United Auto Workers heated up at a Flint, Michigan AM plant. The Flint plant had been taken out on strike by Auto Workers Union, which had idled all North America productivity of autos, trucks and busses.

All Advance Motors operations at the Fedron parts plant where Sara was employed were to be shut down, with the exception of Lean Lines, Toyota, Saturn, and NUMI. Through all this, Sara's position as an assembler working on Fedron parts for AM cars would be furloughed from working due to the strike.

This series of developments enabled Sara to set into action a plan she had been formulating at work -- an escape route. She decided to use the free time to take a vacation, and drop Bobby off in California.

After another moment's sullen silence from Bobby, Sara said, "You know, Bobby, that the Flint strike has cut production to the assembly line where I work, and I've been furloughed."

He kept his gaze focused on the television as he asked, "So?"

"So, I've decided to take the time off for a vacation.

He looked away from the television screen, a panicked

expression in his eyes as he said, "Where's that going to leave me?"

"With me -- I mean, can you come with me?"

He smirked. "Where to, West Virginia?"

"Well, you're partly right; I was thinking of west, but out West -- all the way to California?"

His interest suddenly piqued, Bobby punched the button on the remote and the television screen went dark as he turned his full attention to Sara. "That'd be great, Red. I've got to call David in Monterey, and Aunt Betty, and my sister in Phoenix.

Within a few moments, Bobby was on the phone to his sister; from the way the conversation went, Sara could tell Bobby was being interrogated with all kinds of questions about her. Then she heard, "Well, yes, she is a year or two older than me."

There was a brief pause, and Bobby replied, "No, she's not that way at all. No. Well, you'll just have to meet her then. All right, we'll see you on the trip out. Bye."

As soon as he had hung up the phone, Sara said. "I could tell by the way you two were talking that your sister was giving you a real questioning about me."

Bobby grinned and nodded, saying, "Yeah."

"And she asked you about my age?"

"Yes -- that too."

"And then she had accusing words about me?"

"Well, uh, not really."

"Well, uh, really, I'm not going to visit her then."

Bobby just shrugged and said, "Okay, if you don't want to go, we won't visit my sister, although I would like to."

* * *

Thief of Love

As the day of departure drew nearer, Sara's feelings of anticipation became more hopeful for a wonderful vacation, and even to meet Bobby's family -- to answer her questions and, most of all, get Bobby out of town.

Sara called her co-workers and friends to alert them that she and Bobby would be traveling to the West Coast to visit his relatives in Orange County and Monterey, and stop where and when they liked along the way.

The night before they left, Sara murmured her prayers and hastily got into bed for an early departure in Sara's S-10 Chevy pickup that Bobby wanted to show off.

The first day they traveled twelve hours, and, after they had driven over six hundred miles, at the end of the day's journey, it occurred to Sara as they were moving through the Nebraska plains that the towns were fewer and farther between, and the farms seemed to spread out in more acreage. All day the car was speeding between fields of grain and pastureland among groves of trees. They drove on at a steady pace and stopped at a motel by midnight.

The next day they drove as far as Rollins, Wyoming where they spent the second night. They awoke early and the third day traveled through Wyoming, Utah and Nevada. They stopped where and when they liked, such as Elko, Nevada, where they gambled for a while and then rented a motel room.

Throughout the trip, Sara kept asking, "How long will it be? When will we get to California?"

Late in the same day they left Elko, Bobby replied to her latest questions, "We're already in California. Look down to your right. That's Lake Tahoe. We're in the Sierra Nevada Mountains."

Thief of Love

While Sara looked down, twilight was stealing the scenery as she took a quick look at Tahoe, and thought of how big the trees were. "How long do you think it's going to take us to get to Monterey?"

Bobby smiled and patted her knee. "Gee whiz. Relax, honey. We're nearly there, but don't be in such an all-fired hurry. We won't make it to Monterey tonight. I'm going to drive as far as Sacramento, which won't be much longer. We'll be there in a couple of hours, stay the night and start fresh in the morning."

Sara was tired of keeping her chin up and her mouth shut and, besides that, she was famished. "Promise me, when we get to Sacramento, we'll stop for food. I'm hungry. All I had this morning was a bagel with cream cheese and coffee."

"Excuse me; be a sport," Bobby said.

Sara reached over the back of the seat for the paper sack that held some snacks. She found a Hershey bar and munched away, hoping for some instant energy.

Bobby inserted an Allan Jackson tape into the player, and they listened comparable silence for most of the trip.

"We'll have a couple of minutes here," Bobby said about two thirty a.m. as he pulled into an all-night service station where a clerk sat behind six inches of bulletproof glass.

Bobby hopped out and Sara heard him say, "Gas, Camel cigarettes."

The attendant passed a pack of Camels to him through a small opening that received cash as Bobby paid.

While she waited, Sara took in the surroundings. Across the street, a flashing neon sign drew her attention. It said, 'Rosario's Mexican Food.'

Soon Bobby returned, carrying the pack of Camels, which

he opened in the front seat.

"Hey, Bobby, let's eat there," Sara said.

Bobby just grinned and asked, "How are you holding up?"

"Fine," she said, adding, "Starved, but fine."

"Come on," he said, flashing a quick smile as he reparked the truck, and they walked across the street and went inside the adobe brick restaurant.

Sara ordered refried beans and guacamole salad with two tacos. Bobby ordered enchiladas with picante sauce and frijoles. Sara tried to eat slowly but couldn't help gobbling the food with gusto. Fortunately, Bobby was also so hungry he gulped his own plateful down without seeming to notice Sara's discomfort, or, she feared, lack of manners.

"I think I'm too tired to push on tonight," she said after the food was gone.

Bobby nodded. "Yeah, me too."

* * *

When Sara awoke in the nearby motel room the next morning she realized she had been so exhausted the night before she didn't remember much. The old phrase "fell asleep as soon as her head hit the pillow" was almost literally true; it seemed to her that she had just lain her cheek on the cool pillowcase when the next thing she knew sunlight was streaming in through the partly opened window drapes.

Within minutes they were up and on their way; and Sara realized that the summer sun can be deceiving, even when you're used to the many long hours of daylight. It had seemed to her that they left the motel at mid-morning, but after traveling for a couple of hours she was surprised to learn that it was just then nine o'clock.

Thief of Love

They had already covered a couple hundred miles through Oakland and Santa Cruz, riding along in the warm California sunshine, just two middle-aged people enjoying the ride.

Bobby continued to drive in silence while Sara dozed on and off. By the middle of the afternoon, when Sara awoke from one of her many naps and opened her eyes to see the landscape speeding by, a road sign announced: 'Monterey 10 miles.' She checked the clock. It was four p.m.

"I can smell the salt air," she said.

"You slept for nearly one hundred miles, but didn't miss much -- mostly freeways, the backs of businesses, and train tracks," Bobby said.

"How are you riding?" she asked.

He grinned. "Great. We're getting close to Monterey."

"The ocean smells wonderful," Sara said.

Bobby nodded. "I'm going to get fuel and take a cruise to Monterey Harbor in a few minutes. We'll have a couple of minutes here; get out and stretch. I'll get some coffee."

They passed several stores, and a gas station came into view. Bobby kept in the flow of traffic, pulled into the gas station, stepped out and went inside. He hurried back, bringing the coffee, and filled the tank. Sara walked around the truck while Bobby pumped the gas and cleaned the windshield. Within moments they were again passing through Monterey, headed toward Fisherman's Wharf.

After a very few minutes, Bobby was easing the truck into the parking lot at the Monterey Harbor. Here, Sara had her first unlimited view of the medium to deep blue of Monterey Bay, accented by swirling swaths of purplish-brown kelp, like crooked rivers of the floating plants flowing along the surface of the big open bay. Beyond, the vastness of the even deeper blue Pacific

Thief of Love

Ocean stretched to the horizon to the northwest, west and southwest.

He opened the truck and hopped out, calling back to her, "You're here, babe. How'd like to step out?" he asked with a smile.

"I'd love it," Sara said, climbing out without hesitating and taking a deep lungful of the salt-laden sea air as she admired the bay. "I love the sound the ocean makes," she said.

Sara watched the fishing boats and sailboats rocking on the waves as they entered and left the harbor; the fishermen coming in with their daily catch, and the pleasure boats going out to sail. Along the docks, sea lions barked, begging for food; their heads bounced up as they swam about in the choppy waters closer to shore.

"Come on, let's walk out on the pier and feed the sea lions," Bobby said in a soft tone as he led the way.

After the droning monotone of the truck's engine during their tiring journey, Sara felt invigorated as she strode alongside Bobby with a rapid pace, her mind skipping from one thought to another as she looked about the pier and saw a sea lion food dispenser. She put a dollar into the machine, and a bag of food dropped out.

Sara lost track of the time as she enjoyed throwing handful after handful of food out to the barking and begging sea lions.

They stayed on the pier till evening approached, and the foghorn heralded the arrival of a thick, billowing cloud of fog that developed with amazing suddenness in the heart of the bay.

The fog bank remained low against the water and within the bay, to the north of the pier, and Bobby and Sara were treated to an all-too-rare bright sunset to the west as twilight fell. To

Sara, it looked like a huge ball of fire dropping into the suddenly darkening ocean. They stood still as the sun dropped out of sight, with ripples of reflected skylight still shining on the water.

The foghorn moaned louder while the wind picked up, chasing away the warm summer breezes with sudden gusts of chilling night sea air.

"That fog bank will be drifting down here soon," Bobby said as he put his arm around Sara's shoulders, walking her back to the truck. They sat in the misty evening inside the truck for several minutes, watching fishing boats pull in. Sara laid her head against Bobby's shoulder as they held each other, both taking comfort in the sights, sounds and smell the sea.

"Let's wish upon a star, get a good night's sleep and start fresh tomorrow," Bobby said.

The night air was much cooler by the time they got out of the truck at a lodge on Monterey's nearby 'motel row.'

"A nice old man runs this place. There's good food and clean rooms," Bobby said as he got out of the truck and went into the motel office.

Within a few more minutes they had settled in. It was already almost eleven o'clock, so they enjoyed a quick late-night dinner of soup and sandwiches in the small but cozy dining room, then turned in for the night.

As Sara lay on the bed with the patio door slightly ajar, she could hear the wind pick up as the smell of the ocean was getting stronger, she looked over at her travel clock on the night stand. To her surprise, it was already seven thirty in the morning. She looked over at Bobby, who was still deep asleep, his mouth wide open, breathing heavily.

Sara knew the high summer sun was already up beyond the thick drapes, and decided she wasn't going to stay in bed

Thief of Love

when there was so much to see outside.

After a quick shower, she dressed in cut off jeans and a t-shirt, then quietly slipped out of the motel room.

The morning was slightly chilly, with a hazy mist in the air as she strolled down the walkway leading to the beach, where the tide was out, leaving a broad expanse of glistening sands. Overhead, seagulls soared and swooped out over the water. Sara stood watching the for a few minutes, enjoying the view of the bay, the beach, and the mountains and ocean on the horizons beyond till she prodded herself to walk back to the motel for the truck.

As Sara drove in a random pattern on the streets of Monterey, she enjoyed the mix of old Spanish, Victorian and more modern buildings. Turning onto a narrower street, she encountered heavier traffic and looked about to see several quaint and picturesque shops housed in storefronts that looked to have been built before the nineteen sixties.

After a few tension-filled minutes finding a parking place, Sara strolled down the avenue of trendy California retail vendors searching for something unusual to buy when her eyes lit upon woven baskets and artificial tropical flower arrangements in one store window.

Inside, Sara found that pottery and vases from Mexico dominated the shelves in the first room. Walking around, Sara found that the prices that were remarkably low, so spent some time picking and choosing till she purchased three boxes full of colorful artificial tropical flowers, wooden birds, vases and woven baskets, and a Chinese tree in a potted vase. She had to make three trips to her truck, halfway down the block, loaded all three boxes into the back then headed for the motel.

As soon as she walked into the room, the comforting

Thief of Love

spirit of the morning vanished.

Bobby was pacing the floor with a scowl on his face. "Where in the Sam-hell have you been?" It was more of a demand than a question as his voice shook with rage.

Oh, no, Sara thought. Did I come back for this? "I went shopping in Monterey, okay?"

He glanced at her chest rising and falling beneath her t-shirt, then down at her cut-offs, revealing her shapely legs.

Aha, she thought, I don't believe this. "You were dead to the world. I didn't come all the way to the West Coast to just sit in a motel room and watch you sleep off a drunk."

"A drunk?" he half shouted.

"I could smell it on your breath. You must have gotten up in the middle of the night to have a few. You sure had a fine nap." Caught in the act, she thought with scorn.

"Get down, Red," Bobby said, the words blasting out. He strutted once more around the room, lit a cigarette, and inhaled deeply.

Sara sat on the bed where she faced Bobby, and had to meet his eyes.

"I couldn't sleep late either," he said. "I was up as soon as you pulled out. I heard the truck fly out of here so fast I figured you had someplace in particular to go. You sure you don't know anybody in Monterey?"

Sara just met his gaze with a silent stare, so he continued, "I awoke with a start out of a dream in which you were spending all of our money. How much did you spend this time?" he asked.

"Our money, Bobby?" Was all Sara had to say.

He chewed on his thought for a moment, then said, "There better be enough left for the rest of the trip."

Oh, there'll be enough for me to return, Bobby, but not

Thief of Love

you, she thought as, feeling her pulse beating high, she reached for her purse and flipped through her travelers checks. "I have plenty of money, Bobby. I just counted two thousand in travelers checks. We only spent one hundred ten on gas so far from Ohio. We spent a total of three hundred since we left. I spent fifty-three dollars of my money on souvenirs today."

Bobby shook his head in disgust. "It never ends. I told you I wanted to get an early start, if you can recall in your tiny mind that I was going to leave for Salinas before the California armored closed at noon. David's hard to keep up with anyway; if I don't get there before noon, I've lost a day."

"We can still leave and be there on time," Sara said, looking at her watch. She stood and, taking command, told him, "Let's get a move on."

Sara packed up their clothes and toiletries from the room while Bobby poured a drink, called David and said into the phone, "Call David Wilder to the phone and tell him Bobby Johnson wants to talk to him."

Whoa, what's going on? David's supposed to be his brother, Sara thought. She kept her ear in tune to the conversation while she gathered their belongings, to keep up with what Bobby was saying.

Bobby clung to the receiver in silence for a moment, waiting for David to connect. He caught her eyes and mouthed the words, "He's there." Then he spoke into the phone. "How the hell are you? Yeah, man, I'm in Monterey. Can you meet me?"

He hung on for a moment, obviously listening to David, then said, "Yeah, got ya, man. I'll be there."

Bobby hung up the phone and stared around the room with an anxious look, then leapt to his feet. "Come on, let's head on out of here. David's going to meet me this afternoon."

By the time they checked out of the room, it was nearly noon. A cleaning lady pushed her cart and parked it near the front of the door. Bobby approached her and said, "The door's locked," adding, "We'll be back later this evening. Just give it a once-over. The room is decent." He stepped over to her cart and, without asking, removed two plastic tumblers from the top.

The maid seemed surprised, but, before she had a chance to dare comment, Bobby held up a silencing finger, winked, walked over to the ice machine and filled the cups. He returned to the truck and poured himself a drink of whiskey, mixing it with Seven-Up. Then he poured a straight Seven-Up in the second tumbler, handing it over the Sara.

"Thanks," she said. "The Seven-Up is refreshing. Where are we going now?"

"I'm going to drive back over to Monterey Harbor, if it's okay with you."

"Yeah, sure, let's go," she said.

On the way back to the harbor, they exchanged few words; he didn't seem to want to waste any time talking while getting there.

Bobby parked and they got out, again walking out onto the fishing pier, watching the fishing boats and sea lions in the still misty morning coastal air.

Either it was Bobby's earlier tantrum or just that the novelty had already worn off, but Sara felt relieved when Bobby suggested they leave for the nearby Cannery Row.

At the seaside row of former fish canneries -- now become a strip of fast-food and fine seafood restaurants, upscale as well as touristy, trendy shops, and a world-class marine museum -- Sara was pleasantly surprised to find that the surf met

Thief of Love

the deck just yards beneath the Row.

They walked along a wooden pier into one of the better restaurants, where the hostess seated them at a table with a view of the ocean. Sara enjoyed the lavish display of flowers all around on the tables as she scanned the menu while the waitress brought an iced tea for her and a cold glass of beer for Bobby.

"What are we eating?" Bobby asked, adding, "Oh, surprise me. Go ahead order something for me." Then, he stood and went to the restroom. When he returned, the table was already set with garlic bread in a wicker basket, salad, pasta and red wine. He looked at Sara and said, "I love it. You're going to meet David today. When you do, I don't want you to tell him I'm unemployed. I'm going to tell him we got married in Nevada."

"Sure," Sara said with a shrug. It didn't matter to her if he lied to his supposed brother about such a minor detail; besides, soon, he would be spinning his tales without her help.

He put his elbow on the table, reaching for her hand as his patter went into automatic. "I want him to think that bells ring and the earth moves at just the mention of your name -- all of those clichés."

"Got ya," she said.

"I'd marry you today," he went on, adding, "if you'd have me. We've shared so much together in what seemed like such a short time. I love you very much," he told her, rubbing her back with tender firmness.

"I love you too, Bobby," Sara said, her tone now sad.

"If we have faith enough in each other, our faith will change the forces of adversity coming at us," he said.

Sara mentally edited his words, wondering about his true meaning behind them. But, despite her distrust, it bothered her to

Thief of Love

know the day would come very soon when she would have to say goodbye, knowing he could never be her `completer,' although, in some respects, she still had passionate feelings for his love.

The dinner they then enjoyed together was a chance for them to share some happier moments away from all the driving of three days on the road.

By four o'clock, they were traveling at a faster pace en route to David's Seaside Café.

Bobby pulled in front of a bar close to the curb and killed the engine, then slipped out of the driver's seat.

"Sit out here for a few minutes while I check out the place for David," he said as he stepped out of the truck.

Sara nodded and watched him walk inside. She looked about, noticing the bar was a one-story affair, with a white-sided front and the back extending out in a concrete block structure.

The sound of Country Western music drifted through cafe's the windows into the hot and moist air. Just as Sara was losing her patience, Bobby stepped out through the doorway and motioned to her. She got out and followed behind him inside as they made their way past people standing at the bar. A couple, dancing the Texas two-step, caught her eye as she and Bobby walked around the circular wooden dance floor. Sara stopped and stood watching as the man, dressed in Western clothes, swooped his partner up and spun her around.

After a moment, Sara turned away from watching the dancers to see where Bobby had gone. She saw that he was at the end of the bar, talking to two men. One was wearing a biker shirt, the other in a two-piece, dark suit of denim material. Bobby had hooked his arm around the man in the denim.

"Aw, go on," Bobby said to the man and nodded to Sara, motioning toward her as he and his companion lounged on

Thief of Love

stools at the bar.

The man in the denim work suit threw ten dollars on the bar as he looked at Sara, and she in turn got a better look at him up close. She could see that he was tall and thin, with straight, dark hair. He seemed surprised at her appearance and continued to stare at her for a moment.

"Good evening, I'm David," he said, breaking into a big smile as he asked, "Would you like a drink?"

Seeming to suddenly feel threatened, as if he had been left out of the conversation, Bobby said a little too loudly, "This is my wife, Sara. Our wedding was on the spur of the moment. We were married in Elko, Nevada Saturday night."

David surveyed Sara, eyeing her up and down as she nodded in agreement with Bobby's tale.

"What would you like to drink, Sara?" David asked.

Sara noticed that the men were drinking what looked like whiskey as she asked for a diet coke.

Bobby held Sara's hand and played kneesies with her under the bar, which she considered quite a romantic gesture on his part, then realized he just wanted to show David that 'bells rang and the earth moved' because of their relationship. For the moment, it looked like it. There seemed to be a real, deep respect on his part. But Sara knew it would be for all too short a time as she looked at David and asked, "Where do you work? Then she added, "Bobby told me you're a welder."

David puffed out a little laugh as he said, "I build bullet-proof vehicles over in Salinas."

Sara nodded and said, "I work for the automotive industry too, building bearings for the wheels of cars." Then she asked, "These bullet-proof vehicles, are they armored cars -- light-weight vehicles -- or limos, trucks and vans for government

Thief of Love

transportation?"

"Security and government," David said. "But the California Armored Car Company will be moving to Arkansas. I'll be relocating there next month."

There was a moment's silence, then David continued, "Bobby and I go back a long time. We were the best of friends when I was his squad leader at Black Hawk Fire Base, where we guarded stored ammunition in Viet Nam."

"So, you know a lot about him," Sara said, just a hint of a question in her eyes.

David nodded. "Yep. Bobby was the best of friends with a lot of people; he always had a girlfriend even though he didn't work. But I had to have a job to get a girl."

David studied Sara with what she saw were shrewd, penetrating eyes that seemed to read her thoughts.

He laughed and said, "I had the money, Bobby had the girls, and a lot of free time."

Bobby looked at David with irritation, but David just smiled back as he stared at Bobby idly for what seemed like a long time.

"What's wrong?" Sara asked, noticing the tension between them and the sudden sadness in David's face and eyes.

"Bobby saved my life over there once. I guess I'll never repay him enough, and sometimes even give him too hard of a time, considering that without him I wouldn't be here today."

"Bobby never told me he saved anyone's life. What happened?" Sara asked.

"As squad leader, I was checking on the condition of my fire teams on the perimeter. It was late at night -- a favorite time for Charlie to attack, and he did -- overrunning the perimeter while I was between bunkers. I was caught in the open, by myself, trapped. Then, Bobby jumped up and started firing and hurling grenades like a madman, chasing Charlie back into the weeds before I got chopped."

Sara looked toward Bobby and stared at him in disbelief as he shrugged and said, "I had to fight for our lives. Survival instinct took over. I don't really remember what happened, exactly; I just kept pulling that trigger, reloading, tossing grenades out of a box and grabbing and tossing some more." He stopped talking and began staring into space until the images in his mind faded.

Sara bit her lip, not knowing what to say for a moment before she replied, "I'm impressed by Bobby's courage, and his passion, and I've become aware he is capable of violence."

There was an awkward silence for a moment, as if neither man knew what to say in response to her remarks till David held up his glass in toast and said, "There's not a better man in war. He's a hard battler. He saved my life and I'll never forget it."

Exhausted by the day's activities and overwhelmed by the smoke-filled bar, Sara decided it was time to leave, but Bobby and David were still rambling on in lengthy conversations as they reminisced and swapped war stories. Finally, in exasperation she told them, "I'm going out to the truck to lie down in the back and rest awhile."

"Okay, honey," Bobby said, trying to embrace her, but she gently pushed him away. While she didn't want to be babied and fussed over, she was irritated, even though she also realized Bobby needed the time to be with his old friend.

In the truck, Sara dozed uneasily, on and off till after the warm California sun faded into the horizon.

As twilight glowed, Bobby came out the door with David following behind. The stood just outside the truck and talked.

Thief of Love

Sara strained to listen, but to no avail. Then, David walked away from Bobby, jumped into a Chevy Blazer, floored the accelerator, spinning the tires, and careened toward the state highway.

Bobby hopped into the truck, followed David to the corner, then turned off, breaking away from David at the intersection, heading back toward their motel.

Sara laid her head back and tried to relax till, at dusk, they rolled into the motel parking lot.

After a good night's sleep, Sara woke up before daybreak and lay thinking about where the day would take them. She looked over at the still sleeping Bobby, gave him a gentle nudge and said, "I'm going to take a shower. Come on, Bobby, get up. Let's start fresh."

She unpacked a Western t-shirt with two horses embroidered on it she had purchased in Rollins, Wyoming, a pair of cut off jeans and clean underclothes, then stepped into the bathroom, showered, and returned fully dressed.

She paused to retrieve a tube of lipstick and comb from her purse and, looking in the mirror, she saw that Bobby was up, scanning a road map while pouring himself a shot into a plastic cup.

"When will we be in L.A.?" she asked.

"Mid-afternoon Wednesday -- in about two days from today."

Sara thought that seemed like a long time, then remembered that California is a very large state.

Bobby drank his whiskey then hurried into the bathroom with fresh clean clothes. While he was shaving and showering, Sara rushed around, packing and carrying of their luggage out to the truck.

By the time the sun came up, burning off the patches of

Thief of Love

early morning fog, they left Monterey, getting back onto Highway One -- Pacific Coast Highway.

Only minutes from Monterey, as they moved inland, the hot summer California sun glared into the windshield of the truck and Bobby turned his sun visor down. They were already passing Bixby Bridge and the two-lane road sloped uphill then began a zig-zag climb as the terrain quickly grew more rugged.

Bobby continued driving at a moderate speed, attending to the road ahead.

As they rounded a curve near the summit, Sara looked back over her shoulder at the panoramic view. The sea blended into the sky at the horizon with no line of demarcation because the haze in the ocean air blended them together. Below the coastal mists, the surf made a meandering line of frothing silvery-white along the rocky shore where the waves broke. Inland, the landscape swept away in series of jagged peaks and steep-sided but tree-covered ridges.

Along the road, Sara couldn't help being awed by the magnificent scenery. The trees were getting taller; on the mountains to the left were towering redwoods, with only slightly smaller pine trees scattering along the cliffs. The air was fragrant with a tangy mixture of dry sage, fresh pine oil from the living trees and the pungent odor of fallen pine needles, dry cedar and hot earth.

"Where are we?" she asked, adding, "My ears are popping."

"We're in Big Sur country -- the great California coastal highlands. Your ears will adjust to the change in a minute or two," he said, reaching for his tumbler of whiskey and Seven-Up.

When they were almost at the crest of a steep ridge, Sara looked to the side and saw the ocean far below. The engine growled in low gear. She shivered with fear, holding fast to the seat, knowing they had a long stretch ahead of mountains and coastal cliffs. She tried looking down over the side, but fear kept her gaze on the road ahead. The truck was still at the bend when she suddenly heard the sound of a laboring motor as a SUV approached from around the curve.

The occupants of the other vehicle, a man and woman, looked Spanish. When the man driving caught sight of the pickup truck in the southbound lane, he slowed. When the vehicles passed each other, everyone wave and, distracted, Bobby swerved out of the lane, the truck dipped to the right and careened onto the shoulder.

Sara cried out in fear as she imagined that they would plummet off the side of the mountain and tumble onto the jagged coastal rocks far below.

Bobby started to turn back onto the road, but, when a quick glance at Sara showed him the tears pouring from her eyes, he instead braked, and shoved the gearshift into park. He let go of the wheel with one hand, causing her to yelp in panic once more, and seized her around the waist, giving her a squeeze as he looked at her with an amused expression.

"What is wrong with you?" he asked.

Sara glared at him. "I don't believe this," she said, her chest rising and falling and her heart pounding out of fear. But his arm around her waist, the bemused expression on his face and the fact that he had safely driven them across the United States all combined to make her suddenly ease up a little. Sara laid her head against his shoulder and relaxed for a moment, then straightened, slid away from his side and nodded for him to drive on.

Bobby put the gear shift into low and continued down the

grade at a slow speed, the transmission growling smoothly again.

As they once more approached a sharp turn in the road near precipitous cliffs, Sara looked straight ahead of her. Suddenly she became conscious of the nearer view. The sheer rock walls on the left, the expanse of blue sky to the right, the puffs of clouds -- not coastal fog but high-elevation clouds -- on all sides of them, brought home to her just how high up they were. The ephemeral and wispy masses of clouds appeared abruptly, rising up in front of them from what looked like a straight drop off from the cliff into the Pacific Ocean far below.

"My Lord!" Sara gasped, as she sank back in the seat and closed her eyes, feeling dizzy and nauseous while Bobby slowly steered the truck around the curving edge of the cliff.

"You're driving too close to the edge," she said, her voice quavering in fear.

"I am not. The truck is in the middle of the lane," Bobby said with a scowl.

"I hate this ride," she said.

"Oh, be quiet and let me drive," he said.

"Why did you bring me on Pacific Coast Highway? Those little guardrails are no security. There's hardly enough protection to keep a car from going over these sheer cliffs."

Sara turned and buried her face against his shoulder, swallowing hard as she found breathing difficult.

"I said shut the hell up!" Bobby shouted with a growl, gripping the steering wheel and clenching his teeth as they came to another sharp turn.

Sara was overcome with the fear that she would never see anyone she loved and cared about if they went over the cliff; and, even if anyone ever did find their bodies, they would be unrecognizable, bloating in the ocean or eaten by fish.

Thief of Love

She let out a moan as Bobby pulled a bottle of Black Velvet from beside the driver's seat, opened it with both hands while steering with just his knees, and took a gulping drink. "Want to drive?" he asked, scorn in his voice, adding, "If you don't shut the hell up, you're going to drive me over the edge with your bellowing." He turned his attention to the road again as he continued, "You're totally tripping me out."

Realizing that what he said was partly true -- that her yelling at him would only distract him from driving, Sara resigned herself to the situation, just laid her head back and rested, keeping her eyes closed for most of the next hours.

When her weakness had passed, Sara opened her eyes to see they were coming out of the rugged, mountainous coastal section, and a feeling of greater security for a more pleasant trip swelled within her.

"How are you riding now? Bobby asked with a grin.

She wasn't sure if the road ahead would get better or worse, so said nothing.

"We're coming into San Simeon in about a half hour. I was there on a work detail for Randolph Hearst for about seven years."

Sara looked out at the coast road ahead, relieved to see that they were now at a lower altitude, closer to the water, and that the surf was now off to the right, not at the very edge of the road; between, cattle grazed in the coastal flatlands just a few dozen yards above the sea. Her mind eased, she felt able to renew their conversation. "I remember reading about Patty Hearst. Her father was very wealthy, and she was abducted by a rebel army and held against her will. Then, they brain-washed her or something, and she teamed up with them in crime. I remember seeing a tape of her on TV, robbing a bank with the rebels. She was swinging a machine gun as she made her escape, walking out backwards."

Bobby nodded. "I knew her then. She used to come up to the castle and swim, across the road, at the nude beaches Hearst owned along the coast. She had a knock-out body, and didn't care who looked."

The smell of the salty ocean air was strong as they entered into the tourist town of San Simeon, where Bobby stopped so Sara could admire the scene.

"I know, how about if we take a tour of the castle?" Bobby suddenly asked as they admired the surf crashing against the coastal rocks and washing up on the wide and long San Simeon State Beach.

"Could we?" Sara asked with delight.

"You bet," Bobby said.

He drove up to the state-owned parking lot and historical center, where they bought tickets for the tour bus up to the renowned Hearst estate.

For the next two hours they toured the Spanish-style 'castle,' and villas, garages, even an indoor swimming pool, within the compound which sat on the one hundred twenty-three acres at the crest of the 'Enchanted Hill.' On the vast estate beyond, zebras, gazelles, antelope, buffalo, cattle and horses walked about, grazing on the lush green hillsides.

Within the main compound itself, palm trees gave the area a Mediterranean atmosphere. The terraced grounds included balustraded patios, stone fences of Greek and Roman-style columns, statuary from around the world, well-tended gardens and raised beds of pansies, geraniums, roses, birds-of-paradise, and a wide variety of other blooming plants and blossoming trees from many climates. The concrete walkways among the sculpted

Thief of Love

fountains and pillared walls circled around and between the bungalows and out-buildings in a bewildering maze.

A huge outdoor, cross-shaped swimming pool with rounded ends was overlooked by stone-pillared, open-sided, curving walls and gazebo-like, domed half-crescents both alongside and over one leg of the pool. A wide, curving expanse of stairs entered another branch of the pool, descending from the bright white tiles into the blue-green depths below the glass-smooth surface of the water.

Sara and Bobby took in the sights and listened to the tour guides as they told about the three adjacent guesthouses with their forty-six rooms, gave out dates when ground was broken and concrete was poured for the swimming pool and the castle, and explained that within it were thirty-eight bedrooms, fourteen sitting rooms, thirty-one bathrooms -- one hundred rooms in all.

Their tour group seemed to include people from most of the world -- Europe, Asia, Latin America, Africa and the Middle East -- people of all colors, races, and nationalities, many dressed in their distinctive national or cultural garb.

To Sara, the two-hour tour was like an adventurous trip to another world.

Thief of Love

Chapter 17

The sun was high in the sky by the time they returned to the parking lot. Sara was glad she had brought her sunglasses and worn her sandals during the tour; but Bobby had worn his heavy jeans, a plaid shirt and cowboy boots, all of which made him hot and irritable.

"Come on, let's get the hell out of here," he said in a mumbled growl as he headed for the truck.

But Sara wasn't anxious to return to the road, recalling how closed in and cramped she felt in the truck.

"Aw, have a heart, Bobby!" Sara cried. "Let's stay outside for a while longer."

"Come on, let's go. It's too damn hot."

Sara looked to the souvenir shop. "I want to look inside the shop."

Bobby shrugged and Sara led the way into the store.

Inside, Sara's gaze fell upon souvenirs as she sorted through the t-shirts. Somehow, she was finding all of her favorite styles and colors.

Bobby slipped his arm around her shoulder. "Quit buying so much," he said.

Sara, determined to take advantage of the shopping stop, ignored him and kept sorting through the merchandise. "I figured you'd say that," she said.

For some reason, Sara suddenly became convinced that now more than ever there was much more from Bobby's past she needed to know. She was trying to maintain some sense of order and self-control, but it was becoming more difficult. The call of adventure did not come to the rescue of her dropping spirits.

She turned on her heel and walked briskly to the cashier.

Thief of Love

As she paid for several t-shirts and post cards, Bobby went out the door and to the truck, leaving her to carry the bags out to the parking place, where Bobby now occupied the driver's seat

The engine was on, with country music blasting out of the radio. Irritated by his selfishness, Sara couldn't hold in her anger any longer. "Let me drive," she demanded.

He ignored her.

"I'll drive out of here; now, move," she said, her tone firm.

Bobby didn't budge. "That so, Red?" he asked in challenge, flashing her a keen glance as he continued, "I'm driving -- pressed for time. So, cool the dumb shit. I have a time limit."

"Time limit for what?" she asked, deciding to let the confrontation wait till another time, and sliding into the front seat.

"To the rodeo -- bareback riding, bronco riding, bull dogging, calf roping, bull riding, and barrel racing; you name it, I'll ride it."

This guy really thinks he's a winner, Sara thought.

She laughed. "You talk like you'll be riding in this rodeo."

"I am, by the weekend. I have to get to Paso Robles by four o'clock for registration for the Professional Rodeo Cowboy Association's championship rodeo riding, where the preliminaries are being run off for the grand national. I'm kicking off the California Mid-State Fair Competition." He paused and lit a cigarette, sending a thick billow of blue-gray smoke toward Sara. "Then, it's on to the national finals rodeo in Las Vegas this December."

Sara thought that Bobby sure had himself built up, then

groaned inwardly at the realization that he was developing a new course of action -- unanticipated when she began this journey.

She sat in silence as he started the truck and again headed south along Highway One.

Sara watched the road signs as they passed: First, the town of Cambria, just over a five-hundred-foot ridge from the deep blue of the Pacific. Then, at State Route Forty-six, Bobby turned east, and away from the ocean. After passing over a three-thousand-foot but wide and flat-topped grade surrounded by pine tress, they descended into rolling hills covered with eucalyptus and sage.

The smells of Eucalyptus, hot sun, and sage were heavy in the air by the time they arrived at Paso Robles.

Bobby seemed lost in his own fantasy world as he pulled the truck into the California Mid-State Fairgrounds.

Above the entrance, a billboard announced various rock, country and jazz concerts, as well as the upcoming rodeo.

Bobby seemed filled with a sudden burst of energy as he said, "I'm on my way to kick the dust. I'll be back in a jiff." Parking the truck just outside the gates, he hopped out, taking off by himself, leaving her inside.

Sara could see that the fairgrounds were packed with trucks, trailers, campers, and tents. Labor crews worked diligently, setting up rides and outfitting stages and displays.

A moment later, Bobby reappeared, talking to a man with shaggy hair and a blond moustache who wore baggy jeans and a striped sleeveless shirt, looking more like a carnival barker than a rodeo cowboy. As they stopped a few feet away from the truck, she overheard Bobby asking his companion, "How's the town look? Has it changed much?"

The man shook his head and said, "Looks the same -- two

men to every girl."

Bobby laughed, went to the truck, hopped in and drove off, all without saying anything to Sara. She thought something might be bothering him so she remained quiet.

The town was full of visitors -- tourists, cowboys, ranchers and stock men. The first two motels they tried for lodging were full. The third motel was next to a bowing alley. As Bobby pulled into the parking lot and shut off the engine, he turned toward Sara, flashing her a warm smile with his eyes as well as his face as he said, "If you will please, honey, go inside to the office and pay for one night for a smoking room. The rooms are fairly decent here. Over the years, I've stayed here several times." He reached over and rubbed her shoulder, then kissed her cheek.

She flashed a lazy smile.

"Tired, baby?" he asked after kissing her.

"Kind of," she said with a nod as she opened the door and headed for the office.

When Sara returned from renting the room, Bobby was already out of the truck, standing behind, taking out luggage. On impulse, she picked up her two pieces, which were lying next to his duffel bag, and noticed that there was a pile of clothes and things inside the cab.

Bobby was digging through the clutter, moving boxes and packages of souvenirs when he said, "I'll be in after I straighten up inside the truck. So go on in."

Sara carried her two pieces of luggage into the room, set them on the luggage stand, and then sprawled across the center of the bed, overcome by a pounding headache, too exhausted to move and too unsettled to sleep.

By the time Bobby came into the room, walking past her,

Thief of Love

he mumbled something about pressing his clothes. Sara could see his shirts were badly wrinkled. He studied her, as if trying to figure out if she would iron them. She wouldn't. As far as she was concerned, the idea was out of the question.

Bobby's attitude immediately soured. He poured himself a whiskey and sulked as he drank until he apparently finally realized that she was tired and beat. "Well, I'm going to shave, shower and change," he said as he stepped into the bathroom.

Sara became aware that she had dozed off when she heard Bobby saying in a loud voice, "I talked with Dale Pickens over at the fairgrounds food service concessions. The first trailer has his popular bagels, three kinds of freshly baked buns with all kinds of sweet rolls and pastries. The next trailer has his French-fried veggies, Italian sausage, and subs with fries and cokes. Directly in back of the two trailers are his gyros with all kinds of Greek dishes, including Greek pastry desserts. There will be an area under the shade trees with picnic tables and benches where the people can eat and occupy a seat."

"Make you a deal: If I can accept this, he'll put us up in his one-hundred-fifty-thousand-dollar motor home he has parked at the fairgrounds. What's your thought, sweetheart?"

Sara's tone was firm and feisty as she said, "I'm not staying in a motor home at the fairgrounds with people I don't know while you work concession stands. You know that, I hope!"

"It's a thought, Poppins. Think about it. I can pick up money. Anyway, I was offered another job opportunity over at the B. & B. Amusements. I've had several offers."

"I know you'll spend your time with your Carney friends ; yes, indeedie, the good ol' boys and me," she said. "Anyway, I thought you said we were on our way to L.A., not a cowboy circus. In your heart, Bobby, you must realize that you haven't given your old life a fair break."

"It doesn't matter in the least to you or to anyone out here what or who I am," he said, anger in his retort as his face clouded with rage and he continued, "Well, you all can go to blazes! And listen, Sara; after I take care of some business over at the fairgrounds concerning the P.R.C.A. Pro Rodeo for a contestant card, we're going to L.A.."

"What does P.R.C.A. Pro Rodeo mean?" Sara asked.

"Professional Rodeo Cowboy Association. Those that have won at least one thousand dollars as P.R.C.A. cowboys and cowgirls who make their living out of sanctioned rodeos in a limited number of P.R.C.A. rodeo years. I'm not a rank amateur. I've won some big purses."

"Oh, what a formidable list of achievements!" Sara exclaimed and sat in silent anger.

"I need to ask you a little favor, hon," Bobby said.

"What now?" she asked in disgust.

He stared at her with a cold expression as he lit a cigarette, coughed into his hand and shook his head, apparently bothered by the feeling in his lungs.

"I'll pay you back next week if you loan me eighty-five dollars. I need the money -- seventy-five for a contestant card, and ten dollars for a twelve-pack. I need to get over there as soon as I can to test the waters and kick up the dust with the rodeo cowboys. Uh. . . I'll probably be gone two or three hours, so don't get all uptight if I don't rush back. I need to get the feel of the competition."

Sara's mood fell at the thought of being left alone in a motel room in a strange town. "Things are going from bad to worse," she said with gloom in her voice, adding, "You don't

Thief of Love

want me to go along, so go on and do your own thing, Bobby. What difference does it matter to you what I feel or how I say what I'm thinking? You're on your own turf in sunny California. Do as you wish." She laid eighty-five dollars on the edge of the bed, looking at him with imploring eyes as she said, "You're drink mad, pleasure mad, money mad."

Bobby looked up and off to the side, anger glistening in his eyes. He snatched the money up, counting the bills, and shoved them into his pocket then stood in silence for a few seconds. "All right. That settles that. It's been tough, honey, but I've been on my own for ten years plus, and I'm not used to having anyone at such close range. You make me edgy. I don't know about you, girl," he said, looking at her with a smile in his eyes now. "Look at the big picture. The big picture is, I won five thousand last year in team roping and calf roping. When I win next week, which I'm sure to, it might lead to your good fortune too. You'll have your money back, including more. I'm putting it strong because I want to make us strong. Besides, I'm making this up to you. I promise."

"Whoopeeee!" Sara suddenly shouted. "When are you expecting all of this to happen?"

He paused for a moment, eyebrows going up. "You just wait and see on August seventh and eighth. I've got it down, and planned out our course. We'll leave in the morning for L.A. We'll be there about one o'clock and be back here by Friday at the latest. Allan Jackson will be performing in the grandstand with Deana Carter. If you want, I can get you a backstage pass to meet all the performers, including Allan Jackson at the grandstand."

"How can you do that?" she asked, suspicion in her tone.

"Shucks, in a way it's in your favor. I know a couple of

girls over there who are in charge of the fan clubs. When I see them at the fairgrounds, they'll set me up with a couple of passes. How will you like that, baby doll?"

Sara could see new complications ahead, and that began to gnaw at her mood further. "Well, that's something to make one think," she said. "Backstage passes given by your female buddies. Is that so, Bobby? Really, Bobby, I resent the fact you have to go through your California babes to get me a backstage pass."

"Wha-what did you say? I don't need to be told that! Excuse me. I beg your pardon, Poppins. Anyway, what's on your mind?"

Sara didn't answer, knowing she couldn't give her emotions away now that they were this far.

He loped awkwardly across the room toward the door, looking at her quickly to try to catch her eye.

She turned her head away, refusing to return the gaze.

As soon as he stepped out, Sara raised up from the bed and parted the blinds, watching him leave. He didn't look back as he pulled out of the parking lot and into the intersection, peeling rubber.

A bizarre feeling of isolation and helplessness overcame Sara, and she felt she needed to erase the tension and distance herself from the abandonment she felt -- forlorn and homesick for the first time. Her home and her mother were now on her mind.

She looked through her souvenir packages and sorted through the postcards, settling on a Hearst Castle picture postcard to send her mother. She wrote a brief note to her on the card, then switched on the TV; one of her favorite talk shows was on, but she barely paid any attention to what was being said as she stared at the screen, recounting the entire trip to California in detail.

Finally, when the program ended, Sara asked herself, <u>Are you going to sit in this motel room being a deadhead while the beautiful California sun is shining outside</u>? She knew far better than anyone else that Bobby was enjoying his time in California and asked herself, why shouldn't she?

Sara went to the door, looking out at the sparse crosstown traffic during this, the quiet time of day. Her attention drifted to the bowling alley next door, which seemed to be busy. <u>I'm so bored</u>, she thought, <u>maybe I'll take a walk over there</u>. Then she remembered Bobby had forgotten his motel key and would be locked out if she left; and if she left without locking up, he'd be on her case really heavy when he returned.

<u>What do I care what he thinks</u>? Sara thought. <u>At least I'm thoughtful enough to leave it unlocked for him</u>. She hurried to put herself together with makeup and casual clothing, and went out to the bowling alley before she changed her mind.

When she stepped into the air-conditioned lobby, the tension and discomfort of the oppressive summer heat in central California left her immediately. Through the open door into the lanes, she could see by all the movement inside that the place was busy with bowling leagues.

Sara stepped into the main salon and walked to the far end of the bar. There was no seating available so she stood and turned to survey the room. About halfway down the lanes Sara saw a table with four unoccupied chairs so she went right over and laid her purse on the table to show it was now occupied. Next Sara returned to the end of the bar, to try to catch the waitress.

After a few minutes, a harried-looking waitress in a pale

Thief of Love

green uniform carrying an overloaded tray of empty glasses and beer bottles returned to her serving station at the end of the bar. "Sorry to keep you waiting," the waitress said, smiling. "I'm just part time -- kind of slow."

Sara returned her smile. "I'm not irritated with you," she said. "I can see you're busy." Then she ordered a pizza with double cheese and a diet coke.

The waitress nodded. "Where are you sitting? I'll deliver your pizza as soon as it's finished."

"Sure thing," Sara said. "I'll be over there," she added, pointing to the table where a couple of cowboys had taken her spot and were drinking beer.

As Sara stepped back to the table, she glanced up at the pair. She asked in a nonchalant tone, "Can you hand me my purse? I left if here a few minutes ago." She spoke with a silent wrath in her eyes.

"Oops, fiddlesticks, sorry about that," one of the cowboys said. He wore a Western-style white shirt with pearl buttons, wrangler jeans, and fancy, engraved cowboy boots. He shifted forward in the straight-backed chair, clasping his hands loosely between his knees, his expression pleasant.

Sara froze in sudden amazement. He seemed genuinely pleased and eager to meet her. She thought about her skin-tight cut off jeans, black sandals and soft, loose, lavender v-neck t-shirt, and how her red hair fell around her shoulders. Well of course this handsome and healthy cowboy should be eager and pleased to meet her she thought.

With a shy, uplifted glance, Sara said, "Even though I'm not with anyone right now, as you can probably guess, I feel out of place sitting with two men I don't know."

As Sara spoke, she surveyed the cowboy who had spoken

to her with an easy courtesy, even as she realized she hadn't paid the slightest attention to his friend.

"My name is Cid." He stood and pulled out a chair for Sara, still eyeing her up and down with friendly interest as she hesitated to sit for a moment.

"Come on, we won't hurt you," he said with an easy laugh. "I turn into a pumpkin at midnight."

Sara giggled, seeing that he was humorous and yet seemed respectful. She sat and looked at Cid's partner for the first time. He was an unadorned and pleasant-looking, laid back sort of cowboy who wore a loose, white Western-style shirt, black jeans and plain brown cowboy boots.

The more plainly dressed cowboy noticed her curious inspection and said, "My name's Steven," adding with a relaxed smile, 'You'd've knowed that by now if my rude friend here'd introduced us."

Both men laughed as Cid said to Steven, "Sorry. I wanted to keep her all to myself."

"I knew that," Steven replied and all three of them laughed.

Drawn by their apparent easy-going attitudes and charm, Sara immediately opened up to them, smiled and said, "My name is Sara. Are you locals?"

Cid shook his head. "No, we're not, by golly. We came in a hundred miles, from around Fresno, where I have a livestock ranch. I left a while back; pulled a two-horse trailer with livestock."

"How is the cattle business right now?" Sara asked.

Cid smiled. "Picking up. I'm runnin' about forty thousand head, and not selling any this year. That's on a hunch about next year's prices. Where are you from?" he asked.

"I'm not a local person. I drove through the central route across the U.S. -- from northwestern Ohio. I live along the shoreline of Lake Erie, an hour west of Cleveland and two hours southeast of Detroit, Michigan."

Cid raised an eyebrow. "Um, um, Cleveland, Ohio. The Rock and Roll Hall of Fame. Been there?" he asked.

"Sure, when I take in an Indians game at Jacobs Field, I stop there from time to time."

He reared back, looking at her in appreciation.

"You're an Indians fan?" he asked, his tone joyful.

"Nothing but," she said with a firm nod.

"Strange whereabouts," he commented in a casual tone, asking, "What brings you here all the way from Ohio?"

"Well, bad luck, one way -- I guess I'd say a lemon," she answered with a wild laugh -- so wild it made her feel almost like a rowdy. "My boy friend, who is a local person, is over at the fairgrounds to sign an entry to be a P.R.C.A. competitor with the mid-state fair here in Paso Robles. We're here for his participation. I guess in his mind the fact that we're out here in the West means everything gravitates to him. Back East isn't rodeo country for his riding competition, so we headed west; but he's not willing to give up the old life, which is what it takes to make the grade."

"Ah, then you know about all this? That's ironic," Cid said with a disbelieving shake of his head. "I came for the same reason -- anyway, for my championship-quality horses. My Elly -- an Arabian mare, and Will -- my Appaloosa, will be on exhibit this week and all of next week."

"Are you registered for the riding competition too?" Sara asked.

"For sure, ma'am," Cid said. "I'm in it for the big time."

Thief of Love

Sara raised her eyebrows. "Which event?"

"I'm in the bull rider's invitational," Cid said with an easy grin, his tone proud.

Sara smiled as she looked in his eyes, noticing their deep brown color. "I'll have a great time cheering for the bull riders, won't I?" she asked.

He held her gaze as he replied, "You'll be cheering on a winner. I have twenty years experience. Nonetheless, I'm in hard competition with tough youngsters; but I'm not getting older, I'm getting better."

Sara allowed herself to laugh.

There was a commotion at the far end of the bar and Steven's attention strayed. He went over and watched. In the meantime, Sara's pizza was served.

Sara watched while Cid pulled out a fifty. The waitress took the bill and went back to the cash register. They shared the pizza and drank while the evening moved along, enjoying each other's company.

When they'd finished the pizza and their drinks, Cid asked, "Would you like to play a couple games of pinball with me?"

"Sure, sounds like fun to me. I like to play pinball," Sara said without hesitation, rising to the occasion.

Cid stood and put his arm around her waist with the finesse of one who had the technique down to a fine art. Sara didn't remove his arm or step away, enjoying their closeness.

He leaned his face close to hers. "Give me just one; I dare you, girl," he said, color mounting in his cheeks.

Her eyes answered, 'I'm a taken girl,' leaving him in limbo.

Cid carefully disengaged his arm and remained the

perfect gentleman as the evening progressed, and they played several pinball games. She won; he won. They had fun.

"Well, you play a pretty good game of draw for some strange cowboy, you know," he said as he looked into her eyes.

Her eyes widened as she tried to play down their mutual attraction.

"All right, Cid, you win, not me."

"I dig the hell out of you," he said, adding, "I'd like to spend more time with you. How would you like to step out tonight?"

Despite her attraction to and liking for him, Sara's immediate first reaction to his question was, <u>No! A girl can't lift her eyes or smile without some Western dude thinking stuff</u>! She told him, "Frankly, this was really not how I planned this evening."

But what was happening greatly excited Sara's curiosity. "Are you married?" she asked.

His expression turned sad as he shook his head and said, "I was, but I'm not. My wife was killed in an auto accident last September." He stood still, very quiet, watching her carefully.

Sara's mood changed to sympathy and regret -- sympathy for his loss, regret that she had reminded him of a painful subject. "I'm so sorry to hear she was killed. You're a great person, and I enjoyed your company tremendously. However, my boyfriend will be frantic with me when I go back to our room. I've been gone since five o'clock. I'm sure he's there by now."

"By glory," Cid said. "We're up against it, sweetheart, unless you can give him the slip. You've got me figured wrong," he continued, his tone convincing her he was earnest. "Can you hang on for a minute? I'd like to show you my two champions. I know I've monopolized you long enough."

Thief of Love

"For a minute, that's all," Sara said with a smile and a nod.

"You don't think me lovely or wonderful or anything?" Cid asked with a smile.

Sara laughed and replied, "We'll be leaving early in the morning for Orange County. Bobby, my boyfriend, has relatives there. We're spending a few days of vacation with his family."

"Come on," Cid said. "Let's get going so you can get your rest for the morning."

The moon loomed large on the western horizon as they left the bowling ally and bypassed the entrance of the motel by going around the back to his big, two-horse trailer.

Cid opened the trailer doors. Inside, a beautiful Appaloosa stallion and equally gorgeous Arabian mare leaned against the sides of the stall, light from the now setting moon falling across their backs.

"Wow," Sara said as she stepped inside and petted both animals' flanks. "Your horses; oh, they're adorable. They're beautiful. Champion-grade horses excite me too. Thank you for showing me your horses. Are you staying the night at the motel too?" she asked, watching him demurely as he stopped and turned to watch the last of the moon's yellow orb creep below the western horizon.

The moon down, Cid turned toward her and fixed her eyes with a wistful gaze. "Yes, we're staying the night. At daylight we'll check in at the fairgrounds, after we enjoy a Western breakfast. Would you like to join us?"

Sara shook her head. "I wish I could, but I can't. My boyfriend is a hothead. He's far from being a real law-and-order type, and he's very jealous of me so we'd better call it a night. I'd suggest that you don't interfere -- "

Cid cut her off in mid-sentence. "Say, are you razzing me? Doggone me," he said, adding, "I'm pretty much the same with my girl. He's no different from anyone -- if he believes like a Western man."

Sara remained silent as she smiled, showing Cid very plainly her quiet, affectionate side.

"Well, thanks for the good time," Cid said, "I'm hopin' we'll meet again during the rodeo, if not before or after. Good night now." He turned and went to his trailer, and she walked back toward the motel, torn between regret at having to cut her good time with Cid short and dread at Bobby's probable reaction when she got to the room.

As she'd expected, Bobby was there, standing at the door peering out at the lights of the passing traffic shining into the room from the street.

She walked past him without saying a word, smelling whiskey on his breath.

He was silent for a moment, then whirled around and slammed the door shut, his temper flaring like lighter fluid squirting on an open fire. "For land's sake, you crazy fool! You up and do something just for spite. What in the Sam-hell do you think you're doing staying gone? You left the door unlocked! So I'll tell you, I specifically warned you not to." His hand shot out and he pointed a shaking finger in her face.

"I know it's sticking in your craw, Bobby, but I'm not taking any flak," Sara said. "I left the door unlocked for you. I took my traveler's checks with me, so what's the big deal? Anyway, the evening had been spoiled by you. Was I included on your agenda, Bobby? Was I? Certainly not!"

Sara could see Bobby's frustration, and saw that he was on the verge of a rude comment, then, he hesitated before saying

Thief of Love

in a quieter tone, "I reckon you were mosyin' by yourself; but you piss me off, Poppins. Anyway I was worried sick over you."

"Oh, so you've changed your mind about me? I'll explain to you why I left: I was bored to death."

"Okay, I'll bring you up to speed. Is this any proof, Poppins?" He held up some papers. "I paid my annual dues. I'm a permanent member by earning P.R.C.A. sanctioned rodeos before I came to Ohio. The seventy-five-dollar entry fee I borrowed from you I paid here in Paso Robles." He waved the paperwork and smiled. "I'm a contestant card member, so I'm in. I can pick up a couple of grand easy as long as I keep beating them. It's darn hard to pick just one though."

The news sent a warm glow through Sara's darkened mood. She nodded and smiled. "That's super, Bobby. When are you going to be in competition?"

His answer was quick. "Next weekend -- the eighth and ninth."

Sara realized that she'd better clarify the situation for him. "Bobby, I'd like to explain something to you. While you were gone tonight, I met a couple of ranchers at the bowling alley I'd like you to meet. Although we only spent a couple of hours together, we had clean fun, playing pinball."

Bobby stiffened, looking puzzled, then shrugged. "Nature could make a woman flirt, even when she was innocent and unconscious of it," he said, as if to himself.

Sara shook her head. "You needn't look so flustered. I look forward to watching you. Cid, one of the ranchers, will be riding at the bull rider's invitational at the fair. He also hauled two champion horses for exhibition and judging. I can cheer for the bull riders and ropers, can't I?"

Bobby hesitated, then nodded. "Okay, Sara, you're an

Thief of Love

encouraging gal," he said with another shrug and a sigh. Then he continued, "Well, honey, I have a wonderful time planned just for your enjoyment and pleasure you won't forget. It's 'who you know.' Everything is complimentary for Sara from Bobby the event planner. I have backstage passes to meet all of the entertainers, and any and all concessions on the midway. All rides and all food services are yours for the asking. I have you set."

"Kindly resolved," said Sara with a laugh, then added, "Terrific, Bobby. It sounds like we're going to see a lot and do a lot of fun activities."

"Not too late, by jingo," Bobby said with a smile, then frowned as he added, "but don't upset me."

"Good heavens! Keeping company at rodeos. These westerners are a democratic, free and easy people -- not at all strong on formality. I like their simplicity and sincerity," Sara said.

Thoroughly tired and more relaxed than she'd felt for a long time, Sara changed, murmured her prayers and hopped into bed, only to lie there with wide-open eyes as, over and over again she relived the day.

* * *

The temperature was already ninety degrees when they awoke at eight thirty. While Sara was putting herself together, Bobby got out the maps and road atlas, penciling in marks to towns they would be traveling through while he also anticipated the time of day they would arrive in L.A.

Sara walked around the bed, picking up soiled clothing and tidying up the room a bit, then remembered an advertisement for a restaurant by the bowling alley.

"I have an appetite for a Western-cooked family-style

breakfast, Bobby," she said.

"Well, I have something planned for you, if you can hang on. I'd like to bid my farewells to a few carnival buddies and rodeo cowboys over at the fairgrounds, baby. I'll treat you to a breakfast that's out of sight." He rose and stepped toward the door, turning toward her to say, "Let's hit it."

"Hang on just long enough for me to put my makeup on," Sara called to him as he walked to the door while she retrieved a tube of lipstick and comb from her purse and finished up.

Bobby was already behind the wheel of the truck with the engine running when Sara got in beside him. He gunned the truck into motion and, within minutes, they arrived at the fairgrounds.

Inside, Bobby drove along a dirt road at a creep alongside a six-foot fence in a corner of the fairgrounds toward the camping area. As they approached the collection of campers, pickups, trailers and SUVs, the smell of fresh-cooked bacon filled the air. Laundered clothes hung over the fence along the way. In the distance, cattle the pens were bawling.

Between the vehicles, the fair participants, rodeo entries and carnival people were preparing their breakfasts on open fires.

Bobby beeped the horn at a group of more than a dozen carnies. The campers acknowledged his presence, waving him through. He pulled into a campsite where a tall man, about six foot four, stood brushing the wrinkles from his pants. He wore a straw hat but was bare-chested. He appeared to be in his mid-forties. His skin was tan and his sandy-blond hair was shot through with gray. As he waved, he grabbed at the cigarette that had dangled from the corner of his mouth and shouted, "Of all people! Look who's coming."

Bobby parked and got out of the truck.

Thief of Love

"Howdy, Bobby. I sure am glad to see you all," the man drawled.

"Howdy, yourself," Bobby said in a pleasant tone and turned to Sara. "Let me introduce one of Ohio's real ladies. This is my wife, Sara; and, Sara, this is my old buddy and road dog, Mark."

Mark took long strides over to the truck and removed his hat, all the time warmly regarding her. Without waiting for her to speak, he thrust open the door, reached over and helped her out of the truck. "Mornin', miss. So, you're married to my rodeo partner, Bobby? Ma'am, glad to meet you," he said.

"Good morning, Mark," Sara said with a smile.

As they exchanged hello's and how-are-you's, Bobby watched them in silence.

Mark drew on his cigarette, inhaling deeply, then flicked it into the fire. He reached for a lawn chair from beside the camper and set it before Sara, inviting her to sit with a wave of his arm.

Bobby sidestepped around the fire, suddenly agitated. "I keep my wife at a slow walk; when she tries to gallop, I pull in her reins -- that's quite often with this one."

Sara thought that he appeared to anyone a poor, asinine, masculine clod, saying more than he obviously meant to reveal. With a slow motion Sara sat in the lawn chair without saying anything, her mood suddenly subdued as she tried to ignore his comment, but found that she couldn't. Shaking her head, she said, "We're sure getting an earful. Bobby, don't try to make fun of me now. You may know how to push my buttons, but I'm not your bootlicker." She fixed his eyes with hers as they blazed scorn.

Bobby was preparing an answer when Mark said, "He has

Thief of Love

the crust of a buzzard." He smiled as if hoping the remark would calm things down.

Sara watched as Mark's smile widened, deepening the creases in his leathery-looking face; she thought there was nothing forced, moody, or brooding about him.

Bobby looked to Mark, sighed in frustration, pursed his lips, then shrugged, looked around the camp and said, "Yeah, fiddlesticks; I see you noticed."

Within moments the situation had been smoothed over as Mark poured them both cups of coffee from a pot sitting by the edge of the fire.

Sara sipped her coffee slowly, becoming thoughtful as she surveyed the scene around her, and watched Bobby, whose energy seemed to kick into high gear -- like a rough-and-tumble cowboy kicking it around. It seemed he couldn't have been happier as he walked over to a couple of old timers who were lounging under a shade tree playing cards. He fairly towered over them as he spoke to the one on the left, who had a round face and whose pale blond hair was streaked with black soot and dust.

"Hello. How the hell are you?" Bobby asked and sat down, grabbed the whiskey bottle that sat opened on the table, took a big swallow, wiped his lips with his sleeve, slapped a couple of crumpled bills down and said, "Deal me in."

Sara sat in patient silence while Mark busied himself around the campsite and Bobby played a couple of hands, hustling a few quarters as well as quite a few gulps from the whiskey bottle.

Finally, the other old timer, who had gray hair and a beard to match, scowled at Bobby and said, "Dad-blame you." He fixed Bobby with the boldest blue eyes Sara had ever looked into, even from as far as across the campsite. "You killed the bottle."

Bobby frowned, shrugged, laid the money he had won in the poker game on the table. "Well, you needn't look so flustered, old timer; you have your money back. Keep the change; we're even. I'm out of here."

The old man couldn't argue further because Bobby just went to another campsite and started hanging out there.

Sara asked Mark, "How long have you known Bobby?"

"Met him in Utah, at a rodeo about five years ago. We were both working with horses, which gave us deep personal satisfaction. So we just joined up as a team and started wrangling horses through Montana, Wyoming and Utah. Bobby had dedication. He had heart and soul."

"Sounds like you captured wild horses for trade."

"We could when it counted for profits. Bobby knew every technique. We learned the highways extending north and south. With him, we shared more campfires than I can count going to McDonalds for a Big Mac. He was high-spirited, flying high. I had to adopt to his wild way of survival."

"He's never been too deep or personal with me about his past," Sara said. "What did you do with the wild horses?"

"Sold them at fairs and stock shows where wealthy men dealt in such matters."

"That's cool," Sara said. "Sounds like a real big, money-making time to me. You're a rodeo man too, I take it?" she asked.

"Nothing but. Life was good, and I lived it to the fullest. Been traveling a three-state rodeo circuit, participating in rodeo events ever since I left the ranch. I'm a native of Wyoming, raised on a cattle ranch in a high plains cow town. I saddle-broke my first wild captive when I was ten." Although prideful to his roots, Mark was congenial and warm-hearted.

"How would you like some breakfast?" he asked.

"Sure would. I've been ready ever since I came through the campgrounds and smelled the bacon open-fire cooking."

Mark went to the campfire and fried some bacon, hash browns, and scrambled eggs. When he finished, he took a bite and savored the taste.

Bobby suddenly reappeared, saying, "Man, I smell food."

Marked passed over a couple of tin plates to Bobby and Sara, saying, "Make yourself at home."

Bobby spooned out a modest portion of bacon, scrambled eggs and fried potatoes onto the tin plate and handed it Sara, then served himself a generous helping on the other plate. Without hesitating, Bobby dug into the food with gusto while Sara ate more slowly, savoring the rich flavors of outdoor cooking, and eating. The instant Bobby was done wolfing down the first serving, he jumped up and used his fork to help himself to an even bigger second portion.

Then, as soon as we was done with the second plateful of wholesome food, Bobby set the tin plate on the ground near the fire, hopped up and raced through the campsites, giving his goodbyes.

Mark motioned Bobby back to the camp, brought out a bottle of Jack Daniel's and poured each of them a drink in a paper cup. There followed some more general chitchat about the broncos they were going to ride in the rodeo.

Sara learned something about carnival people that morning -- they were the most sharing people in California, maybe the whole country.

As the morning was creeping by and the sun beat down, they left and drove back through Paso Robles to State Route 46, and merged onto U.S. Highway 101, heading south.

After driving in a southwesterly direction for over two hours or so, Sara could once again smell the salt in the air, so she knew without seeing the Pacific that they were close by it again.

Bobby exited 101 in San Luis Obispo and cruised through the town, which was mostly small, old adobe structures, with madrone trees bordering many of the avenues. The old, Spanish-style architecture -- with stuccoed arches and painted deep pastel tan, beige and sandy earth tones, with red Spanish-tile roofs -- contrasted with the ornately and intricately carved woodwork of the mostly medium to darker blue, green and brown Victorian homes and more modern small commercial buildings.

Steep ridges on the north and to the east, and rolling hills to the west, all covered with the thick growth of chaparral and forest shrubs and trees, formed a country background to the cozy, central California community. Downtown, the store fronts were painted in dark shades of blue, burgundy and gray, with matching awnings arching above the windows.

The distraction of the beauty of San Luis Obispo suddenly faded as Bobby headed toward the coast, on Highway One, but not south, in the direction of Los Angeles, but north again.

"Bobby, where are we going?" Sara asked.

He remained silent, intent upon the road ahead.

"You haven't spoken but a few words since we left the fairgrounds," she reminded him. "I'm curious about this lovely town and I'd like to do some sightseeing and visit the mission, okay?"

But Bobby just gazed out through the windshield with an intense stare that made it obvious he wasn't following the conversation.

Thief of Love

"What are we doing here?" Sara asked.

"Don't worry about it," he said, looking dead serious as he fairly spit out the words.

Sara could see a strange-looking mountain on their left as Bobby accelerated north along Highway 1. On one side there was a steep slope, covered with madrone, redwoods and pine, but the other three sides were almost sheer walls of redddish-purple volcanic rock, giving the peak an eerie, almost spooky appearance.

As the mountain slipped behind, the countryside became more open, with the rolling hills and ridges pulling back from the road.

Bobby remained silent as he suddenly veered off the highway and into a wide driveway with a concrete divider that included a sign that read, `Atascadero State Men's Colony.' He then pulled into a large but almost empty parking lot in front of a five-storey-high wall that seemed to extend for miles. The wall was surrounded by three, fifteen-foot-high cyclone and barbed wire fences. The wall and fences were all topped with coiled razor wire. At the corners and along the walls and fences, uniformed guards manned watchtowers.

Bobby parked near the entrance, above which a sign in red script warned: `Attention. All Persons entering or leaving this institution must present a valid photo identification prior to being allowed admittance or trespass.'

Bobby sat in without speaking and looked toward the compound; then, to Sara's surprise, she saw that he started weep in silence.

Her mind whirled as, unable to control her curiosity, she asked, "Do you know someone here?"

Bobby continued to cry without sound, then, suddenly, he

spoke in a sob. "They buried him back there." He pointed toward the far corner of the prison.

"Who's buried there?" she asked.

When he didn't answer her simple question, Sara felt she needed some further clarification about Bobby himself. "Have you been in prison?" she asked.

Sara waited a few minutes until Bobby composed himself, then said, "There's someone and something in your past you haven't told me about. I want to know."

Bobby nodded absently, his gaze still far away, then he said, "Bob Haynes is buried back there. The wrong he had done long had been atoned for." He sighed and continued. "This is a middle-of-the-road coastal prison, about three and a half hours south of San Francisco and about three hours north of Los Angeles. Atascadero Men's Colony is a two-part prison, with a minimum-security unit for older men and a medium-security facility for younger men, divided into a four- and six-hundred population."

Sara caught his eye in a quick glance. He had become greatly mellowed. His face in this unguarded moment seemed infinitely sad.

"How do you know so much about this place?"

"The worthless creeps," he said. He pounded his fist on the dash, staring into the distance beyond the hills.

"What caused Bob Haynes' death?" she asked.

Bobby sighed, puffing out his cheeks and scowling as he said, "AIDS." Then, his expression shifted to one empty of emotions. He looked over to her and said, "Let's get the hell away from this place. You can drive for an hour or so."

Bobby got out and went around the truck as Sara slid over behind the wheel while a voice whispered to her, <u>I'm lost as</u>

<u>much as he is.</u>

Then Bobby got in and said in a dry whisper, "Take the Pacific Coast Highway -- Highway One, south for a while. I need to get my head straightened of bad thoughts. After I rest, I'll drive the coastline."

Sara glanced at the truck clock. It was just past noon. She started the engine and drove out of the parking lot, and, after a few anxious moments trying to turn left between eighteen-wheelers on the busy highway, headed south. As she drove into San Luis Obispo and followed the signs directing her south on Highway One, which was now also U.S. Highway 101, Sara meditated on the events of the day, her mind replaying what had happened at the prison. She looked over at Bobby's sleeping form, now more suspicious than ever, and negative thoughts and feelings bombarded her, un-soothed by the salt sea air and the tangy fragrance of dried sage.

Thief of Love

Chapter 18

Bobby continued to sleep, and Sara drove on for several hours. Along the way, scenery varied from the coast at Shell Beach and Pismo Beach, then through wooded slopes, rolling hills, open fields, then more rolling hills and wooded slopes, to open beaches again as they neared Santa Barbara.

Driving the long afternoon in the heat, Sara's mood wasn't lightened by the weather reports on the truck radio, which advised triple-digit temperatures across the state.

As the hours and miles dragged by, the heat as well as constant driving made Sara tired, till she slipped into exhaustion.

I can't handle this any longer. I need a break, Sara thought as she slowed, approaching one of the many Santa Barbara County beaches. The sun beating down through the windshield made her just want to find some shade. She pulled off the highway at El Capitan State beach, drove under the old wooden railroad trestle, and swung into the parking lot after paying the day-use fee at the ranger's guard house, then found a place near the sand where shade trees drew her. She parked the truck and, taking advantage of the stop to get a little exercise, climbed out.

There was a paved walking course just above the beach, which would take her out of Bobby's immediate view, but she didn't care. The moist but salty, slightly cooler sea air refreshed her as she turned toward the surf, taking in the beauty of Santa Barbara Channel, with the Channel Islands beyond looking like the wooded ridges of San Luis Obispo but rising out of the Pacific Ocean. She stepped toward the white-silver sand.

"Hold it right there!" Bobby shouted from the truck.

Sara froze and looked back. Hair messed up, eyebrows

Thief of Love

sweating, Bobby stumbled out of the truck, leaned over the hood and said, "You're not getting by with this -- going off on a sightseeing adventure while I'm asleep. You're not deserting me in this God-forsaken heat. You know better. . . Where are we anyway?"

Tired and frustrated, Sara couldn't help shouting back at him. "Hey, it's Wednesday! Wake up; we're in California!" She arched an eyebrow and continued, "Who knows -- maybe Highway 101."

Bobby scowled and shouted again, "Thanks for your great thinking! Where did you get the brainpower?" Bobby spat out the words.

Sara's body language signaled defiance, but, despite herself, she turned and headed for the truck, telling herself that, anyway, she had to continue on the trip to dump Bobby off in California, as soon as possible. But she had no intention of driving, at least not for a while.

"I'll drive," Bobby said.

Good, Sara thought, but said nothing.

He got back into the truck, in the driver's seat. Sara crawled into the passenger's side. Bobby started the engine without delay, then hit the gas a shade too hard, spitting up the sand along the side of the road. A cloud of dust trailed behind the truck as he pulled onto Highway 101, then really stepped on it.

Sara looked over her right shoulder toward the Santa Barbara Channel. A navy ship plowed along in the opposite direction, and overhead a white floatplane flew out above the sea, probably going to one of the Channel Islands, she thought.

Soon, lulled by the sound of the engine, pressed down by the heat, and tired from all the driving, Sara dozed off.

Thief of Love

When she awoke, more than an hour later, Sara asked, "So, how long from here to L.A.?"

At first she thought he wasn't going to answer her as he just inserted a tape into the cassette player. Then, he looked over and said, "Honey, we still have a couple of hours before we're in Orange County. We'll soon be coming into Malibu, then Pacific Palisades, Santa Monica, Venice, and Marina Del Ray before L.A. He pressed the `play' button on the cassette and laid his hand on her shoulder as George Strait's voice filled the truck cab.

Within the hour, they started passing through Malibu. The settlements along the highway were more numerous and prosperous looking. Concrete piers extended out into the ocean from the wide expanse of sandy beaches. On the coast side, upscale shops and manicured lawns gave the shoreline a more Mediterranean appearance.

The frontage road alongside the highway to the right was crowded with cars, and the sidewalks were alive with the hustle and bustle of shoppers, strollers and beachgoers. Sara noticed they made her casual Ohio, Eastern attire fit into the trend of the leisurely California style: boxer shorts, tank tops, thongs, with baseball caps and sunglasses.

As they slowed for the traffic congestion, the colorful merchandise of one store caught her eye. The entire storefront of Malibu Beach Vendors was blocked from view by rows of radiant, fluorescent t-shirts in brilliant colors hanging from portable racks. Her attention captured and riveted by the energizing, dazzling rainbow of pineapple yellow, island green, ocean blue, and sunset orange, Sara said, "Let's stop. Three t-shirts for fifteen dollars is a good deal. This is awesome."

Bobby started to shake his head, then looked over at her,

Thief of Love

and at the t-shirt display, then shrugged as if he had no problem with that and pulled off the highway onto the frontage road, looped back and, with amazing luck, parking in a spot vacated just as they arrived.

They got out and went down the sidewalk, which was thronged with a mixture of shoppers, tourists, walkers and locals -- the latter mostly younger adults swiftly passing by, carrying surfboards toward the beach, narrowly avoiding shoppers toting bags of souvenirs.

Sara went into Malibu Beach Vendors, where she became lost in time amid heaping piles of t-shirts in what became an hour- long shopping spree.

At the end of the hour, she made her way back to the truck, carrying three bags containing of a total of twelve t-shirts ranging in size from small to triple-x. Surprised to find Bobby hadn't waited in the truck for her like he always had before, she left the bags on the front seat and went back up the street.

Within a few minutes, she came upon Bobby, bent over, head turned to one side, petting a well-groomed, white French poodle.

The dog's owner, at whom Bobby was looking, stood motionless, holding her pet's diamond-studded leash. She was an attractive, well-dressed, middle-aged woman with blonde hair piled on her head, in a matching outfit of shorts and halter top in the purest white, and matching spiked, high-heeled pumps.

Sara thought the woman wore too much makeup, and also flashed an excessive amount of diamond jewelry -- hairpins, finger rings, armlets, bracelets, necklace and earrings, even an ankle bracelet -- all for a walk near the beach. She also couldn't help noticing, as Bobby no doubt had, that the woman's ample bosom and long legs were well-tanned, as one would expect of a

California beach dweller.

The woman, who had been smiling at Bobby, looked up at Sara and watched her without expression as she stood behind him, who continued petting the dog, saying, "Nice FiFi. Good doggy; and so pretty, just like your master," talking to the dog like a friend, straight from his heart.

"Hello, Bobby," Sara said from behind him.

Bobby ignored her greeting, but looked up and around, over his shoulder.

After another moment with neither Bobby, the woman nor Sara saying anything, she asked, "We have a deadline, don't we?"

He continued petting the dog, who stood still, enjoying the attention, as he asked Sara, "What deadline?" It seemed to Sara he was just taking his good old time, concerned first with his enjoyment and pleasure in petting the dog, and visiting with the woman.

Finally, he stood erect, looked to the Malibu blonde and said, "Excuse me; I've got to go."

She smiled at him and said, "Bye, Bobby." She looked at Sara with a cold, dead expression as she added, "Call me when you're back in town." Then, she turned on a spiked heel and sached down the sidewalk, her hips swaying in an exaggerated manner.

Sara glared at Bobby, and asked, "Having a good time, Bobby?"

"You needn't bark at me like that," he said, turning away from her and going to the truck.

Sara followed in silence as he got into the truck and started the engine, barely waiting for her to climb in and close the door before he took off into the traffic stream heading toward

Thief of Love

Highway 101 southbound once more.
    Now, Bobby hardly slowed, except for the heavy traffic. They exited the coast road at Santa Monica Boulevard, heading toward the Santa Monica Freeway and Los Angeles. It was rush hour by the time they hit the Los Angeles downtown freeway interchange -- known at 'the five-level,' where the traffic-laden ribbons of concrete were stacked five layers deep. In the unusually hot, heavily congested traffic, everyone seemed frustrated and angry. Drivers shouted out their windows, shaking their fists, making rude gestures and blowing their horns.
    Bobby became emotionally involved, returning a middle finger salute to people who honked their horn as he kept one hand on the wheel, guiding the S-10 through L.A.'s rush and onto the freeway they needed to head toward Orange County.
    They were only minutes from Anaheim Convention Center and Angeles Stadium Junction when Bobby exited to East Lincoln Street and pulled into the parking lot of a third-rate motel of stuccoed, one-story multi-units and parked by the office.
    "We're close to my aunt's place," he said. "Go ahead and register. We'll stay here tonight."
    Sara nodded and said, "Okay," got out of the truck, went to the front of the motel and stepped inside. No one was at the office desk, so she rang the buzzer.
    Smoothing out the wrinkles in her dress, a Hispanic motel clerk came into the office. "Need a room?" she asked without a trace of accent.
    "Yes -- a room for two for one night, possibly two."
    The woman nodded and went behind the desk. "It will be sixty-five dollars a night. We change all the bed linens before noon daily. All long distance phone calls will be only used with your phone card or credit card, and I need to see your driver's

license for proper identification," she said, then asked, "Your method of payment will be what?"

"I have travelers checks," Sara said, retrieving some from her purse and handing them to the woman, who studied them carefully.

After a moment, she looked up, handed the checks back and said, "Sign and date, please."

Sara signed over one fifty-dollar and one twenty-dollar check to the 'Royal Crown Motel' and handed them to the woman, who placed them in her cash drawer and gave Sara two room keys. "I'm sure you will enjoy yourself here. We are minutes from Disneyland and Knotts Berry Farm, while we are also located in a convenient location to restaurants and a shopping mall. We have, for your convenience, entertainment guides along with picture post cards and brochures on the rack here. Take some if you like."

Sara reached up for several and leafed through them as the woman continued, "We hope you have a pleasant stay with us."

Sara nodded and skimmed the material rapidly as she stepped back outside and went to the truck.

"I have the keys. Are you ready?" she asked.

"Just hang on," Bobby said as he rummaged through one of his bags packed behind the seat. "No, go on inside. I'll be in there as soon as I sort through some of my personal belongings."

He stepped out of the truck and took out several of her suitcases, which she picked up and carried to the room. She put the key in the door and pushed it open. The room was dim, without sunlight. She stepped inside and flung open the curtain hanging over a big picture window, to let in some California sunlight.

Thief of Love

<u>Don't they dust around here</u>? Sara wondered as she smelled the musty air. She went to the glass sliding door and opened it wide, hoping the smell would leave and the air would clean itself of the odor. Suddenly tired, she lay down across the bed, her feet dangling off the side, and tried to relax, but almost immediately started wheezing from the dust; it was not a good sign.

Bobby came in, carrying her luggage along with his things. "We'll have an hour, no longer here. Come on, get up. Get yourself together, honey, as soon as you can. I'd like to visit my Aunt Betty while the sun is still out."

"Yes," Sara whispered with a sigh, averting her face. With more apparent vigor than she felt, she got up off of the bed. "Should I wear nylons and a dress? I have an off-the-shoulder sundress in my garment bag." Removing the dress from her garment bag, she held it up to herself. "How does it look? Will this be fitting for the occasion?"

Bobby glanced over. "That'll work," he said. "Wear it, foxy lady! Been falling in love with you ever since you put on a dress. And if you will, honey, can you please remove my black dress pants from my suitcase? Match it up with a shirt, please, too."

"Give me twenty minutes while I shower, Bobby," Sara said as she slipped out of her clothes, wrapped a bath towel around herself and walked to the bathroom.

Minutes later, Sara stepped from the shower and back into the room, the towel wrapped around her again. Then, the musty, dusty air got to her. Promptly overcome with an asthma attack, she struggled to breathe, her lungs air passages suddenly shallow. She gagged, gasped, coughed, struggling to get the next words out as she said, "I need to get to a pharmacy right away

Thief of Love

for relief."

Bobby reached out and took her in his arms till the attack passed. Then he stepped to the air conditioner and switched it on. Within moments, the airflow from the air conditioner and open door eased her symptoms.

"Hold on until I shower and dress," he said. "You can hold on until then, can't you? We aren't far from a pharmacy at the mall."

"Okay," she said, taking in a deep, wheezy breath.

She sat down, trying to relax and regain her breathing.

After a moment, she had recovered enough to sort through her clothing, taking out her nylon stockings, shoes and dress, and putting them neatly on the bed. Then, she selected his clothes, as he'd asked her to do before the asthma attack.

As she dressed, Sara listened to the water run in the shower for a few minutes. While Bobby came out and dressed, Sara pulled the comb through her hair and doused on some sweet French perfume.

In a few more minutes they left the motel room and headed for the nearest shopping mall, parking near the entrance.

Twenty minutes later, Sara had taken her medication by inhaler; she could breathe deeply and comfortably again as they went toward Bobby's aunt's house.

Thief of Love

Chapter 19

In just over another half hour, Bobby turned off the freeway into a residential area in the city of Orange. Sara was astonished to see that they were now driving through an affluent neighborhood. Butterflies lurched in her stomach as realized at that moment the Johnsons were wealthy people.

Bobby slowed the Chevy S-10 into a circular driveway and parked. Toward the back of the well-tended lot, lush with tasteful arrangements of palms, banana trees, and other subtropical plants, the house was behind a three-car garage. The home itself was of a `D' elevation architectural design, trimmed in white with a rough, wood-grain style of siding.

Bobby took Sara's hand and held it for a few seconds, in a state of rare nervousness.

Sara met his eyes, but made no response. She was feeling extremely nervous as well.

Finally, he asked, "Are you ready for the introductions?"

"Of course," Sara said, nodding with a smile. "I do want to meet your family."

"Come on then, baby. Let's do it." With deliberate slowness and grace, Bobby stepped out of the truck, walked around to the passenger's side and opened the door for her. Sara assumed that his gesture was calculated to give off an air of respect and gentility for his well-to-do relatives.

As they walked through the beautiful rose garden leading them through the courtyard, they giggled with great excitement. Bobby put his arm around Sara and she held onto his shoulder.

Bobby reached for a stem of roses and held it toward Sara's face, and she inhaled the fragrance.

"How does that smell? A rose for my lovely lady -- you,"

Thief of Love

he said.

Their mutual happiness made Sara's heart glow.

Bobby led her up to the door and rang the bell, calling out, "Anybody home in there?"

In a few moments, a petite older woman in an expensive-looking but bland, pale blue dress, her hair pulled back in a bun, answered the door. She greeted them with a terse expression, indicating that she was put off by their arrival. Sara had expected her to be welcoming, at least gracious, but was taken aback.

"This is my Aunt Betty," Bobby said in his most formal tone of voice.

Betty leaned forward and said, "Robbie, whatever brings you here to Orange Groves?" There was no warmth in her voice, and the critical and bold gaze she ran over Sara was just as cold, causing Sara to shift in discomfort.

After a few seconds hesitation, Bobby said, "My special lady, Sara, is a Christian and she follows a TV evangelist program from in Tustin. I brought her out here so she could sit in the live audience and watch it."

Betty laughed -- an arrogant laugh. "Victimless crimes. Why don't you take her over to Universal Studios, Robbie? It won't cost her as much money," she said, her tone mirthless.

Sara swallowed and looked at her, wide eyed.

"What did you say your name was, Miss?"

"Sara."

"Well, Sara, please come in. Let's go into the great room."

She led them inside, making a quick stop in the doorway of an anteroom, saying, "I'll have the maid bring us a refreshing drink.

Sit down, Sara, and make yourself at home," she

Thief of Love

concluded as they entered the 'great room.' Betty gestured them toward a pair of large, wingback chairs.

They sat, and Sara found the chair very comfortable as she looked around in a quick survey, focusing on the large fireplace crafted of a beautiful white brick she had never seen before, which matched that on the pillars and corner supports outside the house. The mantle was made of bronze and glass. In the center of the room, a crystal chandelier hung from the cathedral ceiling, which made it in fact a 'great room,' which took on the appearance of the inside of a church sanctuary. Toward the front of the house, a moon-shaped picture window allowed the bright California sunlight into the spacious home.

"Where's Brian?" Bobby asked, rising again to walk over to Sara and place a protective hand on her shoulder.

Aunt Betty's smile was stiff as she said, "I'll find out if you like." She picked up an elegant, gold and white telephone receiver and dialed a number as an attractive, young Hispanic maid brought in iced tea on a tray and served them; apparently, Betty's offhand remarks as they passed the small room in the entryway was enough of an order for the maid to understand without being asked directly. Sara knew that for this surprising finesse, the maid was probably paid very well.

Sara, Aunt Betty and Bobby all took the glasses of tea from the tray, each offering thanks to the maid, who kept her eyes down, and nodded and curtsied with a slight smile before backing away.

As the maid was about to turn and leave the room, Bobby looked her over and eyed her up and down. The maid's eyes lingered on Bobby for the merest instant, then she looked at Sara's outfit, averted her eyes and left.

Sara sipped on the iced tea and pretended to ignore their

Thief of Love

interaction.

"Ah, there you are, Brian. Robbie's here, and he wants to talk to you," Aunt Betty said into the phone, then extended the receiver, adding, "Come on, Robbie. It's Brian; take it."

Bobby stepped over to her, took the phone and said into it, "What's happening, man; where are you? Yeah, it's me." He covered the mouthpiece with his other hand and said, "I'm going to meet Brian out in the courtyard. He's calling from his cellphone, out in back."

Then, he abruptly hung up, turned, and passed by Sara, winking as he walked out, leaving her on her own with Aunt Betty.

Without wasting a moment, Aunt Betty fixed Sara with a steady gaze as she asked, "Has he told you about his record?"

Sara didn't know how to react, and hesitated in her reply. "I know some of it. I try to believe the best of him as there is a lot of good. I didn't know he spent time in prison, or did he?"

"He's not a man to follow the rules of law," Aunt Betty said, wringing her hands. "It's terrible how life's ordinary things become heartbreaking."

Sara could see that this visit had opened old, deep, all-but-forgotten wounds.

"With the escapades he pulled in here Southern California, he put my dear sister-in-law into an early grave. It was a sin and shame how Robbie could torment her so. It's hard to imagine that he could hurt so many. I suffered the agony right along with the family." She shook her head in disgust. Sara watched in silence.

"Mary Stein was a special person, from the top of her head to the bottom of her feet, inside and out, a true lady with class all her life."

Thief of Love

"What did Bobby do?" Sara asked.

Aunt Betty's crusty exterior weakened as she cast a despairing look at the floor before answering. When she spoke, her voice quivered with emotion. "Back then, he posed a deadly threat to law enforcement officers in Los Angeles County, where he lived with his foster parents, and where he lived with his natural parents. He was charged, prosecuted, found guilty and sent away for ten years to a coastal prison about four hours drive from L.A."

"What?" Sara asked, shaking her head in disbelief. "What were the charges?"

"He's physically assaultive when he's drinking. The alcohol makes him enraged!" Aunt Betty said, her face and voice filling with anger. "A twelve-pack of beer was the fuel for his attempted murder, mayhem, aggravated assault over a bar robbery. He's crazy when he drinks."

"I didn't know this," Sara said, her skin suddenly hot as she flushed, perspiration breaking out on her forehead. "I wondered how much he was holding back. I know he's a man given to drinking and violent rages, but he's been very private with me about his past life in here in California."

"He doesn't need advance planning when he fights; he's in it for the violence," Aunt Betty said.

Now Bobby's reaction at the Atascadero Men's Colony came into a clearer focus for Sara. "I guess he treated me no different from other people, which was disdainfully, even abusive, especially when he was drinking."

"I just have one thing to say, and that might lead to a few things," Aunt Betty said, her voice dripping with irony. "He is an expert at deception. He can talk a blind woman out of her seeing-eye dog." Aunt Betty stood, eyeing her. "He's a compulsive liar, but a powerful one in many ways -- cunning and prolific."

Sara met Aunt Betty's eyes, but remained silent.

Aunt Betty shook her head in disgust. "I'm fed up with the greedy adult yet childlike Robbie waiting for everything to fall into his lap. He cons all his friends into believing in his flamboyant persona instead of working to make a decent name for himself. He runs his silver tongue, grabbing and taking from others, falsifying, living as a carney, traveling in carnival circuits. He couldn't squabble over an inheritance as his sister, Megan, was made executor of the estate."

"Bobby told me had a substantial inheritance," Sara said.

"If there is a trust fund, Robbie got zip. Recognize that, because there's nothing in it for you."

Sara was outraged that the woman thought she was trying to take advantage of Bobby, especially since he had been doing just that to her; but, before she shot out an angry retort, just then, Bobby returned. At his side, a slightly younger man whose appearance fit a laid-back Orange County, California style -- cut off jeans, tank top, thongs on his feet. "This is my cousin, Brian," Bobby said as he walked with him over to Sara. "This is my wife, Sara," he said. "Our wedding plans were spur of the moment. We were married in Elko, Nevada on Saturday."

Aunt Betty fixed her gaze on Bobby, then looked over to Sara. Sara drew in a deep breath and clasped her hands, holding in her irritation.

"Are you working, Robbie?" Aunt Betty asked.

Bobby's reaction was fast as he began talking with a quick answer. "I've had some jobs in Ohio, including working in a motorcycle shop for Russ for a while." He thought for a moment, then said, "You know my passion! While we were in

Thief of Love

Paso Robles, I registered for the P.R.C.A. rodeo next week."

Aunt Betty shook her head and fairly tsk-tsked as she pursed her lips and spat out the words, "Rodeo hopping! Ridiculous! Absolutely absurd! Get a real job, Robbie."

When he remained silent, she added, "You get out of this life what you put into it."

Brian came to Bobby's support, putting his hand on Bobby's shoulder giving him a nudge as he said, "Robbie, you were always a good rodeo man, and top athlete in school, with a fair arm in boxing. You're good, man!" He turned toward Sara. "What part of Ohio are you from?" he asked, obviously intent on changing the conversation around to focus on Sara.

"Northwest Ohio, near the Lake Erie shoreline."

Brian smiled and nodded. "Ohio. You've come a long way. Ohio is a three-day long drive from here. I'm sure you enjoyed traveling through all those states."

Brian went to a window facing the courtyard, opened it, and called through it. "Hey, Ella, come on in here. Robbie's come to see us. He's been in the Ohio valley for the last six months where he met his wife. They're here on their honeymoon."

After a moment, a side door to the courtyard opened, to reveal a dark-haired, dark-complexioned, equally dark-eyed, pretty young woman with a heart-shaped face. She hurried inside, carrying a small child. As she stood near Brian and Bobby, Sara could see that her eyes, while dark, were very bright, almost shining. Sara thought she was probably about twenty-one, and also probably Native American, but taller than most she had met. Bobby arched a brow as Ella set the child, a girl, on the floor, who ran into Aunt Betty's waiting arms. Ella sat on the white leather couch near Aunt Betty as the older woman

Thief of Love

ruffled the little girl's dress and played with her dark and thick curls, her eyes lighting up in admiration.

Brian stepped to the couch and sat beside the woman as he said, "Sara, this is my wife, Ella, and my daughter, Jill." He was obviously very proud of both. Then, he looked toward his wife and said, "Ella, meet Bobby's wife, Sara."

Sara inclined her head to Bobby condescendingly.

"I'll take my darling granddaughter,' Aunt Betty said, reaching for Jill and a quick embrace. "Bless your heart child," she said, as she stood, nodded to everyone and stepped away into another part of the huge room.

Ella looked toward Sara and said, "Sara, tell us how Ohio is these days. Brian and I traveled through Ohio valley on our honeymoon to Niagara Falls."

"About five years ago, in the springtime," Brian added with a nod.

"Ohio was chilly in the springtime," Ella said with a mock shudder.

Bobby snorted and said, "Tell me about it! Just about everything there, including the spring weather, sucks in Ohio, even the tulips have a hard time coming in. We shivered all through the month of April."

Aunt Betty returned to her seat and listened quietly.

Ella nodded. "I know it's a bit cooler, Bobby. We drove through Dover, Ohio to New Philadelphia on the way to a one-hundred-sixteen-acre working farm near Walnut Creek, Ohio. I remember the area well. The rolling hills were out of sight."

"That's in the foothills of the Appalachian Mountains," Sara said.

"I didn't know that," Brian said. "I thought the Appalachians were in the coal mining states of Kentucky and

Thief of Love

West Virginia. I'd like to fly there to the Amish Country and drive a rented truck back with Amish-made furniture. I saw some of the highest quality Amish-crafted furniture in oak, cherry and some walnut while we were there."

"I have some Amish furniture in my house that I bought from Amish carpenters," Sara said. "Did you see the world's largest cuckoo clock in Alpine Alpha, in Wilmont, Ohio?" she asked.

Brian nodded. "We ate in the Amish restaurant there."

"What did you eat?" Aunt Betty asked.

"We ate Swiss, German, and Amish cooking at Sunday buffet. There was a choice of ham, chicken or roast beef, mashed potatoes, two side dishes on large platters, with homemade pie for dessert. The food filled us up quickly."

Bobby shook his head. "No doubt. With those Amish living among Ohioans they most likely include fillers while they're preparing the food. You can't trust Ohio Amish either," he said.

Sara repressed an angry reply by compressing her lips.

"People think Amish are sheltered from the outside world, but the temptations are there," Brian said.

Bobby laughed and shook his head. "Amish Republicans. I read in the newspaper that two Amish men were indicted on charges of buying drugs from the Pagans motorcycle gang while I was in Ohio."

Sara could restrain herself no more, especially when what was being said was untrue. "That's the state of Pennsylvania -- the city of Philadelphia's Pagans motorcycle gang. Got it, Bobby? Not Ohio, okay!" She was half-shouting by the time she'd finished.

Aunt Betty joined the conversation by saying, "I would

think the Amish out there are the standard image of conservative religious values, horse-drawn buggies, like maybe in the movie, `Witness.'"

"Well, if the prosecutors are right, the two found common ground in cocaine trafficking. The two Amish men were indicted on charges of buying drugs from the motorcycle gang and distributing them at dances in their Lancaster County communities in Pennsylvania," Sara said.

"What's your denomination, Sara?" Aunt Betty asked. "I hope you're not going to tell us that you're Amish," she said with a laugh.

"She's not Amish, Aunt Betty. She's a born again Bible thumper," Bobby said, disgust in his voice. "She's never been taught the proper prayer etiquette. She's one of those existentialist people, if you get my drift!"

Sara felt herself losing control, but she sat perfectly still, her heart banging like a fist against her ribs.

Brian put a new spin on the conversation. "Man, I'm surprised to see you back in Orange County, Bobby."

"You're probably about as surprised to see me as I am you," Bobby said, unfazed.

"That so? The last visit, you spent time here in L.A., till law enforcement escorted you out for a ten-year visit to San Luis."

"Shame on you," Bobby said. "Your memories are unfortunate. Yeah, man, I'm living among people where cops treat you with respect -- people who when you need help, they speak to you and help. The case is closed. Hey, the case is closed. Let's quit talking about that."

Changing the subject again, Brian asked, "Bobby, what are you doing living in the Midwest? Ohio is a laid-back state and, by nature, you're a man of action."

"Like I said," Bobby said, "I get respect."

Sara's eyes met his, but made no response as she thought about the developments of the day.

Brian shrugged, rose and crossed the room, going toward the back of the house, calling back to Bobby, "How about playing us a jam on the drums? Can you still hit a beat?"

Bobby considered for a moment, stood, and followed Brian, holding up his hands as he said, "I have the main elements." He laughed, following Brian out of the room. Ella rose and followed with the baby, while Sara remained sitting in the great room.

The sounds of drumming and guitar playing emanated from the back of the house while Aunt Betty took advantage of Sara's being stranded alone to show her an album of family photos.

After what must have been just a few minutes but seemed like hours, Brian and Bobby came back into the room.

Aunt Betty rose and went to a desk, retrieving a road atlas from a drawer. She returned and handed Bobby the atlas, saying, "We're not far from Megan's, in Phoenix."

Bobby opened the atlas and studied it while Aunt Betty fixed him with her stare.

Bobby looked at Sara and said, "We're going to Megan's."

Sara studied Bobby quietly, angry as well as surprised. "You can't be serious, Bobby. We already talked all this over before we left Ohio."

"What makes you say that?" he asked.

"I said, we're not going to Phoenix." Sara said the words with obvious tension, her voice quavering.

He shook his head slowly. "Ohioans are a little slow." He stared holes in her, then said, "She's about two quarts low, Aunt Betty -- most Ohioans are."

Sara gave him a final, furious glance. "One more word," she lashed back, "come on, one more." The corners of her mouth were beginning to curl.

For a moment, no one knew what to say.

Sara saw dark anger in Bobby's eyes as he said, "She's jealous of Megan's career in her executive position."

When Sara didn't respond, he continued. "Sara works in a factory," he said, testing her. "She's out on strike, without any pay from her job. Ohio isn't paying out unemployment benefits. I told you Ohio is a cheap, Republican state. Oh, you Ohioans certainly have a poor opinion of yourself," Bobby said, taunting her.

"Yeah," Sara replied, her tone now strong and positive. "If I had, it evidently couldn't be as poor as yours of me. I work for the largest corporation in the world. That's true, we are on strike for what I believe are political reasons. The strike is in Flint, Michigan. I can't blame the company though. The government has laid the ground for the company to pursue global marketing and outsourcing. Most big companies are downsizing to be competitive. Our U.A.W. union is working to get our Ohio unemployment benefits."

Aunt Betty asked, "What religion did you say you were?"

With a hand trying to steady her thumping heart, Sara gazed over at her. "I didn't say what my denomination is."

Bobby started in on her then. "Communication is a two-way street. Why don't you pass it along to us? Say something. My aunt asked you a question. Sing hallelujah, jump, shout. Put some drive in your country. Try that."

Thief of Love

"Excuse me," Sara said. "For the record, let me be very clear with you in what I'm about to say." Sara could feel herself losing it, thinking that with this type of person you can't try to reach any kind of medium ground. You have to throw it back. "At least I worship with those who know who the mediator is between God and man." Sara struggled with what little strength she had left. The confrontation brought old wounds to the surface. A kind of paralysis had taken possession of her.

Aunt Betty shook her head disapproval and said, "Sara, although Robbie hasn't kept kosher or gone to the synagogue regularly, he has kept the family traditions of the temple with sensible faith."

Bobby cut in, and the insults kept coming. "She looks sweet and innocent, but she's really crazy. She's a righteous Christian, Aunt Betty; she sends money to those TV preachers out here. She even let one bilk her out of a thousand dollars for Lifetime Harvest, a ministry down there in the Bible thumper belt in Texas. I read the letters," he said.

He smirked at Sara's shocked expression and continued, "She gets a form letter back that they send around the country to the tens of thousands of other sucker Bible thumpers that God is blessing her good faith seed offering and God is scheduling miracles as a result of her offerings while the praise of them flows like cool, refreshing waters out of the springs of her righteous, religious mouth."

Sara had to defend herself. "I have a job that pays well. I own my own home. I must be doing something right. That's more than you can say, isn't it? Haven't I even paid the fee for your entry to the rodeo?"

Sara felt blown apart, and was sweating all over as she continued. "And, just for the record, you people all better be grateful. I have Christian standards, but I know I'm not partaking of biblical blessings while I'm not living by the rules. I admit I'm a carnal Christian -- and a woman who casually prayed publicly."

Bobby looked to his aunt.

Sara was shuddering helplessly.

Aunt Betty, looking overly burdened, stood and walked the far side of the room.

Sara thought, I need to get out of here. I need to get some fresh air.

She sprang to her feet and turned on her heel. Realizing she had to pass them, with bated breath Sara strode with a rapid pace and marched out the door, down the garden walkway to the truck, and climbed in, slamming the door.

How could I be so stupid? Sara continued to berate herself. An hour later, she was still sitting in the truck, hyped up with anger.

Then, Bobby finally came out. He stood in the garden and gestured animatedly for Sara to come back inside. Aunt Betty followed him out, stood by the door and watched. The coolness in her eyes told Sara she wasn't the kind of person to turn to for sympathy. She immediately confirmed Sara's thoughts by saying, "I need you to hear this -- both of you. I'll speak frankly. It's possible to have members of your family you've shared tremendous times with and yet feel unattached from them." Her gaze was pitiless as she looked from one to the other, then back again, as she added, "Now, I think you should leave!"

Bobby turned to look at his Aunt Betty, eyes and mouth wide in shock. He pointed toward Sara in the truck and said, "There's your trouble. She's a load, Aunt Betty. I mean a full

Thief of Love

day's work."

"What do you know about work, Robert Johnson?" Sara shouted out the open truck window.

Aunt Betty lit a cigarette in one hand and held a glass of something resembling Scotch in the other. She went to the doorway, leaned close to the intercom and yelled into it, "Brian, hurry! Come out here. I want you to vent the attack on some domestic conflict that's heating up with Robbie and Sara, quick and hectic."

Bobby didn't say goodbye as he dashed to the truck, hopped in, started the engine, put it in gear and drove out.

Engulfed in a fog of pain mixed with an eerie fear, Sara's silent tears fell as Bobby drove wildly through the well-to-do neighborhood.

His steel-blue eyes snapping, Bobby shouted, "Bitch! You're going back to the motel."

In a rage, Bobby sped out of the exclusive neighborhood, turned onto the boulevard, and drove like a maniac on a rampage back to the motel.

Thief of Love

Chapter 20

Chaos erupted when they returned to the motel room. Bobby paced like a caged animal and raged at Sara, at his family, and, inside and maybe even without realizing it, Sara suspected, at himself.

"Never in my life have I had a tramp disrespect me in front of my family like you have tonight, whore!" he shouted, pounding on the table, adding, "I hope you burn in hell, bitch!"

Overwhelmed with her own anger and Bobby's blatant cruelty, Sara broke down in tears. She couldn't think clearly, she knew, but felt she had to answer. "I have high hopes, Bobby, that you and your rich, high-class Aunt Betty Johnson drop in an El Nino sinkhole!" she shouted back.

Bobby's reply was to jump away from the desk and knock over a chair, breaking a lamp.

Seeing his escalating rage, Sara looked for a way to escape. She rose from the bed and dashed to the glass sliding door, heart pounding, giving it a quick nudge.

"Move and you're dead meat," Bobby warned, his fist clenched.

"Oh, no," Sara muttered breathlessly, frozen in place. It was then that Sara realized the severity of the situation. She couldn't believe it was really happening -- this kind of thing was only supposed to happen in crime stories.

Given the nature of his past criminal behavior, she had no doubt he meant what he said. He came lunging quickly toward her. His hand reached for her arm, tightening around it while the other hand gripped her ear. Sara skidded backwards while he slung her onto the bed, ripping her pierced-loop earring through her earlobe.

"You dizzy bitch. I should think that you, of all people, would understand how much my family means to me. We're not going to Phoenix; do you hear me? I'm not taking you to Megan's!"

He picked up one of her shoes and threw it, knocking a small glass souvenir cup she'd purchased onto the floor, breaking it into pieces. Then he stopped suddenly, short of trashing the room as though restraining himself.

Sara lay huddled on the bed near the wall and yelled, "Help! Somebody help me! He's a madman! He's going to kill me!" She kicked at him, then suddenly screamed. Her screams echoed off the walls and ceiling, but Sara knew no one heard, or heard and didn't pay attention; for no one rushed to her rescue, or even called out for them to be quiet.

Sneering, Bobby grabbed her wrist and her ankle, and roughed her around on the bed. In spite of her struggles, he shook and pulled her arm and leg till they hurt.

"If you don't shut the hell up, I'll tape your mouth shut with duct tape. Lie still or I'll tie you to the bed." Then he grabbed a pillow from the head of the bed and held it to her face.

Sara struggled to breathe, and fought back, till he pulled the pillow away, giving her a chance to draw a breath, before holding to her face once more, and again she tried to push it away; but he was stronger. After another suffocating moment, he tossed the pillow aside and stood, towering over Sara, showing her that he had the power of control over her.

"I'm not the kind of man to hurt a woman, but I will if you don't sign ownership to the S-10 over to me, which I'm about to take, along with two hundred fifty dollars from your purse."

As Sara watched, paralyzed with fear, Bobby tore through

her wallet and removed the cash, then whirled around and pointed a finger at her, shouting, "You're dead!"

Sara knew she was going nose to nose with a hardened criminal and was unsure how to respond. She wanted to escape, but she also knew he wouldn't let her. Desperate and in despair, she lashed out. "Let me go! You haven't been straight with me, Bobby. You've lied to me all along. You're a criminal. There's no way in hell that a rebel will fade in the sunset with my possessions."

She rubbed the back of her head, wishing she didn't feel so dizzy and weak.

His angry scowl deepened. "What did you say?"

"I've been horribly deceived, Bobby," she said, forcing herself to sound calm. "You lied to me about being in prison. You lied about so much. And I believed in you. . ."

His eyes bored into her as he took a deep breath. "You asked questions after I told you not to get personal about my past. I warned you that the case was closed."

Sara fell back against the wall, tired by trying to reason with him.

"I didn't press your aunt for information. She spat it out as soon as you were out of sight, Bobby. She grilled me. I'm the one who should be angry. I never even met the woman before!"

He turned away, pacing across the room as he spun around again and said, "Why did you disrespect me. Why did you do that?"

He said the words almost in a whine and, for a fleeting moment, Bobby looked to Sara like a lost boy rather than a crazed man, but knew she knew better than to let that fool her.

"I have nothing to apologize to your aunt for. She was the one who made snide, insulting jokes about my religion and

Thief of Love

my religious expression. She provoked me. You argued with me, teaming up with her against me; you went right along with it. She threw us out like two cast-offs who were social enough to prefer drowning together."

"Nonsense. My aunt treated you with the utmost respect," he said, his voice dry and cracking, almost a croak. "Had you not been with me, I guarantee you that she wouldn't open the door for me." He laughed; it was an eerie laugh. "We both know that I don't fit into the Johnsons' upscale world in Orange, California."

Sara slowly started to regain her strength and sat upright. "Your aunt molded her own opinion against you; she needed no further prompting from me. I know you've been vague with me since we met, so much so that I didn't know you spent time in prison -- in Atascedero Men's Colony -- right, Bobby Johnson? I'm not about to roll over for that kind of trash easily." Sara said the words with increasing strength, her adrenaline pumping.

Bobby laughed suddenly and shook his head, saying, "Hell has no fury." He grabbed her shoulder, regarding her for a long moment, as though trying to decide if he should take the money and run, or stay with one of the few people in the world who cared.

Sara waited, wondering what would happen next.

Finally, he went to the desk, then turned and handed her a pen. "Get your truck title," he said.

Sara set her jaw. When she spoke her voice quivered with rage, not fear. "I hate you, Bobby Johnson," she said.

He chuckled and replied, "That's all too obvious." He pushed her roughly, knocking her back down on the bed.

"I'd lie here and die before I'd let you," she said, turning her face away, then looked back and continued, "I think you have some serious mental problems. Are you crazy? I don't have my truck title with me. Even if I did, I owe a mortgage on that truck. The lender has a lien on the back of my title. So I couldn't do it if I wanted to." She knew she would have to appear to be submissive, with him in control.

His expression hardened. He leaned over, bringing his face close to hers. Then, as if throwing a switch, he smiled and pressed his mouth against her dry lips.

After the brief peck on her mouth, he said, "What do I have to do to prove I love you?" Then, he kissed her again, more roughly at first, then less so; still passionate and not gentle, but with less harshness.

Sara submitted to his kiss, all the while wondering about how to get away from this monster. As soon as she did get away, she'd call the police. She mentally calculated how she would leave and the time she would get to the police station as she remembered seeing one on the way to the motel.

After the first kiss, Bobby tried to get romantic, but Sara rolled away. She heard him sigh in frustration, then get off the bed to make himself a drink.

Over the next few hours, Bobby finally calmed down and drank himself into a sleepy stupor.

During the night, Sara counted the hours. She knew Bobby seemed to sleep with one eye open, and that in the event she made a frantic effort to escape from the room he'd be up and on her at once.

When it was about two o'clock in the morning, and she was certain he was asleep, Sara attempted to roll slowly out of bed.

"Don't tip your target until all of your ducks are in their rows. Don't try it; one foot on the floor and you'll find yourself

Thief of Love

laying on it like a smashed pancake."

Sara turned toward him and said, "Either I go to the bathroom or you'll be sleeping on a wet mattress."

He said nothing but opened his eyes all the way and watched silently as she went to the bathroom and returned.

As she lay down again, Sara resigned herself to the fact she was a prisoner until at least morning. The spell of silence and fear continued on through the night.

Thief of Love

Chapter 21

The next morning dawned clear and warm, a stark contrast to the cold and murky hell Sara was experiencing in the motel room. They sipped on lukewarm water from the tap for breakfast, and Sara decided again to try and reason with him.

"You can't lie to me anymore, Bobby. I need to know the truth. Based on all the things I've heard about you; hearing all that, I know you were in prison. Now why don't you tell me exactly what happened?"

Bobby's eyes widened. He looked directly in her eyes, his gaze sharp, like an eagle, then stood and paced back and forth across the room, fidgeting, before he answered.

"You want the truth? Well, let's start by saying that I didn't want to put you through it, but since you wouldn't let me bury the ghost, everything fell apart. I took those L.A. cops apart, but I didn't try to kill any of them. That's not what it was about."

Sara sighed. "Well, why don't you tell me what it was about?"

Staring out the window, he said, "I'd been home from Vietnam less than six months. I returned home like a time bomb that could go off at any time. It was a Saturday and I'd been drinking in an L.A. tavern. It was a mixed crowd -- bikers, drug dealers, family guys; a place where you could make a contact to buy dope.

I looked over and this guy yells out, `turn off the music.' I didn't like his attitude, and I just knew he was a queer. I didn't listen and so he kicked a chair across the room after I had dropped two dollars in quarters in the jukebox. I yelled across the room, `Is that so, faggot? I can't hear very well. I don't have

Thief of Love

my hearing aid turned on. What did you say, bitch? I held my right hand to my ear. I raised my left hand and gave him the finger.

The bartender warned me to chill, but instead I flew to the bar with my beer bottle and slammed it down on the bar. `Man,' I said, `are you running a queer joint?' `Out! You're barred! Out!' The bartender warned. `Give me a twelve-pack to go and I'll be out of this queer punk dump. `No,' he said. `You've had enough. You're cut off.'

When he told me that it blew my mind. I stormed out to my car, opened the trunk and moved my spare tire. Then I reached for my loaded revolver. Hell, has no fury. The front door swung open and I was back.

"The bartender tried to beat me to the phone cubicle. I held the gun at him until he was intimidated and moved back to the bar. He was so focused on the gun, he failed to see I came back for my beer. `

Now give me a twelve-pack of Bud,' I demanded. He hustled around, shaking in his boots. I reached into my front pants pocket and pulled out the money, which he snatched up resentfully and tossed in the cash register. Then he brought my beer."

Sara closed her eyes, trying to visualize the event, then she stood up and shook her head.

"But, Bobby, didn't you think the bartender felt threatened because your behavior was so antagonistic? You walked in with a gun!"

He lifted his head automatically, but was faster with his words, "Just let me finish, Sara.

"Keep your hands where I can see them, real nice and easy,' I said. By the way, keep the change.'

Thief of Love

By then, everything was quiet in the bar, with others slipping out the door, fleeing. I was calmer by then and left. I drove off knowing that no one knew me in the bar and didn't follow me, but every passing car seemed to direct its headlights into my face. Several police cars passed me while the sweat poured off my forehead into my eyes. Thirty minutes later, I arrived home.

"The following morning, I left L.A. county en route to the San Gabriel Mountains. I entered the 210 freeway in Orange County, passed through Glendora, Azusa, and Montevideo, and arrived at Newcomb Ranch before noon. It was the ranch and residence of my cousin, Brian Johnson.

"I had no idea the heat was on or, when I returned, what would happen when I did." His voice was developing an edge.

Sara already had a multitude of questions.

"Bobby, how did the fight start with the police? I learned real quickly in life you have to be docile as possible with law officers."

Bobby sat on the edge of the bed, blinking.

"The night after I returned home, my eyes zeroed in on the local news story in the paper, and I knew the heat was on."

Sara sat silently, trying to show she wanted him to continue without interrupting him.

He continued, "It said that local law enforcement investigators hoped to identify the mystery man in a bar robbery; that a man fled the bar after robbing it of a twelve-pack of beer, at gunpoint. A witness had grabbed the phone and called 911, the detective said. The man was already talking to a 911 dispatcher as the robber pulled out of the parking lot, heading west. The witness tried to stretch the phone cord as far as he could, but all he could see was the taillights.

Thief of Love

"They said the investigators following up on some leads and were asking that anyone who knew the suspect or his whereabouts to contact the detectives at the Los Angeles County Sheriff." Bobby looked at the floor, then said, "It was ridiculous. Turned out that faggot knew me; knew who I was."

With tearful, tragic eyes, he looked at Sara, then Bobby's voice grew hard. The muscles around his mouth tightened when he said, "I was clearly the object of a witch hunt. The bartender took my money. I didn't rob anyone!"

Despite her earlier anger at him, Sara now felt sympathy for Bobby.

"The cops were looking for me on the bar robbery. I was at a pool hall near home just about to shoot an eight ball when they came in by surprise and started to jack me around with tough talk. I held my pool stick up and warned them, 'If you don't have a warrant for my arrest, buzz off.' I was frustrated, trying to keep my mind on the game.

"Then they came at me by force. The first cop was very fast. He hit my side with a baton. I was instantly transported back to Vietnam, and survival situations. I kicked in his head and then his ribs. He went down on the floor.

"Another cop rushed in. He whacked me on the side of my head. I was used to trading pain for pain, and I felt like I was in warfare, fighting for my life. I caught the baton in a vise-like grip with one hand while the heel of my free hand shot toward the officer's neck in a karate chop. The blow missed slightly, which is good or he'd have been dead, but the baton caught him in the neck. I could slash a windpipe or pierce a heart with cold speed and efficiency, but I can't square it with my conscience. I didn't try to do it, but I heard his neck crack. Before I knew what I was doing, I had inflicted heavy punishment."

Sara's eyes widened, suddenly apprehension at hearing about the violence Bobby could commit.

"I was ready to haul ass, but beating up cops gets reactions from other cops. When I got outside I heard shouts from more police all around me, but I went through the line of cops. I out-distanced them in the foot chase; but some were in patrol cars. One used his radio to call for help from all available units. Within a minute, a whole lot of police cars joined in. I was good at out-maneuvering my opponents though, till I got cornered. I made movements with my feet to confuse them, kicking the closest one to me in his knee. He fell to the pavement and I took off again.

"I jumped in my car and gunned the engine. I wouldn't have trouble outrunning a single police car; but more wailed in with their sirens and blinking lights. I had to stop. They had roadblocks set up around a two-block perimeter."

"I could see the cops were preparing for battle -- no questions asked. At gunpoint, I was ordered out of my car. Then a big cop jumped at me, swung a baton into my gut, and then to my ribs. He kicked me and shattered my arm; and of course I was in no condition to fight any more."

Sara knew that Bobby had known when the incident happened what he was doing, and he still did it. This made her more uneasy about his capacity for violence.

He continued rambling, annoyance flickering across his face. "From there I was shackled and hauled into the Los Angeles County Jail. In there, I was accused of the attempted murder of an L.A. cop."

Sara couldn't help asking, "You sure didn't keep cool under fire, did you, Bobby?"

"Would you have kept cool? Would anyone? I was put

Thief of Love

in isolation, still shackled, and left on a cold concrete floor. Two of their heavyweights came in. One took off his jacket, revealing a gun. He pistol whipped me with it, and I bled a lot."

Bobby started to sweat. "Then the other grabbed me in an arm lock, and put pressure on my carotid artery." Bobby paused, then remained silent.

Sara watched Bobby's face, as he seemed suddenly perplexed.

"After the beating, I was taken to the interrogation room without them reading me my rights. I made a confession."

Sara thought his entire story over, unsure exactly how to respond. As appalled she was by Bobby's behavior, she was also appalled by the strong-arm tactics of the police.

"Bobby, under the First Amendment, you had the right to express your point of view. Every citizen in the United States has that right, while, under the Fifth Amendment, you also have the right to remain silent until your attorney is present, or to remain silent altogether. They didn't have the right to pressure you like that. I can't say you were wrongfully imprisoned -- I don't know that; but I do know the zealous prosecutor should have reopened the investigation that implicated you in the bar robbery. Your Fifth Amendment rights were violated by the police in forcing a confession, and made worse by the police hiding behind the powers of the state."

Sara thought there was simply no way to deny the dramatic impact of how Bobby had been wronged, even though he had done wrong himself.

"No! Hell no! I didn't rob him! He took <u>my</u> money. I wasn't about to stand still and get beat by cops with sticks either. I wouldn't give up my ground easy. I did it! I confessed it! It was self-defense." Bobby raised his arm to give the finger to the wall as he continued. "The police gave testimony that I tried to drive my car in the direction of officers coming at me on foot."

Sara interrupted him to re-channel his thoughts.

"I would think your story would turn the heads of news and talk shows across the country, shining the national spotlight and raising concerns about the integrity and professionalism of the L.A. police, Bobby.

"Robbing a bar of a twelve-pack of beer at gunpoint and being on the run for it. It's a bizarre case, with the news media reporting you went berserk, fighting against attacking law officers with martial arts and karate kicks.

"That was a story for national interest," she said, the images racing through her mind.

Bobby looked up, his gaze angry and grim.

"Say no more," he said. "Statements varied. They reported to the news I went berserk, grabbed a night stick from the officer and began attacking the other police."

"During the trial, my attorney was determined not to put me on the stand or introduce those issues I thought were a crucial part of the case in regards to police brutality. I just wanted the truth to be looked at."

Sara sighed. "Bobby, the risk to a lawyer is high in trying to prove police brutality without a video. Attorneys have to be cautious; they have to work with the police, judges, district attorneys every day. It's not credible to anybody, and probably made the jury angry. You know the public fear of escalating violent crime."

"Tell me about it!" Bobby shouted. He paced around the room again. "The prosecution continued its case on charges of attempted murder upon law enforcement officers, mayhem, aggravated assault and armed robbery."

Thief of Love

"Bobby, weren't you offered a plea bargain for lesser charges? People usually get impulsive under pressure, don't they?"

He waved his arms as he said, "I protested my innocence all the way through trial, standing up for what I believed in -- what I thought was the right thing to do. I wanted to tell the truth and get everything off my chest. Yeah, you bet I could have copped a plea. They tried to rattle me by keeping me held in jail without bond. They created the scenario that I was mentally abnormal with a personality disorder as an excuse."

"It sounds to me, Bobby, they used your mental condition as a bargaining chip. Why didn't you cop out? Under the law, you were entitled to reasonable bail," Sara said, rubbing her arms with her hands to keep her circulation going. She gave Bobby a look as if she thought maybe he was crazy. He looked away.

"Bobby, if you're crazy, what do they do with insanity cases?" she asked.

"Yeah, right." His tone was cocky. "Don't get funny, Sara. I'm trying to be civil. Why don't you meet me halfway?"

"Isn't the burden on the prosecution to get beyond a reasonable doubt?"

Bobby picked up a plastic tumbler and handed it to Sara, asking, "Honey, will you pour me a drink?"

Bobby was silent while Sara mixed him a seven and seven and handed it to him.

After a big swallow, he said, "Society's sentence; it's all about the public's interest and opinion."

"Personally, I strongly disagree in the main stream of society on that, Bobby. We live in a free country. That's a magnificent way to live. I think you should have opted for a trial before a three-judge panel instead of a jury trial. You understand the implication of that, don't you?"

Bobby lit a cigarette, took a drag and put it in the ashtray before he continued. "My attorney was slated to sign-on to a jury waiver."

Sara shrugged. "It wouldn't have been a lengthy trial, Bobby, and no one would feel the emotional aspect of the situation of the crime."

"No, Sara. There were strategic reasons. Basically, he thought it would be more favorable with a jury trial. Doing battle with cops doesn't sit you up high on the ranks of noble achievers with the court. A three-judge trial for any violent acts on state officials I don't think so! That's classic downtown L.A., where the rule of prosecution is turned on public interest."

"I would think, though, it would have moved away from the emotional aspect," Sara said.

"The prosecutor handled it and went from there. The public has no idea how much discretionary power the D.A. has to determine indictments."

Bobby was now primed and ready to continue talking about the case. "I looked around the court room. It was packed with lawmen with their sneering faces throughout the trial. The first officer wore a neck brace, and a cast around his right arm as he took the oath and shuffled up to the witness stand. Oh, man, it was like a theatrical production!" Bobby half shouted in disgust.

"I knew I was really going to pay hell for it. The jury was outraged from the start. The judge eyed me like I was a wild animal. The prosecutor called about a dozen witnesses. As the case plodded along, the second cop was setting the stage for more two-bit acting for the benefit of the jury. He gave a long statement in his testimony to the prosecution. This show was for the record -- talk about a national spotlight for the cops to drum up more support. By the end of his rambling speech, he was claiming that I left him medically disabled and unable to return to work; that he was permanently and totally disabled with a fifty-percent disability from trauma to his back -- with severed, herniated disks -- and head injuries. Those two were carefully drilled as to each word; and my defense attorney didn't make a single objection, even though I kept bugging him to say something -- anything -- about the show trial they were putting on. It was trial by ambush."

Sara nodded. "I've heard police officers lie, Bobby, while they're giving testimony on the stand."

"Yeah, they do! You're right about that." Bobby nodded vigorously as he continued, "Especially when they're playing the disabled role, with the state paying. Rip-off artists!"

"Such hypocrisy," Sara said, her tone soft, hoping it would help calm him down.

Bobby looked down at the ashtray, stabbing out his cigarette. "I was told later that there were strong apprehensions in the jury room after the three-day trial. It took them another day and a half for several hold-outs to be persuaded."

Sara raised an eyebrow. "Hold outs?" Her eyes remained locked on his.

Bobby nodded. "People with different views or different interpretations."

"Oh, I see," she said, leaning toward him as she lowered her tone further. "How long was the sentence? Obviously, they mulled over all the issues, and some doubts, for a day and a half."

"The jury doesn't sentence you. It was up to the judge. He said he reviewed the trial transcript and a full probation investigation, then imposed a sentence of fifteen years to life."

Thief of Love

His final word was almost cut off by Sarah's gasp as she held a hand to her mouth, her eyes wide in shock and horror. After a moment she regained her composure and asked, "Had you been in juvenile hall or jails before? That seems like a very big sentence for a first crime."

"No!" Bobby shouted, then fumed silently as he took a few deep breaths, sighed, and stared at her.

Turning to the subject of his actual incarceration i prison, Sarah asked, "Was it rough, Bobby?" She waited in silence as she continued to watch his face going through changes from at first seeming lost in the distance to anger, then perplexity.

"I don't call doing time in a six-by-ten-foot cell staring at the walls the right, easy place. It's so stifling hot -- no way for air to circulate. It's not what the big hand's on and what the little hand's on that counts; that's not time. Time is what you do and when you do it. Adjusting doesn't come easy; every minute of the day has to be counted as time of your freedom taken away. It's the real world in there -- the heart of the real world: good people, bad people; selling drugs, using drugs; gambling, drinking." His tone was half joking, half serious.

Sara shook her head. "I shudder to think of myself in that type of situation." She looked away from the contempt in his eyes as silence settled over them in a subdued stillness. Finally, she said, "Respect is the most important thing in the world."

Bobby laughed. "I got deep respect in there. No one messed with me. Doing battle with cops set you high in the rank and file in the prison population. Tension runs enough in there.

Sarah frowned. "Did you have confrontations with other inmates?"

Bobby shrugged. "I got respect. No one messed with me. If you have enemies -- you don't want enemies either -- they can

Thief of Love

follow you when you go to the bathroom at one a.m., beat you or stab you." He stood suddenly and started to space. "I told myself, 'life is sending you trials and tribulations.' I felt anger, not fear, when I thought about the danger. Being in there taught me a lot about handling things, protecting the rights of the old-timers, and whatever my conscience dictates. When they put the hurt on the old men, it was more about instinct than anything." Bobby shook his head, as if to be rid of unpleasant memories.

"Survival dominated my moral horizon. I was given two disciplinarians. I had to follow the rules, but found myself quick to intervene in protecting the old-timers. The anger got to me when I did that, and I kept ending up in 'the hole,' which made me angrier."

Sarah furrowed her brow. "What's 'the hole'?"

Bobby kept pacing as he lit another cigarette, blowing the smoke through his nostrils, mentally fuming as well as he said, "A stripped-down disciplinary cell with no TV or radio, and nothing to read. I worried most about losing my sanity, my knowledge, and losing my faith. It could have been a worse place, I guess, but at the time, it seemed nothing could be worse. I felt cold and dead inside."

Overwhelmed with sympathy, Sara rose and went to Bobby's side. She reached out and touched his hand, a sad smile on her face as she gave his fingers a squeeze. "Bobby, people are sent to prison, and we on the outside say 'Throw away the key; they have no future. If I were in there I'd want someone to come visit me and pray for me; someone to help me find the answers." They stood in silence for a moment before she said, "I feel a great loneliness in you, Bobby."

Bobby nodded, and they remained still for another moment till Sarah asked, "Did your wife visit you regularly?"

Thief of Love

He sighed. "She drove three-and-half-hour trips to come see me. She wrote. We exchanged letters once a week; and once a month she would come up for a conjugal visit. As it happened, her coming so regularly, she became pregnant for the third time with our youngest son. During the holidays, she came with my Aunt Betty and mother. They also brought my two sons.

"Then one day she wrote unexpectedly. 'I don't love you anymore,' her letter said. I had to accept her wishes, and let go." The silence deepened; Sarah could hear the ticking of her own watch.

"At my best, I felt good," Bobby continued. "At my worst, I felt terribly alone. People want someone to hold; to be with. No man is an island." As he said the last, his tone became weak, forlorn, pitiful.

"If you can't provide for your family's needs; well, then, I guess for some people, it's out of sight, out of mind."

"It is very unusual, Bobby. You said your wife became pregnant while you were in prison," Sarah said, trying to hold on to every bit of focus.

"I seen him once," Bobby said quickly -- Sarah knew he meant his youngest son. "When you're locked up, you're forgotten. She just quit coming to see me!"

"Is it true, Bobby, that when men are in prison some of them have male lovers?" Sarah asked and turned to study Bobby's face.

"When you're locked down, you're forgotten!" Bobby repeated, his voice thundering. "Loneliness can cloud your judgment. The sheer weight of loneliness draws intrusive thoughts into what should be kept private. Drop it, okay!"

"I can scarcely imagine how shameful it must be, and so public," Sarah said, contempt in her eyes. "There sure as hell

Thief of Love

nothing sane about that! I shudder," Sara said, actually shudering as she said it, "to see myself ever in that type of situation."

"There's not that much; you make a big deal out of it."

"How about at night, when everything is dark? How about in one's cell?"

Frustration and anger showed on his face. "My celly's weren't. . . `funny.' Drop it! I kept myself stimulated lifting weights and building my body. I could bench press four hundred pounds."

Sarah's suspicions were not dispelled, although Bobby did admit to some homosexuality behind prison bars. His openness to the emotional state at San Luis Obispo Men's Colony brought back Sarah's her doubts about Bobby's friend Robert Haynes, who had died in prison from AIDS. She remembered the clothing he brought with him when he first came. The name `Robert Haynes' on the front shirt pocket stood out. That Bobby couldn't deny. Sarah knew should couldn't put a lot of credence in his words.

After a moment, Bobby took a deep breath and continued. "I was allowed out of my cell to eat and go outside to the yard at times; but prison relationships are often tense, and tension breeds hostility. The fierce irony makes you go off. Men weren't in the joint during the seventies for all the drug- related crap of the nineties. They were there for more serious crimes of passion; and the explosive, self-absorbed paranoid skits, so -- the real deal!"

"Amen for honor status," Bobby said. "Thank you for the work! Thank you, Jesus. I was allowed to work after seven years -- outside the prison walls and inside fenced-in boundaries. I functioned well in a work detail for several years."

"Where at?" Sarah asked.

Thief of Love

Bobby smiled as he said, "I worked for the California Forestry Department, and Metro Parks on a work detail for Randolph Hearst on his properties at San Simeon State Historical Monument, which at that time was Hearst Castle."

"That's how you knew so much history of the place; when you were there you learned all about the property!" Sarah exclaimed.

His smile widened as he said, "The guards trusted me. They even brought me a drink of whiskey at Christmas. Their wives would make me a Christmas box of candy, cookies, and cheeses from their homes. It was phenomenal to have such a favor; they could've been fired for that."

Sara realized why he was in the good graces of the guards. He carried himself with so much self-confidence. He just loved who he was, and showed it to everyone, and it worked its charm.

"Were you in prison a long time before you were paroled?" she asked.

Bobby nodded. "Eleven years," he said.

"Several affidavits had to be prepared for each yearly hearing. The state of California recruited a clinical psychiatrist and expert in prison classification to evaluate my behavior and mental state."

"In his evaluations in his affidavit, he pointed out that I am a man of conscience. I'm intelligent and have a good understanding between fantasy and reality, and understand the concepts of violence and performance, of death and murder. He also found that I have a good understanding between right and wrong. He believed I didn't harbor any bitterness toward the system. I accepted responsibility for the crime and didn't insist on my innocence, and that I was remorseful about my assaults on the police."

Sara analyzed his body language. He seemed relaxed, but his posture was firm. "He'd have to know how to manipulate minds," she said.

Bobby nodded. "He raised the question about when the police came to the pool hall -- that I had been drinking all day and the alcohol triggered my rage. He said that something had come over me when the police used the baton to strike me. I retaliated in an imperfect self-defense. He said this was a common action, often caused by flashbacks from the traumatic events of war. He also compared a profile of adults with a history of child abuse cases, who maim their parents after they reach the age of accountability in an imperfect self-defense. He said that I suffered with post-traumatic stress disorder. He added that I was tested by a professor of psychology and I was extremely open to the issues while under hypnosis. Then the big day came after eleven years of no freedom. When I came before the parole board to either give me freedom or deny my request for parole, in the hearing, a spokesperson proceeded with the hearing. He spoke in a loud, clear voice. He addressed the transcript -- of my removal, my arrest, trial, and conviction, and the Judge imposing sentence.

"I kept silent," Bobby said. "He went on full steam. saying: `Eleven years ago, Robert Johnson was violent, brutish and self-absorbed. He maimed and attempted to murder police officers while they were trying to investigate him for a robbery allegation. At that time, he knew what he was doing, and to this day, he still knows what he did. He is a man who was found guilty of multiple felonies and did his best to elude capture.'"

Bobby shook his head. "I could see it coming. A dramatic conclusion. Robert Johnson overpowered their peaceful investigation. He used martial-arts-type karate kicks to their heads and bodies, dropping them to the floor in critical condition. He tried to flee the arrest in his car as officers approached him on foot. He drove into their path, swerving toward them, trying to run over the officers with his car. The officers moved quickly, narrowly avoiding the car running them over. The officers returned to their cruisers and radioed for help. Police cars were close by. They closed in. The police set up a perimeter in a two-block radius, eventually subduing him and placing him into police custody. He was taken to Los Angeles County Jail where he was charged with attempted murder, aggravated assault, armed robbery, and mayhem. He was acquitted of the armed robbery but found guilty of the other charges by jury trial in Los Angeles County Superior Court."

"Then the prison social services spokesman read assessments by the prison social service."

"'Robert functioned well in a work detail for several years, and his past work experience indicates that he will be a good worker. He has leadership abilities.'

"I spoke last. I rigidly faced the parole board side of the table. I said all I planned to say: 'I have learned in prison to control my temper. I learned in prison which people you can tease and which ones blow up. If you let me out,' I said, 'I promise not to be back. The only fear I've had for eleven years is that I would never get out. I'm sorry for the criminal acts on police.' I looked straight ahead.

"They studied every word in the affidavit material carefully and looked over the tops of the page at me -- heads up, chins up -- protruding toward me. We were all seated around a large, circular mahogany table, in the big meeting room at the main prison. There was silence for a while.

Thief of Love

"I tried to be relaxed in my mind, but there was a tight feeling in my stomach. There were several social service staff present. Among them were the warden, criminal justice experts, state clinical psychiatrists with social workers for the men's colony. The chairman announced that the parole board would then retire to render a decision. They gathered their reports and moved from their seats. A guard came for me as the door to the cellblocks opened. I was back again in another world.

"They took me back to my tier and my cell. I tried to get my thoughts together: Where would I go and who would I ask to be paroled to? I meditated the rest of the day." Bobby sighed heavily. "My instincts told me I would get paroled this time."

Sara found she now had a deeper understanding of Bobby. She could see things in a more clear prospective after all he had told today. She could at last see that these experiences had been destructive to his feelings of self-worth, and how hard it had been for him to put his life back together. Her heart ached with empathy as she could feel what he had been feeling all this time.

After a prolonged but not uneasy silence, Sara said, "It seems to me you're holding up remarkably well. It must have been terrible, Bobby. You're not a cold, calculating man." Yet she could also see how he lived in a fantasy world -- he had to live above that season of his life, and where he thought was his rightful place of station.

Bobby's eyes widened and he suddenly looked away.

"After they assessed the fact that I was rehabilitated and could live my days productively as a citizen in society without being a threat, I was paroled to David. I was released to Monterey, California. I didn't return to L.A. My wife had someone else."

Thief of Love

As she stood beside Bobby, Sara realized he couldn't discuss his ex-wife or his children's lives in any detail without him losing his composure. In moments like this, even though she was next to him, he was all alone.

Thief of Love

Chapter 22

The tension had worn Sara out, and, as the day went on, she felt in desperate need for some sleep. She sat heavily on the bed, fell back on the pillow and slept over three hours before she awoke with a start, and her mind wandered back to the veiled threat to her the night before. For now, she resolved just to focus on how she would leave Bobby behind when she went back to Ohio.

Rolling over, she saw that Bobby was sitting on a nearby chair, staring at her. He seemed aware that she was overcome by worries and dwelled on deep thoughts. "The nerve of you," he said, his words a renewed challenge. He studied her with shrewd, penetrating eyes. "People know how to take advantage of my feelings," he went on. "I'm just a misguided man who was lured to a Republican state by a woman who made me believe she loved me. I uprooted my life and gave up my job at the ranch, for a lady that didn't have honorable intentions. She's just a mercenary woman," he concluded, his tone bitter.

Sara's intentions to put up a phony front immediately fell away. She felt she could no longer deal with the falsehood with which she had started this journey, and to just leave him here. Sara suddenly sat and said in a clear, commanding tone, "If I were you, Bobby, I'd concentrate on staying in California. You're better off here."

The range of emotions on his face -- confusion, shock, fear, rage -- gave her the willies. She doubted any woman would want to be with him very long after they found out how criminal-minded and downright unstable he could be; she knew she no longer did.

Bobby blinked, smiled and said, "Why don't we go back

and visit Aunt Betty again?"

Sara laughed, "It's hardly worthwhile to drive over there for half an hour only to find her so hostile."

"Tell you what: I'll take you to your Movie Land and Knotts Berry Farm, then we'll visit Aunt Betty again, okay?"

Sara considered, then thought she was at least getting what she wanted out of him for a change, so she shrugged, and gave a slight nod.

They managed to get their belongings in order in a few minutes, left the motel and drove to Movie Land in Anaheim.

Sara was impressed and pleased that the exhibits covered so much movie history and featured so many stars of not just today and the recent past but the earlier days of the feature film industry.

Time seemed to reel back on itself as they strolled through a museum building set up like an old-time street from vaudevillian days, and they suddenly came upon a life-size wax figure of George Burns. He was standing at the curbside as an old-fashioned Yellow taxi pulled up in front of him as he waited, holding his famous cigar.

Sara and Bobby had their picture taken as they stood on either side of the smiling George, an impish glint in his eye as he seemed to cast a flirtatious glance toward Sara's figure.

Farther along, in a section devoted to horror films, Bobby was himself impressed with the ample form of Elvira in her revealing, low-cut, skin-tight black dress with its thigh-high open side. This time, it seemed the evil glint in Elvira's eye was directed toward Bobby as they had another picture taken there.

" She could be your twin sister, except not as sexy," Bobby said with a laugh.

Sara blushed, then said in a small voice, "What a sweet

thing to say." Then, after a second's thought, she added, "Treat 'em like a witch and they'll throw you out like a bitch." She was instantly embarrassed but hadn't been able help herself -- the words just popped out. She started to laugh. Then Bobby did too, and the photographer, who had also heard her remark, had to step away from his camera because he too was laughing so hard.

After their tour of Movie Land, and a visit to the old Western atmosphere of Knotts Berry Farm -- with its old-time steam train, lumberjack's log-run water ride and wholesome, small-town Old-West setting -- they both felt relaxed and happy as they had ever been on their trip to the Golden State. As mid-afternoon waned into evening, they drove past Disneyland on their way to Aunt Betty's house once more.

Bobby pulled up to the security gate, jumped out as he braked the truck to a halt, killed the engine and punched in the security code.

Within a minute, a chattering could be heard as the double doors opened. It was Aunt Betty and Brian having a heated discussion, probably about Sara's and Bobby's return, Sara realized. Sara wanted to avoid getting out of the truck and contending with a possible chaos, while Bobby went inside. But Brian came out to talk to her, and his personality was strong.

"Aren't you coming in?" he asked. He seemed genuinely concerned, his manner gallant.

Sara was skeptical. She swung her hair over her shoulder in nervousness. "No, I'll just wait out here," she said without further ado.

Brian launched into a defense of Bobby. "Look," Brian said, "Bobby is a regular guy. He's human. Give him a break. The biggest problem is that the general public sees rodeos as a traveling carnival show or something. Bobby lives and breathes horses, boots, hats and rodeos. I've always believed in the best for him." Brian's spirited defense of Bobby had a certain bravura appeal for her.

"It's deeper than that. He needs to do something about his alcohol abuse problem," she said in a firm voice. "I've done my friendship duty, my loving duty; I've done it all," she added, her tone weakening and quivering now. "I've given him enough chances," she continued. "My conscience is clear from now on. I know he's a real cool customer," Sara concluded, a tiny ball of anger fusing inside her.

"Hold on, hold on." The fire in Sara's eyes caused Brian to raise both palms toward her. "Just give yourself a chance to get to know him better before judging or making rash decisions," he said, adding, "Think about it."

Sara tried to think how to answer tactfully, but couldn't. Brian was such an ebullient, fast-talking man, with a quick intelligence.

Brian eased off and went back to the door, where he and his aunt stood waiting. After a few moments, Aunt Betty came out to the truck. All the mockery and antagonism was gone. There was something new in her eyes as she tried to make an amends. With great poise, she reached in the truck and put a protective hand on Sara's shoulder. "Will you relax," Aunt Betty said, her tone easy and relaxed. "I'm the one that should be nervous."

Aunt Betty's words lifted a weight from Sara's shoulders, and she sighed in relief.

"It's okay," Aunt Betty continued, her tone soothing, adding, "Everything's going to be all right."

"You told me to watch out for Bobby," Sara said, her tone wary. "You said he'd rob me all the way to the bank."

Thief of Love

Aunt Betty smiled and held up some papers she'd had hidden in her other hand, and extended them to Sara.

Sara looked into Aunt Betty's eyes, took the papers and glanced at them. What she saw there made her stop and examine them more closely. "This is senselessly tragic -- incredible," Sara whispered as she felt confused emotions rise within her. "He was a heroic soldier," she could only say through a sigh.

"Such a waste. His moral strength; the ability to respond to crisis the way he did." Sara slowly lifted her eyes to meet Aunt Betty's once more.

"David Widler. . . Isn't that Bobby's brother, in Salinas or Monterey?" she asked.

Betty laughed and shook her head. "Bobby doesn't have a blood brother, only a sister Megan in Phoenix, Arizona."

Sara was shocked and more confused now than ever. She looked down at the papers and reread from them:
`A Bronze Star Medal has been awarded to Corporal Robert A. Johnson, who served in Vietnam with company B, 3rd Battalion, 21st Brigade. The award was presented for heroism in connection with military operations against a hostile force in the Republic of Vietnam.'

"Corporal Johnson distinguished himself by exceptional, valorous action on July 8, 1968 while his company was conducting combat operations in Tam Ky Province when they suddenly came under intense fire."

`During the initial action, Private Johnson's company became widely dispersed and sustained heavy casualties. Johnson was a member of an eight-man squad that was sent to aid another squad that had been surrounded by the insurgents. Without hesitation, Johnson ran through the intense enemy firing, noticing a wounded man lying in an open rice paddy. Corporal

Thief of Love

Johnson ran through the hostile fire and brought the injured man (David Widler) to safety.'

'Johnson's personal heroism and unselfish concern for his soldiers and devotion to duty were in keeping with the highest traditions of military service and reflected great credit upon him, his unit, and the entire United States Army."

'The Americal Division and the United States Army proudly award this citation."

Sara caught her breath. It had been painful to read, but she had been unable to keep from reading it again. She now knew Bobby could be an unselfish person when it came down to another person's life.

This visit went better from that point on. Aunt Betty and Brian remained gracious and polite. After an hour of talking over Bobby's sister Megan's problems with her husband, and their impending divorce, Bobby kissed Aunt Betty goodbye and shook Brian's hand. They gave Sara a good send-off as well. The sun was lowering in the west when they headed back up Pacific Coast Highway, U.S. 101, back toward the motel by the bowling alley in Paso Robles.

Arriving late, after a peaceful and restful night, they were up early and on their way to the fairgrounds. As midmorning heightened toward noon, Bobby wheeled the S-10 Chevy pickup into the carnival entrance. The parking lot was now filled with cars, trucks and vans. Crowds of people walked in a bustling throng toward the front gate.

Passing the ticket booths and driving slowly along the dirt road for fair participants, they approached the area where pickups, vans, trailers and recreational vehicles were parked in the shade of a few live oak trees.

Bobby drove alongside the fence, searching for familiar

Thief of Love

faces. The truck bumped along, half on the side of the dirt road, half in the ditch along the fence. They followed a dusty, marginal route that took them away from the carnival gypsy encampment and toward the horse trailers and motor homes driven by the stockmen and rodeo goers, where they passed happy-faced, jocular and robust cowboys who waved at them as they engaged in good-natured teasing, shouting and Western bantering among themselves. Sara noticed the wide smiles and flirtatious glances Bobby received from several healthy-looking, pretty, farm-fresh cowgirls.

Finally, Bobby found the last remaining shady spot, pulled over and parked. He popped his seatbelt, resting his forearms on his thighs. He turned toward her and held her gaze, leaning back against the seat.

"I suppose we'd better go, in a minute," he said, rolling his head closer to her.

Sara looked out the windshield, to the sky. It was a perfect, clear and deep blue overhead, paler and without haze closer to the horizon.

He sighed deeply, and smiled. "I like being with you," he said, his voice a murmur as he shifted one hand to her thigh.

She looked down at his hand resting on her knee; it looked much darker than her own, enormous and strong. "I like being with you like this, too, Bobby -- when you're not drinking."

He shrugged, took his hand away, opened the door and hopped out as he asked, "When are you pulling it off?" The words, as well as his movements exuded a crisper, hard-edged vitality.

She got out of the truck, where he had already gone around to her side, "It's not over until it's over," she said.

Thief of Love

"Come on, I'm ready to go." She patted him on the shoulder and they set off.

"No problem," he said as he took her through a path boxed in on both sides with tents and trailers. Large kettles swung over what she could only think of as gypsy fires.

They entered the participants' gate, and Bobby's mood accented his outfit -- Levi jeans, Western shirt, cowboy hat -- as they spent a few hours listening to the Country and Western music -- tones that set their toes tapping, hands clapping -- and enjoyed some good, old-time fun of rides, games and shows, and hot dogs, ice cream and sodas.

"All I wanted at one time in my life was to do the rodeo circuit," Bobby told her. "This is my home base. I had my goals set that someday I could be number one and set out to prove that I was right. But now that I met you," he said, "my sights are set on making you happy. Where would you like to go? I'll show you around some more. Where to?"

"The Gypsy Encampment," Sara said without hesitating. "I'd like to get my fortune told."

Bobby's eyes opened wide. "Are you sure? The gypsies aren't all that fancy."

She nodded.

"Come on," he said. "I'll take you to the supernatural reading of your future."

As they continued through the fairgrounds, Sara's mind was filled with everything and everyone. She kept a keen eye on the large crowd: people talking, waiting for rides on the ferris wheel and the thrills of the roller coaster and witch's wheel.

People were waiting at concession stands for carnival food while others were walking about eating hot dogs, gyros, candy apples, and drinking from cartons of milk or cans of soft

Thief of Love

drinks while playing games on the midway.

Sara felt as excited as a child as she took in the bright, varicolored, flickering lights at the carnival while vendors and attendants worked the circuit of games.

Bobby led and she followed as they left the midway, turning onto a path that took them to a small cluster of tents in what she discovered was a real gypsy encampment. They approached a tree with a sign on it that read, `Fortunes by the Famous Zemaga -- Seventh Daughter of a Seventh Daughter.' There was another sign below it with a large red arrow pointing toward what looked like an old army medical tent -- like those seen in the old television series, "M*A*S*H*. Yet another sign affixed to a post just outside the tent's open flap doorway read, `Witness Master Performer Dissolve the Boundary Between Reality and Illusion: Objects and People Appear and Disappear at Bidding, and Battles Sinister Villain. Promise Mysterious and Marvelous Things to Come."

A gypsy queen, apparently Madam Zemaga herself, stood just inside the entrance. Her first noticeable feature was her dark, skin. The scarlet and yellow scarf tied over her head contrasted with her olive complexion. Her dress was loose-fitting, and had an intricate orange, burgundy and gold pattern that reminded Sara of a Moroccan design. Around her thin, graceful-looking neck, strands of purple, green, red and dark blue beads accented the golden bangles on her wrists and her gold, coin-shaped earrings.

Zemaga smiled, stepped aside, raised one arm and made a sweeping gesture inside as she said, "Come in."

Bobby continued to lead the way as he and Sara followed the woman inside.

"I'll read your future," Zemaga said as she gestured for them to sit at a small table in the center of which a satin cushion

Thief of Love

supported a crystal orb almost as big as a soccer ball.

Sara sat across from where the woman assumed her own seat on the far side and Bobby took the chair to Sara's left.

The woman flashed Sara a brief but warm smile and immediately focused her gaze upon the crystal ball, seeming to look into its depths. Sara swallowed hard, looked to Bobby, and whipered, "Bobby, is this New Age Eastern mysticism?"

Bobby grinned and whispered back, "This is the real deal." Then he turned toward the gypsy woman and said, "My lady, Sara would like her future read."

"Do you do Taro?" Sara asked.

The gypsy madam smiled, reached under the table and brought out a vase, which she held out.

Bobby fished in his Levi's pocket, then dropped in a ten dollar bill from left over money he had already taken out of Sara's purse back at the motel room.

Zemaga continued to hold the vase out.

Bobby frowned, dug in his pocket again and added another ten dollars to the vase.

Zemaga nodded as she set the vase on the floor, and retrieved a deck of Taro cards from somewhere under the table, which she shuffled, had Sara cut, and began dealing.

Zemaga looked up at Sara as she said, "I see death." She continued to lay out the Taro cards, saying, "Someone in this room will die within two years."

Sara jerked back in fright.

Madam Zemaga did not hesitate as she continued, "If you dare to look into the past, present, or future, I will continue."

Somehow Bobby failed to notice the dark, cloudy spot Sara could plainly see in Zemaga's crystal ball as he said, "Go for it!" He looked irritated as he pressed, "Go ahead, continue."

Thief of Love

The woman looked from Sara to Bobby and back again. Sara gave a little nod as she glanced at Bobby, noting the suspicion edging his eyes.

Zemaga fixed Sara with her gaze as she said, "You think God is punishing you, Sara."

"How did you know my name?" Sara asked.

Zemaga smiled, "The gentleman mentioned it when you first came in, and you called him 'Bobby.'"

Sara and Bobby looked to each other as Zemaga continued.

"But, Sara, it's not God -- it's people. God is love. Satan works through people. Satan is not a person you can see or touch, but you can hear him. He is a demon spirit who works through those who he wants to destroy," she said, glancing into Bobby's eyes.

Sara was overcome with horror, suddenly engulfed in fear.

Bobby scowled at the gypsy woman. "Let's go," he said. "I've heard enough from this charlatan."

Reluctantly, Sara let Bobby lead her away as he stood, gripped her wrist, tugged her to her feet and towed her outside.

He led her back up the path to the midway, and tried to keep her busy with games of skill and chance, attractions and rides for the rest of the afternoon, becoming his most charming self; but Sara was still spellbound, bewitched for a time, by the idea of what fate held in store for her, or him -- perhaps both of them. The uneasiness stayed with her the rest of the afternoon.

Finally, as the day wore on toward evening, Bobby said, "Come on, let's find some food."

He again led the way as they went past most of the attractions and rides on the main midway, passing food

Thief of Love

concessions of succulent barbecued ribs, gyros, gourmet burgers -- hot grease from the vats snapping inside.

"I'm gonna pass most of these food stands," he said. "All we need is a shot of carbs -- carbohydrates; something that won't fill us up too heavy. I need to keep myself burning energy off my own body fuel."

They passed the Italian sausage stand where a crowd stood in line waiting. Bobby snorted in contempt as Sara drank in the delicious aroma there. "I don't need the calories," he said, then stopped, adding, "but I'll just have one. My buddy who runs this trailer will fix us up. I'll order us a couple. There goes a couple leaving the picnic table under that shade tree. Let's take a break over there." He pointed as the couple stood and walked away.

"Do you want Paco Paco sauce over the onions and peppers?" he asked.

Sara shook her head. "Just onions and peppers, and a Pepsi, please. Thank you," she said as, tired of so much walking, she made her way over to the picnic table and sat before it was taken.

As she sat and waited, Sara and noticed Bobby's intense stare out at the midway. She followed his gaze and saw that he was looking at an attractive young woman in her mid-twenties.

Sara watched as the young woman looked at Bobby, and walked toward him. He gave the girl a slight shake of the head and motioned with his chin ever so slightly in Sara's direction. The woman glanced at Sara, then fixed her eyes on Bobby's as she walked past, giving him a 'just wait and see' look, a smile, and a surreptitious wave.

Sara continued to watch as Bobby held his fixated stare on the retreating backside of the young woman, who seemed to sense his eyes on her as she gave her hips an extra swagger while she strutted her stuff on and away, soon becoming lost in the thick crowds.

A sudden and terrible rage flushed hot and overpowering through Sara as she leapt up, the concrete beneath her feet hot, but not as hot as she was feeling inside, with her tail feathers ruffled. <u>What a miserable, rotten skirt chaser</u>, she thought as she inhaled deeply, to save her breath for what was to come.

Bobby headed back to the picnic table, seemingly unaware of the change in Sara's mood as he bit into the end of an Italian sausage sandwich. He smiled as he set the food on the table and sat, saying, "Have a seat, Red, before it gets cold."

Sara harrumphed and said, "I don't want that sandwich."

Bobby looked up at her in surprise.

Sara nodded toward where the girl had strutted away, fairly spitting out the words as she said, "Give it to <u>her</u>. You've always liked your girls on the trashy side, haven't you, Bobby? Even her jeans are grubby."

His anger up now, Bobby fairly snarled as he shouted, "You damn she devil!"

Bobby hopped out off the bench and threw the sandwiches in a nearby trash can. "What the hell kind of crap are you programming into your little brain now?" He shook his head as he continued. "She's not dressed up right now. She doesn't look ultra-chic, but she works a polished and professional business. Quit being so reptile. She's not a factory worker, but that doesn't mean she's no good either."

"Well, big deal. What exactly does she do then?" Sara asked. She could tell by the nervous darting of his eyes that he was trying to come up with a good answer, no matter how untrue.

"She's a professional horse braider, fixing up the manes

and tails of show horses. She works long nights grooming horses, helping get them ready to show."

Sara suddenly became uneasy as the thought occurred to her that perhaps she'd over-reacted to an innocent exchange of friendly but not lustful glances and expressions. She turned away to allow herself a moment to reconsider.

Bobby stepped around, so they were now face to face. He shook his head and sighed. "Your jealousy is going to destroy us," he said. "Why can't you believe me? My love for you is true."

His expression was so completely sincere that Sara had further doubts as he said, "Come on, let's go," and started walking down the food stands toward the livestock stalls and exhibition arenas.

Reluctant at first, Sara followed about a dozen steps behind, then increased her pace to catch up to Bobby and match his stride.

As the sun was starting its gradual drop toward the western horizon, the sound of drums acted as a beacon, drawing crowds -- and Bobby and Sara along with them -- toward the free concert at the Ponderosa stage.

Approaching the stage, they heard the united sound of many loud voices from the gathering audience, who began chanting, "Hey-ya-hey-hey-hey," like an old-time Native American religious or social gathering.

In front of the grandstand in the center of the arena, a man dressed like an Indian chief danced around the yellow flames of a small bonfire that flickered and flared into the open air.

The crowd chanted louder and the man danced at a faster tempo. Sara soon felt herself caught up in the atmosphere by the rhythms of sound from the jangles of bells and slapping of leather of his costume in time to his movements as he paced, stomped his feet, leaped and spun about. The power of the experience resonated through Sara's inner being till she thought she must have some American Indian genes in her, so strong was the feeling that she'd felt it all before.

Sara was so engrossed by the performance that she became disengaged from the concept of time. She didn't know how long she'd been lost in the hypnotic mood of the music and dancing when she noticed that Bobby was no longer nearby. A quick scan of the bleachers revealed that he stood on the far side of an arena entrance, and she suddenly realized that she didn't remember entering the arena, but there she was, engulfed in the mystical charm of the Indian chief's dancing.

Sara noticed that Bobby removed his sunglasses and scanned the spectators as if in search of someone, but not Sara, she was sure, for he'd been near her side before moving off while she had become lost in enjoyment of the Indian dance.

A loud whistle cut through the sounds of chanting, music, bells and leather. After a few seconds, the whistle again pierced through all other sounds. Sara searched for the source of the whistling. As her eyes scanned past the fiery orb of the setting sun, its glare dimmed and blurred the images of people in the chanting crowd and the dancing Indian chief they cheered on.

One step toward the bleachers put her in the long shadows of late afternoon as it approached sunset. There, above, in the dark pool of shadow in the bleachers, just behind the rail and in the center stood Cid.

Instantly, Sara's heart increased its pace, almost matching the tempo of the drums and chants. After a moment's confusion, Sara realized the whistling was intended to her attention. She looked to one side of Cid, where a hand gave a casual wave. It was Steven. He whistled again and Sara blushed as they exchanged a meaningful glance, and she laughed in nervous embarrassment.

Steven stepped away from Cid, going down the steps from the bleachers and along the wide aisle, weaving his way among groups of men who stood about smoking, talking and laughing as he made his way toward Sara. He tipped his hat in the common cowboy style as he drew within a couple of paces of her.

"Evening, ma'am," he said, looking straight at her. "I believe we met before." Sara immediately sensed that he was changed somehow.

Sara cleared her throat while she also cleared her mind. "Ahum-hum. Good evening to you, Steven. We have met before." Sara stopped as she found her emotions were a combination of surprise and reluctant admiration. She noticed that Steven wore a gold-inlaid, silver trophy buckle five inches across. On it was inscribed, "All around cowboy." His wrangler jeans were tucked down into his fancy, snakeskin cowboy boots.

"A lot of things need to catching up," she said. "The timing is perfect."

"It isn't bad at all, is it?" he asked and winked. "You're just trying to high-hat me." He started chewing on a matchstick, but his attention seemed focused on her, and was powerful and immediate. "You know, baby, I could go for you in a big way," he said, his entire manner persuasive. Conflicting emotions suddenly left Sara in something of a flutter.

Looking away from Steven, Sara saw that Bobby had spotted them. He shifted his weight from one dusty boot to the other, trying to see who she was talking to, but a man's back was all he see from where he stood. Sara hoped Bobby would think it looked innocent as it was, although he would recognize that there was a familiarity between them.

A sudden anger flared in his eyes, and she imagined that he was thinking that all her ex's aren't in Texas and that someone was messing in his world. He stomped toward them and, as he got closer, swung off with a swift, hard, savage swing of his heavy boot, kicking dust and stones toward where Sara and Steven stood.

Steven spun around for a look at the source of dust and stones, his jaw tensing as he faced Bobby.

Sara felt her throat clench and heart race as she realized trouble was on the way while Bobby marched toward them, completely fearless, full of bravado.

Cid stepped down from the bleachers and headed toward the pending confrontation, giving Bobby a searching glance as he called out, "Crazy cowboys and rank stallions excite me too, Bobby!" The remark was made with warmth, and in a mischievous tone.

Sara refrained from trying to appear innocent, which would only heighten Bobby's suspicions and set him off.

"You dawg gone ornery hawse! You again?" Bobby drawled.

"You know him?" Sara asked, tensed up, expecting double trouble.

Cid jostled Bobby's shoulder.

Bobby glared at Cid, then grinned and shook his head. "Do I know him?" he asked Sara, clearing his throat.

"Where have you been at?" Cid asked Bobby.

"It's a pity -- Ohio, of course!" Bobby replied, then turned to Sara and said, "He's the hottest thing going in the circuit. He's the richest, orneriest, no-goodest son of anger and nicest

Thief of Love

guy I know in the sport." Bobby said it in a voice he meant to carry into the stands.

Cid smirked. "Wasn't it during the jazz capital internet to-do that you left the circuit last September in Monterey, with. . . ." He thought for a second. ". . . Lori. You left the circuit with Lori. Am I correct?" Bobby paused an instant, as though weighing the pros and cons of lying.

"Skip it!" Bobby half shouted. "By gawd, man, I met a girl by the name of Lori. She flirted with me and I took her to dinner. She was into the internet stuff and partying when I left the circuit to be with her. It was a big mistake. She was a tramp. Anyway, who cares about Lori? This is my lady, Sara," Bobby said with a nod toward her. "She's my one and only sweetheart. I'm terribly indebted to her; she rescued me from Lori."

"She has a lot to learn about rodeoers," Cid said. "They're fast workers, especially with the ladies. She'll learn the ropes."

"Lay off me, you bruiser. I'm on to you," Bobby said in a harsh, rasping tone. His retort focused everyone's attention on Sara.

"They have very little regard for tomorrow, or taking girls into the future with them," Cid said, his reply even and controlled.

Bobby's focus was squarely on Cid as he said, "I'm not used to cowboy humor, but I know the difference between fun and insult. So knock off the B.S." He said it in a bellowing tone.

Sara saw how Bobby's pattern went on automatic as he continued, "Since I met Sara, I don't want another woman. I've settled down with the lady of my life. I thank the good Lord about for a good Christian woman. No better woman ever walked the earth. I've got all I need or all I could ever dream of

Thief of Love

in a lifetime. I'm blessed," he said.

Ludicrous as his words were, considering their source, Sara had won his unwilling admiration. She took it all in, noting that he was trying to sell a bill of goods and not the goods themselves, like a Mountebank would, though the bill of goods he was trying to sell her was himself. She couldn't help blushing at his boasting about her, but everyone ignored her reddened complexion, or didn't notice it as they settled in a semi-circle in the area set aside for the show people.

In the center was Cid. He took off his hat and stood bareheaded as he spoke to them.

"I met Sara over at the motel in Paso Robles last week. She bowled a few challenging games with me at the bowling alley. I didn't have the faintest idea you were the boyfriend she told me was rodeoing at mid-state competition," Cid said in a cheerful voice.

Bobby faced Cid in silence with cold, narrowed eyes and hard lips. Cid fell silent too for a moment.

Finally, Bobby said, "Cattlemen have the same thing to deal with, pretty boy. Stop obstructing my love life. So you're that dude tenderfoot my lady has honestly and openly told me about."

"I guess he is," Sara said, fighting a slight sense of anxiety. "I'm on the level; but I don't care to prove to you anything else," she said, her tone like ice.

Cid took his handkerchief from his pocket, smeared away the dust and perspiration from his brow and said, "Sara's an Easterner -- new to the rodeo. She wasn't sure what you're riding. What events are you competing in at the R.C.A., Bobby?"

Bobby pursed his lips and said, "Steer roping, bareback

riding, team roping."

Cid nodded. "Uh huh. You still have that flamboyant style though. Bareback riding is a young man's sport, Bobby. The life expectancy in competition isn't as long as for other events. Why do you keep on keeping on?"

"I'll be responsible for that," Bobby said with a scowl. "I know it's a strain on my body, but I can hang in there as long as a twenty-five year old pro-rider. I have the body; my lean muscles can respond to the moves of a quick horse, and I still have the wild freedom to be in control."

"Whose horse are you using for competition?" Cid asked.

"Pat McDonald's, most likely," Bobby said.

"Yeah, what if Pat didn't bring a trailer?" Cid asked.

"Yours then," Bobby said. "Did you bring Lucky Times Two?"

"Of course. I pulled a trailer with two show horses Tuesday and my partners brought down a three-horse trailer Monday."

"I like Lucky Times Two's attitude. Maybe I'll get lucky with Lucky," Bobby said. "What else can I think?" Then, after a moment's pause, he asked, "Can I borrow your rigging and your riding gear?"

Cid nodded. "Sure can. I'm guessing the gear will fit you. I've drawn a money bull," Cid said, thinking about the bull he would be riding in the bull events.

"There's enough Brahma to give him size and power. I couldn't ask for a better combination, with the mother Angus bundle-stub shorthorn."

"You can't ask for any more speed and heart than that," Bobby said with a nod.

"It better be," Cid said. "If I can make it to the top

Thief of Love

thirteen in North America, I'm qualified for the world championship. That's something I've been close to for the last two years. I won in N.F.R. in Vegas. This event here is only practice," he declared with a smile.

"Congratulations, Cid," Sara said, not bothering to hide her admiration. "That's quite a big accomplishment. I didn't know you were in the world championship competition until I saw your belt buckle."

"Thanks," Cid said with an embarrassed grin. "I pride myself in being a bull rider."

"If you want to, you can make money, Bobby," Cid said. "If you work at it, it comes pretty fast when it happens. When you don't own a car, when you're lucky to buy one hamburger a day and make it on three bucks a day, you work on concession stands setting up rides for the carnival. You do what ya gotta do. Well, where are you staying at?"

Bobby looked around and didn't respond.

"We have a room over at the motel," Sara finally said for him.

"Motel? That's too much money. Would you like to strike up a deal? I could use your help, Bobby."

Bobby shot Cid a suspicious look. "Doing what?"

"Working for me. I'll put you two up in my deluxe motor home, or trailer. The trailer will sleep ten. I have three bedrooms, so I have the room for you. I'm in a bind for a day or so." Cid didn't try to hide the urgency in his voice.

"What is it, man?" Bobby asked, his suspicion faded into a sudden concern.

"I need to move my horses to the stable in the show ground. The vet's going to check them out over there with the other horses that are participating."

Thief of Love

"We'll do it," Bobby said as he curled up his tee shirt sleeves another notch, adding, "Let's go, man."

Cid held up his hand. "Wait a while longer, Bobby. I was hoping I'd run into my partner over here,' he said in an exasperated tone.

"I'll wait around until this place clears out after the show. My partner slipped off on me this morning accompanied by a rich southern gal from Louisville. She's got a problem who's here with a couple of show horses. She's been here before, and always enters her horses in classes where she knows her horse outclasses everyone else's -- afraid of the competitive world," he said.

Bobby shook his head, taking it all in. "That's a cheap trick. They're probably hustling around trying to buy off judges."

Cid scuffed his feet in the sandy dirt. He glanced at Sara. Bobby's eyes were quick, picking up on it right away, and he gave Cid a `Get back, Jack' look. He circled his arm around her waist, pulling her close to him as they walked through the crowd to the horse shelters.

The path they took circled around back of the building, past the regular workers who came to get things ready for the show horses.

Bobby tipped his hat and reached inside a door next to the horse stalls. He took a halter and lead rope from inside the tiny tack room, and walked to the Appaloosa near Cid.

"Consider it a favor," Bobby said to him as he looked toward Sara. "This is my hideout. I come here to get away from the crowd when I can't get a little peace and quiet."

Bobby led the horse to the main building, and from there they all went to Cid's motor home for a restful evening.

Thief of Love

Chapter 23

The following daybreak, the light of the rising sun shone through the bedroom window, and the sound of mooing in the distance snapped Sara awake when the cattle called from the stalls in the livestock shelters. For a moment, she fought the urge to go to the bathroom as she felt uncomfortable being in Cid's motor home at that time of day. She'd rather have been at the motel room, with more privacy.

Sara slid out of the bed and crept with quiet steps past Cid's room, which was on the way to the bathroom. She side-glanced into his room as she went by. He lay on his side, apparently asleep. She regarded him with uncertainty -- feeling a need to talk with him and tell him she'd be leaving. After a moment of hesitation, Sara changed her mind though, since she didn't feel really safe giving out that sort of information because he and Bobby had been on such good terms.

Recovering her composure, Sara crowded back into the bed with Bobby for one last time. She let her head slide sideways onto his arm and, without a word, he drew her to his side so she could pillow her cheek on his chest. She knew this wouldn't be the only morning she'd want him and not be with him. This would be the day she planned to leave for Ohio.

Bobby suddenly twitched around in the bed, and sat with an abruptness that literally cast Sara aside onto the pillow and mattress as he arose, slide into his pants and boots and said, "I'm starting to feel how the ride's going to be. I need a surge of adrenaline going through my veins, not alcohol. What I need is a cup of hot, black coffee strong enough to cut through this blah."

Cid had gotten up in the meantime and put on a pot of regular perked coffee, then went back to his room, rustling

Thief of Love

around and dropping things on the floor.

Within moments, Bobby and Sara went into the kitchen, and Cid joined them there.

"Cid, you needn't be so flustered," Bobby told him, adding, "Relax your mind, man."

"Say, are you razzing me, Bobby?" Cid asked, then said, "What I need is an hour's worth of this stuff pumping through my blood and I'll make it through the day. My nerves are raw; I feel like an animal." That said, he went into the living room, and they followed as he threw his riding gear, leather chaps, soft conchos, and rigging bag on the sofa.

"Try these on for size," he said to Bobby as he unfolded a tattered blanket and flung it next to the riding gear.

Sara eyed all of the leather Bobby was carrying as he stepped into the bedroom. She took one of the Danishes on the countertop, and poured some coffee, spilling some, then wiped it up with the towel Cid handed her.

Bobby came out after a moment, high stepping and holding in his hand a ticket that permitted him to enter any of the contests.

"You never been at a rodeo, you're sure?" he asked Sara. Au-da-fan! You're going to see eight rounds of ranking spurs, flapping chaps, and a bucking, twisting, wild critter under me, down and up, downward an upward again, then side to side, jerking me every which way but loose. You're going to think I'm having an epileptic seizure; but you're going to be my support. You're my cornerstone."

Cid broke out his ropes and stretched the travel kinks out of them. "You know, Bobby, you're the finest of horsemen wonders with a rope."

"Sure I am. Rustle now," Bobby said.

Thief of Love

"Haw! Haw! Tonight's the night, by jingo!" Cid half shouted. "If you win tonight, you get a check. I want to win this go- around tonight and the second go-around Thursday, and from there, the finals Friday."

Bobby unzipped Cid's rigging bag and removed the rigging, reinforced rawhide, twenty inches long, ten inches at the point where the handhold was attached, and tapered to about six inches at the D ring.

"Do you have a glove with you?" Cid asked.

"Yes," Bobby said.

"What's it made from?"

"Horsehide. It has little resilience, but it won't stretch."

Cid watched as Bobby turned his glove inside out.

"I don't use buckskin riding gloves. That glove has to fit right or you lose a lot of power," he said to Sara. "The glove and rigging are the only two things between the rider and the end of his existence when he rides."

"I'll go with you," Sara said as show time approached, when Cid donned his cowboy duds, except the chaps, and they sallied forth.

Within minutes, Bobby was inside the high fence where he encountered cowboys he knew, and with the prevailing good-natured Western raillery was checking his equipment as Sara sat in the bleachers just outside the circular fence. She watched as Bobby stood behind the chute, holding onto a post. She admired his denim shirt, with a paper number "forty-two" pinned to the back. His shapely feet were encased in high-top, intricately carved and richly decorated boots. His riding glove was tied loosely to the strap closing the front of his chaps.

It was time for him to mount the animal and Bobby slid his buttocks forward, up against Cid's rigging. In a moment he

Thief of Love

pushed, moving his feet ahead, putting them on the chute, all ready to set his spurs in the horse's shoulder as it turned out of the chute. He grabbed his hat, which set the tone for the ride and gave it a yank. Everything was ready. The gate swung open.

Sara was full of excitement. Then the horse burst out into the arena with a pounding clip-clop of hooves. Bobby bounced and bumped around, and threw his legs up in the air for an eight-second ride, and scored high points, which at the time was tops.

Sara was full of pride as she cheered. Then, a sudden seriousness settled over the arena; the bull riding events would begin soon.

In a short time, it was Cid's turn to risk injury or death on the back of a powerful animal.

Bobby was near the chute as he handled Cid's bull rope. He took the loop, threaded the end through it, and pulled the tail of the rope across Cid's palm, giving it a twist, then took it around the back of the rider's hand and across his palm again, giving it two more twists.

Cid positioned his body, and hunched a little to set his hips.

"Get set, cowboy! Hustle man!" Bobby yelled through the gate. "Hook, man. Hustle!"

The bull upon which Cid was mounted suddenly went wild, bucking, kicking and lurching around. The force of the animal's tremendous strength broke Cid's arm hold and he was thrown off, his hand still tangled in the rope. The bull raised up and caught him in the air, but he couldn't release the rope as he fell to the ground with a sickening thud, finding himself looking at the bull's privates and watching the sharp hooves coming down.

A rumble of voices in the crowd swept around as word

Thief of Love

spread that a rider was down in the pen. The excitement and euphoria that had engulfed the crowd turned to a tense feeling of dread.

The announcer yelled, "Get out of the pen!" as, in a split second, Bobby leaped into the pen, putting himself in mortal danger as he rushed to help while Cid was wriggling and squirming, struggling to get his gloved hand free of the rope.

Bobby reached down with both hands and twisted and wrenched Cid's hand this way and that, until it was out of the glove and freed from the binding rope. Bobby pulled Cid away from the two-thousand-pound bull and to the fence, struggling himself to stay on his feet as Cid leapt onto the fence and vaulted over it.

Behind and below, the bull came driving hard, slamming into the fence just as Bobby lunged, got a grip on the top railing, and propelled himself up to stand atop the uppermost bar, where he faltered, swayed, regained his equilibrium, turned and, balancing precariously above the enraged, thrashing bull, raised both arms and looked up at the crowd.

At the spontaneous outburst of cheering and applause, Sara caught her breath. It had all happened so unexpectedly. The spectators continued to roar with glee and began chanting, "Bob-by! Bob-by! Bob-by!" while stomping their feet, making the stands shake with a rhythmic beat.

Bobby waved his hands, hushing the crowd while still straddling the fence. The bull backed up and charged once more against the fence landing terrific blows, knocking Bobby off-balance and sending him tumbling once more into the pen. The bull swung around, his head down, horns thrashing. He charged at Bobby, knocked him down. Bobby rolled, scrambled to his feet, then fell as the bull caught him from behind, pushing him against the side of the pen. Then, before Bobby was crushed, the bull backed up, raised its feet in the air like a rearing horse, and started to fall toward Bobby. But Bobby whirled around, gripped the top railing again and pulled himself up, while the bull kicked savage blows to his body.

Bobby climbed over the fence this time, and hopped down from the other side, without fanfare; but the audience gave him sustained applause as he limped off, vowing as if to himself that, "My ambition to be a rodeo star is completely squelched."

Cid gripped Bobby by the elbow and led him toward the first-aid station.

Sara's thoughts bucked and reeled almost as much as the wild bull had. She felt terrible now about her secret plans to leave Bobby, but made her way to the first aid station and went inside, lacing her hands together to lessen their trembling, regarding him with a vague uneasiness.

"I hope you're not badly hurt. Bobby' you look terrible. Are you all right?" she asked.

With a grin, he said, "Does a Texas twister look all right? Thank you; never mind. That bull almost kicked the piss out of me! Man alive! Never again!" His words came out in a harsh rasp. "I was just about freight-trained by a Brahma bull!" he concluded with a pant and a shake of his head.

"Bobby why did you go into the pen after the announcer told you to get out? You took it so lightly. Why?" she asked, half in tears.

Bobby sat on the gurney, fell back, then looked up at her, a strange melancholy in his tone, as if the incident lay uncharacteristically upon his spirit, like a mantle.

"I had to get Cid free from that monster, and then I was trying to fake him out so my partner could get over the fence.

Thief of Love

How did I know Cid was so much faster than I thought such an old man could move? As long as I got up and got out, that's all that counts, okay?" With the last, his old, bitter, mocking self returned.

"Sport, I admire your nerve," Cid said, then laughed. His voice had a pleasant depth, with an intonation that reminded Sara how different he was from Bobby as he continued. "Bobby, I thought you were one tough customer, so get yourself up and out of here. You dawg gone ornery hawse. Talk about an old man. Can't you stand on your own two feet?" Cid said in his Western drawl. "Go on, man, get yourself back in action. Even the best players never hit five hundred. They always mess up more than they score, Bobby. It ain't the way you ride that counts, it's stickin' on. You're as big a competitor, finest of horsemen, a wonder with a rope; but you're unreliable, if you know where I'm coming from, man!"

"Or as I am," Bobby said and snorted.

"Takes one to know one," Sara said in a teasing tone as she took advantage of the moment to slip out of the first aid station and melt away into the crowd, finding an escape route that would lead her back to Cid's motor home. Bobby didn't make any apparent attempt to chase after or even locate her.

The sun was still high in the Western sky as Sara searched through the vehicles and motor homes, finding Cid's after what seemed like more than an hour had passed. Going inside as fast as she could, Sara packed her belongings and threw everything in the cab of the truck, then flung herself inside and started the engine without hesitation.

With both hands on the wheel, Sara pulled out of the parking lot of the fairgrounds, conscious of several conflicting feelings without looking back, leaving Bobby in the dust and dirt

Thief of Love

and the roaring of the crowd of the rodeo on a midsummer midafternoon.

Sara turned onto Riverside Drive, then made the turn onto twenty-fourth, with less than a tank of gas as she started down the road, leaving Paso Robles and emerging onto Highway Forty-six east, the now lowering sun to the west, behind her.

At last, Sara was alone, perfectly free, speeding along an open road into unknown country as she continued down Forty-six east for about twenty-five miles, which took her out to a rural area. She saw a resemblance in the Western range that seemed in her imagination like Timbucto, with the only movement in the stark and dry landscape an occasional eighteen-wheeler whizzing past on the sole east-west route.

Ahead, amid a cloud of truck-stirred dust, Sara could scarcely see the driver of a semi-tractor trailer truck that had captured her attention as it turned into a parking lot next to a building alongside a flickering sign that announced: `Jack Ranch Café.'

Sara watched as she too turned in, trailing behind the dust of the eighteen-wheeler. The truck driver parked the semi near a large tree off to the side of the café. She parked three spaces over, by two cars.

The trucker had gotten out of his semi and walked around a flagstone, circular path toward a wall of stainless steel and copper that circled a monument. The monument itself was made from stainless steel, wood and copper.

Sara didn't go to read the plaque on the monument that no doubt announced its purpose, but she instead headed for the restaurant.

The restaurant building was old, possibly from the 1920's, tan in color, trimmed in green. Sara went inside and made a

Thief of Love

walk-through inspection of the café, wandered around and carefully surveyed the place. An old piece of farm equipment, a seeder, which had once been pulled by horses in rural areas, made up the centerpiece of the decor inside. The carpeting on the floor in the dining areas was forest green. A floor-model old-fashioned juke box was playing happier Country music from the 1950's, Rockabilly, she thought, noting that the mood wasn't the same as the somber, depressing music so prevalent in country tunes in recent years.

Sara wandered around to the cash register and sorted through an odd collection of old James Dean magazines written in Japanese. She sifted through old photos of James Dean and picked out a dozen souvenir post cards, paid the cashier, and went back to the cafe at the front of the building.

"Good evening," the trucker she had seen outside said, raising a brow.

Sara widened her eyes in surprise, but didn't speak until the waitress seated her at a table, when the trucker walked over and found a seat for himself opposite her.

The waitress brought a pot of coffee.

The trucker, certainly seeming courteous and wholesome, made a casual nod. "I see you don't mind me sitting with you. I'll buy," he said. "I have a schedule to keep by midnight at Pacific Palisades," he said. "I don't have time to wait for formal seating."

Sara had noticed.

The waitress poured two cups of coffee. The trucker sipped from his cup, and Sara saw that his fingers were decorated with Black Hills gold-nugget rings, without a wedding band.

The menu was mostly Mexican food and hamburgers. Sara ordered a hamburger, and the trucker ordered Mexican food

-- tacos, refried beans, tortilla chips. He watched Sara as she looked through the James Dean post cards, but she paid little attention to him as she just studied the pictures.

"The legend lives on," he said, half joking, half serious, munching on a tortilla chip as he mixed chili sauce with it.

Sara's glanced up at him. He was clean-shaven, wearing his black hair in a ponytail. He had a diamond-studded earring in his right ear. He wore denim Levi's and a t-shirt with a Western design -- cactus on the desert, in earth-tone colors. He looked muscular, but not heavy. His eyes were brown and bold in expression. When he extended a leg to scratch his knee, she saw that he wore brown Western boots.

"What's with all this James Dean stuff around here?" Sara asked.

"Don't you know where you are?" he asked in return, giving Sara the benefit of a searching glance.

"Nooooo. . . not really," she replied, confused. "I left my boy friend back at the rodeo in Paso Robles. He's participating in the R.C.A. there, but his base is southern California."

"That's cool about your boy friend. Well, ma'am," the trucker said, "You're in Shalom, population less than seventy-five, surrounded by the hills of the Diablo Range, near where James Dean was killed, a mile from here at the junction where Forty-one and Forty-six come together. Didn't you know you're in an historical place? The memorial is out there in front. Didn't you check it out?"

Sara shook her head, then thought about his question and remembered the walled monument around what looked like a sculpture.

"I saw the monument, but I came inside without going over. There was a truck driver walking around a circular stone path," she said.

"If you're keen about seein' it, we'll stop as we go out." The trucker stared at her for a second. "That was me. I saw you pull in out there."

He pointed to the post card. James Dean was driving a low-slung silver Porsche with the racing number 'one thirty' painted on the side.

"If I recall the name correctly," the trucker said, "Rolf Weuterich, his German mechanic, was riding with him. They were on the way to the races in Salinas, roaring down Route Forty-six when, at the intersection of Forty-one, a car driven by Donald Turnspeed, a college student, made a left-hand turn. James Dean swerved to avoid the car, but the two vehicles collided head on at the fork in the road. The student and the mechanic survived, but James Dean died in the ambulance on the way to the hospital in Paso Robles."

"I know all about James Dean," Sara said. "Then you also know that he was famous for his speed and fearless, reckless driving," she added, sorting through the post cards.

The trucker nodded. "Two hours before his death, Dean was given a speeding ticket in Bakersfield. The authorities who investigated the accident estimated he averaged a speed of seventy-five miles an hour up until he crashed. That means he had to be doing more than a hundred a lot, considering the time it takes for stops for gas, getting that speeding ticket, traffic slowdowns and the like."

Sara handed him a post card. "Look at this one; it's of James Dean on his five hundred Triumph Trophy motorcycle." On the card, a caption read: "You've Got To Live Fast."

The trucker shifted his chair around the table, until he was alongside Sara, and placed his arm along the back of her

Thief of Love

chair while he studied the picture.

"What brings you out here while your boy friend is back at a carnival in Paso Robles? You should be with him, hon."

Sara shrugged. "He's there, I'm here. I guess that's how I got to where I am now," she said in a soft tone. "It's too late to turn back now. I'.m kind of lost out here in the hills of the Diablo Range. When I left, I was in a hurry. I didn't use a map; I just turned away from the lowering sun when I got onto Highway Forty-six east."

The trucker looked at his watch.

"Normally, I drive late, to be minus the traffic and hectic pace of daylight hours. That way, I try to pick up my load in the evening. I needed a break from the road when I pulled in," he said.

"I can appreciate that," Sara said. "Do you ever travel to the Midwest, through Ohio?" she asked.

He seemed to be assimilating a startling thought, then said, "My ex-wife lives in Pittsburgh, PA. I take the Ohio Turnpike about once every six months. Passing through, I stop off for a day to see her. She remarried, so we have to be discreet and find a secret place at the Comfort Inn or where we can be alone. It's worth the effort though. Not ego," he said, shaking his head, "just good sex; just confidence in something good," he added, smiling, then laughed. "She thinks I still have the touch; but, from then on, I relearn what leaving feels like," he finished in a gloomy voice.

"Why did you leave," Sara asked, "if you had such a good thing going?"

"She tried to get me off this road I'm on. The only way that would ever happen would be nothing short of breaking down my rig."

Thief of Love

"Do you ever stop at Stony Ridge Inn Truck Stop in Toledo?" Sara asked.

He thought for a moment. "Stony Ridge, off Exit Five on the Ohio Turnpike, by Route Two Eighty? Right on," he said. "So, you know about Stony Ridge, huh?"

"Yeah, that's the place," Sara said in an excited tone.

"Oh, why sure!" he exclaimed. "There's a Country Western band at the night spot, restaurant, motel and truck stop out there. I used to meet my semi-lover at Stony Ridge whenever I was in Ohio. Whenever we'd be within a hundred miles of each other, we'd get a room in back of the restaurant for a night together. She drove for Challenger Truck Lines out of Port Clinton, Ohio. I drove for a trucking company out of Tulsa, Oklahoma. We seemed to often interchange in Michigan or Ohio, back to back," he said.

"She was a lot of fun for one-nighters," he continued. "I'd love to be with that semi-lover again, but she drives for an independent company now."

Sara recalled old memories too. "I met a few truck drivers myself from time to time at Stony Ridge Inn. I like to go over there for the evening for two-stepping Country Western music. It's about a sixty-minute drive from Sandusky, where I live. I take the Ohio Turnpike, get on Exit Seven, got off Exit Five."

"I know. The dance floor is perfect for two-stepping," he said.

Sara nodded. "Most of the truckers I met were good dance partners. Whenever they came into the area, I'd get a call from one or another, and I'd drive over for the evening, nothing serious though. I don't take truckers seriously. I know truckers have a gift to gab, just passing their time to the next truck stop."

She laughed. "I do know some truckers take their women cross-country with them."

"Some of the best truckers for dancing partners come in from all over the South and West with their women. They dress up for the evening and take a night out for dancing. I remember their women dress Western style -- out of sight -- I mean jeans and a casual look, but stylish -- good taste in clothes."

"My fiancée rides with me cross-country sometimes. Now, I only have one fiancée," he said, "you remember?"

"Where does your fiancée live?" Sara asked.

"Out by Dallas-Fort Worth Airport, west of Irving, Texas. She has a career with a cosmetic company. She drives a pink Cadillac," he added with obvious pride.

"Got you," Sara said, then asked, "Does she work for Mary Kay?"

"You bet," he said. "She draws a six-digit income, but has nothing to do with what this man falls for."

"Isn't the corporate office in the Dallas area?" Sara asked, then continued, "I was at a World Wisdom Conference with an evangelist ministry at the IX Atrium. We always held our luncheons in the Peacock Banquet Room. We couldn't hold our signal's luncheon in the Atrium II as the Mary Kay convention had taken priority over all the dining rooms that were first class. That was the last for that. We stopped having World Wisdom Conferences in Dallas."

Sara decided to not talk about that anymore, but couldn't decide what to say next, so a moment of silence followed, till the driver asked, "So you've been to Paso Robles?" I read the preliminaries were being run off before a half-filled grandstand Tuesday. You've been at the biggest little fair anywhere.

"I'm going there tomorrow myself. I purchased front row

Thief of Love

seats for me and my girl, Katie, to see an outdoor concert with Allen Jackson and Dean Carter."

"I wanted to see Allen Jackson and hear Dean Carter sing 'Strawberry Wine,'" Sara said, "but it was bad timing for me. I have to get back to Ohio as soon as possible. The AM plant where I work has laid three quarters of the people off because of a strike in Flint, Michigan. The strike is now over and the employees were notified to start back to work on their regular shifts. I'd like to be out of California by noon tomorrow; I need to get on Route Eighty, near Sacramento."

"You're a long way from Route Eighty," the truck driver said, shaking his head, drawing a pen and pad of paper from his shirt pocket and proceeding to draw her a route to Interstate Eighty that truckers take to save time.

"You're about sixty-four miles to Hanford and about eighty-four miles to Fresno," he said. "I suggest you get a room for the night. There are several rooms down there in Hanford; it's closest. On the map I'm drawing, you'll see the way basically takes you out of Hanford."

"I wouldn't go to Fresno anyway," Sara said. "One of the cowboys I left, I mean one of the bull riders back there, was from Fresno. He could show up there, but, I'm trying to leave the past behind."

"Well, if I see them, I won't tell them where you are," the driver said and laughed, then continued. "I'm dropping off a load in Huntington Beach; after that, I'm picking up my girl. She lives our near Trabuco Canyon."

"Where's that?" Sara asked.

"On the way to Cleveland National Forest. I'll park my truck there and come back in to Paso Robles for the fair tomorrow in her jeep. We can pick up a tent, and cooler of beer for a couple days, do a little camping and rest up for the home stretch back to Dallas.

"Well, babe, time flew," he said. "Time to shake a leg," he added, pushing aside his empty plate and sticking a toothpick between his teeth. He took his wallet, which was secured by a chain from his belt, out of his back pants pocket, and laid a twenty on the table.

"This is for both," he said. "Don't forget to tip the waitress!" He winked. "I'll just say adios; have a safe trip back to Ohio. If you get tired, pull over and rest. Don't drive if you're sleepy. You have a long trip ahead of you."

"Thanks for the map," Sara said with a smile. "And I value your concern for me in my safe trip back home to Ohio."

He chewed idly at the toothpick as he rose, turned on his heel and left with a few quick steps.

Sara paid at the cash register and went out the door. It was dark outside now, and she scanned the parking lot quickly as the scary thought occurred that Bobby could be about. The moon loomed large on the eastern horizon and, after moment, she felt safe enough to follow the trucker.

He pulled out onto State Route 46 as she was getting into her S-10, and he trucked off. All she could see were the taillights disappearing into the night, heading toward Paso Robles. Sara sighed, thinking, There goes another `Mother Trucker.' He's never going to be true to any one woman. Typical trucker -- got it down to a fine art.

On the way to Hanford, Sara halted at a corner gas station to fill up, then continued onto a hotel farther down the road, where she checked in for the night.

The next morning, feeling anxious but refreshed by a night's sleep, Sara was on her way home with hope that yesterday's events would fade as far behind her as the distance over which she had come. As Sara drove along the road her mind seemed both busy and absent. How good it was to be free from Bobby.

Once on Interstate Eighty, Sara drove absent-mindedly across the western states and, on day three, the S-10 was speeding through Ohio. Farmhouses stood among cornfields and groves of trees along the Ohio Turnpike. How beautiful the countryside looked, she thought.

It took her time to regain some semblance of normality when she finally got home and back to her daily routine of going to work.

Bobby's memory was still on her mind though, as she thought a woman can only take so much. Would she be glad if he returned? If he came back, would he be a hero to her -- brave, strong and courageous -- to venture forth; or would he be just a wounded creature. What he was really about?

Thief of Love

Chapter 24

Fall had arrived in full force, it was the first week of October in northwest Ohio and the trees were turning from green to first the brilliant then washed-out and burned shades of fall colors. Every day the leaves got a little brighter and deeper in hue, and the nights were getting chilly, the days shorter.

Sara was preoccupied when the phone rang. She had been planting spring flower bulbs since the early morning -- Tulips, Hyacinths, Daffodils -- and the midday sun was at the peak of brightness. She propped the shovel up against the white picket fence, interrupting her planting job.

Feeling relaxed, humming to herself, Sara rushed inside to answer the phone. She checked the time; it was two o'clock.

"Can I talk to you? It's me, Bobby. Please don't hang up on me!"

Sara thought Bobby's voice revealed a note of loneliness, so, after a moment's hesitation, she asked, "Where are you? I'm kind of surprised to hear from you."

"I'm in Sandusky, Ohio," he said. "I'm fine -- doing good -- working in Akron, Ohio."

"Why call now? It's been a long time, and it's peaceful around here. Anyway, I thought you'd forgotten me by now."

"I'm back," he said, "because my heart won't let me forget you. Regardless, I've been doing well."

Sara took in what he said but wasn't touched emotionally. "How long are you staying?" she asked, thinking, <u>Exactly what I need after a hard week's work.</u>

"Not long," he said. "I have an efficiency apartment in Akron, so I'm just on a visit here to see Sandy and Rob, along with a few others. I did hope to see you, so I thought I'd ask, if you weren't busy, if I could stop by before I head back home. I won't stay long." He sounded sincere.

With mixed feelings, Sara hesitated and thought, It's not starting all over again. A moment passed, then two.

"Why are you staying in Akron? Isn't Akron a long way from California?"

"You mean where you dumped me off?" His tone held a note of bitterness. "I have a job there as a handyman. I wouldn't feel good about coming here today if I couldn't come to see you. Just be honest with your feelings," he said. "It's okay. Do what's best for you. If you don't want me to stop by, I can understand."

"Bobby, you know, I don't have a lot of time for you or anyone today. I'm working outside," she said, her voice cool, then added, "But, okay. Bobby, you can stop for a little while."

"Thanks," he said. "I'm on my way, in my Chevy Monte Carlo."

About forty-five minutes after his call, Bobby pulled into Sara's driveway in a 1994 Chevrolet Monte Carlo. He parked, stepped out of the car, shut the door, and walked over to where Sara stood with the shovel in her hand. "I'll take over," he said, his tone warm. "What are you planting next -- where at?" he asked and cupped his hand gently over hers.

Seeing him was almost painful; he had changed so much -- looking shrunken and suddenly so aged in just nine months. More than fifty pounds had melted away from his frame, which had been strong and muscular, but was now thin and wan.

"Have you been sick?" she asked in a concerned tone.

He shook his head. "No. I'm not sure what my problem is. I quit riding in rodeos about eight months ago. I lost so much strength and energy so quickly, I had to walk away from the

Thief of Love

circuit.

Sara's mind raced. "You left the rodeo circuit eight months ago? Where have you been for the last nine months?"

"I left with a carnival in Nevada that slowly brought me back to this area." Bobby said, adding, "I tried to call you different times, just for general chit-chat, but I never connected. I guess you were out with your boy friend. I wish you would have been home."

"I'm preoccupied with work, Bobby, okay? I don't have a boy friend."

"I wasn't far from here, in Sharon, Pennsylvania during the Anheiser Busch Beer Festival. You've seen the Clydesdale Belgian horses, haven't you?"

Sara nodded. "Yes, I've seen the Clydesdales, on TV in parades, many times.

"They're awesome in person," he said.

Sara nodded again, then asked, "How did you get from Sharon, Pennsylvania to Akron, Ohio?"

Bobby pushed the shovel into the ground and said, "I met my landlady, who's from Akron. She was at the festival with her son and granddaughter. I met them at the children's rides. I was so weak at that time, I was put on light duty in order to keep my job. I was about to put Becky, her four year old granddaughter, on a pony when I collapsed right in front of everyone. She knew I needed a caregiver, so she just took me under her wing."

"And you're staying with a woman in Akron?" Sara asked with reluctance, feeling a slight sense of anxiety.

Bobby shook his head and said, "She told me she'd give me a place to recover, and a job -- something easy -- helping her with her apartment rentals until I could manage when my health got better."

Thief of Love

"Are you sure she was feeding you?" Sara asked in concern. "By the way, where did that Monte Carlo come from that you drove here?"

"It belongs to my landlady's son, Franky. He has two sets of wheels, but mostly drives his S.U.V. He gave me the keys so I could come see you, and, frankly, he told me, 'Bobby, have a good day!' He knew I needed to see you."

Bobby lingered, and they talked for another hour, while he dropped hints that he wanted to stay longer, so Sara showed renewed interest in her yard work. A strange feeling came over her, with Bobby being there, with both knowing he was no longer wanted. Her return to gardening chores and distant expression relayed the message, and he soon took the hint and left.

After he had been gone for a while, Sara had a sudden uneasy feeling; just then, the phone rang again, and she hurried inside to answer.

"Hello? I need to speak with Sara," a woman said.

"This is Sara," Sara answered.

The woman calling introduced herself as the owner of the Sundown Motel, five miles east of Sara's home.

"I was given a message by Robert Johnson," she told Sara. "He was just taken to the police department, and he asked me to call you. It was very important to him that you know."

"What did he do? What happened?" Sara asked.

"He went off the road and rammed into a public phone booth out front here, then plowed through the wall of my motel before his car came to rest."

"Was he injured?" Sara asked.

"I don't think so," the motel owner said, adding, "He was coherent, but he must've had too many shots of Crown Royal. They took him to jail. He has a lot of answering to do with my

Thief of Love

insurance company and to the police for all this damage to my property." As she disconnected, Sara was suddenly overwhelmed by shock and anxiety.

A scant sixty seconds passed before the phone rang again, and the voice on the line said, "This is MCI with a collect call from city jail from Bobby. Will you except the call?"

"Yes, I will," Sara said.

"It's me, Bobby. Can you come get me?" he asked, his tone anxious. "After I left your house, I was headed for the Ohio Turnpike when a car cut in front of me, forcing me off the road. Franky's car was impounded, and I was taken to the city jail. Can you please come pick me up?"

"How did you get out of jail?" she asked.

"I signed my own recognizance bond, but I have to come back in the morning and make an appearance in court. I called Sandy and Rob to come get me, but they're not home. They took Johnny and Jerry to the mall. Can you please come down here?"

"Are you going back to Akron after court?" she asked.

"After court," he said, "I have work to do."

"I'll pick you up, but you're not staying at my house." Sara spoke so firmly her voice broke. She thought, <u>Bobby, you're not getting your foot in the door.</u>

"I know I can't stay," he said, "but it doesn't sound like a bad idea. I need to get some stuff out of Franky's car before it gets dark outside."

"Where's your friend's car impounded?" Sara asked.

"It car was towed into the salvage pool at Martin's Auto Wrecking yard. I have the address." He read it to her, then asked, "Do you know where that is?"

"Yes," Sara said. "I'll take you over there and drop you off wherever you're staying tonight, but not at my house. I want

Thief of Love

to make that clear before you get in my car. I'll have a delay though. I need to clean up and it'll probably take about an hour."

"I'll have to wait? Well, hurry then; please try to hurry."

"Be patient, Bobby; hang on. I'll be there shortly -- at the Sandusky Police Department, right?" she asked.

"Right," he said. "Hurry up."

Sara hurried herself along and arrived at the police department and city jail within the hour, and the desk officer called for Bobby to be released.

Sara could hear the heavy metal doors unlock through several lockdowns. After a few moments, Bobby came out in high spirits, showing a ghost of a smile.

"Where to?" Sara asked, anxious to leave the jail.

"Martin's Auto Salvage Pool," Bobby said, lighting a cigarette as soon as they stepped outside.

Sara noticed that he looked stern and as if life had battered him around even more lately.

They headed for Martin's Auto Wrecking as dusk deepened. Arriving at just before full darkness, they checked in with the gate guard then pulled into the back, searching the lot for Bobby's borrowed car, driving through a maze of wrecked vehicles -- busses, cars and trucks, even farm and construction machines, that had been totally wrecked.

"Where's my Cadillac?" he asked.

Sara cruised around, looking for a Cadillac. "I don't see your Cadillac," she said, adding, "As a matter of fact, I don't see any Cadillac. If I remember correctly, I believe you were driving a Chevy Monte Carlo."

"Excuse me," Bobby said in a sarcastic tone, "a ninety-four model. I believe it's past tense though -- it was totaled out. Look." He pointed. "look at it!"

Thief of Love

Sara stopped the car. They got out and walked around the wrecked car. "It can be rebuilt by a good auto body man," Sara said. She checked the out-of-county tags to make sure he was telling the truth about where he was staying.

Bobby went to the car, reached through the now missing window, withdrew a duffel bag and three pieces of beat-up, ragged army bags and dropped them on the ground.

Sara looked at him with skepticism. "You said you were living in Akron. What's with your clothes here?"

"One thing's missing," he said, ignoring her question.

"What's missing?" Sara asked, glancing around.

Bobby stomped his foot in the dirt, and slammed a fist into his opened palm. "I hope whoever has it drops dead. I bought myself a beaver hat with my state pay when I was released from prison. Me and that beaver hat go back some time and along some rough roads."

"Did you have it with you when the car crashed?" she asked.

He didn't answer. Sara thought he might be stalling, or making up a good story. "Get on with it, Bobby, okay? I have stuff to do tonight." She got in the car and waited while he loaded his luggage and climbed inside.

As they drove off, Bobby looked at Sara and half-shouted in a defiant tone. "It was stolen in Nevada by a skin-head wannabe who acted tough, but backed down when I challenged him. He ripped me off when I was down! He came back to my camp like a coward while I was sleeping."

She shook her head and asked, "Where to, Bobby -- Greyhound Bus station or homeless shelter?"

"I'm not Greyhounding it, or hanging out at a homeless shelter! I have money for a motel room. Just take me around the

Thief of Love

corner to the motel we passed a couple of minutes ago. I can get a ride in the morning. . . Thank you!" he added, his voice laced with bitterness. "I'll go to traffic court with Rob. He'll pick me up."

"How about your apartment in Akron?" Sara asked as they approached the motel.

Bobby nodded. "By golly, I'll make arrangements with my landlady, Carol McKay. Carol will keep a watch on my mailbox and hold down the fort until I can make it back. I need to get through all the court stuff first. I'll come up then, if it's all right with you, Poppins," he said his tone slipping into sarcasm. "Can I keep my stuff in your car until I get out of traffic court tomorrow? I'll check out of the motel in the morning, so I won't have a lot of time for transferring clothes around. If I could, I'd really appreciate it." He waited for her acceptance.

Sara wondered, <u>What did he bring his clothes with him for? He ignored me when I tried to impress upon him that he isn't staying at my house.</u> Another part of her guessed he might ask her for a ride back to Akron. She nodded and said, "Just make sure you call me after court. We can transfer everything and I'll take you wherever you're going."

Bobby stooped, opened his duffel bag and removed shaving cream, razor, toothpaste and brush, and deodorant, then sorted through for a change of clothes, put his stuff in a tote bag and rose, mumbling. "This is a bitch. Just what I need!"

Sara said, "Make sure you call me before noon; my shift at the plant hasn't changed."

"That'll work," he said. "I'll call you right after court, okay?"

Sara agreed to wait for his call and left for home, bombarded with thoughts of too much and too soon again -- once

Thief of Love

more contending with Bobby and his problems.

Thief of Love

Chapter 25

In the morning, Sara waited for Bobby's call. Nine o'clock passed, then ten o'clock, and eleven. She was anxious and angry by the time he finally called, at just after noon. She snapped up the phone and fairly growled into it as she said, "It's about time. Where have you been?" You know my job and schedule haven't changed. The only difference is I work for Fedron Automotive Services. AM spun Fedron off as an independent company, but, that's beside the point now, except that I'm running late because you didn't call sooner."

"Whatever," Bobby said in a bored tone. "The reason I'm calling late is I've waited all day for a public defender to counsel me. I pled not guilty in court this morning and I was given a continuance. My public defender filed a motion for me that had my recognizance bond continued. So don't worry about me; I have legal stuff to take care of today."

"What about your clothes, Bobby?"

"I'll have Rob bring me out to get them tomorrow," he said.

"I thought you were heading back to Akron this morning. Are you still going?"

Bobby ignored here comment and question, saying, "I'm fighting the charges."

Taken aback, Sara asked, "Are you prepared for that?"

"I think I can expect almost anything to happen in this state and city," he said.

"Same old, same old," Sara said. "Have a good day. You'll do great. Call me tomorrow so you can get your clothes." She disconnected and planned out her time as she hurried to get ready for work.

Thief of Love

While Sara worked a productive day, Bobby called and left a taped message on her voice mail, in which he said: "I know you're at work so I'll just leave a message. It's six o'clock. The reason I called is my attorney worked for me to participate in a D.U.I. school and an alcohol abuse treatment program. I'm in the program, so I'll call you when I get squared away. Later." He sounded like he was choking a couple of times before hanging up.

As the week passed, Bobby kept a low profile. Sara hoped he'd call so she could remove his clothes from her car. Her frustration grew as she waited and, finally, as impatience overcame her, put his things in her garage herself.

During personal time at the plant Shea Robinette came into the break room when Sara was there.

"How's your night going, Shea?" Sara asked.

"Okay. How's your week, Sara? I haven't seen you around the plant for a time." While she waited for Sara to answer, Shea fumbled through her purse and found a stick of chewing gum.

Sara engaged in herself in mental monologue, thinking, Shea doesn't have a clue as to what I'm about to tell her.

"Everything was going well up until two weeks ago, last Sunday. . ." Sara took a deep breath and hesitated.

Shea looked at Sara, eyes opened wide. "Well, what then?"

Sara exhaled, swallowed and continued, "Bobby Johnson's back in the area." Sara couldn't continue as her eyes began to mist.

"What in the Sam hell is he back in Ohio for?" Shea exclaimed in a demanding tone. "He's just like a bad quarter that keeps coming back."

Thief of Love

Sara turned her face so Shea wouldn't see her tearful discomfort, and embarrassment. "I was surprised myself he came back to Ohio, as much as he's verbally black-balled this state. He tells me he now has an efficiency apartment in Akron though."

"Does he have a job?" Shea asked.

Sara nodded. "He said he did. He told me he works as a handyman. He also told me he works off his own apartment rent. He said he had been with a traveling carnival, but lost so much weight for unknown reasons he let the carnival in Sharon, Pennsylvania, at the Anheuser Busch Beer Festival. He looks like he lost over fifty pounds. Shea, he's either doing without eating or has an illness. I think he's sick because that's how he looks -- kind of like a death-pallid look. It made me start to worry."

"Oh my Godfather!" Shea said in an outburst of rage. "He probably has full-blown AIDS. I'm sorry for you, Sara. Be careful around him; don't let him use any of your glasses or dishes -- you know, body fluids and stuff like that."

Sara's feelings plunged into despair.

Shea looked her in the eyes and continued, "Look, he deserves to have AIDS!"

Sara glanced at the wall clock. "Excuse me, Shea. We'll have to get together another time; but Bobby Johnson does not have AIDS!"

Shea shrugged, took out a hand mirror from her purse and started to repair her makeup as she said, "Well, see you later then."

After Sara returned to her department, she could hardly wait for her shift to end. She drove straight home for rest and relaxation, immediately taking her shoes off and putting her feet

Thief of Love

up on the footrest in front of her couch.

Sara remained resting in her living room for fifteen minutes before she noticed the light blinking on the telephone answering machine. With a sigh, she reached over and pushed the 'play' button. Bobby's voice promptly filled the room; but, instead of his usual feisty or confident bragging tone, he seemed almost to be weeping as he asked, "Can you come to the hospital? I . . . I . . . I . . . need you to call me at Packard Community Hospital." His tone was sad yet urgent.

Sara immediately wondered what was wrong, thinking, <u>He sounds as though he's had another accident.</u> She reached for the phone right away. When she was finally connected, Bobby answered in a near whisper.

"What's wrong, Bobby? I just found your message on my machine," Sara said.

"I can't swallow; it's the most God-awful pain. I can't even eat a light meal. I just can't swallow; the undigested food is backing up like sewer water in my throat. I had to leave rehab."

Sara didn't respond but continued to listen.

"I'm scheduled for an upper G.I. endoscopy. I was admitted into the surgery wing. In the morning, I'm scheduled for a photographic procedure of my esophagus, stomach and duodenum. So far all I really know is that something is really wrong with me. Can you please, please come?" he finally pleaded, his tone laced with frustration and fear, his voice quivering.

Sara felt a twinge of pity for Bobby and asked, "What time have they scheduled the procedure?"

"Nine a.m.," Bobby said. "Come early. I need to talk with you before I go under a sedative."

"I'll be there early for support, so don't worry, okay?"

Thief of Love

Sara said.

"Thank you for being here for me," he said. "I need you more now than ever. I'm really scared to death," Bobby concluded before they said good by and disconnected.

All the sudden stress and worry that came with Bobby's return was catching up with Sara. <u>And now this,</u> she thought.

Thief of Love

Chapter 26

As the night sounds faded into silence, Sara slipped under her covers and closed her eyes, trying to retreat from all her worry and concern for Bobby. Then the phone rang.

Sara picked up the phone and heard the voice of a woman she didn't recognize. "I need to talk to Bobby Johnson's ex-wife," the woman said, her voice catching before she concluded, "Sara Johnson, please."

Sara's reply was sharp in tone. "There is no ex-Mrs. Bobby or Robert Johnson's wife at this number."

"I'm really sorry. I thought you were married to him," the woman said.

Sara laughed aloud. "God forbid," she said. "Something serious has happened to Bobby though. Do you know what's wrong with him?"

"My son is trying to reach him at the hospital," the woman said.

Sara felt her stress level immediately rise. "I know he's in the hospital, but who are you?" she asked.

"I'm Carol McKay. I'm calling from Akron. Bobby's been living with me."

Sara bit her lip and refused to give the caller the satisfaction of a display of anger. "You're his landlady from Akron?" she asked.

Carol hesitated, then said. "I'm really sorry; I just had a feeling you could give me some information about Bobby. My son and I are worried. Bobby called and told me he was in the hospital."

"Bobby told me he had an apartment in Akron. Are you his landlady?" Sara asked again.

"How can I answer such a ridiculous question? And how can you treat Bobby so mean?" The woman's tone was bitter as she continued. "Bobby told me a lot of stuff about you."

"Like what?" Sara asked.

"That when you were together, he built you a new Cape Cod house. Is that true? You live in a 1990's vintage Cape Cod?"

All Sara could do was laugh aloud again at the idea of Bobby Johnson building her a Cape Cod house. Instead of answering such an absurd question, she asked one of her own. "How did you get to know Bobby? He's not from Ohio."

"I know; he's from California, but he's been living with me and my son as my live-in boy friend, until he took you back."

Her hands began shaking as Sara said, "Took me back? I don't believe this!" She drew in a deep breath, stifled any more outbursts and instead hung up the phone.

The rest of Sara's night was restless and troubled, but she was up early to fulfill her obligation to see Bobby.

It was between shift changes at the hospital, nearly seven a.m., so the day shift and night shift nurses were all active as Sara arrived.

As she stepped into his room, Bobby rolled over in his bed and reached out his hand for her comfort as she read the longing in his eyes. She responded and edged closer, reaching for his hand in turn.

"Try to relax, Bobby," Sara said.

At seven twenty-five a registered nurse came into the room and handed Bobby a pill and water, both in small paper cups. He was in such a rush, he nearly bobbled the water.

Then, a few moments later, a lab nurse entered the room. Bobby squeezed his eyes shut.

Thief of Love

The lab nurse began to explain. "Don't be afraid. The procedure goes quite fast. You'll most likely go to sleep immediately and probably won't even remember talking with your doctor. There will be no difficulty in your breathing during the test. Your doctor will spray your throat and you'll go to sleep almost immediately -- within seconds. The endoscope will pass through your mouth and then turn through your esophagus, duodenum, and stomach. Bobby's expression softened as she explained.

Sara could see the tranquilizer begin to take effect, and Bobby drifted into a state of being half-awake, half-asleep.

Within a few more moments, two hospital orderlies entered and wheeled Bobby out of the room, still lying in his own hospital bed. Sara followed as Bobby was transported into the procedure room, near the surgery wing.

For fifteen minutes, Sara sat in the visitor's waiting room when suddenly a door opened and Bobby's doctor -- Doctor Bakker -- entered. Sara noticed as the doctor approached that he had a strange expression on his face as he began to speak. "I found a large, ulcerated area on his esophagus." He avoided looking at Sara directly as he said, "Growing out of the ulcer is a large tumor, which has been closing off his throat." The doctor looked into Sara's eyes as he said, "In my past experience as a doctor, I found that we're looking at a metastasized cancer of the esophagus.

The word 'cancer' sent a shockwave through Sara. She recalled the sequence of suspicions she held up until the doctor revealed this terrible news. <u>Two and a half years ago I met Bobby. I suspected he had an illness. I took him for a medical checkup. He was constantly spitting phlegm into a cup. This pain and suffering persisted even after he was diagnosed as</u>

having a stomach ulcer.

"Oh my God!" Sara finally said, then asked, "Will this take his life?"

In a somber tone, Doctor Bakker said, "The cancer is advanced. I find it hard to understand how this wasn't treated two and a half years ago. He may have had a successful treatment if it had been found then. In my professional opinion, it will probably take his life.

"It's all in God's hands," Sara said.

Doctor Bakker nodded. "And it's all in our hands -- the medical profession's -- to help perform that miracle. I'll meet with a team of doctors this afternoon to start an aggressive treatment program. For now, I've ordered a CAT scan."

Sara said, "Thank you, doctor. Bobby's not from Ohio. I have to call his family."

Doctor Bakker nodded, gave Sara a small wave, turned and went back toward the procedure room.

Sara spotted a pay phone across the hall as Doctor Bakker left. She hurried over to the phone and with some nervous fumbling with coins and buttons, called southern California.

The phone rang several times. The delay with no answer after each ring was disheartening, draining Sara of much needed strength just when she wanted someone to lean on. After six rings, a woman whose voice Sara didn't recognize answered the call.

"I need to talk to Betty Stine," Sara said.

"This is Betty Stine," the woman told her.

"I'm sorry, I didn't recognize your voice, Aunt Betty. It's been a while, I know, but I need to discuss something very important with you."

"Well, who am I speaking with?" Aunt Betty asked.

Thief of Love

"This is Sara Bringard, from Ohio -- Bobby Johnson's friend. I was at your house last summer. Remember me?"

"I remember you," Aunt Betty said, her tone colder now.

Sara continued without delay, before Aunt Betty might decide to disconnect. "Some things happened today. I don't like to be the one to tell you, but you'll have to prepare yourself for a crisis. I was just given a bad medical report about your nephew."

"Where is Robbie?" Aunt Betty asked.

"He's at Packard Community Hospital, in Sandusky. He just went through an upper G.I. endoscopy and I was told he has malignant cancer of the esophagus."

"Am I hearing you correctly?" Aunt Betty asked, then repeated the word: "Cancer? Robbie has cancer?"

"Yes," Sara said, "I was told by a specialist."

"Cancer! It can't be true," Aunt Betty said, adding, "I need to talk to his doctor. I hope his suffering isn't bad. I can't bear the thought. I'll talk to Bryan and Megan about this, and I do hope you keep us posted."

Sara agreed; they said their good-byes. After the conversation, Sara went back to Bobby's hospital room, dazed and broken now as she sat and waited for him to return.

Two hours after the endoscopy procedure, Bobby was brought back in. He lay in silence, staring as if through the far wall.

Then, after a few moments, Bobby suddenly broke the silence with the declaration, "I'm going to die," in a bitter tone. "The cancer has traveled into my bones."

Sara shook her head slowly. "You don't know that for sure." She worked hard to get the next words out. "Have faith in God. He can heal you."

There was a long silence. Then Bobby closed his eyes

Thief of Love

and said, "I can't beat the odds, even with God's help. When I left California, I just knew I put the past, with prison and Vietnam, behind me; but I have a dark cloud following me over my life. You'll never be my wife, nor will we have a long life together. It's over! I'm a dying man!"

Sara wondered if she could be a strong enough person to be there for Bobby as a friend, and didn't know how she could get through it all.

Noticing that Bobby had fallen asleep, Sara left the room, walked down to the gift shop and began to peruse the card selections, reading verses in the cards that spoke of dreams of the future, and her mood darkened. There was no card she could find to bring Bobby encouragement. <u>God only knows where Bobby will be next year at this time,</u> Sara thought; and, with that realization, she thanked God that He had given them a little more time to be together. She then silently vowed she'd spend as much time as she could with Bobby.

Throughout the day, Sara cried softly and often had to leave Bobby's room to regain her composure. She didn't want him to see her weaken.

About five thirty, Doctor Bakker entered Bobby's room, accompanied by a tall, dark-haired man in a fashionable business suit. A registered nurse followed.

The well-dressed man stationed himself next to Bobby's bed as Doctor Bakker said, "Robert, I'm here with Doctor Richard Crawford, who's an oncologist. He'll be part of our team of doctors working closely with you. Another doctor -- Doctor Roshon -- has ordered a small tissue sample -- a biopsy."

There was silence from Bobby, who wasn't familiar with medical terminology. Doctor Crawford examined Bobby while the nurse set up an easel nearby, upon which she posted film of

Thief of Love

Bobby's CAT scan photo.

In silence, Sara and Bobby studied the photos of the protruded tumor, which showed as a filmy area. Bobby worked his jaw slowly as he looked, then winced, but whether from pain or the sight of the cancer growing within him, or both, Sara couldn't know, and dared not ask.

* * *

With the exception of the following days of Bobby's hospital stay, Sara wasn't aware that the coming weeks would be the most difficult in her life.

On the fourth day, between lunch and dinner, Bobby was released from the hospital with a prescription for the pain medication ibuprofen, with the narcotic pain suppressant codeine added.

On the way home from the hospital, Bobby asked Sara to stop at the liquor store for a fifth of Black Velvet. She did so, and took him to her house, where, as the long day finally drew to a close, she was now willing to let him spend the night.

Sleep for Sara proved impossible. Bobby lay awake, choking and coughing. He was up and down, back and forth to the kitchen, gulping down straight glasses of whiskey. Sara couldn't really comprehend the indescribable depths of his pain, but she certainly realized that a sleepless night lay ahead for both of them.

In the middle of the night, Sara crept down the hallway and tentatively knocked on Bobby's door. He didn't answer her knock, but she heard his rasping cries and loud moans. She returned to her room and snapped on the light switch. A glance at the clock showed her it was one thirty a.m. Thinking something was probably wrong with Bobby, Sara rushed back to his room and pushed the door open. Bobby was thrashing in the bed, sweat covering his face and bare chest.

Sara hurried to the bathroom, removed a clean towel from the shelf, and ran cold water on it. She returned to his bedside where he lay suffering and stayed there for him, sponging his face, neck and chest. The pain suppressant pills didn't seem to be lessening Bobby's agonies.

"Can I call the rescue squad for you, Bobby?" Sara asked, adding, "You need a pain shot; then you'll be able to manage better if you do go to the hospital."

"No," he said, his voice low and his words almost mumbled. "Don't do that."

Sara could see that he was undergoing another wave of pain as the muscles around his mouth tightened.

For the next half hour, Sara encouraged Bobby to go to the hospital again. He finally agreed and, on his own, managed to get up out of bed. Within an hour, they were at the hospital emergency room.

Once inside, Bobby received immediate attention. The intern on duty made late-night morning call to Doctor Crawford's home, and Bobby's prescription was changed to doses of liquid morphine.

By two thirty, Sara had put Bobby back in his bed, resting, hoping to find the hours till daybreak without pain.

Sara tried to rest herself, but, before the sun rose, she was drawn back to where he lay in bed.

Bobby's breathing became erratic and labored, and Sara gave him another dose from his morphine prescription, but it seemed to barely help.

A tear ran down Bobby's cheek, then another, and more as he began to cry, still sweating profusely. Once again, Sara convinced him he needed to see the doctor for further observation.

When they arrived at the hospital, Doctor Crawford was busy, but compassionate, and worked Bobby in between regular appointments.

Sara sat with Bobby in the waiting room. Bobby was called into Doctor Crawford's office within twenty minutes, and Sara went with him. When Doctor Crawford entered, Bobby began to cry again, begging for relief. Doctor Crawford patted him on the shoulder and proceeded to check his blood pressure and vitals.

"We want to keep you as comfortable and pain free as we can. Robert. I'm changing your prescription to Dilaudid, a painkiller commonly prescribed to cancer patients. The drug will relax your breathing, and it won't be too long to take effect. Your pain will be managed very soon." The doctor paused, then added, "Dilaudid is a class four narcotic. You'll have no driving privileges because your judgment and reflexes will be affected. You may lose sleep for days, along with a burst of energy. These are the major side effects of the drug."

"I won't drive," Bobby said. "Just give me something strong enough to help me deal with this God-awful pain," he pleaded.

"Robert, there is a very serious thing you must be aware of while you're taking Dilaudid. You need to be careful where you keep your pills. Drug addicts could steal them from you, so be careful who you're around. These are not street pills."

Bobby nodded.

Doctor Crawford continued. "I'll write you a prescription for one hundred Dilaudid capsules. Fill it today. Cancer services will pay for them. I'll give you the number to call."

After the consultation and treatment, the discussion

centered around resources to pay medical bills.
"What medical coverage do you have?"
Bobby shook his head. "Only V.A."
Sara spoke up with her own plan for a course of action. "I'll take Bobby to get his benefits started -- V.A., Social Security and Medicaid, sometime this week."
Doctor Crawford looked toward Sara, nodded and said, "As this moves along, hospice funding will pay doctor bills and pay for all Robert's medicine, like painkillers." He turned toward Bobby. "Cancer services will pay for your prescriptions out of United Way funding. Robert, I want you to start with your radiation therapy right away. Doctor Littlejohn is expecting you. I have you scheduled for tomorrow." He wrote the phone number, address, and time schedule on some notepaper and handed the sheet to Bobby as he added, "We're going to shrink the tumor down so you can swallow again."
By day's end, the painkiller took effect and Bobby's suffering eased. Rejuvenated, Bobby puttered around through the house in high gear -- washing walls, doors, cleaning windows and continually moving as though he would never stop and never go to sleep for the night.
Finally, at two a.m., Bobby sat on the living room couch and began drawing on a piece of paper with a pencil. After all his hyperactivity, Sara was more exhausted than Bobby -- she was tired, apprehensive, sleepy and uptight. Bobby hadn't eaten all day or slept for far into the night. The new painkiller made him more comfortable, but the side effects were a new issue.
The next day, about ten a.m., the day's agenda started with an appointment with a Social Security specialist. The following day was spent at Veteran's Administration Services, where Bobby took in his army discharge papers, Medicaid

Thief of Love

papers, and a CAT scan photo of the tumor on his esophagus, which guaranteed that a rush was put on the processing of his claim.

At the beginning of Bobby's interview with the specialist to consider his eligibility for Social Security benefits, Bobby was asked for an employment history, and she called up his records, to which she would refer back on the computer screen at her work station. Sara could see the display, which read: Universal Studios as a grip, nine months; window cleaner in Orange County, three years; semi-truck driver, six months. His official working contributions added up to a total of four years, while the carnival work was under the table -- work not performed as a Social Security taxpayer.

If eligible, Bobby's disability benefit would be S.S.I. -- Social Supplement Insurance. He didn't qualify for regular Social Security benefits because of his apparent lack of work. During the interview, Bobby never even mentioned his ex-wife or his sons. Sara wondered why.

By the time the Social Security specialist left the room for a moment, Sara was confused.

"Why haven't you given her any information on your ex-wife?" she asked. "Or why haven't you given out any information on your three sons? You know, they'll be eligible if you are. They can draw from your benefits, I'm sure."

He answered right away. "If I wanted to include them, I would. That would be my choice, but I choose not to give them any part of this. My sons aren't deserving."

"Why aren't they deserving?" Sara asked.

"They disowned me," Bobby said, "when I went to prison."

At this point, Sara totally believed, and was still clinging

Thief of Love

to his lies and the delusion that he had previously been married and had three biological sons. She realized now, after all the questions and all the answers, that if he had a wife and three sons, their social security numbers would have shown up on the computer. Sara knew she had been deceived again.

The week was full of running back and forth with all the necessary information required to get the process started for Bobby's claims.

From all the running around and taking care of papers, they both were worn out and uptight by the next office visit with Doctor Crawford. Bobby wore creased jeans and a turtleneck underneath his flannel shirt, with his usual Western look.

While they waited, Bobby took out a notepad and pencil. He sat scribbling, head and eyes down, when Doctor Crawford came in the room. Doctor Crawford looked toward Sara and they exchanged a smile. He looked at Bobby again. Bobby continued to scribble.

"How is the pain management, now that you're taking Dilaudid?"

"What pain?" Bobby asked, adding, "I can't feel a damn thing!"

"You can't?" Doctor Crawford seemed surprised, and confused.

"Even my pee-pee doesn't feel anything. It doesn't get hard anymore."

Bobby's dry sense of humor drew laughter from Doctor Crawford. "You look rather sporty today, Bobby," Doctor Crawford said, still smiling.

"I know I do!" Bobby said as he continued to scribble on the notepad.

Sara looked up. "This is the Robert Johnson, Doctor

Thief of Love

Crawford -- his behavior as usual. He puts his ego and sense of humor out there every opportunity he can, at any cost!"

"So what?" Bobby asked, continuing to scribble.

After the visit with the doctor, Sara took Bobby to her house, then went on to work. But she found it difficult to concentrate on her job. Her thoughts revolved around Bobby and the other questions on her mind. That night at the plant, hoping to find daybreak and safety, she was hit with an amalgam of emotions -- surprise, pride, sadness, and remorse.

Thief of Love

Chapter 27

Early on Monday, Sara packed Bobby's tote bag and they left for the hospital, with his attitude now stressed with the will to survive.

As he began intravenous chemotherapy, Bobby vomited profusely the first two days. He also suffered from a loss of balance, even if he just tried to walk to the bathroom, and was too dizzy to stand for a long time. But still, even with the treatments, he continued to lose a pound a day.

Although Sara found it burdensome, seeing him so sick, she did her best to be pleasant and sympathetic. She realized his care would be a heavy burden as his cancer advanced, and it weighed on her mind. Sara knew Bobby should be with his family instead of with her, so she called Aunt Betty.

"I'm not so sure I can take all this with Bobby. He's in the hospital, and they've started his first aggressive chemotherapy." Sara told her.

"Yes, we know all about it," Aunt Betty said. "He's receiving treatment for five days of aggressive intravenous chemotherapy, right? He called to let us know, and also gave us the hospital phone number."

"He's too hard to take! It's too much for me. Can you people come get him? I don't want to watch him die," Sara said in a pleading tone.

Aunt Betty dodged the question. "Robbie is capable of making decisions, Sara. I'm sure if he weren't competent, he'd be placed in a nursing home by his cancer specialist."

"That's only partly true. If you were here, Aunt Betty, you could see for yourself what I have to deal with. He sits for hours scribbling on a notepad in a state of perpetual motion without turning the page, or he washes walls in the same spot. He's just too much for me. My nerves are frazzled. He won't sleep. He's awake day and night -- hyper, jumpy, and really mean."

They continued to talk for some time, but the conversation ended without any hint of productive help from California.

About noon, the same day, Shea Robinette called. "Why haven't you been at work, Sara? I haven't seen you in the break room lately."

Sara sighed and said, "Shea, I've put in so much time and energy lately with Bobby -- taking him to his appointments with medical, veteran's benefits and Social Security. For now, I've taken personal leave from the plant. With some of these people I have to deal with, taking him to all these appointments has really stressed me out. The salaried director, Tully Washburn, from cancer services, who gets paid by donations from United Way funding, has no sensitivity for the friends and family of cancer patients when we have to come for help for a requisition or a prescription to be signed for United Way assistance.

"She makes our appointments for nine a.m., for example, but doesn't arrive until eleven. She stops to shop at the mall on her way in from Huron, fifteen minutes away. So the Easter Seals lady gives me a seat to wait in her office until the pokey bitch comes on the scene. When she arrives and finally sees Bobby, she makes a big phony scene as though she cares about him. He's vulnerable and can't see what she's all about," Sara said.

"I wonder if all the cancer patients have to put up with such an inconsiderate bitch," Shea said, adding, "If I were you, Sara, I'd call the veteran's home and get a professional, paid service to take care of him. He's not your husband, your brother or your relative. Get him out of your house, out of your life. He's costing you lost wages, and a lot more."

"It's hard for me to do that, Shea -- to watch this man who once was so full of life and vigor living his last days so helpless and vulnerable. I'm hoping his veteran's benefits or his Social Security speed up. Then he'll have money to pay for a room of his own. I've asked him, Shea, to consider going back to California, and he refused, of course. I also pointed out to him that when he passes on, his place is with his family."

"What did he say?" Shea asked.

"Get ready for this one, Shea! He told me they're Jewish, and with their deep religious practices, wouldn't have any part in burying him. Ultra-orthodox Rabbis control all the laws of family life, he said. So I called his Aunt Betty, and she gave me some friendly family advice, which was to keep him here till he dies. Veterans bury their fellows who have no one to take care of their burial needs. My emotions are tied up and wrung out. He has no appetite since they started shooting the radiation. He's lost most of his muscle mass, his skin sags and hangs on him, and he has the night sweats."

"How many treatments has he had?" Shea asked.

"Thirty, with one aggressive series of chemo-intravenous inpatient treatment, which has been a nightmare too. After treatment, he vomits and trips all over, and after I encouraged him to go live at the veteran's home, he reacted very disturbingly toward me. He started to leave threatening, intimidating notes around like, `Make me leave, bitch, you're dead', or `Bitch, I'm coming back to haunt you when I'm dead.'"

"When will he go back for chemo treatments?" Shea asked.

Thief of Love

"Next week, on Monday," Sara said.

Shea hesitated, then said, "Sara, if I were you, I'd just dump him at the hospital, and when they release him they'll have no other alternative than to put him in a nursing home if you don't pick him up. His cancer will spread and progress. Let's face it: he's a dying man. Cancer travels; he'll be bedridden. Do you want to put diapers on him, or wipe his butt?"

"Shea, I just can't bring myself to do that. He still has the will to live. The radiation therapy has been successful; the tumor has shrunk down, and he can swallow. I'm awaiting his V.A. disability benefits, then he'll be able to pay his own way in his own apartment."

Shea said, "You better do something, Sara, before you find a dead man lying in your bed. You know the Jewish burial practices? Traditionally, Jewish people do not embalm their dead; they wrap the body up in a white sheet."

"What?" Sara asked, adding, "Bobby's not Jewish, even though his family is. There's no support from California, or Phoenix, from his sister Megan. She'll send a card, and once in a while will call. But Bobby calls them often. He places the calls from my telephone and charges them to me. I called his Aunt Betty and had a one-on-one conversation with her from my heart, and she just said if he dies, leave him here. They wouldn't bury him or have any other Jewish person eulogizing his funeral. Anyway, I would never just wrap Bobby in a sheet! If I made the decisions for Bobby's funeral, he'd be buried in a suit and placed in a casket."

Shea said, "If I didn't detest the man so much, I could feel sorry for him; but there is no way on earth, for love or money, that $\underline{I}$ would allow this to continue! Just call the V.A. and get rid of him, now!"

Thief of Love

Sara thought about placing Bobby in a convalescent hospital, and it lay heavy on her mind until the next day. But, prompted by Shea's reasoning, she called Veteran's Administration Services, explaining, "This is Robert Johnson's caregiver. Things around here are getting to the point that Robert is a hardship on me. I can no longer deal with the responsibility or take care of him. Can you please find him a cottage on the veteran's property or at the dormitory so he can establish residence there?"

The benefits clerk, a Mrs. Thompson, paused and said. "If this is your choice, then you must stay determined, with the will to see this through. As long as Robert is able to walk, bathe himself and eat at the table, he's eligible for placement immediately at our government facility. However, if he's going to take that step, I would advise that he would be making a decision based on this informed choice. If he lingers on with his illness, puts it off and doesn't recover, we'll have to put him on the list to be placed in our veteran's hospital, and he'll have a long wait. The list for vets in Ohio awaiting a hospital bed is nine months. My advice for him would be to take up residence now. Later on he may not get in here."

"I'll talk with him tonight about this. Thank you for your time," Sara said, adding, "I'll get back with you later."

Thief of Love

Chapter 28

During the first part of his illness, Bobby had been isolated, but began interacting with other cancer patients in support groups like "New Beginnings"; and he resumed watching TV. Soon, Bobby began to perk up, and to spend time away from the house. Sara questioned a few things, such as the sudden disconnections when she would answer her telephone.

One night, a phone call came in at midnight. "Who would be calling so late at night?" Sara asked Bobby while they sat on the living room sofa watching TV.

"I'll answer the phone!" Bobby half-shouted, rushing to pick up the kitchen phone.

Sara drifted into the kitchen, lingering at the refrigerator and trying to eavesdrop, giving the appearance of bewildered innocence.

Bobby turned his head away and spoke in a low tone.

With a shake of her head, Sara regarded the episode as a waste time and energy, and she returned to the living room.

A few minutes later, Bobby returned to the sofa and looked out the picture window into the night. A moment passed, then another. Bobby rose in silence, went to the front door and walked out into the night, closing it firmly behind him.

Sara too rose and followed, waited at the door and looked outside to see where he went. A small station wagon pulled up, facing the house two lots down. Bobby stepped out of the shadows and went toward the parked car. Sara watched as Bobby leaned down and had a conversation with the driver for about ten minutes before he stepped back and the station wagon drove away.

Sara went back inside and closed the door, and when

Thief of Love

Bobby returned he glanced away from her. He kept silent as he walked through the house to the bedroom where he could be alone. Sara sat on the sofa, returned to her thoughts for a while and then went to bed.

The next morning when she awoke, Sara immediately headed to Bobby's room, and found a note taped to the door. It read:

'Don't make me leave. I'm afraid to die alone.
I need you, baby, Please, don't make me go.
I want to die with you at my side, in our
house. I love you. Bobby.'

Later that day, much to Sara's surprise, Bobby remained absent after his radiation therapy. He wasn't at the doctor's when she went to pick him up, so she scouted around. He wasn't at the 'New Beginnings' support group or the E-Z Does It nightclub either. On her way to work, Sara took an alternative way, selecting a detour away from downtown. She passed Perkins Plaza, and crossed Columbus Avenue when, seconds later, she saw Bobby leaving an electronics shop, having a hard time carrying a box the size of a VCR machine.

A light-colored Ford Escort wagon parked in in front of the store. Sara couldn't catch a glimpse of the driver and, to her surprise, Bobby suddenly got into the station wagon, and the driver pulled out into traffic and sped past Sara's car. Briefly, she made eye contact with the driver, whom she recognized at once.

"Oh, no! It's Mark Shephard!" Sara exclaimed as she saw the driver, and her heart lurched. Mark Shephard was a notorious drug addict and small-time dealer who had once worked at her plant and been fired for drug abuse and failure to complete any rehabilitation programs, before the union

Thief of Love

intervened and got him reinstated, with one more chance to go through rehab.

In the instant he drove past, Sara could clearly see Mark's eyes dilated to pin holes as he wiped perspiration from his face with his sleeve. Then she realized: Bobby had been coming up with money for incidental things. Could it be possible, she wondered, that he was selling his pain pills? The pills were disappearing too quickly after each prescription. She'd been monitoring his pills and noticed that he had three prescriptions, with twenty-five pills missing from the first.

Overcome with anger, Sara she sped home and emptied the dresser in the guest bedroom where Bobby was staying, then went to the garage where most of his clothes were sitting in the corner in his beat-up army duffel bags. Within a few moments, all his belongings were out the door. The thought of him selling his pain pills at her house enraged her further, and, too upset to perform well at work, she called in sick.

After about an hour passed, at around four thirty, there was a knock at the door. Without an instant of hesitation, Sara marched to the door, wrenched it open and shouted at the completely surprised and startled Bobby, "I want you and your narcotics out of my house!"

Taken aback for only an instant, he smirked and ignored her, stepped around her and walked past into the house.

Utterly surprised, Sara stood in shock for a moment, then turned and followed bobby into the living room, saying, "You caused me to miss work again. No, dope pusher, you're not staying here anymore. I've monitored your pills -- three prescriptions, and I've discovered twenty-five gone from your pill vial within three hours after I brought your first prescription to the house. Why are you sneaking around with a known drug

Thief of Love

addict? I know why: You're selling narcotics."

Bobby was visibly trembling as he said, "You're wrong -- totally wrong. Just as I left the hospital I saw Mark parked in the middle of the street. He was out of gas."

"Sure, Bobby -- right! What a coincidence. Just at the same time you were leaving the hospital, you walked past, balancing yourself with your three-pronged cane. It brings to mind an old country song, `Just walk on by. Meet me on the corner.'"

"I'll pay you half my money, for room and board. I. . . I . . . I have close to two thousand dollars hidden."

"No! You won't cut me a deal with your dope money. Didn't you get my message? You can't stay here anymore. You're nuts for selling your pain medication."

Overcome with anger, Sara dashed into the kitchen, snatched up the phone and pushed 911 for an emergency call. Bobby tried to stop here, stepping toward her and grabbing the phone cord, pulling it from the wall outlet. Weak and wobbly, he fell into a chair, one leg hanging over the side, still clutching the phone cord.

Responding to the 911 call, five minutes later, two deputy sheriffs entered Sara's house unannounced and went directly into the kitchen. The older deputy came toward Sara and Bobby. The younger officer stood in the doorway and they both watched Bobby as he sat crookedly in the chair, leg still hanging over the side, as he lay lopsided.

Sara immediately said, "I want this man, Robert Johnson, out of my house. He's only a guest here. This is not his residence."

Bobby squirmed, then worked himself onto his feet, smiling and trying to appear innocent as he said, "I love the hell out of this woman, officer, even though she doesn't want me anymore. You see, officer, I have cancer of the esophagus. I'm going to die soon, and now she wants me out."

Sara's stomach tightened as she said, "Don't try to make me look like a creep. Tell the officers the truth. You've been gone from Ohio for nearly a year. I left you off at a carnival in Paso Robles, California, and came back alone, but you found your way into my home uninvited, afflicted with cancer! I gave you support and help.

"You told me you rented an apartment in Akron, Ohio, then you delayed returning to Akron. I considered your motives, as one delay after another prevented your leaving. By the way, your live-in from Akron called here while you were in the hospital -- Janet, your landlady you made it with!

"I spent six weeks of my personal time away from my job, taking you from doctor to hospital over to Veterans Administration Services and to Social Security, trying to help you with your medical needs and resources for disability benefits."

Sara looked at the officers and continued, "Look at my phone; he ripped the cord from the wall outlet. Now he refuses to leave. He has one problem after another delaying his exit from Sandusky."

The officers exchanged glances.

"He can't stay any longer," Sara said.

Bobby sat, putting his hands on his chest, trying to appear weak and innocent.

The older officer said, "Let's just step outside peacefully, Robert."

Sara said, "Officer, those are his clothes on the front steps."

Thief of Love

Bobby frowned and said, "Get me outta here. I'm a liability to society. Get me out of her house. Take me to the Volunteers of America homeless shelter."

The older deputy took Bobby by the arm and eased him to his feet as he said, "We're in sympathy with your medical problems, Robert, but you must leave now. The lady wants you out of her house. We're taking you to a homeless shelter, downtown."

The younger deputy told Sara, "We're taking him. If he comes back, call."

Sara's face creased with worry as the deputies took Bobby outside; voice trailing as he left, tears in his eyes as he said, "Take me to the V.A. shelter." He wobbled, holding onto his cane, to the police cruiser and climbed into the back. Moments later, they drove off.

Thief of Love

Chapter 29

By midmorning the next day, Sara felt the surges of conflicting emotions as, in despair, she considered calling Bobby's sister, Megan, in Phoenix, then finally made the call.

At first Megan came on as a concerned family member, saying, "I haven't spent much time with Robbie over the last ten years. I can only recall moments from our childhood. Even with the memories, I can't say I know him very well. He's nine years older than me, but I do know he's very emotional. Robbie did call me a lot and share his concern and feelings about dealing with cancer and death.

Robbie was adopted by our Jewish family, but he hasn't adopted our Jewish beliefs. Before I was born, my parents received legal custody rights when he was eight, after his biological parents were killed when a drunk driver crashed into them. Robbie's last name -- Johnson -- was kept, although our name is Stine. Robbie's father worked as a delivery man in our father's -- Stine's Furniture -- store in L.A. I guess my parents had gratitude for his father's labor. Robbie was taught the Jewish culture and our customs of faith. But Robbie was ashamed of being raised Jewish, especially in southern California. He didn't respect the customs we held dear. Even at a young age, I was struck by my parents' grief.

When Robbie reached his teen years, he gloried in California's sunshine and the lure of the street people living in California's fastest lanes, until he was drafted into the army and went off to war, still with his mental problems. He should never have experienced Vietnam.

After he was discharged from the armed forces, his mental

problems grew greater and deeper. Though Robbie intentionally would never hurt anyone, he always put himself out on the front lines for his friends and family and even people he didn't know. He had proved that; he was given a medal for saving another soldier's life. Robbie always saw the poor, drug addicts and alcoholics as people who deserved respect and dignity at times when they didn't really deserve it. Most of those people were ungrateful lowlifes.

Whatever was done, though, my parents felt sorry for him losing his real parents so young. But Robbie learned not to appreciate things he didn't have to work for. He saw life through rose-colored glasses, with my parents giving him too many material things."

Sara said, "I ended our two-year relationship last summer by leaving him at a fair in Paso Robles, California. Things happened, and eight months later, he came back to me sick; but that doesn't change my human obligation to him, although it's getting to be too much for me. I believe Bobby's place is with his family."

Megan replied, "Our family grieves over him, and believes he should stay in Sandusky where there's a lovely veteran's home, and Bobby can enjoy the company of other retired vets."

Sara said, "I've tried to persuade him to return to California with his family. He wouldn't listen to me. He's changed since taking all the painkillers in very high doses. I don't know if I can take much more of the stress and worry he's put on me! I had him put out last night by the sheriff. Bobby is criminal-minded, and he's not capable of any rational decision making."

"What do you mean?" Megan asked in a flat voice.

Thief of Love

"It may not be easy for you, hearing this about your brother, Megan; and it may be hard for you to comprehend, although I have facts to substantiate it -- he's selling his hydromorphone pills to a known drug addict. I also have a strong suspicion that he's doing more than drug trafficking."

Megan scoffed with a sigh.

Sara continued, "Bobby walks around really hyper, with a three-pronged cane balancing him from a fall, but he moves fast. I think if I were to pinch him he wouldn't feel it. I believe his brain is numb from the pills, or something stronger!"

"This story sounds calculated and orchestrated. I'll tell you what I intend to do," Megan said in an angry tone. "I have Robbie's cancer specialist's name and phone number, and I personally can assure you of one thing -- I'll bring other people into this. I'll call his oncologist, without talking to you any further about Robbie's record, troubled aspects or family ties. I feel this is a private family matter -- personal. This conversation hasn't accomplished anything for you! I'm busy. Goodbye." She disconnected.

Sara called Bobby's cancer specialist, presenting herself tactfully. She didn't want to give Doctor Crawford any indication that Bobby was selling his narcotics and then substituting them with a lesser painkiller such as Percoset, Darvosette, or Tylenol with codeine. Sara knew the past trauma Bobby had suffered and wanted him to remain pain-free.

"Hello,' Sara said in an urgent tone, "Bobby Johnson isn't at my house anymore, Doctor Crawford. He's living with a street hustler -- a throwback from the hippie days -- a doper." She didn't tell Doctor Crawford Bobby was selling his pills. "I called to tell you about my suspicions about Bobby's pills being abused."

Thief of Love

Sara didn't know then that Bobby was one step ahead of her, already leaving a message at the doctor's office that implied Sara was stalking him, and stating he didn't want her in his personal life.

Taking a deep breath, Doctor Crawford seemed to realize Sara may be giving him solid information.

"You better watch him with those pills," Sara continued. "Bobby's taking too many at one time, and I'm afraid he could overdose."

Doctor Crawford said, "Robert has called for prescription refills. He informed me that he lost a prescription on a plane coming back from California. Later, he's called at different times with different excuses."

"Bobby hasn't been on a plane. He's being taken advantage of by unscrupulous characters in his affliction and vulnerable situation. I can't tolerate that," Sara said.

Although Doctor Crawford didn't say so, Sara could tell from his tone that his suspicions were aroused by Bobby repeatedly claiming he'd lost his pain pills.

Thief of Love

Chapter 30

As Sara waited for Shea to come over and help plan a function at the plant celebrating the fall production season ending, the doorbell rang. When she opened the door, Sara saw a woman whom she had never met before.

"Hi! I'm Bonnie Bennett, with a personal message for you today. Nice to see you, Sara," Bonnie said.

"You know me?" Sara asked.

"I know of you," Bonnie replied. "You don't know me, but I know of you."

The strange woman had a friendly smile. She was dressed hippie-style -- in jeans, flannel shirt and tennis shoes. Her hair was long, straight and dark, and parted in the middle.

Sara hesitated for a moment, then asked, "What's your message?"

"I have a deal to make with you regarding a friend of yours."

"Come on in," Sara invited, adding, "but I have a prior commitment. What's this about, anyway?" Sara asked, escorting Bonnie into the kitchen and seating her at the kitchen table so they could discuss the matter at hand. She glanced at the clock, wondering when Shea would arrive -- it was already ten thirty.

Then Bonnie dropped the bombshell. "I was sent here by a dealer, and he needs to make a connection with Bobby Johnson. His plans are to eliminate the middleman, Marcus Siebert. Do you know him?" Bonnie asked.

Sara was unsure of what might happen, so she decided to play along while concealing as much as possible. "There's little I know about him. Perhaps I could be more helpful if I knew what this was about," Sara said.

"Marcus is ripping Bobby off. You do know Marcus Siebert?" she asked again.

"I do," Sara answered bluntly, "but only through association. I met him a year ago at the hospital when his father was fighting cancer for his life. His father shared a hospital room with Bobby."

Sara thought for a moment, then asked, "What do you mean, Marcus is ripping Bobby off?"

"This is the deal," Bonnie said. "For three, number four Dilaudid, I'll make a direct connection. There's something you should know, if you aren't already aware of the situation Bobby is involved in," she continued. "Marcus and Bobby are wholesaling Bobby's Dilaudid -- twenty pills off the top as soon as his script is filled and dispensed."

Sara mulled over the conversation, and was optimistic, considering Bonnie a drug informant, maybe wearing a tape recorder for a drug investigation.

"Marcus is wholesaling twenty of his Dilaudid for three hundred dollars, while Bobby gets only fifteen for one pill. He's ripping Bobby off royally and Bobby isn't even on to his game."

"I know Bobby's not as street smart as he thinks he is," Sara said. "He's easily influenced by friends with rebellious behavior," she added, "and now he's afraid of dying. I guess he's reaching out for a friend, no matter what the cost. I do know this: Bobby was a softy in his healthier days. I've personally seen him being used."

Bonnie seemed to want the pills badly, and she brought up the drug deal again. "For just for three, number fours, I'll get Bobby together with the dealer, Elmore -- you don't need to know his last name. They both know about each other, even though Marcus keeps them apart. Bobby's losing money," she said, "and Elmore wants to deal with Bobby directly."

Sara thought, I can turn them all in to the drug task force of the Sandusky Police Department without any regret. Then again, she knew Bobby had been coached by Marcus to protect the supply of narcotics rather than to cooperate with the drug task force in putting the drug addict hustlers away. So why bother? she thought.

For the next hour, Bonnie tried diligently to persuade Sara to talk with Bobby about the money he would be have. Sara scoffed silently, aware that even if she had been inclined to become involved with drug dealers, a setup like this with these people would mean Bobby wouldn't be ahead at all, without his pain managed.

At eleven thirty, Shea Robinette finally arrived, ready for planning the celebration and union events. When Sara saw Shea coming through the door, she livened up. She always drew energy from Shea's company.

Shea came into the kitchen carrying a cassette tape recorder, briefcase, and demo tapes, including those of local Country and Western bands.

"Hi," Shea said to Sara's visitor before they were introduced. As always, Sara gave Shea the scoop of the day, the agenda, and her conversation with Bonnie, to bring Shea up to speed about the purpose of the woman's visit.

Shea became controversial immediately. "It's like playing Russian Roulette," she said. "Most of the cylinders don't have bullets and most people won't get killed, but some will; and some will go to jail for these drug deals."

"But there's money in it," Bonnie argued. "Bobby Johnson is losing three hundred dollars for every twenty DiLaudid Marcus deals."

Thief of Love

The subject of money set Shea's mind reeling, as always. Money talked, and Shea always felt she wanted to be in control of decisions made about money.

"He's losing money?" Shea asked Bonnie, then turned toward Sara and said, "You best relay the message so Bobby can decide for himself if he wants to deal directly with the dope man." She turned to Bonnie again and asked, "Has Bobby sold his prescriptions to any other drug addicts or dope dealers?"

Bonnie jerked her head up and stared ahead of her, looking put off by the words, 'Drug addict' and 'dope dealer.'

"We don't like to be called drug addicts or dope dealers. We're 'users,' okay? To answer your question though: Marcus is using at least half a script after they wholesale twenty pills to Elmore. I'll take that back. Sandy, a stripper over at the Quarters Tee House, gets her freebies. She's a dancing lady there Wednesday through Saturday. She stops off about seven thirty daily on the way to work for a free buzz."

<u>No wonder he goes without his pills so often,</u> Sara thought, and she lowered her head till her chin touched to her chest. Her eyes closed with sadness, then she opened them in embarrassment. She looked at Shea and caught her wearing a smile of pleasure and enjoyment. Shea knew Bobby was a womanizer, even up to his last living days.

"Bobby gets Sandy high on pills?" Sara asked.

"Why not!" Bonnie asked in reply, saying, "Sandy uses top- shelf drugs. She likes D's, and heroin too! But then again, we all do. The closest place to buy heroin is Toledo, but T-town is too far away. When you have money to get high who wants to wait when you need a buzz? You want a fix right now -- no waiting. You have money, you go buy at the closest drug house. Sandy uses her tip money from her customers and goes directly

Thief of Love

to the dope man. Just the thought of dope -- feeling the rush coursing through your veins -- you can't wait. You get sick to your stomach if you don't get high."

"She's on heroin?" Sara asked, "and Bobby's pills too? What does she look like anyway?"

"She's tough," Bonnie said. "You can see for yourself any night at the Quarters Tee House. You can't miss her or have a hard time with finding her in a line-up because she's the tallest stripper in the house. She has raven hair. Her stunts on stage demand the full attention of every man in the audience."

"I'll keep a low profile and just stay out of the place. Since Bobby's joined in the circle of street people, I've chosen to distance myself from him. Bobby can deal in it!" Sara said. "Anyway, I'm not emotionally prepared to concern myself with any issues involving other women, especially women in that class."

But, despite her words, Sara seethed with jealousy.

"She's not a street person! And what do you mean by 'that class?'" Bonnie asked. "She has a beautiful life. She lives in a beautiful condo on Lake Erie. She has a man who works and takes care of her. He's a black dude with a high middle-class standing of living. He works at Avon Lake Auto Assembly Plant." Bonnie waved away the remarks, stood, went to the sink and faced Sara again, woman to woman, as she continued. "Sandy is also a fitness instructor. She teaches yoga and stress-reduction therapy to cancer patients, so they'll know how to balance the body and quiet the mind."

Sara bit her lip and remained strong and focused.

Shea rose and walked over to Bonnie, her face flushed, saying, "I'm not sure if I like the version of Sandy as a doper prostitute as opposed to New Age Eastern meditation, Yoga instructor-therapist." She rolled her eyes. "Maybe I'm being too personal with you; however, I am curious; the picture you painted of her Eastern mediation is an illusion of her own making. She's a junkie." Shea held up her fingers, counting the many hats Sandy supposedly wore. "She's into New Age Eastern mystic religious practices, yoga and chanting, helping cancer patients to cope, stripping, prostitution and drugs. Get real! How is she going to teach stress reduction with a monkey on her back?"

Anger stirred in Sara and she asked, "How does this Sandy manage to keep seeing Bobby while she lives with her man?"

"Hustle is the name of the game. It's easy!" Bonnie boasted. "Don't be stupid. She drives herself over. Her man knows she hustles for dope. He's accepted her lifestyle and learned to deal with it. Anyway, he gambles whenever he can in Windsor, Canada; and at the slot casino, and Detroit."

Sara blinked. "Does Sandy have sex with Bobby for pills?" she asked, her emotions in turmoil. "I . . . I . . . I don't believe this. You can't be serious. How could he in the condition he's in?"

"He stays stoned on DiLaudid and after he deals his pills, he buys heroin."

"What?" Sara asked, amazed. "Heroin?"

"Of course," Bonnie said. "He shot dope even before he came here to Ohio."

Sara shut her eyes and swallowed, plunging into depression. "Then the whole thing revolves around Bobby's pills and dope, as you put it! The pills are one enemy, but with the money Bobby has many weapons."

Bonnie continued, "Sandy plays up to Bobby, and he loves her attention. He digs Sandy's jazzy style."

Thief of Love

"It's quid pro quo -- something for something," Shea said. "What do you expect?" Bonnie asked. "We're all hippies from the sixties," Bonnie said in a boasting tone as she bragged. "We all believe in love! If we can't be with the one we love, we love the one we're with," she continued. "Sure, Sandy has her vices. So be it! We all do!" she declared. "About a dozen of us are in the same drug flow nevertheless. We're all survivors -- long-term users of opiates, but we have hobbies, interests and emotions like other people do. We're huggers and lovers who have fun and good times, but our first love is our drugs! We're chemically dependent on substances made from opium, and with the dependency we have to hustle because our habit is top-shelf and expensive. We're not cheap, but roughly taught," Bonnie continued. "As they say, we're flower children -- hippies from the sixties and seventies, hooked on music, flowers, beads, rock concerts, the pungent odor of marijuana, and the simple notion love could solve all the problems in the world. We were and are all that, and more!"

"I know about the relics that were unearthed in the sixties and seventies by dope addicts," Shea said.

Hearing Shea calling her friends dope addicts, Bonnie returned to her earlier attitude. "We don't like to be called dope addicts. We're users -- dependents. We've been down that road before. I must say I'll tell you we don't need a title. I'll tell you about it: You think you're cool and life is such a ball at the preliminary development in your drug use, and then you break down your moral code until nothing else in your life is important -- not your mother, not your father, and not even your boy friend. You'll sell your soul for dope. That's why we call our dope 'the thief of love.' Only about twenty percent of us have survived. We've lived to tell about it. For twenty-five years, when others

Thief of Love

in our circle overdosed and died years ago, or died of hepatitis, we all participated as addicts through methadone government programs. Meth was the closest we could take when heroin left the Midwest. We were all strung out big time on heroin, or 'smack' as it's called on the streets. After all the meth programs, we began to use street pharmaceutical drug pills -- barbituates, quaaludes, marijuana -- anything we could find."

"What kind?" Sara asked.

"Pot, turpin-hydrate and codeine cough syrup gave us a buzz. Downers -- mostly Valium; Percadan, Demerol and Dilaudid were all the top-shelf drugs. We love the rush, though, when we shoot pills. We shot bams -- a speed in the seventies and eighties, and used black beauties before they took them off the market. We don't like speed much. Heroin filtered back into the streets in the mid-nineties -- pure stuff, easy to overdose on, more now than in the seventies. Competition for it is strong in the big cities."

"What's as popular as Dilaudid?" Sara asked. "Why do hard drug users use Dilaudid frequently?"

"For an alternative to heroin. They're top-shelf pharmacy pills," Bonnie said, adding, "Dilaudid is a derivative of opium -- the poppy plant -- synthetic heroin, really -- good high though for a pharmaceutical pill. Heroin is the junk left from the poppy plant after all good stuff has been taken out. We call it junk."

"How about crack?" Shea asked. "Are you crackheads too?"

"Never! Oh, no! We stay away from crack. That's some evil stuff. You use crack, you take the devil's dose. We stay with what we like -- opiates."

Sara thought, <u>They'd use anything they could to get high if they couldn't get opiates, the way she's presented herself.</u>

Thief of Love

Bonnie continued. "Heroin doesn't make you want to kill to keep high. It's just painful when you're trying to quit jonesing -- every muscle, every joint, every nerve ending is unbelievably painful. Just the thought. . . " Bonnie hesitated, opened her purse and removed an eight-ounce brown bottle of terpin-hydrate and codeine cough syrup. She turned toward the kitchen cupboard and removed a plastic drinking tumbler.

"Do you have orange juice or Pepsi?" she asked. "This stuff takes the edge off and gives me a buzz until I can shoot dope, but it lays heavy on my stomach."

Sara opened the refrigerator and took out a pint container of orange juice, pouring some for her uninvited guest. Bonnie slugged down two big gulps of the eight ounces of cough syrup and used the orange juice for a chaser. She rolled her eyes back into her head as she swallowed, puckered, choked and cleared her throat, then started to sweat.

"Tell me about Marcus Seibert," Sara said.

"Well," Bonnie began, "I made an emotional investment with him since my sixteenth birthday. We've hung tight together ever since. Marcus taught me my street values in my hippie days. He taught me how to be a survivor in the hustle for my dope -- knowing how to feel people's sensitivities. When you can get a person's feelings you have it made. Marcus taught me that you can play on their weaknesses. He taught me that everyone has weaknesses and strengths; you have to sharpen your defenses when you know the difference. Then you have street smarts! We had our energy jams over the years through life's learning process -- treating crises. When one of us overdosed, we never jumped ship. We never left the scene; or if one of us was tripping or turning blue from lack of blood circulating, we would sit their body in ice-cold water with fans blowing on them until

Thief of Love

they passed from death's door and came down from their high. Anyway, though, the higher your trip, the closer to death's door you get and the more you enjoy the trip into ecstasy."

Shea couldn't take it any longer. She jabbed a finger at Bonnie's chest, nearly shouting as she said, "This is sick! You're getting close to death and you brag about how you enjoy the trip into ecstasy! You need help!"

Bonnie laughed and nodded as she looked at the floor. "You're probably right about that." Then she opened up more boldly and continued to lay out the cold facts of the drug protocol. "Marcus knows a lot of johns out at the plant where he works. We have to hustle to keep our habit satisfied. This is how I get my money -- tricking johns. I can make a couple of hundred bucks with one john. I can fool around a couple of times in an hour or less. If I shot dope before I made it sexually, I have to work real hard to get the john off, but in the sex act I've gotten myself off a couple of times too! I enjoy sex with a good partner. Some are a lot of fun in bed. Some even go south, but then again I will too! It takes two people enjoying it together, It takes me three hours to get Marcus off. He stays so numb he wears me out!

"I have sex with Marcus sometimes when we're hanging tight together, but I have to be aggressive with him. He never makes the first move. He won't split a pill with me either; his high comes first. When he fixes me up to trick, he has me get a front so he can get high. That's why I have to make two hundred dollars. He tells me, when he fixes me up, 'Bonnie, don't take all the johns' money. Leave them some too. Just take two hundred!' His principles are strong like that. His street values are fair.

"Marcus can read me inside and out. He can look into my

Thief of Love

eyes and soul. If he picks up on my sensitivity;, if he knows I hold back on money, or if I take too much from the John, he'll bitch-slap me!"

"How can you allow all this? How can you let him have that power of control?" Sara asked. "That's totally wrong -- what he does to you." Sara shook her head and continued. "I'd say your drug buddy, Marcus, is a pimp. Drugs rule his life. What a waste. You know, Bonnie, all this may be your personal taste and style, but you've lost your self-respect along the wayside, living your doper lifestyle. Maybe it's your freedom of choice -- your first love, as you put it -- but look at what drugs have done to you. You're into prostitution and crime, insensitive to Bobby's medical condition, without a conscience for his pain management; all you want is his pain pills. Why don't you get clean, instead you're just bragging about how your first love gets off on dope? You don't have to be a jelly brain the rest of your life. Quit justifying yourself."

"We don't want to get want off drugs," Bonnie said. "We can't function in the natural sense. If we wanted to quit, we would have a long time ago."

"So you just stay numb!" Shea said, her face reddening.

Bonnie ignored her insult, saying, "It's a good feeling mentally. You can be carefree. You don't go through stress. You can't feel disappointment, living day by day."

"What now?" Shea asked, leaning forward, peering hard into Bonnie's eyes.

Bonnie wouldn't be intimidated. She took a piece of paper from her purse and said, "When you see Bobby, give him this message." She wrote down her name and phone number. "By the way," she added, "This is Bobby's address." She wrote down the motel and room number Bobby was trying to keep secret from Sara.

    Bonnie headed for the door as she said, "For just three Dilaudid..."

Thief of Love

Chapter 31

At work the next day, Sara couldn't keep her mind centered on her job. She asked for a relief on the assembly line about seven fifteen and headed for the motel to talk with Bobby.

Sara circled the motel, watching his room for activity. A slight fall breeze blew. The remaining leaves trickled down from the treetops, then darkness descended and the air cooled. She parked near the office and watched Bobby's room for ten minutes. The light outside his room was on.

In a few more minutes a van pulled up and stopped near Bobby's room. A woman dressed in skimpy clothes stepped out of the van, hurriedly went to Bobby's door and knocked twice. Someone parted the drapes and quickly opened the door. Sara could see that it was Bobby as the woman went inside.

Sara shifted in the seat with impatience, wanting to get out and barge into the room on impulse, but she controlled herself and peered at the door, still watching and waiting. After an hour of enduring the anxiety, she worried and was stressed -- convinced that was Sandy inside. Sara was imagining the two of them in there for all the wrong reasons -- seeing his face hungry for her touch. Unwilling to imagine any further and having no need to, Sara got out, stepped over to the van, wrote down the license number, then returned to her car.

The moment Sandy stepped out of his motel room, Bobby's outside light turned off. Sara waited till Sandy drove off, got out of her car, her knees like rubber, walked to Bobby's door and knocked. She waited a few moments, but there was no answer. She turned the doorknob. It was locked. Bobby parted the drapes again and peeked out. When he saw it was Sara he unlocked the door and yanked it open in a jerk. Losing his

Thief of Love

balance, he almost fell.

"How did you find me?" he asked.

In an angry tone, Sara said, "The road is widening Bobby. A lot of people know where you are, and among them is Bonnie."

Bobby just stared.

Sara continued. "Bonnie asked me to stop by and see you and to let you know that you're getting ripped off on the Dilaudid you're selling for fifteen dollars. Marcus is selling each Dilaudid for thirty dollars. You're losing three hundred dollars for every twenty pills you sell." Sara stepped inside and stood in silence, looking around the motel room with a few quick glances. A baseball bat near the door stood upright within reach near the door. <u>Maybe he expects an ambush or a drug deal gone bad or maybe a bludgeoning,</u> Sara thought, feeling uneasy for Bobby. He turned his back to her and slammed the door shut without asking her to sit, but she did anyway.

<u>What a big surprise,</u> Sara thought as she saw a dozen fresh, beautiful red roses were in a vase on a small coffee table next to a neatly made sofabed. On a nightstand an opened box of chocolate candy with a few pieces taken out caught her eye.

"What are you trying to do, romance her?" Sara asked.

Bobby hesitated and backed away from her, saying, "Marcus brought the roses for his girl. She was just here a little while ago."

Sara noticed Bobby's style had changed -- his clothes were designer sportswear, with a Nike logo on the shirt that sagged on his shoulders. <u>He's trying to dress in the groove,</u> she thought. Even though he did try to adopt a more youthful look, his pants bagged on his back end, making him look old and decrepit. He wore a gold chain necklace with a Star of David pendant around his neck. He also wore Nike high-top basketball shoes.

Bobby must have seen the look in her eyes and said, "Get used to her coming over. She's Marcus's lady, and she's been invited over by both of us -- doctor's orders! My doctor has given me orders for therapy in yoga for stress reduction and improved concentration. Sandy is my therapist."

Sara knew it would be cruel to say she didn't care. She told it like it was. "Did she shoot up before or after therapy? You're the dope man, Bobby, aren't you?" Sara asked.

"Leave, right now," Bobby said in an angry tone, adding, "Marcus doesn't want you here."

Sara said, "Tell the devil's advocate that the dope man wants to connect directly with you! He wants to eliminate the middleman." She held her gaze steady on Bobby. His eyes struggled to hold hers, but he looked away. She fumbled in her purse and gave him Bonnie's note with the drug dealer's name, phone number and address.

"Please do call. Don't be used like this," she said as she turned and left.

As Sara went toward her car, Bobby slammed the door shut behind her.

Thief of Love

Chapter 32

A week later, Sara tried to be happy once again as she looked out her kitchen window and enjoyed the beauty of the last of the fall foliage. The morning sunlight shone brightly in a clear blue, cloud-free sky. Sara sat at her kitchen table in deep thought, feeling the fall breeze coming through her window as she looked out at the brilliant colors of the late November fall season.

She rose and went into the living room, looking out the front window as, suddenly, a car pulled up to her mailbox. The passenger leaned out the window, opened her mailbox and began to sort through the day's early-morning mail delivery.

Without hesitation, Sara jerked open the front door and stormed across the porch and down the front steps. As she headed toward the car, she saw that the invader of her privacy was Bobby Johnson. Walking quietly, Sara approached from behind when the driver, Bobby's new partner, Marcus, said, "Peace be with you. We came on friendly terms." He made a peace sign hand gesture, adding, "We didn't come to steal your mail. We're trying to track down Bobby's disability checks."

Sara looked at Marcus and said, "Nothing yet," adding, "I don't know what to tell you."

"I signed up over a month ago for my V.A. disability pension. My check is long overdue," Bobby said, bellowing, then, gripping his stomach, he opened the car door and vomited onto the pavement. Bobby leaned back against the seat as Marcus took some tissues from the car's center console and gently wiped Bobby's face and mouth, showing compassion. He then proceeded to take a damp rag from a plastic bag and washed the perspiration from Bobby's brow. Sara was touched by

Thief of Love

Marcus's kindness to Bobby. Before she realized what she was saying, Sara invited them both into her house.

"Come inside, and we can call Veteran's Administration and find out the status of your benefits."

Bobby pushed himself out of the car, obviously determined to walk on his own. But, as he began to step, he lost his balance and came close to falling, supporting himself with his cane.

"He's dizzy from the pills," Marcus said as he too got out of the car. "It takes a while to get used to Dilaudid. His equilibrium is off-balance with the change." Marcus put his arm around Bobby so his weight was on Marcus's shoulder and walked him through the yard, into the house and to the recliner where he set him down.

Bobby was obviously fatigued, resting for a few moments, but perked up long enough to call the V.A., to be told that everything had been approved and was ready to be sent out in the immediate future.

After a strangely cordial half-hour visit, Bobby and Marcus left.

Three days later, Bobby called again. Sara noticed that his breathing was shallow and sounded obstructed.

"You sound terrible," Sara said. "You haven't told me where you're living now. I don't have your new phone number, or an address. I'm very concerned that you're moving around too much. What's going on?" she asked.

"I need you to help me fill out a paper you have to sign, and a household receipt stating that I've paid bills since I signed up for Social Security Supplemental Income, because of my disability."

"How are you getting here? Who's bringing you?" Sara

asked.

"I don't know," Bobby said.

"I'll sign the paper," Sara said, adding, "But I have to go to work and can't take you there." They agreed that he would stop by the next day before work, after he arranged transportation.

The next morning, as Sara sat waiting and watching TV, an unfamiliar man dropped Bobby off at the door, then left.

Bobby shivered involuntarily as she let him in. He looked drawn and under-medicated. His now weak-framed body seemed to sag as he made his halting way inside, then collapsed onto the living room couch.

Overcome with empathy for Bobby's state, Sara tried to comfort him by placing extra cushions around him; then she spotted an abrasion on the inside of his elbow. She checked his right arm; the same slightly purple bruises and crooked streaks were there.

"These look like needle tracks, Bobby. You're not shivering from being cold; you're going through drug withdrawals. I know what you're doing; I can see the needle tracks. You're mainlining your pills, aren't you?" she asked in a challenging tone.

Bobby struggled to speak; his voice was barely audible as he finally said, "Please don't start with me now. Call my doctor, please. I need my prescription filled."

"How long has it been?" Sara asked.

Bobby wouldn't answer her for a few moments, then finally said in a half-mumble, "I'll get drunk on whiskey if you don't call. I tried whiskey earlier and it burnt my throat like hell, but if that's all I have then I'll take it." There was just enough agony in his voice to put Sara on the defensive.

Thief of Love

Her resolve crumbled, and Sara picked up the phone and called Doctor Crawford's office. The call was forwarded to a medical answering service and Sara was told Doctor Crawford was out of town. They gave her Doctor Ben Miller's number; she placed an immediate call to him.

"I'm a friend of Robert Johnson -- a patient of Doctor Richard Crawford. I need to talk with Doctor Ben Miller," Sara said.

"Doctor Miller speaking," came the reply.

"Doctor Miller, Robert Johnson is here with me, suffering without pain medication. He has cancer of the esophagus, and he uses Dilaudid."

"Hasn't he already been prescribed his pain killer by Doctor Crawford this week?"

"Yes, on Thursday," Sara said, looking at the label on the pill vial. Sara thought from the doctor's tone that he'd go by the book.

"I couldn't prescribe a controlled substance this soon," he said. "It's only been two days, for a hundred pills! What did he do, sell them?"

Sara was silent as Doctor Miller continued, "If he's completely out of his pain killers, I'd suggest he have someone go to the pharmacy nearby and pick up some over-the-counter pain reliever for Mister Johnson to use until Doctor Crawford comes back on Monday." That said, he hung up.

Sara knew Bobby's discomfort would become agony without a high dosage of his painkiller, so she acted on impulse.

"How much money do you have?" she asked.

"I have enough money," he said in a desperate tone, placing his hand in his pocket.

"Let's face the facts, Bobby. Without Doctor Crawford's

Thief of Love

approval, no other doctor will refill your prescription this soon. So, if you have money, you'll no doubt have to buy from the streets. I know Marcus has the connections, with his everyday narcotics habit. Do you want me to call Marcus?" she asked.

"Please call," Bobby said. "That'll work. I'll buy from the street." Bobby wrote Marcus's phone number on a notepad. His hand shook; his writing was barely legible.

It bothered Sara tremendously that Bobby would have to resort to buying his medication on the streets, but this wasn't the time to pressure him about it. Without another thought, she called Marcus, and was surprised at how fast he made it to her house.

When Marcus arrived, Bobby was weeping and struggling to breathe.

"You're jonesing, man!" Marcus said. His eyes shifted back and forth from Bobby to Sara, stopping on her. "On the streets, we call drug withdrawals 'jonesing.'"

Marcus crossed the room and stood in front of Bobby.

Bobby looked up and asked in a pleading tone, "Can you cop me one Dilaudid?"

Marcus shrugged. "A pill for a pill. It's going to be a hundred bucks."

Sara could see Marcus knew he was in control and enjoyed it.

Bobby gritted his teeth, stifled an angry retort and dug into his pocket, pulling out a roll of money, which he gave to Sara. "Count out a hundred," he said, his tone weary, yet eager and expectant.

Sara took the money and counted out five twenties. She knew it was wrong and even criminal to be involved in all this as she gave the money to Marcus.

Thief of Love

Marcus took the money, shoved it in his field jacket, went to the phone and called the dope man.

"This is Marcus, Elmo. I need two, number fours."

Marcus left. Time wasn't on Bobby's side, or Sara's. He was completely open to the pain and she was helpless in giving him aid. He waited and choked in fearful silence and, after an hour of misery, Marcus pulled back into the driveway. He hopped out of his car and ran up the front walk to the house with a new energy level and showing a more pleasant expression.

Sara knew by sight and attitude that Marcus was high. He stepped inside without knocking and removed a pair of pantyhose from his field jacket. The nylon stocking was wrapped around two hypodermic needles and a stained black teaspoon. He stood for a moment.

Sara glared at the drug paraphernalia in his hand as Marcus moved over to Bobby and gently took his arm, helping him to stand.

"Come on, man. Get up, Bobby," Marcus said. "One step forward, man. You can make it. You're almost there, Bobby," Marcus said, easing Bobby forward to the bathroom.

The thought of them using her bathroom for a drug shooting gallery made Sara irate, and played heavily on her conscience. She felt weak and guilty for not telling them they should commit their crimes somewhere else. She listened carefully and could hear the bathroom water running as she endured a nerve-wrecking silence. Realizing they were absorbed in what they were doing, Sara quietly crept close to the bathroom door, which was ajar. She stood in silence, looking at them, not moving.

Bobby sat on the commode, his left arm bent and his elbow resting on the vanity. The nylon was tied tightly and knotted around his arm above the elbow. Bobby made a tight fist.

Sara opened her mouth as she watched with shock and disbelief.

Marcus stood next to Bobby, peering at the syringe that he held upright, then tipped it to make sure there were no air bubbles in the yellowish liquid inside the vial. He flipped the needle and held Bobby's wrist down flat with the other hand as he held the syringe, like a doctor. He made one shot into the vein, injecting the dope very professionally.

Bobby's eyes rolled back in his head as he felt the rush toward ecstasy, sending him into a semi-comatose state, without knowledge of his surroundings.

Sara rubbed her eyelids. Then her right eye twitched. She stepped away with care, her feet heavy, her heart frozen.

Moments later, Bobby and Marcus came out of the bathroom, both in a good mood. Marcus began rubbing the tip of his nose. Bobby showed a relaxed look, breathing deeper and moving with a painless walk, thoroughly ignoring her. He opened the front door. They both walked through, and shut it.

Sara realized she had been used again. Her kindness was once more taken as weakness, and now she had permitted drug abuse on her property. She suddenly became concerned that they could have AIDS or Hepatitis, so she disinfected the entire bathroom with hot water and bleach. Exhausted, she called in sick from work through the eight hundred number at the plant. Now Sara felt rejected and ashamed; the pleasure she had once derived from helping Bobby was once again shattered.

Sara's anxiety kept her awake most of the night. She wondered if she should she call the police, or go see Doctor Crawford Monday herself. Despite her troubled conscience, Sara decided to give it more time; she didn't want to see Bobby put in jail for the last days of his life. She prayed to God that He would give her an answer as she turned it over to Him for Bobby's correction, judgment and accountability.

Thief of Love

Chapter 33

Sara was restless all the next day. In a drawer she found a letter Bobby had written to Cid, but never mailed. The unopened letter kindled her interest, so she opened and read it. The letter didn't say a lot, only that Bobby may be coming Cid's way for work, and asking him if the phone number he had was up to date. Cid's number was written in the letter. <u>I must keep up the momentum,</u> Sara thought. <u>Someone has to care for him enough to get him away from the dopers taking advantage of his condition.</u> She decided to call the ranch. Cid was out in the field and was called on his pager. He answered in about four rings.

"Cid, this is Sara, from Ohio. You met me at the bowling alley in Paso Robles during the mid-state fair last summer. You do remember me, don't you?"

"Oh sure!" Cid said in a friendly tone. "How have you been? To what do I owe the pleasure of hearing from you, lovely lady?"

"You've been on my mind a lot lately," Sara said. "I'm not prepared for all that's been happening. You see, well, Bobby is going to die."

"Bobby Johnson is going to die? Why do you say that?" Cid asked.

Her tone anxious, Sara said, "He has cancer of the esophagus. I've tried to deal with Bobby's family in California, and have learned from them that he allegedly caused them ethnic intimidation over the years on account of their Jewish culture, and the flamboyant lifestyle he lived on the wild side of California's fastest lanes. They've chosen to not come here to be with him, or have him return to California to die."

Cid sighed. "I can't believe it. Bobby is going to die?"

he asked again.

"I'm sorry, Cid, for not letting you know earlier that Bobby has been diagnosed with cancer. In October he started radiation therapy. There's a large tumor on his esophagus. They had to shrink it down. It was closing off his passageway and he couldn't swallow. He's now in chemotherapy too."

"Is he in the hospital now?" Cid asked.

"No," Sara said. "He's staying in a motel with a long-term drug addict whose now become dependent on Bobby's painkillers. There are also women involved, whom Bobby's friends use for sex; and they all talk with humor about overdosing, and reselling stolen goods to pay for their drug habits."

"I heard about those types of things that go on with drug addicts. If they can, they'll push, pull and drag, piece by piece, everything you own out of your house and put it in a moving van or grocery cart, along with your food," Cid said.

"I know," Sara said, "they're trouble. You can't trust them. They have no integrity. I made Bobby leave when I found out he was trafficking narcotics at my house. He's so vulnerable and easily taken advantage of now. He's been taken over by three drug addict hustlers. He does without pain relief while they sell his pills, and he lets those parasites use his pain pills for their drug habit. They buy heroin with the money he gets selling his pills."

"What's that?" Cid asked.

"I watched them while Bobby and his friend shot up in my bathroom. Bobby was sitting on my bathroom commode while his dealer and junkie partner was sticking a hypodermic needle into Bobby's arm."

"This is bad news -- very bad news," Cid said. "Have

Thief of Love

Bobby call me. Please."

"Cid, I'll try, but he is in an insane state, with all the pills. I find it hard to talk to him sensibly. I can't get through to him."

"Maybe you should stay away from him," Cid said.

Sara continued. "I had the police escort him out of my house about two weeks ago, but he calls me when he's out of pills, gasping for air at times with his shallow breathing, like a fish on dry land. Whenever he's out of pills he haunts me with a phone call and shallow breathing. But his respiratory system relaxes when he takes his medication regularly."

"I hate to hear this about Bobby," Cid said, his voice low. "Bobby is a complicated person, but this is too much."

"Complicated isn't the word," Sara said. "He's nuts for selling his pills and giving them to drug addicts while he suffers. He has a relationship right now with a stripper who's also a drug addict. I caught her coming out of his room higher than hell after she shot up his pills in his bathroom at the motel where he stays. Bobby tells me she's the therapist his doctor sent over to give him treatment with yoga.

"That cowboy is something of an odd critter, with women of all ages falling for his lines. He more or less used them all for cigarettes and alcohol, and now drugs or whatever else he can get. He could talk them out of it. He knew just what the girls needed and wanted. You should see him now. He's lost over seventy-five pounds, his skin sags and he looks almost like a seventy year old man. His face is sunken in and he can't even wear his dentures; they fall out of his mouth. Even his bones have shrunk," Sara said.

"That's a damn shame," Cid said. "He's had a hell of a way to go. Look at it! He'd been kicked around as a child by other people who made slurs about his Jewish family. His civil

Thief of Love

liberties were violated by the L.A. cops, and then he was prosecuted and sentenced to prison for ten years, where he was locked up with violent schizos. His wife found a new love and forgot the jailbird husband, divorcing him. When he finally gets paroled he's lost ten years, a wife and his self-esteem. So he stayed soaked in booze, without any goals, traveling with a carnival and rodeo, sleeping in tents, trailers and cars. Then suddenly he's at the age of forty-four, diagnosed with a terminal cancer with a short time left to live. Then he's taken over by a drug ring for his pain medicine. He doesn't deserve to be taken in by these drug hustlers after all he's been through. He has the freedom of choice, whether we like it or not, but I don't intend to take this easy."

As they finished talking, Cid told Sara he wanted to be kept informed, but that his schedule wouldn't let him come to Sandusky; he was needed at the ranch. They agreed they would talk again after Sara had more information.

Thief of Love

Chapter 34

The next week, thoughts raced through Sara's mind about whether or not to tell Doctor Crawford what was going on with Bobby's pills. Doctor Crawford was up against a con man who was practiced enough, knew enough and was assertive enough to hustle his way to get large volumes of drugs to sell.

After all her agonizing, Sara decided to alert Doctor Crawford, and she made an appointment to see him. "I was approached by a woman who told me she wanted me to help her connect a drug dealer with Bobby so they can eliminate the middleman -- Bobby's pusher -- Marcus Seibert, who's wholesaling Bobby's Dilaudid," Sara said.

Doctor Crawford looked at Sara in surprise and then with an expression of deep thought. "This certainly isn't good for Robert's best interests. He needs his painkillers, day and night."

"He seems in unbearable agony whenever his pills are used by others. When he calls me, his breathing is shallow and he cries a lot," Sara said.

Doctor Crawford frowned. "Robert's medical prognosis was poor. We knew the potential for abuse when I wrote his prescription. We knew he had dependency problems, and he was counseled and received treatment for drug abuse." The doctor thought for a moment. "We've been successful in shrinking the tumor down so he can eat a bland diet, and he's maintained his weight for two weeks now."

Doctor Crawford pursed his lips and looked directly at Sara. "There are a few inconsistencies in the statements between Robert and you. But there are many facts as well. I've talked with Robert's family in California and his sister Megan in Phoenix. They've shouldered much family grief; they're on call, if need be."

"I've spoken with some of them myself," Sara said. "His sister Megan -- his closest confidant and protector, he tells me -- will probably be mindful of him, but when he dies the family won't take any responsibility for any of his medical liability or his memorial and burial."

"That's not the way I heard it," Doctor Crawford said. He looked away, as if something was on his mind.

"I'm worried about Bobby being drawn into the drug world's corruption," Sara said. "I'm bringing you this information for his sake, not my own. You're the doctor. I'm telling you first, not the police or his family, or anybody else. Bobby is living with drug addicts who have been convicted of crimes. If this drug dealing with his pills doesn't stop, I'll take it to the authorities," Sara concluded, meaning what she said -- that the doctor had better do something to appease her.

Doctor Crawford nodded and remained silent as he rose and stepped out of the room

Sara left the office and prepared herself to get ready for her afternoon shift at the plant. She began to feel weak and congested, and her head ached, as if she had a flu bug coming. During her break, she went down to the plant medical office, and the nurse gave her throat lozenges and a package of ibuprofen pain reliever. Then the nurse directed her to go home and get bed rest. Sara asked for a pass from her supervisor and went home.

She hadn't been off work for an hour, when, as she lay on her sofa watching TV, her phone rang. When she answered a man whose voice she didn't recognize asked, "Is this Bobby Johnson's old lady?"

"Who's calling?" Sara asked.

"My name isn't important. I'm calling to forewarn

Thief of Love

Bobby Johnson that Marcus Seibert is just about to get set up at the plant."

"Set up?" Sara asked.

"Marcus is selling Bobby's pain killers all over town, and now he's dealing at the plant. He's being set up to get busted. When he does, he goes to prison. Bobby Johnson will go to prison right along with him because Bobby is the supplier and Marcus is the pusher."

Every muscle in Sara's body tightened. The caller hung up before she had a chance to ask questions. She put down the phone and stared at the bedroom ceiling, almost paralyzed with indecision. She considered going to warn Bobby, but continued to lie in bed, thinking, I don't want to go back over there. But she was convinced Marcus was set up to take a rap, but would probably make Bobby take a fall with him if he could. Sara lost sleep as she wondered most of the night just how deeply involved the police were in this setup.

By morning Sara's flu had vanished, while the anonymous telephone message weighed heavily on her mind. But her nervousness caused her to have an extraordinary burst of energy. She rummaged around in the house, going through drawers and sorting through the papers and other stuff Bobby left behind, until she found a plain manila legal-sized envelope.

Sara opened the envelope slowly. Inside she discovered drawings of a livestock corral Bobby had once sketched as part of his big dream to open the largest cattle ranch in the state of Ohio.

As Sara stared at the drawings, her heart was heavy. She wasn't sure what to do with her weekend off from the plant, but with the remaining burst of energy, she continued to clean the house.

An hour before dark, it being a good time to relax, Sara

Thief of Love

took a drive to watch the boats and the sunset into Sandusky Bay. A few leaves were still dangling on nearby branches, silhouetted by the setting sun. The temperature immediately fell and it was suddenly a bit nippy.

Sara thought about the caller the night before, and about Bobby being arrested. He would face trial and almost certain conviction because he'd keep the truth from coming out, protecting those who bore the guilt while he spent the few last days of his life in a prison cell.

Sara realized she was naive to think if she warned them they would listen. She decided to go nevertheless, circling Bobby's place twice to look over the motel parking lot and the shadowy alleyways of the addicted. After her brief surveillance, Sara parked, got out of her car and knocked on the door.

Marcus answered it. His shirt was off, and he was sweating. He wore jeans with a belt, his big belly hanging over it a bit. Marcus smiled and opened the door wider. He pointed to the only chair. The TV was on.

"Where's Bobby?" Sara asked as she entered and sat on the chair, facing Marcus, who sat on the bed.

Marcus nodded toward the bathroom. She could tell he was flying high. His eyelids drooped like he was feeling a good buzz; and he was rubbing his nose.

"Would you like a cold Pepsi?" he asked.

"Sure," Sara said. Marcus retrieved a Pepsi from a cooler next to the bed and poured it into a plastic tumbler. She sipped from the glass while Marcus continued to watch TV.

A few moments later, Bobby came out of the bathroom. His hair was damp. He cradled his left hand around his throat and wore a dazed look, Sara thought. He turned his head sharply when he saw her. His legs were obviously weak, and shaky -- he almost tripped over a shoe lying in the center of the floor.

"I'm in no mood to hear a lecture," he said. "You should have had some respect and called somebody over here before you stopped by. I'm not feeling well. I need rest. You'll have to go."

Well, at least he was frank and to the point, Sara thought as she felt the heat start down around her toes and rise to her face. "I need to talk with you, Bobby. I was given a message by an unknown caller, but he seemed anxious for me to pass it on to you. He called to warn you that something big is just about to happen." Her gaze locked with Marcus's.

Marcus's eyes bulged. "What was it he said?" His expression and body language indicated he was starting to have a bad attitude.

"I'll start from the beginning," Sara said. "A hyper man with a warning called and said he knows Bobby and asked me if I was his fiancée -- "

Marcus said, "Get to the point." He lit a cigarette and inhaled deeply.

Sara realized Marcus had no patience with people, especially her. She continued, "He said he knew Marcus and Bobby, and this message was meant solely for both of them. He said Marcus is selling Bobby's painkillers all over town, and at the plant. He said Marcus is about to be set up and sent to prison, and Bobby is going right along with him. He said it's because Marcus is the pusher and Bobby is the supplier."

Marcus drew deeply on his cigarette, the veins popping out on his neck and forehead. Bobby looked gripped with fear.

"Obviously, he had access to unlimited information about you both," Sara said.

Marcus shot a look over to Sara, then held his gaze on

Thief of Love

Bobby and, without blinking, said, "This is bullshit! Man, don't listen to her, Bobby. She doesn't have a full story, with any facts, names, or details." Marcus's eyes went hard as he looked toward Sara. "Hey, you! Don't put my business out in the street. Keep my name out of your bogus story."

The room was silent. Sara was scared, knowing what Marcus was capable of if he lost the supply of Dilaudids. She decided to leave and, still in silence, she quickly rose and headed to the door. She opened it, paused and she said, "I just came to tell you you're about to get arrested." Then she went out.

Behind her, Sara heard Bobby struggle to his feet and push the door shut with all his remaining strength as she went toward her car. It made her angry that he bluntly ignored every warning she tried to bring to him. Sara agonized over the situation as she headed for home.

Thief of Love

Chapter 35

On Saturday, Bobby called Sara at her house. His voice sounded weak and troubled although he accepted the offer to meet Bonnie the next day. Sara was surprised that he called.

After their brief conversation, Sara called Bonnie and made arrangements for her to come about noon on the following day. Bonnie arrived on time. Sara opened the door to find Bonnie a bundle of frazzled nerves, appearing to be jonesing.

"Bobby called a while ago," Sara said. "He said he'll be late."

The news didn't rest well with Bonnie.

Bonnie Scowled. "That isn't what you told me yesterday." Then, she shrugged. "If that's the case, I need to take the edge off. Go to the pharmacy for me and sign for a bottle of codeine cough syrup."

While Sara decided whether or not to do as she demanded, Bonnie cleaned out her purse and pockets, counting out six dollars in change and fifty pennies. "I can't buy a pill, just a bottle of syrup," she said, handing Sara her change.

Sara's first thought was to tell Bonnie to come back later. She considered, then asked, "Where would I go to get it?"

"It's no biggie," Bonnie said. "Drive us over to the medical center pharmacy. You may need a picture ID when you sign. It's simple though. Just make sure you check the date and time. That's important. I watch that closely. I did five years probation on felony drug abuse for illegally signing two days in a row."

Sara checked her watch. Her emotions were mixed; she wasn't sure if she should do this or not.

"We still have time," Bonnie said. "Let's get a move on."

Thief of Love

The day was cold. A freezing drizzle came down while Sara slowly drove to the medical pharmacy. The parking lot was one quarter full of cars. There was a crowd inside. Many scruffy-looking people scurried by, nodding to Bonnie or smiling at her while Sara went inside and to the pharmacy counter.

The pharmacist, a middle-aged man, stepped up to her. "Can I help you?" he asked.

"Yes," Sara said. "I'd like a bottle of turpin-hydrate and codeine cough syrup."

The pharmacist gave her a knowing look as he handed Sara a clipboard with a form on it for her to sign. "Read this," he said.

The notice read, `Under the Controlled Substance Act, the federal government requires a signature and date when the purchase of a controlled substance is made." The pharmacist hadn't check Sara's ID, but she was on guard, and checked the date when she signed below the names of the twenty people who had already purchased controlled substances that day.

Sara paid for the cough syrup and took it outside to Bonnie, who promptly unscrewed the cap and slugged it down in four big gulps, chasing it with sips from a can of Pepsi Sara hadn't seen before. Bonnie cleared her throat several times, rolled down the window and spit outside as Sara headed back toward her house.

A half-hour later, Bobby pulled up in the driveway in a delapidated car driven by two men who looked like Mexican farm workers.

Bobby was weak and tired and had a ghostlike pallor as he staggered into the house. Bobby took Sara aside and, speaking in a low tone, said, "Doctor Crawford cut my pills

Thief of Love

down. I'm short forty pills on my script. Tell Bonnie I can't deal."

She turned and saw that Bonnie had been nearby, but Sara didn't know if she had overheard Bobby. He decided to talk to Bonnie directly and said, "I can't deal with you. My pills are cut down."

"So what!" Bonnie said. "I don't care if your pills are cut back. I don't care what you need. A deal is a deal!"

In frustration Bobby pulled the top off his pill bottle and shook out one Dilaudid, which he handed to her.

Sara looked at Bobby. "How did you get away from Marcus? I thought he trained you well."

"There aren't not enough pills for Marcus anymore. It's down to him or my cancer."

"I knew it would come to this. Why did you allow it? Oh -- that's right, Bobby -- he's your mentor and you're his protégé."

Bobby fumbled for an answer. Just then, Marcus pull up in the driveway and shut off the engine. He moved fast as he got out of the car and entered Sara's front yard.

"What does he want here?" Sara asked. She felt uneasy as she went out with Bobby, staying by his side as they went down the steps.

Marcus aimed his penetrating eyes at Sara, trying to intimidate her to go back inside. He walked up to Bobby. Sara remained to listen to the conversation even though she was frightened.

"I told you to buzz off," Bobby told Marcus.

Marcus just stood there in menacing silence, hovering over Bobby.

"What are you doing? Stalking me?" Bobby bellowed.

"I need a pill, Bobby," Marcus said.

"No way in hell, man! You owe me five thousand in front," Bobby said.

"Bobby, just one pill. Trust me for just one pill." Marcus's voice was high and his hands were shaking as he shifted his weight from one foot to the other.

Sara knew Marcus was humiliated, but she wondered how far Marcus intended to let Bobby slide by. He needed a fix, and might get violent. She thought Bobby's safety was on the line; that Marcus would overpower Bobby, bitch-slap him and grab his bottle of Dilaudid. Bobby was too weak to fight back now.

But, no matter what, Bobby's mettle was forged long ago in prison; he was a hardened criminal. Bobby took the bottle of pills out of his pants pocket, opened it and removed one pill.

Marcus's eyes shifted and bulged. Even though Bobby was physically challenged, he still was in command. Acting on impulse, he threw the one tiny Dilaudid into the grass. "Crawl, man!" Bobby shouted.

Marcus was desperate, wasting no time getting down on his hands and knees in the grass. He began crawling, rooting and sweeping the ground, like an animal hungry for prey, until he found the pill. He raised up, stripped of his pride. His street macho image taken as he grabbed the pill, got in his car and drove away without a word. Marcus had won after all though; he got what he came for -- a pill to get high.

Sara shook with anger as she told Bobby, "You opened the door to all this! You should've known better."

Bobby ignored her outburst and said, "I want to come back and stay here with you."

"No. I can't let you, Bobby. It's too dangerous for you, and me -- for just one pill to these addicts. Any of them could come back and break in here. Wherever you go, they'll find you. Look there." She pointed to the porch. "That's an example." Bonnie stood on the top step, watching them.

"If I can't stay with you, I have a buddy, Richard. He told me he'll move in and share a duplex at Bay Bridge with me within a few minutes of here. I'll be nearby. My buddy will keep Marcus away, and the rest of them. We won't want anything going on like that. Anyway, my buddy worked as a cook. We'll eat good."

"Does he have a job?" Sara asked.

Bobby nodded. "He works as a machine operator in a factory, but he's taking a buy-out for his employment. He's planning to relocate to Arizona to be in training at a motorcycle mechanic school."

* * *

For a few days after Bobby moved in with Richard, he disconnected, not even calling Sara. This gave her a sense of finality. She thought maybe it was her signals to him that she'd had more than enough of him that caused Bobby to stay away. Even so, when Sara came home from work she passed by the duplex Bobby and Richard were sharing, slowed and side-glanced out her windows, watching for extraordinary activity or traffic in the neighborhood. Every night, a red glow light coming from an upstairs bedroom told her Bobby slept in. Things looked quiet, Sara thought.

After several more days, Sara stopped by to see how Bobby was doing. She knocked on the door. When he answered he was quiet, subdued, almost polite -- as polite as Bobby could be. He even seemed nervous during the first part of their hour-long visit. Then, he left the room and went upstairs, seeming more relaxed after he came back down.

Thief of Love

Bobby brought out a few collectors items he was saving: cigarette lighters with the Joe Camel logo, a crossbow he said he planned to use deer hunting, other odds and ends of this and that.

Then, an hour after Sara arrived, she looked out the window as a van pulled up. Two men and a woman hopped out, then helped one more man into a wheelchair, which they pushed up the driveway. He was very large, and fat, and wore a black leather jacket, jeans, motorcycle boots -- all the biker garb. The woman appeared street wise, and street worn. She wore jeans, a sleeveless t-shirt with a leather vest over it and flat shoes. Before they made it to the door, another man, whom Sara presumed to be Richard, pulled up behind the van with a willowy brunette at his side. When everyone entered and exchanged greetings, Sara was shunted aside in the shuffle of newcomers. Bobby seemed to completely forget about Sara and didn't even introduce her to them. She sat quietly off to one side of the sofa for a few minutes, avoiding looking at anyone or moving in their line of vision. Soon, they all adjourned into the kitchen.

From her seat, Sara could see the paraplegic pull a syringe from his boot. He seemed to possess a considerable influence among the others in their group. The woman laid a folded paper on the kitchen table, which she unfolded, revealing a yellow-colored, powdery substance. Everyone in their group gave her money in exchange for part of the powder. Sara knew she was on dangerous ground, and promptly left, driving at once to Bonnie's house for some questions and answers.

"The woman you saw is Lynny, from Toledo. She brought down heroin from T-town to deal in Sandusky. She's been around since Thursday. I copped some myself last night," Bonnie said.

"Were there other people with her?" Sara asked.

Thief of Love

"Marcus, Bobby, and some people from T-town," Bonnie said.

"Who was the woman with Richard?" Sara asked.

"Her name is Shelly. She's a hooker from Cleveland. Rich thinks she's his girlfriend, but all he is to her is a trick. He's her john. Richard has taken a buy-out on his job for seventy-five thousand dollars. He's going through his money fast, buying heroin. They brought down some good stuff -- pure heroin, not cut.

"Last night, about one thirty, Marcus overdosed on heroin from the Toledo supply. He played up to Lynny. She gave him as much as he wanted, and he pigged out. He used a whole teaspoon of pure dope, took in a deep breath and fell on the floor. We thought we lost him. He seemed dead for a few minutes. In that time he lost his bowel movement and urine. One of Richard's customers came in with Fat Tammy and gave CPR and brought him back to breathing. We cleaned him up and put fans on him. He was wringing wet with sweat until he came down after about three hours. He wanted to shoot dope again."

"Oh, that's awful," Sara said. "I thought he was street smart. Where's Sandy at these days?" Sara asked. "You didn't mentioned Sandy's name at the shooting gallery."

"Hasn't anyone told you?"

"Told me what?" Sara asked.

"Sandy's terminal," Bonnie said. "She's a carrier of Hepatitis C, which has laid dormant since she was nineteen. She found out a month ago she has pancreatic cancer. The doctor gave her some medicine. Sandy didn't tell him about the hepatitis and the medicine caused the cancer. She's not expected to live very long. The drugs aren't any fun anymore. It's only a matter of time. Hospice is coming to her home daily."

Thief of Love

Sara decided she'd heard enough and went home for the night.

Thief of Love

Chapter 36

Bonnie called late that night, stoned. "The feds were watching the books closely last month," she said.

"What books?" Sara asked.

"The medical center pharmacy. Fat Tammy illegally signed. She was charged; she's caught a case," Bonnie said, talking fast and buzzing.

"What will they do to her?" Sara asked, worried about her own signature.

"Prison time," Bonnie said. "She's a felon. She'll be charged with drug abuse and do a one to five."

"I can feel the heat," Sara said. "This lifestyle is pretty dangerous and risky. Don't ask me to sign for you anymore. If they changed the pencil color daily, it wouldn't be a risk," Sara said. "They need to arrest the pharmacists who sell that stuff. I saw all those names and addresses on the sheet. Even Cleveland people signed for cough syrup."

"Get real!" Bonnie said. "You know how the system works. All the agencies collect when they arrest you -- the city, the county, the police, the lawyer, the pharmacist. It's all about money, and if you're even under investigation for signing for me, never admit you've bought it for me because if you do they'll charge you for aiding and abetting my addiction. If ever they do pick you up, say you buy turpin-hydrate for your personal use. The feds can't hang you on your first charge anyway. You can plead to a misdemeanor charge."

"This is something else. All your friends are in trouble, or dropping like flies, and now you tell me Marcus OD'd and Sandy is dying of Hepatitis C. Bobby will have more pills for

Thief of Love

himself, won't he?"

"Richard was dealing Bobby's pills from his bedside. He was getting real bold with it," Bonnie said.

"I know Richard isn't street smart," Sara said.

"He's going to get busted," Bonnie said. "Marcus was wholesaling to the drug dealer, but Richard is trafficking out of their duplex a pill at the time -- it's too open. I was there last week, when Lynny was there tricking Richard. Bobby was in deep sleep -- anyway Lynn thought he was. I watched her cross the room like a stalking cat as she sneaked into his bedroom. She lowered her hand and towered over him, reaching for his bottle of pills. When Bobby awoke, he was groggy. He reached out and swatted her hand. 'Get out, tramp,' he said. But, within a few hours, Richard asked Bobby for three D's. Richard came in and Bobby gave Rich three willingly. After that we sauntered down the hall the next bedroom and shot dope.

"No matter what," Sara said, "Bobby is going to maintain, to hang on with these people as long as he's breathing. You keep different hours than I do, Bonnie. It's four thirty. Call back in the morning."

Bonnie laughed and said, "You know how we are. Time has no meaning to opiate users. I'll catch you later."

Thief of Love

Chapter 37

When Sara arrived at the plant the next day, it was on the work grapevine that a big thing happened on the evening shift. Sara and Shea learned that Marcus had been arrested. The talk was all over the plant, so, on their personal time they walked up to the union work center to get some more information.

"A drug task force came out with a warrant and arrested Marcus while on the job," the shop committee man told them.

"What happened -- I mean, how did they do it?" Sara asked.

He said, "The drug task force handcuffed him and took him upstairs to the men's locker room. They searched his locker, I was told, but found absolutely nothing but some empty lunch bags. All hell broke loose though when they searched his car in the plant parking lot. They found enough substance in ten hypodermic needles to charge him with possession of heroin."

Shea shot Sara a smirk and an 'I-told-you-so' look.

"I was going to report Marcus to the labor retention department for stalking me and intimidating me in the parking lot, but I wanted to protect myself from an avalanche of shop talk," Sara said. "I tried to warn Marcus, but he wouldn't take heed, and Bobby threw me out of their motel room. After that, Marcus tried to intimidate me. He would pass through my department, glaring at me. I tried not to look at him, but on impulse I would. His eyes would be bulging. He would stalk me, too."

"He's street smart," the union rep said. "He beat the charges a couple of years ago when he was hit with felony drug abuse for signing for codeine cough syrup too many times. I was told by a credible person that Marcus was offered a deal to set up

Thief of Love

two drug dealers by acting as an informant. That really bothered Marcus. I personally know with this street values as a long-term drug user, there was no way. He got lucky. He didn't waive his rights to a speedy trial. In the meantime there was a change at the detective bureau. They let him slip through their hands."

"How's that?" Sara asked.

"Ohio law requires offenders who have been charged with felonies to be brought to trial within two hundred seventy days. The state failed to meet the speedy trial requirements, and when they finally brought him to trial, he walked. Two hundred eighty days had passed. His lawyer knew his job," the committee man said. "Marcus too. He made out like a bandit. He's going to pay his dues this time. He's out of here. Now they have all the evidence on him. Plant security had him on video camera in the guard shack when he was dealing out in the parking lot, while the drug task force was parked just across the street, when one of his so-called girlfriends came out here and busted him about four months ago."

"I wonder why it took so long to arrest him," Shea said.

"I don't know," the union man said, "but they arrested him on a secret indictment. The county already gathered the evidence. They also brought a search warrant. They knew what they were doing because they put another charge on him. They have two felonies now. He'll never get back in this plant. The international union has made an agreement with the company that if anyone has a controlled substance arrest on company property, and they refuse treatment and don't end their habit, they'll be terminated from their job and the union won't protect them or bargain for them."

"I can't say I feel sorry for him," Sara said. "Shop rumors get spread fast, you know."

Thief of Love

"We came in here for transfers to other AM facilities," Shea said. "We need to get into the system in AM's placement center for another AM job. Fedron Automotive Systems isn't where I'm going to retire. We don't want to lose our AM benefits. We'll probably transfer to a service parts plant, maybe out in Reno, Nevada."

"There is a service parts plant there now," the union rep said. "AM is building some new warehouses around here too. Why don't you put in for one in Columbus, Ohio?"

"We're not interested in that," Shea said. "We're going west."

Sara smiled and nodded. She rubbed her eyes, put her safety glasses on and gave Shea a little shrug. They headed for the break room to look over the list of possible locations for transfer.

"I hope they send all those dopers away," Sara said. She couldn't concentrate on any other thought but that now.

"Right!" Shea said. "I hope they send the whole doper ring away, including the supplier."

The thought of Bobby touched a nerve in Sara. She knew who Shea meant by supplier -- Bobby.

"Bobby is going to church Sunday, Shea. "I've been praying for him," Sara said.

Shea whirled around, as if expecting to hear Sara talk of Bobby's religious conversion.

"I believe he's going to be born again and repent before he dies -- make things right with the Lord," Sara said, hope in her voice.

"I doubt that," Shea said. "How can he, with the influence of those people around him?" Shea rolled his eyes. "He's hell bound! Seeing him is a mistake. Stay away from him."

"I have faith in God that He will take Bobby from all that," Sara said. "He has a friend in California who's very supportive and working on all this for his best interest. Anyway, I talked with Reverend Miles. Reverend Miles called to let me know Bobby told him he'd like to see him come worship at services on Sunday. Bobby's been truthful with me about his Jewish upbringing, and he's said he'd also like to attend an interdenominational service."

"Well, good luck with all that," Shea said.

* * *

The next Sunday, Sara arranged for Bobby to join her at the service presented by Reverend Miles.

Bobby pulled up in front of her house in a G.T.O. at nine a.m., beeped the horn, then leaned on it till Sara came out. He looked bad -- drawn, haggard, thin and weak. He was dressed in layers -- a dark brown corduroy sports coat, sweater, warm wool dress shirt, jeans, and dress shoes.

"Bobby, Doctor Crawford told you not to drive when you take medication," Sara scolded him as she stepped into the car. "You're legally under the influence. Your driving privileges are taken away from you!"

Bobby ignored her. "Let's go," he said.

Sara closed the door and hadn't even fastened her seatbelt when he ripped the gears into low and sped off, heading for church. Moments later, he wheeled the car, nearly out of control, and it hurtled into the church parking lot. He parked, they got out and headed for the church side door, where they were greeted by a young male usher who took them to sit near the center aisle, in the seventh row back from the pulpit. The Reverend Miles was reading Bible scriptures as Bobby sat and began scribbling

Thief of Love

on a church program and hymn guide.

The reverend asked anyone in the congregation who didn't know the Lord to raise his or her hand. Bobby raised his hand. The organ played a low and slow melody, and the reverend called an invitation for Bobby to come forward to make a profession of his faith openly and publicly -- to repent of his sins.

Bobby looked to Sara, who nodded in encouragement. Then, after another moment of hesitation, rose from his seat. Two elders of the church came up the aisle and escorted him to the pulpit, where he stood, composed.

The reverend asked his name, and introduced him as Robert Johnson to the congregation, then with a gesture and by stepping aside, invited Bobby to stand beside him, at the podium, and speak.

"The <u>old</u> man is dead," Bobby said. "I'm a new man now -- reborn and returning to the Lord."

There were affirmations of witnessing, a few cheers and many shouted words of encouragement from the congregation as the church elders laid hands on Bobby and prayed with him. He made many professions of his faith. Most of the congregation were moved to tears.

After the service, when they were back in the G.T.O., Bobby looked at Sara and said, "The <u>old</u> man <u>is</u> dead. I'll call Cid. I'm going to the ranch for one last roundup." His breathing became shallow and he became nervous and fidgety as he drove Sara back to her house, where they found Shea waiting to see Sara. Without much in the way of a good-bye, Bobby burned rubber as he sped away, down the otherwise quiet Sunday afternoon streets of Bayview, Ohio.

"Oh my God," Shea said. "He had to get back to the

duplex to shoot up after church."

"No, Shea... That is... Oh, I can't deny it any longer. You're right. He declared that he had found God and returned to Him, and prayed and professed and testified; but, I guess he's just the same old Bobby Johnson, even with all his talk about the old man being dead. Maybe I'll write a book Shea, with all the knowledge I've gained in my experience with him, and the company he keeps, so others can know about the misuse of a cancer-stricken patient's pills by evil people who pretend to be caring and supportive. I'm not a journalist, I know, but I can write about what I experienced."

"The story will touch the hearts and minds of people who need to know," Shea said with a nod, "about exposing the dangers of drug use and street life."

"If we can help someone," Sara said, "Bobby Johnson's legacy will be a catalyst for ending the dopers praying on terminally ill people. The story will be a memorial to Bobby."

"Go for it," Shea said. "We're living in a day when everyone is writing books."

Thief of Love

Chapter 38

It was hard for Sara to stay away. For a month she would detour to drive past the duplex on Bay Bridge on the way home from work. At first everyone there seemed to be in seclusion, but then suddenly a big Harley Davidson sat parked in front of the G.T.O. at night.

A few days later, the Harley was gone and replaced by a Honda, about ten thousand dollars less expensive. It was evident Richard's buy-out money for his fifteen years of service to the company was being used up fast.

A few days after that, Bobby started to call again. His manner and tone of voice were rushed and irritable as he spoke in a raspy whisper.

Overcome with concern, Sara called the local hospice, and learned they were paying regular visits to Bobby. Sara then called Reverend Miles and reported his behavior, since he was spiritually preparing Bobby for the afterlife.

Although Sara talked sensibly with Reverend Miles, he had already been conditioned by Bobby. "Your ex-husband has a very short time to live," he said. "He tells me you're causing him emotional stress and pain. As his spiritual advisor, I must ask you to refrain from carrying on this vendetta against Robert."

Sara involuntarily I jerked her head back at the words, staring at the phone for a moment before she said, "Ex-husband? Let me tell you something: He is <u>not</u> my ex-husband but a wanna-be husband who's allowed himself to slip into the company of the lowest form of human life -- drug addicts."

Reverend Miles was silent so Sara continued. "In that environment Bobby is their prey; they want him there with them. His roommate, Richard Redman, is using Bobby's Dilaudid for his own drug addiction. Bobby needs to be taken out of that environment and put into a nursing home or assisted living place. Independent living is not for him."

After Sara finished, Reverend Miles adopted a slightly arrogant tone as he said, "Robert has signed his last will and testament. Every personal possession he has will be given to Richard Redman after Robert passes on."

Sara never expected any repayment from Bobby for all her numerous kindnesses; the reverend's words hit her like a slap to the face. The idea of Bobby, and the reverend, thinking she wanted anything of Bobby's was more than an insult -- it was an attack on her integrity, she felt, so she told him how she saw the situation. "I understand that those pills Bobby are given, and Richard uses for his own dope habit, are purchased with charitable donations from people who care about and support cancer patients. Don't take this too lightly. I'm taking this situation to the local drug enforcement task force if you don't do something to stop this aiding and abetting the habits of known drug users, right away."

Reverend Miles coughed, apparently because he didn't know what to say for a moment. "That won't be necessary. I'll have this investigated through the hospice, the church and the cancer patients' support group." That said, he promptly hung up; their conversation was over.

Thief of Love

Chapter 39

A few days later, Sara got a phone call from Cid, who said he wanted to meet her in Ohio as soon as possible. Sara immediately agreed and met him.

Sara drove to Cleveland's Hopkins Airport. Cid had already arrived and waited at the departures area outside the terminal, wearing Western boots, a leather jacket, jeans and a plaid shirt.

Sara's outfit was casual -- a pants suit with a black velour collar, black boots and black leather jacket. She wore her hair in a French twist.

With a gentle grip, Cid caught hold of her arm as he asked, "Would you like lunch?" pointing to the Bomb Squadron Restaurant.

Sara agreed; they went inside and were seated at the bay window facing the runways, where they could watch the jets land.

Sara felt the warmth of Cid's presence, but avoided looking into his eyes.

"You never really got over him, did you? Do you still love him?" Cid asked.

Sara's thoughts turned back to the times they had been together in California, but there was no feeling of irreparable loss. "I can't say I ever had an 'I'm yours, you're mine,' kind of relationship with him. Our relationship was platonic. Actually, he had been a problem to me since day one," she said. "A TV talk show called my house in hot pursuit to include Bobby. They were covering the Romance Hot Line. Bobby seemed to be their preference in and style and trash. I had already been psyched after two months of conversations with him on the phone about

Thief of Love

his flamboyant personality." Sara reached up to toy nervously with an earring.

Cid's eyes scanned her, but he remained silent.

"The talk show wasn't the type of human exploitation 'entertainment' I thought needed to be helped along. I was troubled and humiliated by the sleazy business of calling my house, invading my privacy and Bobby's, from the day he arrived. They wanted to fly Bobby and two of his girlfriends to New York, ferry them around in a limo and put them up in a fancy hotel to flaunt the goodies around before airing all the gory details of the Romance Hot Line and the hustlers who become involved in it. They were trying to reach the lowest common denominator, and it became clear it would be a tragedy to an audience, but an amusing one. To enhance the story, they tried to use me and flaunt his escapades in my face, but I refused to go or allow him to go either."

Cid listened with what Sara was sure was sincere interest. She felt privileged that he would take the time to do so, and continued. "I called his aunt, sister and cousin in California. There was no help there, as I explained to you on the phone. I can't tell you how much I appreciate you coming all the way out here and listening to what I have to say. Aren't you tired?" she asked.

Cid shook his head. "I couldn't get tired in a picturesque place like this. The planes drop down and seem to land right outside the restaurant windows."

Sara continued as Cid watched the planes coming and going. "It wasn't long after Bobby was diagnosed with malignant cancer that I was approached by a drug addict. She said she was sent by a drug dealer who wanted to make a connection with Bobby directly, cutting out a middle man who was pushing

Thief of Love

Bobby's pills. I went to the doctor with the information, and he cut Bobby down from one hundred pills in weekly prescription to sixty."

"I admire you for that, and the loyalty you've given Bobby; but you were on some dangerous ground. Did they know you were the reason he was cut?" Cid asked.

"No," Sara said. "If they would have, all hell would have broken loose. I thought at first Bobby was being victimized, but he was making money selling his pills. I thought it was temporary, until he got all his benefits, V.A. disability and S.S.I. But he didn't stop. When he received his back pay he used the money to buy a car from one of the drug addicts -- the one he's living with now -- but he was ripped off royally. He bought a car without a notarized title. The owner signed his name off and Bobby signed his name on, but the title was never legally changed over."

After dinner, Cid telephoned Bobby at the duplex and they agreed to meet at three o'clock to be together for perhaps their final visit.

Bobby arrived at Sara's house on time, but kept mostly silent after the beginning of their conversation. Cid tried to convince Bobby to focus on going back to California. "Bobby, I came here to take you out of this mess. I have no qualms about stepping over the boundaries of the drug protocol to put these offenders where they belong."

Bobby started to say something, then apparently changed his mind and remained silent. Sara prepared a meal. Bobby ate little, smashing his potatoes, meat and carrots, and ate small bites. He chewed slowly and then suddenly choked while trying to swallow. Before Sara or Cid could react, Bobby turned pale,

Thief of Love

then white and suddenly fell out of his chair, collapsing on the floor. Cid bolted from his chair, leaned down, lifted Bobby and laid him on the couch. Sara called 911. By the time the rescue squad arrived, Bobby's lung, damaged by radiation therapy, had collapsed. The paramedics were able to clear Bobby's blocked esophagus, stabilize his breathing and get him to the hospital, where Cid sat shoulder to shoulder with Sara at Bobby's side till after midnight.

In the deepest post-midnight hour, when late night becomes early morning, Bobby woke, groggy, then seemed to revive as he looked first at Cid, then Sara. He took a couple of shallow breaths, then a deep one, and breathed no more. He had met a peaceful, quiet end.

After the burial service, Bobby was cremated, and Cid and Sara carried his ashes back to Paso Robles, California, where they were scattered at sundown. Cid took great care to plan the kind of memorial Bobby wanted -- simple, and, above all, not costly.

When the plane flew over, sending Bobby's ashes down, Cid put his arm around Sara. She leaned into his embrace and knew that their hearts had touched forever, and that God had brought their spirits together.

"He was rough around the edges," Cid said, then added, "He has his rightful place now, as a free spirit."

Later, when Bobby was eulogized, Cid read Bobby's last words, spoken just a few hours before he died. "Please remember me when you're here at Paso Robles, at the mid-state fair. When you see the bucking bronc, my spirit is near you, in the dust and the dirt, and the roaring of the crowd."

Thief of Love

EPILOGUE

Bobby's family was notified of his death. They lit candles at their home, but didn't come to his memorial service.

The local newspaper reported, "Cops and Court:" `Man faces felony charges for false prescription cards. A man faces multiple felony charges for allegedly falsifying a deceased man's prescriptions. Richard Redman, forty-two, tried to fill a prescription at a pharmacy around nine p.m. May six, when a skeptical pharmacist contacted the police. Police searched Redman and found hydrocodone and carisoprodil, a muscle-relaxing drug. Hospital emergency stated both drugs were dangerous. All items were sent to the bureau of criminal investigation and identification laboratory. Redman had been forging prescriptions issued to his former roommate, Robert Johnson, now deceased. Redman is being held in the county jail on thirty thousand dollars bond, and is scheduled to appear in Municipal Court Monday.

Marcus Seibert was also arrested and charged in the case, and will be returned to serve the remaining term of his sentence for an earlier conviction on drug abuse for two to five years in Ohio State Reformatory."

Shea Robinette transferred to Reno, Nevada, with AM.

Sara accepted Cid's proposal to marry him, and relocated to live with her new husband on his large ranch near Fresno, California.

THE END

Thief of Love

About the Author

Gerald Roy Cramer, an elusive individual born in Tampa, Florida, raised in an auto sales family business. During his younger years he practiced his motto, "If you don't make dust, you eat dust."

Racing professional flat track motorcycles from New York to Ohio, to California and in between, most of the time trying to lead, not to be second best. He was critically injured in a race on September 9, 1979.

Still wanting to make dust and not eat dust, he met Bobby Johnson in the PRCA "Rodeo Cowboys Association," as a competitive bare back rider. From cycles to saddles, he decided to travel with cowboys and cowgirls who make a living out of the sanctioned rodeo circuit. He didn't want to give up the dust, dirt and the roar of the crowd, so he chose another form of high stakes competition in the rodeo.

After achieving recognition, he's thought to be traveling the world on a one way journey. "Remember: if you don't make dust, you eat dust."

Thief of Love

Photo Listing and Credit

The author gratefully acknowledges the use of pictures from the following sources. Great effort has been made to trace the proper copyright holders of the photographs and/or to acknowledge the photographer of record.

Author's Collections:
Sandusky Ohio Bus Station
Jackson Pier
Peelee Island Fairy Boat
Amish Country
Mid State Fair, Paso Robels, California
Cowboy/horse's tail

Cycle Photos: Gerry Cramer Collection
                    RT
Sandy Warner, Jack Ranch Café Management
Chalome, California